Zoran Drvenkar was born in Germany when he was three years old. He has been working as a writer since 1989. He is the author of many prize-winning books for children and young adults. His new adult thriller, *Du* (*You*), has just been published in Germany and will be published by Knopf and Blue Door in 2013.

'*Sorry* is the kind of thriller, the kind of novel, that doesn't come along every day . . . It's that oft-cited but very rare species of novel we call a page-turner, and it brilliantly achieves this because Drvenkar knows how to use all the tools at his disposal, to excellent effect'   *New York Times Book Review*

'For those with quick minds and strong stomachs, *Sorry* is an impressive début'   *The Times*

'A cleverly plotted, switchback read'   *Guardian*

'This thriller breaks with all conventions, topping all expectations . . . Fast paced and in deadly good style. A joy to read, a piece of art'   *Die Welt*

'It's the kind of book for a Friday evening, with the rest of the weekend free, because not much else will be able to compete for your attention'   *wordswithoutborders.org*

'Shocking, compelling, disturbing . . . there are many apologies in *Sorry*, but lovers of the dark side will have no regrets'
MICHAEL ROBOTHAM, author of *Shatter*

'A brilliant story that's as gruesome as it is philosophical'

Easy Living

'It's rare that a book in the crime fiction genre can break all the writing conventions and yet keep you on the edge of your seat until the bitter end . . . Drvenkar breaks the mould with *Sorry* . . . A master of his craft'   *Courier Mail*, Australia

'This is what thrillers should be about. Taut, tense and terrific, *Sorry* is a cracking read'   SEAN BLACK, author of *Gridlock*

'This highly original, dark and sinister thriller breaks all the rules . . . it delivers something thrillingly different'

lovereading.co.uk

'You need to be prepared and ready to read *Sorry*. Ready for the brave experiment in writing not seen before in this genre, and ready for an extraordinary plot'   *Berliner Zeitung*

'One of the best German language thrillers ever. And certainly the most original in years'   *Krimi-couch.de*

'Drvenkar is good at social networks – we believe in his characters and how they relate to one another'   *TLS*

'This is a very clever, dark read . . . Drvenkar [is] a writer to watch'   *Booklist*

'A challenging, insightful thriller . . . Drvenkar adroitly keeps the reader in the dark as he unravels a horrific story of child sexual abuse, savage revenge, and retribution'   *Publisher's Weekly*

srry

Zoran Drvenkar

TRANSLATED FROM THE GERMAN BY
Shaun Whiteside

blue door

Blue Door
An imprint of HarperCollins*Publishers*
77–85 Fulham Palace Road,
Hammersmith, London W6 8JB

www.harpercollins.co.uk

First published in Great Britain by Blue Door 2012

This paperback edition 2012
2

Copyright © Zoran Drvenkar 2009
© by Ullstein Buchverlage GmbH, Berlin. Published in 2009 by Ullstein Verlag

Translation copyright © 2011 by Alfred A. Knopf,
a division of Random House, Inc.

This edition published by arrangement with Alfred A. Knopf, an imprint of
The Knopf Doubleday Group, a division of Random House, Inc.

Zoran Drvenkar asserts the moral right to
be identified as the author of this work

ISBN: 978-0-00-743928-7

Printed and bound in Great Britain by
Clays Ltd, St Ives plc

MIX
Paper from
responsible sources
FSC **FSC® C007454**
www.fsc.org

For all the very good, dead friends.
I miss you.

A good apology is like a farewell,
when you know you won't see each other again.

In Between

YOU'RE SURPRISED how easy it is to track her down. You've been hiding in such a deep hole that you thought nothing was possible any more. You lost yourself more and more, and when you thought you'd never see light again, his other address book fell into your hands. He had two; you didn't know that either. There was so much you didn't know about him.

One address book is bound in leather, the other is an octavo notebook like the ones you had in school. You happened to find the octavo notebook among a stack of magazines on his bedside table. It's full of names. You counted them. Forty-six. You're still filled with longing when you see his handwriting. Sloping to the right, with the despair of the left-handed. Your fingers wandered over names, addresses, and phone numbers as if you could sense what he felt as he was writing them down. Two of the names are underlined; they are the only names you know.

The day you found the octavo notebook, light entered your darkness. The names are the signs you were waiting for. Six months of waiting, and then this light. And how could you have known that sometimes one must search for a sign?

No one told you.

One of the two addresses is no longer valid, but that's not a problem for you. You're experienced in tracking people down. Our system works chiefly through information, and these days nothing is easier to get hold of. It took you two minutes. His wife moved to Kleinmachnow. On the map you find out that her new home is exactly three kilometers south of the old one as the crow flies. The new block is very much like the other one. We are creatures of habit. When we turn around we want to know what lies behind us. You wait patiently until one of the tenants leaves the building, then you climb to the third floor and ring.

"Yes, who is it?"

She's in her late forties and looks as if the last few years have been a long, tough journey that she had to travel on her own. It doesn't matter what she looks like, you'd have recognized her anywhere. Her posture, her voice. You're surprised that you've internalized her gestures. You have never had a relationship with this woman, but everything about her is familiar to you. The way she leans forward when she looks at you, the narrowing of her eyes, her quizzical expression. Every detail has burned itself so deeply into you that it's more than just memory.

"Hello," you say.

She hesitates for a moment. She isn't sure whether you're a threat. You'd like to ask her what kind of threat turns up in broad daylight outside a block in Kleinmachnow and smiles.

"Do we know each other?"

Suddenly there's interest in her eyes. You aren't surprised. She's a curious person; even if she can't place you, she doesn't show a trace of suspicion. The most dangerous people aren't suspicious, they're interested. You know that expression. As a child you studied an accident on the highway. All that blood, the broken glass, firemen running around, flames and oily black smoke. Every time you drove past the place of the accident with your parents afterward you felt that same excitement.

This is where it happened. Can you still spot anything? Is it all gone?

She looks at you the same way.

"We know each other from before," you say and hand her the photograph. "I just wanted to say hello."

You know that as soon as she sees the photograph she's going to be filled with panic. Perhaps she'll shut the door. She'll probably deny it.

She surprises you, as she has always surprised you. She's good at surprises, because she's unpredictable.

"It's you!"

A moment later she opens her arms and gives you a warm, safe hug.

In the apartment she explains that her husband will be back around six—there's more than enough time. You know she's divorced, and her ex lives near Bornholm. It's good that she's pretending to trust you. Any insecurity is good.

You sit down in the living room. From where you're sitting you can look out at the balcony. A table, no chairs. Beside the table a sculpture. A boy lowering his head, hands clasped in prayer. You've noticed sculptures like that at the hardware store. Some of them hold books, others have wings on their backs. You look quickly away, you feel dazzled, although the sun shines down pale and weary today.

"Would you like something to drink?"

She brings you a glass of mineral water and sets it down on the coffee table next to the photograph. Two boys on a bicycle. They're grinning, they're so young that it hurts.

"I didn't think I'd ever see you again," she says and leans forward to brush a strand of hair from your forehead. Intimate. Close. You don't flinch. Your self-control is perfect.

"Did you miss me?" she wants to know.

I've dreamed about you at night, you want to reply, but you're not sure whether that's the truth. There are dreams and there's reality, and you wander back and forth between them, struggling to keep them apart.

She smiles at you. Now there isn't just curiosity in her expression, there's also a trace of desire. You force yourself not to look at the sculpture, you force yourself to return her smile. At the

· 3 ·

same time something in you tears. As silently as a cobweb. Her desire is too much for you. And you thought you had self-control. And you thought you could do that.

"I need to use the bathroom."

"Hey, come on, you're not ashamed of me, are you?" she asks.

Your face is red, your fists clenched under the table. Shame.

"Second on the left," she says, tapping your knee. "Hurry up, or I'll have to come and get you."

She winks at you, lascivious and playful. *I'm not nine years old any more!* you want to yell at her, but there's only a cold stiffness in you, and that stiffness lets nothing through. You stand up and walk into the corridor. You open the second door on the left and shut it behind you. In front of the mirror you look up, but your eyes avoid you. It hurts, it hurts again every time. You hope it will be different one day, and that hope holds you upright and eases the pain.

It'll soon be over.

You kneel on the tiled floor and lift the lid of the toilet. You're quiet, no coughing, no groaning, just the sound of a splash. When nothing more comes you take the toothbrush from the toothpaste cup and shove it into your throat to be sure that your belly really is empty. Then you wash your hands and rinse out your mouth. Before you leave the bathroom, you put the toothbrush back and, with some toilet paper, carefully wipe clean all the surfaces you have touched.

Soon.

She's still sitting in the armchair smoking—arm bent at the elbow, head tilted slightly back when she lets smoke escape from her mouth. Even that gesture is so familiar to you that the memories overlay one another like a handful of slides. Back then and today become now, and now becomes today and back then. She holds the photograph in her hand and studies it. When you are standing behind her, she turns her head and her eyes flash. You aim the gas at that flash until the can is empty and she is lying on the floor in a whimpering heap. Then you start removing any trace of yourself from the room. You drain the glass and put it in your pocket. The photograph has fallen from her hand. You pick it up and put it in your pocket. You are careful, you are precise, you know what you are doing. When she tries to creep away, you turn her on to her back and sit down on her chest. Her arms are trapped beneath you, her eyes are swollen. She rears, her knees come up, her heels drum on the carpet. You put one hand firmly over her mouth, and with the other you hold her snot-streaming nose closed. It all goes quickly.

You make a package out of her. You press her thighs to her chest and shove her arms behind her knees. She's not very big. You've thought of everything. Ten days of planning was enough. She fits in one of these black 120-liter trash bags. You carry her out of the flat. On the stairs you meet an old man. You nod at him, he nods back. It's as easy as taking out the garbage.

It's late by the time she wakes up.

You were a bit disappointed when you first stepped into the apartment. It was dirty and deserted, it was nothing like what it had been. You had expected more. Places with a past like that shouldn't be deserted. It's disrespectful. People make pilgrimages to Dachau and Auschwitz, they look at the concentration camps as if they could read something from them, while a few yards from their homes a new form of horror is taking place and they aren't even aware of it.

It was very hard to find the right photomural. You drove all over Berlin, and it was only after the fifth specialty store when you described to one of the clerks exactly what you were looking for that he went to the storeroom and came back with several rolls.

To your surprise he let you have them all for nothing.

"No one buys this kind of crap these days" were his exact words.

Sometimes you wonder if you aren't exaggerating the details. Then you give yourself the only logical answer. This is all about memory. It's about details. Details are important to you. You prize details.

The wall is still wet with glue. At the spot where the metal ring used to be, there's now a hole in the wall. Before you glued the photomural over the hole you had to stick your index finger into it. You marked the spot: the X is exactly at eye level.

The left shoe falls from her foot when you press her against the wall. As you do you get so close to her that you feel ill. Her unconscious body is soft, and it's hard to keep it vertical. Your strength calms you down. You're chest to chest. Her breath smells like cold smoke. You lift her arms up, her feet part a few inches from the floor, you swing the hammer back and strike.

The nail easily penetrates the palms of her hands, placed one over the other. Three blows are enough and the head of the nail is all that sticks out from her wrists. The third blow wakes her, your eyes are level now and she screams into your face. The scream fizzles out in a dull tap against the insulating tape you've stuck over her mouth. You look at each other, you will never be as close to her again. She twitches, tries to kick; your body presses her against the wall, holds her in position. Panic and contentment and strength. Strength, every time. Tears shoot from her swollen eyes and hit your face. You've seen enough and step back. Her weight pulls her down. The surprised expression. Something jerks. The pain makes her tremble, a shudder runs through her body, her bladder empties. The nail holds. She hangs on the wall with arms stretched upwards. Her right shoe falls with a quiet click, her toes scrape over the floor in search of purchase. If looks could kill, you'd be long dead.

It's time to part. You show her where to look. She tries to turn her head. You knew she would do that. It fits. So you walk over to her and place the second nail on her forehead. It's bigger, sixteen inches long, and has a special name that you don't remember. The man in the hardware store told you it twice and you nodded and said thank you. She freezes as the tip touches her skin. Her eyes speak to you. They say you won't do it. They order you not to. You shake your head. Then she closes her eyes tight shut. You're surprised, you expected more resistance. You expected her to kick out at you again, to defend herself.

She gives up.

Your lips touch her ear and you whisper:

"It wasn't me."

She opens her eyes wide. And there's the look, and there's the understanding.

Now.

You drive the nail through the bone of her forehead. It takes you four more blows than the hands did, before the nail pierces the back of her head and enters the wall. She twitches, her twitch becomes a quiver, then she hangs still. Bright blood trickles from the ear you whispered into; a dark thread of blood emerges from the wound in her forehead and wanders between her eyes over the base of her nose and her cheek. You wait and study the elegance with which the thread of blood moves over her face. Before it reaches the insulating tape, you pull it from her mouth. Spittle seeps over her lips and mixes with the blood. Her right eye closes, as if it's weary. You open it again, it stays open. You follow her frozen gaze. It's fine, you don't have to correct anything, everything is right.

PART I

After

IN THE DARKNESS of your thoughts I would like to be a light.

I have no idea who wrote that. I just remember the piece of paper that was pinned up on the kitchen wall one day.

In the darkness of your thoughts . . .

I want someone to come out of the forest with a flashlight and aim the beam at my face. Being seen can be so important. It doesn't matter by whom. I'm disappearing into myself more and more.

It's the day after. My hand rests on the cold metal of the fender. I listen as if my fingertips could hear the vibrations. I need more time, I'm not yet able to open the trunk. Perhaps another hundred kilometers, maybe a thousand.

. . . I would like to be a light.

I get in and start the engine. If someone should ever follow my journey, he'll get lost in its incoherence. I'm moving through Germany like a lab rat in a maze. I lurch and every step is uncertain. I step sideways, turn in circles. But whatever I do, I don't stand still. Standing still is out of the question. Sixteen hours are bundled together into sixteen minutes when you travel aimlessly. The boundaries of your own perception start to fray, and everything seems meaningless. Even sleep loses its significance. I wish there were a light in the darkness of my thoughts. But there is no light. So I'm left with nothing but my thoughts.

Before

KRIS

BEFORE WE TALK ABOUT YOU, I'd like to introduce you to the people you will soon be meeting. It's a cool, late August day. The sun is extremely bright in the sky and resembles the flickering gleam of light switches in corridors. The people turn their faces to the sun and wonder why so little warmth comes back.

We are in a small park in the middle of Berlin. This is where everything starts. A man sits on a park bench by the water. His name is Kris Marrer; he is twenty-nine and looks like an ascetic who decided a long time ago not to be part of society. Kris knows only too well that he is a part of society. He has finished school and his studies. He likes going to the seaside, he enjoys good food and can talk about music for hours. Even if he doesn't want to be, Kris Marrer is definitively a part of it, and this Wednesday morning he feels that clearly.

He sits on the park bench, as if he were about to jump up at any moment. His chin is thrust forward, his elbows on his knees. It isn't a good day today, he knew it wouldn't be a good day when he woke up, but we'll get to that later. What's important at this moment is that he regrets seeking out this particular park bench at the Urbanhafen. He thought a few minutes' peace to gather his thoughts was exactly what he needed. He thought wrong.

A woman sits on the grass a few yards away. She's dressed as if she can't believe the summer is over. Sleeveless dress, sandals. The grass around her looks exhausted, the ground is damp. A man stands in front of the woman talking to her. His right hand is like an axe cutting silently through the air. Sharp, angular, quick. Every time the man points at the woman she flinches. The couple isn't particularly noisy, but Kris can clearly, distinctly hear each of their words.

He knows now that the man has been unfaithful. The woman doesn't believe him. When the man lists all the women he has slept with, the woman begins to believe him and calls him a bastard. He is a bastard, there's no getting around it. He laughs in her face.

"What did you imagine? Did you think I'd be faithful to you?"

The man spits at the woman's feet, turns his back on her and leaves. The woman starts crying. She cries silently; the people react as people always do and look the other way. The children go on playing, and a dog barks excitedly at a pigeon, while an indifferent sun sees nothing it hasn't seen a million times before.

On days like this it should rain, Kris thinks. No one should split up with anyone while the sun's shining.

When the woman looks up, she notices him on the park bench. She smiles embarrassedly, not wanting to display her sadness. Her smile reminds Kris of a curtain that he's been allowed to glimpse behind for a second. *Nice, inviting.* He's touched by her openness, then the moment is just as quickly over, the woman rubs the tears from her face and looks across the water as if nothing has happened.

Kris sits down next to her.

Later he will tell his brother that he didn't know what he was doing. But that's later. From here on it's all very simple. It's as if the words had always been in his head. Kris doesn't have to search for them, he just has to say them out loud.

He explains to the woman what's just happened. He takes the bastard who cheated on her under his wing, and invents a difficult past for him. He talks about problems and childhood anxieties. He says:

"If he could, he would do lots of things differently. He knows he's screwing up. Let him go. How long have you known each other? Two months? Three?"

The woman nods. Kris goes on.

"Let him go. If he comes back, you'll know it's right. If he doesn't come back, you can be glad it's over."

As Kris is talking, he's taking pleasure in his words. He can observe their effect. They're like a calming hand. The woman listens attentively and says she wouldn't have been sure what to think about the whole relationship.

"Did he talk about me a lot?"

Kris hesitates imperceptibly, then pays her compliments and says what you say to an insecure, twenty-three-year-old woman who will find her next lover without any great difficulty the very same week.

Kris is good, he's really good.

"Even though he'll never admit it," he says at last, "you shouldn't forget that he's sorry. Deep inside he's apologizing to you right now."

"Really?"

"Really."

The woman nods contentedly.

Everything starts with a lie and ends with an apology—even this morning here in the park. The woman doesn't know who Kris Marrer is. She doesn't even want to know how he knows the bastard who has just left her. And although she has no other connection with Kris, she asks him if he'd like to go for a drink. The woman's pain is like a bridge that anyone can walk on, if they can summon up some compassion.

Sometimes, Kris thinks, *we're so interchangeable it's embarrassing.*

"A glass of wine would do me good," she says, smoothing her dress over her legs as if the dress were a reason to think about her offer. He sees her knees, he sees the red-painted toenails in the sandals. Then he shakes his head. He didn't do this to get closer to the woman. He acted purely out of instinct. Perhaps it was the banal primal urge of the protector. Man sees woman, man wants to protect woman, man protects woman. Later Kris will reach the insight that he has pursued his vocation—he had an urgent need to apologize. Later one part will find the other and form one big whole. Later.

Kris rests his hand on the woman's and says, "Sorry, but I've got a date."

There's her smile again, but it's not tormented now; she understands Kris, she trusts him.

"Another time," he promises and stands up.

She nods. It's over. The pain of separation has vanished, because she has seen a glimmer of light. A nice man has opened her eyes. And so we leave the woman sitting alone on the grass, and leave the park with the nice man. We are on the way to his job. It will be his last working day, and the nice man is not in a good mood.

"You've got to understand this," says Bernd Jost-Degen ten minutes later and sticks his hands into the front pockets of his designer jeans. He stands with his back to the window, so that Kris can only make his face out as a silhouette. A digital hand twitches between a Chagall and a Miró above a digital clock projected on the wall. The boss's office must always be in semi-darkness, or else you wouldn't be able to see the clock. Bernd is three years older than Kris and doesn't like people calling him "boss," or pretends not to.

"There's a lot of rationalization going on," Bernd continues. "Look at me, I'm up to my neck in shit, as well. The structures aren't the same any more, the world has moved on, you know? Back in the old days, people did good work for good pay. Now they have to do fantastic levels of work for bad pay. And they're supposed to be grateful, too."

He laughs the laugh of someone who isn't one of those people. Kris feels like an idiot and doesn't know why he wanted to speak to his boss again. At his feet are two paper bags that the cleaning woman handed to him after she had cleared his desk.

"It's a market economy, Kris, it's overpopulation. There are too many of us, and our souls belong to capitalism. Look at me. I'm dangling on strings. I'm a puppet. The guys at the top are saying, Bernd, we want twice as much profit. And what do I do? I give you cheaper mineral water and order the cheapest kind of coffee and make cuts wherever I can, so that the people up there don't get rid of me."

"What on earth are you talking about?" asks Kris. "You fired me, you've made me one of your cuts."

Bernd rests one hand on the other and leans forward.

"Come on, Kris, look, my hands are tied, kill me if you want, but my hands are tied. It's last in, first out. Of course you can go straight on to another job. And if you like, I'll write you a reference, I'm happy to do that. Of course. Try the *Tagesspiegel*, they're a bit slow off the mark. Or what about *taz*, they're ... What's up? Why are you looking at me like that?"

Kris has laid his head on one side. His thoughts are focused. It's a bit like meditation. Each time Kris breathes in he gets bigger, and each time he breathes out his boss shrinks a bit more.

"You're not going to get violent on me, are you?" Bernd says nervously, and steps behind his desk. His hands disappear into his trouser pockets, his torso leans back as if he were standing on the edge of an abyss. Kris doesn't move, he just observes, and if he were to step closer to his boss right now, he'd be able to smell his fear.

"I'm really sorry, man. If you want—"

Kris walks out on him mid-sentence and crosses the editorial office with the paper bags under his arms. He's disappointed. Bernd Jost-Degen has never learned to formulate an apology properly. Never say you're sorry and hide your hands in your trouser pockets as you do so. We all want to see the weapons we're being injured with. And if you're going to lie as he just did, then at least take a step toward the other guy and let him feel you're telling the truth. Fake closeness, because closeness can mask lies. There's nothing more pitiful than someone who can't apologize for his mistakes.

No one looks up when Kris walks past. He wishes the whole gang of them would choke on their own ignorance there and then. He's worked closely with them for a year, and now not a single one of them looks up.

Kris sets the bags down on the floor of the elevator and looks at himself in the mirror on the wall. He waits for his reflection to look away. The reflection grins back.

Better than nothing, Kris thinks and presses the button for the ground floor.

The two bags contain all his research and interviews from the last few months, which no one's really interested in. Current for a day, then just some junk that's recycled over and over. *Journalism today,* Kris thinks, really wanting to set the whole pile on fire. When the doors open again, he steps out of the elevator and leaves the bags on the floor. At almost the same time they tip sideways with a sigh, then the elevator doors close, and it's over.

Kris steps onto the pavement and takes a deep breath.

We're in Berlin, we're on Gneisenaustrasse. The World Cup has been over for nine weeks, and it's as if it never happened. Kris doesn't want that to happen to him. He's in his late twenties and after twelve months in a steady job he's unemployed again. He has no interest in looking for another job, and neither does he want to switch, like hundreds of thousands of others, from one internship to the next, getting by on starvation wages and hoping someone takes him on sooner or later. No. And he doesn't want to work as a trainee, either, because he's had training and he's been through university. His attitudes are at odds with the job market—he's bad at begging and far too arrogant for small jobs. But Kris doesn't plan to despair. He won't end up with his head in the oven, no one will be aware of his problems. Kris is an optimist, and there are only two things he can't stand: lying and unfairness. Today he is aware of both, and his mood matches the fact. If Kris Marrer knew now that he has been moving toward a new goal since waking up, he would change his attitude. You'd be able to see him smile. But as he is unsuspecting, he curses the day and sets off for the subway. He wonders how to straighten a world in which everyone's used to standing crooked.

TAMARA

JUST AS KRIS IS leaving the editorial office, Tamara Berger is sitting up in bed with a start. The ceiling is just a few inches away from her head, and Tamara knows she will never get used to it. Like waking up in a coffin. She falls back into the pillows and thinks about the dream that is echoing around in her head. A man asked her if she had made her decision. Tamara couldn't see his face, she could just see the tensed sinews at his throat. So she tried to walk around the man, but his head kept turning away from her until hairline cracks formed at his neck that made Tamara think of dried-out earth. Finally she laid a hand on the man's head so that he couldn't turn away any more. She walked around the man and woke up.

We are in Berlin South, two streets away from Steglitz Town Hall. The room looks out onto a courtyard to the rear, the curtains are drawn, and a wasp is flying tirelessly against the windowpane. Tamara doesn't know how the wasp got through the sealed window. The alarm clock shows 11:19. Tamara doesn't believe it and holds the alarm clock right in front of her eyes before she gets cursing out of the bunk and puts on last night's clothes. A minute later she dashes from the apartment as if the house were in flames.

You'll now be wondering why we are spending any time on a woman who can't even manage to wash her face or put on fresh clothes after she wakes up. Tamara asks herself the same question as she looks at her face in a reflection on the subway. When she got home at four this morning she was far too tired to take her makeup off. The running mascara left dark traces under her eyes. Her hair is straggly, her blouse crumpled and open one button too far, clearly revealing her cleavage. *I look like a tramp,* Tamara thinks and buries her face in her hands. Without a word, the man diagonally opposite hands her a tissue. Tamara says thank you and blows her nose. She wishes she had slept through the whole day.

Even though it's hard for you at the moment, you have to believe that Tamara Berger is an important element in this story. One day you will sit opposite her and ask her whether she's made her decision. Without her we'd have to part now.

The job center is closed. Tamara gives the door a halfhearted kick and walks to the nearest bakery. She eats a sandwich standing up and sips at a coffee that tastes as if it's spent a third night on the hot plate. The woman behind the counter shrugs and refuses to make a new pot. She says what's there has to be drunk first. And no one else has complained. Tamara thanks her for her terrible service, and when the woman turns away she steals her packets of sugar. All of them.

The apartment belongs to Tamara's sister, Astrid. First floor in the front of an old building. Not beautiful, not ugly, just practical. Two rooms lead off to the front, and the third, next to the bathroom, is Tamara's. It has a depressing view of a gray courtyard that has never seen sunlight. In summer the stench of rubbish bins is so bad that Tamara has sometimes woken up choking in the night. When she complained to her sister, Astrid said that as far as she was concerned Tamara could go back and live with their parents if she wanted. Tamara kept her mouth shut and sealed up the chinks in the windows.

We are family, she thought, *that's how things are, you keep your mouth shut and hope things will get better one day.*

Tamara really thinks that. Her father took early retirement, at thirty-nine; her mother spends her days behind the till at Kaiser's supermarket, and in the evening she sits and crochets in front of the television. Apart from Astrid, Tamara has an elder brother who disappeared from home at some point to emigrate to Australia. The children grew up with the traditional bourgeois philosophy that life is no one's friend and you should be content with what you have.

When Tamara gets back from the job center, Astrid is standing at the stove stirring a kind of green cream. The flat smells like the locker room after a game.

"It stinks in here," says Tamara by way of greeting.

"I can't smell anything any more," Astrid replies and taps her nose. "It's like Chernobyl in there."

Tamara kisses her sister on the cheek and opens the window.

"So? What happened?"

Tamara would like to answer that nothing's happened, because nothing actually has happened, but she knows exactly what Astrid means. So she keeps quiet and pulls off her boots and hopes to get away without any further questions. There are days when she manages to do that.

Astrid studies each of Tamara's movements. Not a lot has changed between the sisters since childhood. They might be four years apart, but no one can see the difference. Tamara doesn't know whether that speaks for her or against her. In the old days she always wanted to be the older one.

"Don't make that face," says Astrid. "One of those big book-shops will take you on eventually. Dussmann or someone. They're always looking for people."

Astrid can talk. People with jobs are always hearing that there are jobs everywhere. A year ago Tamara's sister set up a nail studio in the basement of the building. She also mixes up creams and face masks to order. At the end of the year she intends to specialize in massages. Astrid runs the nail studio on her own. Tamara would like to help her, because anything would be better than sitting around idle, but Astrid thinks Tamara is overqualified.

Tamara hates the term. It sounds as if she'd developed an infectious illness after she took her final exams. Normally qualified is always better, it means the employer can pay less. Student is best of all, of course, but Tamara has sworn never to study again. She's glad that school's behind her; she doesn't have to wear the academic invisibility cloak all over again. She doesn't even expect much from life. She just wants to make a bit more money, travel a bit more, and she wants things to be a bit better overall.

"Did you call in and see them?" asks Astrid.

"See who?"

"Are you even listening? Bookshop? Big one? Dussmann? Something'll come up there soon, believe me."

Tamara nods even though she doesn't want to, then stands by the kitchen table and empties all the sugar packets from her jacket pocket.

"Look what I've brought."

Astrid grins.

"So who got on the wrong side of you this time?"

"A member of the working class," says Tamara, kisses her sister on the cheek again and disappears into her room.

Even though she's only been living with Astrid since the spring, it's felt like an eternity. It was Tamara who chose to move in, but sometimes you just go with it and then you're surprised that things happen the way they do.

If you could look around Tamara's room, you'd think the person who lives here is just passing through. Two open suitcases with clothes spilling out of them, two rows of books along the walls, no pictures, no posters, not even any little ornaments on the windowsill. *Having arrived* is a state that Tamara is still waiting for. She doesn't dream of owning her own house with a parquet floor and a husband whom she will bless with three children. Her dreams are bleak and feeble, because she doesn't know what she wants from life. She doesn't feel any sense of vocation, she isn't enticed by a mission. There's just the desire somehow to fit in, but without really having to belong. She likes society too much to be an outsider; she's too much of an outsider to conform.

After Tamara has closed the bedroom door behind her, she listens to the treacherous silence. Through the wall she hears first a quiet cough, then a loud groan.

I've got to get out of here, Tamara thinks, and resists the urge to hammer on the wall. Werner is on the toilet again. Werner is Astrid's current boyfriend, and he spends five days a week at her place, even though his flat is twice the size of hers. Astrid doesn't see him on the weekends, because that's when Werner goes from one house to another with his friends, getting so drunk that he can't be bothered to see anybody. Werner is a high school gym teacher, and he's had hemorrhoids since childhood. Every day he sits on the toilet for an hour and groans. Tamara hears every sound. Except on Saturday and Sunday, of course.

She climbs onto her bunk bed, grabs her headphones and the historical novel that lies open and facedown beside her pillow. Seven pages later the ceiling light flickers on and off. Tamara takes the headphones off and looks down from the bunk. Astrid is standing in the door frame, waving the telephone.

"Who is it?"

"Who do you think?" Astrid replies and throws her the phone.

Tamara's heart starts thumping. There are days when she hopes to hear an elegant, almost tender voice at the other end. She knows it's an idiotic hope, but she still excitedly presses the receiver to her ear and listens. She hears breathing, she knows the breathing and is disappointed, but tries not to let any of her disappointment show.

"Save me," says her best friend. "I'm on my last legs here."

Tamara Berger and Frauke Lewin have known each other since grade school. They ended up at the same grammar school, fancied the same boys, and hated the same teachers. They spent almost all their evenings with the clique at the Lietzensee. From the first kiss to the first joint they experienced everything there—lovesickness, crying fits, political discussions, arguments, and the depths of boredom. In the winter you could see them sitting on the benches by the war memorial. The cold couldn't touch them in those days. They drank mulled wine from thermos flasks and smoked their cigarettes hastily, as if they might warm them up. Tamara doesn't know when the cold took hold of them. They feel it much more quickly now, they whine more, and if anyone asks them why, they reply that the world is getting colder and colder. They could also answer that they'd got older, but that would be too honest, you don't say that until you're forty and you can look back. In your late twenties you go through your very private climate disaster and hope for better times.

Frauke waits by the war memorial, which looms out of the park like a lonely monolith. Her back rests against the gray stone and her legs are crossed. Frauke is dressed in black, and that has nothing to do with this special day. In her teenage years Frauke went through an intense Goth phase. On days like today she looks like one of those innocent women in horror films whom everyone wants to protect against evil, who then suddenly transforms and shows her fangs. Take a good look at her. You can't know it yet, but one day this woman will be your enemy. She will hate you, and she will try to kill you.

"Aren't you cold?" Tamara asks.

Frauke gives her a look as if she's sitting on an iceberg.

"The summer's over and my ass is an ice cube. Can you tell me what I'm doing here?"

"You're on your last legs," Tamara reminds her.

"How I love you."

Frauke slides along, Tamara sits down, Frauke offers her a cigarette, Tamara takes the cigarette, although she doesn't smoke.

Tamara only smokes when Frauke offers her a new cigarette. She doesn't want to disappoint her friend, so she keeps her company. Sometimes Tamara doesn't know if there's a name for women like her. Passive smoker doesn't capture it.

"How did you even manage to get out of bed this morning?" Frauke asks.

They danced the previous night away at a disco, and got so drunk that they didn't even say goodbye.

Tamara tells her about the closed job center and the coffee at the bakery. Then she draws on the cigarette and coughs.

Frauke takes the cigarette from her and stamps it out.

"Has anyone ever told you that you smoke like a fag? People like you shouldn't smoke."

"You're telling me."

They study the few strollers who risk going to the park in this weather. The Lietzensee glitters as if its surface were made of ice. A pregnant woman stops by the shore and rests both hands contentedly on her belly. Tamara quickly looks away.

"How old are we?" asks Frauke.

"You know how old we are."

"Doesn't that worry you?"

Tamara doesn't know what to say. At the moment she has other things to be worried about. Last week she split up with a musician whom she met on the subway. His notion of a relationship was for Tamara to rave about his talent during the day, and in the evening keep her mouth shut when his friends came by for a jam session. Tamara doesn't like being alone. She sees loneliness as a punishment.

"I mean, doesn't it worry you that ten years after leaving school we're still sitting here by the war memorial and nothing has changed? We know this place like the back of our hands. We know where the winos hide their bags of returnable bottles, we even know where the dogs like to piss. I feel like an old shoe. Imagine going to a class reunion now. God, how they'd laugh."

Tamara remembers the last reunion a year ago, and the fact that nobody was doing particularly well. Twelve were jobless, four were trying to keep their heads above water by selling insurance, and three had set up on their own and were just short of bankruptcy. Only one woman was doing brilliantly: she was a pharmacist and couldn't stop boasting about it. So much for high school graduation.

But Tamara doesn't think that's really Frauke's problem.

"What's happened?" she asks.

Frauke flips the cigarette away. A man stops abruptly and looks at the stub by his feet. He touches it with his shoe as if it were a freshly killed animal, then looks over at the two women on the park bench.

"Fuck off!" Frauke calls to him.

The man shakes his head and walks on. Frauke snorts and grins. On days like this it's plain to Tamara that Frauke is still a street child. While Tamara had to fight to leave the house for as much as an hour, Frauke had wandered around freely, taking advice from no one. The girls looked up to her as a leader, while the boys feared her sharp tongue. Frauke has always had both pride and dignity. Now she's working as a freelance media designer, but only takes on commissions that she likes, and that often leaves her broke at the beginning of the month.

"I need a new job," she says. "Just anything, you know? But really urgently. My dad has another new girlfriend, and his girlfriend is of the opinion that I should stand on my own two feet. I mean, hey, am I like fourteen years old or something? He stopped the checks. Just like that. Can you tell me what kind of sluts my dad's hanging out with? Let 'em come and ring my doorbell, I'll tell them a thing or two."

Tamara has the image clearly in front of her eyes. She doesn't know whether there's a Latin name for Frauke's father complex. Any woman who gets involved with Frauke's father experiences his daughter as a Fury. Tamara was there a few times, and the memories aren't good. Tamara sees the father as the problem, not his girlfriends, but she keeps that thought to herself.

"And now?" Frauke asks, suddenly feeble. "What do I do now?"

"We could mug somebody," Tamara suggests, jutting her chin toward the man who stopped when he saw the cigarette butt.

"Too poor."

"We could open a bookshop?"

"Tamara, you need seed money for that. Monetos, capice?"

"I know."

It's always the same dialogue. Tamara dreams, Frauke wakes her up.

"And don't suggest I go to the job center," says Frauke, tapping a new cigarette out of the box. She offers one to Tamara, Tamara shakes her head, Frauke puts the pack back in her pocket and lights her own.

"I have my dignity," she says after the first drag. "I'd rather beg in the street."

Tamara wishes that Frauke's character traits would rub off on her a little. She'd love to be choosier. In men, in work, in her decisions. She'd also like to be proud, but it's hard when you've got nothing to be proud of.

I've got Frauke, Tamara thinks and says, "You will manage."

Frauke sighs and looks into the sky. Her neck lengthens as she does so; it's white like a swan's.

"Look down again," Tamara says.

Frauke lowers her head.

"Why?"

"I get dizzy when people look into the sky."

"What?"

"No, it's true. It makes me really ill. I think it's some sort of nervous disorder."

"You really are a case, aren't you?"

And she's absolutely right, Tamara is a case.

* * *

An hour later they share a bag of chips by the district court building, and wait for the 148, toward the zoo. Frauke is feeling better. She has worked out that she sometimes sees nothing but storm clouds everywhere. When Tamara tells her to take less medication, Frauke doesn't even pull a face and says, "Tell that to my mother, not to me."

At Wilmersdorfer Strasse they get off the bus and head into the Chinese supermarket opposite Woolworth's. Frauke fancies stir-fried vegetables and noodles.

"It'll do you good to eat something healthy," she explains.

Tamara doesn't like the smell in Chinese shops. It reminds her of the hallways in the blocks of apartments with corners stinking of piss, and it also reminds her a bit of an InterRail journey when she got her period and couldn't wash herself down below for two days. But what bothers her most is that she has gotten used to the smell of dried fish after a minute, but knows very well that it's still in the air.

Frauke isn't worried about that. She puts bok choy, baby eggplants, and leeks in the basket. She weighs a handful of bean sprouts and searches for the right noodles. Then she runs back to the vegetables to get ginger and coriander. She doesn't like the coriander. She talks to a saleswoman and asks for a fresh bunch. The saleswoman shakes her head. Frauke lifts the coriander and says, *Dead,* then taps herself on the chest and says, *Alive.* The saleswoman holds Frauke's stare for a minute before disappearing into the storeroom and coming back with a new bunch. Tamara thinks the new bunch looks exactly the same as the old one, but she says nothing, because Frauke is content. Frauke thanks the saleswoman with a hint of a bow and marches to the register with Tamara. The Vietnamese man behind the register is about as nice as the kind of uncle you might imagine trying to grope you under your skirt. Frauke tells him he can stop grinning. His mouth becomes a straight line. Frauke and Tamara hurry out of the shop.

"Plan B," says Frauke, dragging Tamara over to one of the phone booths. Plan B can mean anything with Frauke, but in lots of cases it just means that no Plan A exists.

As Frauke is making her call, Tamara studies the people outside the Tchibo coffee shop. Even though it's overcast they're crowding around the tables under the umbrellas, shopping bags crammed between their legs. Grandmas with a cigarette in one hand and a coffee cup in the other; grandpas silently guarding the tables, as if someone has forced them to leave their flat. Among them are two laborers bent over their tables eating as if they aren't allowed to leave crumbs on the pavement. Caffè lattes and apple tarts are on sale. Tamara imagines herself standing there with Frauke in thirty years' time. Fresh from the hairdresser's in their beige orthopedic footwear, their plastic bags full of booty, lipstick crusted in the corners of their mouths.

"It's been months," Frauke says into the receiver. "I can't even remember what you look like. And anyway my kitchen's too small. I hate cooking in it, is that something you can possibly imagine?"

Frauke looks at Tamara and holds up her thumb.

"What? What do you mean, when?" she says again into the phone. "Now, of course."

Tamara presses her ear to the receiver as well and hears Kris saying he thinks it's nice of them to call but he has no time right now, his head's in the oven and they should try again later.

"Later's not good," Frauke says, unimpressed. "Do you *really* not fancy stir-fried vegetables?"

Kris admits that he isn't in the slightest interested in stir-fried vegetables. He promises to call again later.

"After the autopsy," he says and hangs up.

"What does he mean by autopsy?" Tamara asks.

"For God's sake, Tamara," says Frauke and pushes her out of the phone booth.

*   *   *

Whenever Tamara thinks about Kris, she thinks of a fish that she saw once in the aquarium. It was her twentieth birthday. Frauke had bought some grass from a friend, and the plan had been to get completely stoned and look at the fish in the aquarium.

"You can't beat it," she had said. "You suddenly understand what a fish is really like."

They strolled giggling from one room to the next, got terrible munchies for Mars bars and stocked up on them at a newsstand before entering a room with a big pool. A handful of tourists had assembled, students sat yawning on the benches. Tamara's mouth was full of chocolate when she stepped forward and saw the fish.

The fish wasn't swimming. It floated among all the other fish in the water and stared at the visitors, some of whom pulled faces or knocked on the glass, making the fish jerk backward and swim away. But the one fish remained still. Its eyes were fixed, and it looked through the visitors as if no one were there. Tamara thought, *No one can hurt him.* And Kris is just like that. No one can hurt him.

At the time they all belonged to the same clique. Kris and Tamara and Frauke. There was Gero and Ina too, and Thorsten, Lena and Mike and whatever all their names were. They sailed through the nineties like an armada of hormone-drenched seafarers with only one goal in mind: one day to reach the sacred shore of high school graduation, and never to have to take to the sea ever again. After school they lost touch. Years later they bumped into each other by chance and were amazed at how much time had just slipped through their fingers. They were seafarers no more, neither were they shipwrecked; they were more like the people who walked along the beach picking up flotsam and jetsam.

"What's up?" Frauke asks, turning to Tamara, who is still standing beside the phone booth. "What are you waiting for?"

"Are you sure he wants to see us?"

"What sort of a question is that? Of course he wants to see us."

The last time Tamara talked to Kris was New Year's Eve. Kris described her as irresponsible and incompetent. Tamara is in fact irresponsible and sometimes incompetent as well, but there was no reason to rub her nose in it. She has no great desire to listen to this tirade all over again.

"Today's his last day at the paper," says Frauke. "Wolf mailed me. Kris *has* to see someone, or he'll go off the edge."

"Wolf said that?"

"I said that."

Tamara shakes her head.

"If Kris wants to see anyone, it's certainly not me."

"You know he doesn't mean it like that."

"So how does he mean it?"

"He . . . he gets worried. About you. And about the little one, too, of course."

Frauke deliberately doesn't say her name. *The little one.* Kris, on the other hand, always says the name, although she's asked him not to. And that hurts. They don't talk about Jenni. Jenni is the wound that does not stop bleeding.

Tamara tries to see Jenni twice a week. She isn't allowed to talk to her. She isn't allowed to show herself to her. On especially lonely nights Tamara walks through the south of Berlin and stops in front of Jenni's house. Always well hidden, as if waiting for someone, she looks to see if there's a light in Jenni's room. That's what she and David have agreed upon.

Jenni's father worked his way up over the last two years and now owns a bookshop in Dahlem. Tamara met him at accounting school in Leipzig and became involved for the first time with a man who was grounded and had goals in life. After the relationship had been going for a year Tamara got pregnant. In spite of the pill. Frauke said it was all due to her hormones.

"If your hormones are going crazy, you may as well chuck your pills down the toilet."

Tamara wasn't ready for a child. Although her hormones claimed the opposite, she didn't feel like a mother and wanted an abortion. David fell to pieces when he heard that. He talked about their great love, their future, and how wonderful it was all going to be. Tamara should trust him.

"Please, trust us."

Interminable discussions followed, and in the end Tamara gave in, even though she didn't love David. Being in love with someone and loving someone are two completely different things as far as she's concerned. She can fall in love with a new person every week, but she only wants to love once. David just wasn't the man who totally set her heart alight. He was good to her, he laid the world at her feet, but for true love that wasn't enough. Tamara stayed with him because he had goals and had determined their course

Jenni came into the world, and it was a fiasco. Tamara learned too late that you should never try things out on a child. It's not like choosing a kind of wallpaper, getting out at the wrong station, or entering a relationship. You can take wallpaper down again, there's always a next train, and relationships can be ended—you can't do that with a child. It's there, and it wants to stay.

To make things worse David was the ideal father; he never lost his temper and always took plenty of time, while Tamara was climbing the walls.

She managed seven months before giving up.

She knows it was wicked and mean to go, but she couldn't help it. She didn't feel enough for little Jenni, and was afraid of becoming one of those women who bring up a child who'll spend her whole life in therapy talking about the lack of affection she received from her mother. So Tamara took flight. And it wasn't that Tamara didn't feel anything at all. It was a slowly progressing detachment from herself. She had the feeling of becoming less and less every day, while Jenni was taking up more and more room. As Tamara didn't want to lose herself, she went, leaving father and daughter in the lurch.

David was disappointed, David was furious, but he said he understood and accepted Tamara's decision. He assumed custody on the condition that Tamara gave him the chance of a new start. He didn't want any half measures. He wanted Tamara completely and totally, or else she was to disappear completely from his life.

And that was how Tamara became a ghost.

That same year David married another woman, they started a family, and Jenni got a new mother. For a year Tamara was fine with that, a second year began, and then everything happened as she had been warned it would. By girlfriends, by her family. A painful longing for Jenni exploded inside her. She started to doubt her decision, she started to burn with yearning.

David didn't want to know anything about Tamara's change of heart. He said the door was closed now, and would stay closed.

It hurts Tamara when people talk about Jenni. And for this reason she stays out of Kris's way, because Kris is of the opinion that Tamara should do something about her yearning. He thinks that Jenni belongs with her mother. Regardless of what David has to say on the matter.

"Whatever the two of you agreed on," he said on New Year's Eve, "is completely worthless. You are and remain her mother. It gets on my nerves the way you run around the place suffering. Pull yourself together, damn it. Everybody makes mistakes. You have to stand by your daughter. No ifs or buts."

Everyone makes mistakes.

Tamara understood all that. She gets more advice from all sides than she can deal with. And yet she doesn't want to meet her daughter. Because what if that feeling of estrangement came back one day? Who's to say that Tamara wouldn't take flight again after two days by her daughter's side? There are no guarantees. Tamara would give anything for a few guarantees.

*   *   *

That's almost it. You've met nearly all of them now. Kris and Frauke and Tamara. The fourth member of the confederation is missing. His name is Wolf. He will be the only one that you will meet personally, for just a moment, which is a shame because he's like you. You'd have got along. You both walk through life feeling guilty. The big difference is that Wolf is wrong to feel his guilt, while you are completely aware of your responsibility, which is why you're slowly going mad.

At the moment Wolf is less than thirty yards away from Frauke and Tamara. He is holding a stack of books in his arms, and even though he would never admit it, he'd be really glad for a bit of company.

Let's not keep him waiting.

WOLF

FOR A WHILE WOLF drove a truck. Out in the early morning to the central market, then delivering to the fruit stalls and the little neighborhood grocery stores. After that came a phase in which he did the rounds for various record labels, distributing promo CDs to the shops. That wasn't the right thing either. But he does enjoy selling books outside the university. There are nice female students, who like to haggle and go for coffee. Otherwise, Wolf is in the fresh air and can read as long as nothing is going on. He gets most of the books from Hugendubel or Wohlthat. Today it's Woolworth's turn.

Wolf is one of those writer types who only venture into writing very cautiously. He says he's collecting experiences, but in fact he uses that to hide the fact that he isn't sure what story he has to tell. His first great novel is waiting to be written. Short stories and poems are his bridge to that dream.

Since waking up Wolf has had a brilliant dialogue going on in his head, he just wants to buy this last stack of books before sitting down in a café and putting the words in order. He doesn't know that his course has been predetermined.

On the way to the registers he sees Frauke.

Wolf is about to duck. He has nothing against Frauke, in fact he makes a lot of time for her, they mail one another, they phone, but there's no getting past the fact that there's a lot of history between the two of them, and sometimes Wolf doesn't want to see Frauke. The past can be like a millstone hung around your neck at the most inappropriate moment.

At moments like these.

Men don't like to let their defeats simply happen, they experience them like a bad film, over and over again from the start, and enjoy the bitterness of loss as if it were something precious. When Wolf thinks back to his time with Frauke, he isn't really thinking about Frauke. He is thinking about the woman who extinguished the memory of Frauke. That's exactly where sand gets into the works, and the machinery of his thoughts begins to falter.

Her name was Erin. For two weeks, every hour, every minute, she and Wolf stuck together. *That's what love must feel like,* Wolf had thought then, because everything seemed in focus and super-sharp. His senses were overstimulated, his belly constantly hungry. When Wolf went to the bathroom, he left the door open to go on listening to Erin. And listening was required, because that woman could talk. It was incredible. Wolf found everything she said right and good. Of course a lot of nonsense came out of her mouth as well, but during that brief period it didn't bother Wolf for a second. His head transformed even that nonsense into razor-sharp philosophy. Wolf belonged to her completely.

It was Erin who had sought out Wolf. It happened on the night bus. Wolf was on his way home from a concert. Erin came and stood next to him, said *Hi,* and then said her name. *Erin.* It sounded like a question. *Wolf,* said Wolf, and made it sound like an answer. She took him by the hand, the bus stopped, they got out, and in a deserted playground a few yards from the bus stop they had sex together for the first time. It was very quick. Wordless. Wolf came right away.

"At last," Erin said afterwards.

"At last," Wolf said too, knowing that she would disappear almost immediately and he would lose her forever. He saw himself spending the rest of his life walking around the place with a broken heart. From the beginning Wolf had had that premonition.

They didn't part for a minute. Time existed for them alone. Wolf lost ten pounds because he more or less forgot about eating.

His new life consisted of vodka, television, dope, Pizza Express, sex, cigarettes, Vaseline, music, sweets, baths, talking and talking some more, of sunrises, sunsets, laughing, the best deep sleep of his life and of course one hundred percent of Erin.

On the fourteenth day her cell phone rang. Up until that point Wolf didn't even know she had one. It was three in the morning, and Wolf said:

"Don't answer it."

Erin took the call, listened briefly, and hung up. Wolf wanted to know who was calling at that time of night, but before he could ask, Erin turned onto her belly and stuck her bottom in the air.

"Come on, fuck me again."

Wolf didn't take the trouble to pull down her panties. He pushed them aside to reveal her cunt. He couldn't understand how this woman could always, but really always, be moist and ready for him.

It would be the last time.

Afterwards Erin was in the shower, and Wolf was sitting cross-legged on the lid of the toilet, rolling a joint and listening to her.

"As far as I'm concerned this could go on forever," he said during a pause.

"What do you mean?"

Erin opened the shower curtain. The water sprayed Wolf and slowly covered the floor. Wolf laughed and didn't reply. She didn't have to know everything, after all. Erin turned the water off and reached for a towel. She said she was hungry now. She said the word *hungry* so many times that it lost its meaning. Then she got dressed, took Wolf by the hand, and they went to have breakfast.

Berlin is the only city in Germany where you still feel alive at night. It was summer two years ago, they cycled from west to east and sat down in a café at the Hackeschen Markt. When Wolf crosses the market square today he feels uneasy, as if the tourists are watching him, as if everyone knows that this is the place where he failed.

There was hardly anyone to be seen in the square that morning. There was just a council street-cleaning machine going around sweeping up the dirt from the previous night. Wolf had no idea what day of the week it was. A romantic veil lay over his eyes. Everything about Erin was right—taste, humor, every touch found a perfect echo, no words were out of place, their gestures were almost synchronized. Wolf knew he had found the right woman. *She is mine and belongs to me alone!* He wanted to sing it out loud.

When the first people walked past the café on their way to work, Erin snuggled up to him and he said, "You and me and me and you."

"No," Erin contradicted him. "You *and* me, you *and* me."

She laughed, stood up, and explained she just had to go to the little girls' room for a moment. Wolf didn't follow her. He sat there and played with a beer mat and let five minutes go by. He should have followed her right away. *If only I had . . . Then I would have . . .* Guilt began. Erin didn't come back.

There are days when Wolf sees her in the street, at a newsstand or waiting by a traffic light. Sometimes she sits down next to him on the subway and he doesn't dare look at her. Today on his way to Woolworth's he saw her on a park bench. Her legs were crossed and she had a cell phone pressed to her ear. Of course she paid him no attention, and he didn't stop to chat with her because he had accepted long ago that Erin settled wherever and whenever she felt like it. *She hides in details, she is never the sum of the whole.* Since Wolf accepted that, he has stopped talking to women who are complete strangers.

Wolf is still Wolf. He's a bit broken, he has lost himself a little, but he's still Wolf—a man who thinks that the love of his life is still nearby. He finds her in the tiniest detail. As if her spirit were in turmoil; as if her spirit wanted him to see her.

Wolf found her in one of the stalls in the bathroom. Her head was thrown back, her half-open eyes stared at the ceiling as if there was something to see there. He doesn't know how long he crouched by her motionless body watching her. At some point he leaned forward, closed her eyes, and carefully pulled the needle from her arm before asking one of the waitresses to call an ambulance. When he went back to the bathroom Erin's left eye had opened again. *Automatically,* thought Wolf, feeling hopeful nevertheless, but there was no breathing, there was no pulse. He walked back to the table, sat down, and waited until the police came. He didn't want to know what they had to say. He didn't want to know anything. But he couldn't go. He couldn't simply leave Erin on the toilet in that café. Alone.

For this reason there are days when he even avoids his friends. On those days he doesn't want to exist, or be reminded that he does. He knows it sounds absurd. But the attempt to keep out of his own way is absurd enough already. Wolf just wants to function, with a feeling of guilt by his side and melancholy in his head. The million-dollar question is how long you can go on doing that without feeling like an idiot.

"Look who it is," Wolf shouts across Woolworth's. "It's Frauke!"

Frauke turns around, surprised. Wolf feels his heart contracting.

Such joy.

"Yeah, look," Frauke calls back. "It's Wolf!"

At school Wolf was two classes behind his brother. Little Wolf, so different from big Kris—wittier, noisier, more present. Kris's clique treated him as a mascot. They took him along to parties, watched him bouncing around, trying to get off with girls and puking into the bushes behind the house. When the clique left school, they left Wolf behind like a dog that wasn't old enough to join the pack. The two years till his own school-leaving exam were a torment for him. He wasn't interested in the kids his own age, he listened to different music, spoke a different language. For a while he grew bitter, stole money from his father and drank the evenings away, started fights and had his heart broken by a girl who looked very much like Frauke. During that time melancholy broke out in Wolf like a creeping infection.

He passed his leaving exam with difficulty and went traveling. He explored Scandinavia, spent a month in a dilapidated hut high in the north of Norway and didn't see another human being for six weeks. Then he took a freighter to Canada, where he worked little jobs, felled trees, and cleared snow from driveways. In the summer he slept in the forests and stayed far from civilization. Everything he owned was in his rucksack.

After six years Wolf came back to Berlin having decided to be a writer. No one collected him from the airport the day he arrived, because no one knew he was back. For six months everything was fine, until one day his brother bumped into him in the street.

"And there I was wondering why you didn't answer the phone in Toronto," Kris said by way of greeting.

They looked at each other, they didn't come any closer; something was missing, something had turned the brothers into strangers. Wolf was no longer little Wolf; a strange man was standing in front of Kris. It's always difficult when your surroundings don't change at the same pace as you do yourself. Wolf had gotten burlier, his hair reached his shoulders, his attitude was defensive. And Kris was Kris.

"What are you doing here?"

"Living."

That was all that came out of Wolf. He would have liked to follow it up with another line, he would happily have laughed away the moment, but he had frozen.

"Well, then, go on living," Kris said at last, leaving him standing.

Kris could do that. Kris could draw a line and go on with his life as if nothing had happened. Wolf found that very hard. The brothers remained strangers to one another, and probably nothing would have changed if Erin's death the same year hadn't turned Wolf's world upside down.

Wolf hugs Frauke. The smell of vetiver rises into his nose. Earthy, crude, warm. He feels her breath on his neck and wonders how he could ever have thought of running away for a second.

"What are you doing here?"

"Look to your left," says Frauke.

Two aisles over Tamara is rummaging in a pile of socks. Frauke puts her thumb and forefinger in her mouth and whistles once. Tamara looks up, Wolf waves, and Frauke says:

"Well, if that isn't a coincidence."

Wolf twitches imperceptibly. As far as he's concerned coincidences are an invention of people who can't come to terms with life. The minute something goes wrong they go all helpless. If things are going well they try and find a reason why they're going well. They haven't the guts to say, *This thing and that thing happen to be because I'm the way I am.* Coincidence is Wolf's great weak spot. Since Erin's death he has been trying to find answers to questions that have no answers. *If only I had, I would be.* Nonexistent coincidence caught him off guard and Wolf is hoping for revenge.

Kris greets Tamara and Frauke with a kiss, he's clearly glad of their visit. When the women have gone in, the brothers hug.

"How bad was it?" asks Wolf.

"So-so. My boss couldn't give me a straightforward apology. You know how much I hate that. He said I should give *taz* a call. Can you imagine me doing that?"

Wolf shakes his head.

"Thanks," says Kris, and they walk into the apartment.

Tamara and Frauke have occupied the kitchen. Frauke is

busy washing the vegetables, while Tamara pokes about in the fridge and takes out yogurt, tofu, and sauces. *It's like family,* Wolf thinks, putting his bag of books down on the floor. Kris puts his arm around his shoulders and says something that makes Frauke laugh. Tamara chucks a baby eggplant at Kris and hits Wolf. They laugh. It's as if they have no ballast.

We're approaching the start. You are now ready for the present and know who's going to be crossing your path. Over the next few days you will learn more about Frauke, Tamara, and Wolf. Kris, on the other hand, will remain a mystery to you. He'll get close to you, but he'll still stay out of reach. All your efforts to uncover his motivation and his background will trickle into the sand. You won't be able to bridge the distance between you and him until the finale. But you don't need to worry about that now.

In a few minutes it will all begin.

It's midnight.

Four people are sitting in an apartment. They've talked a lot, they've eaten and drunk and they're glad they've met up again. The singing of Thomas Dybdahl comes out of the speakers, the wail of an ambulance siren rises up from the street, then it's quiet again and Berlin goes on breathing. Calm and resolute.

Four friends are sitting in an apartment. They have more defeats than victories to show for themselves. They live on their overdrafts, hope for the love of their lives, and shop at Aldi, even though they hate Aldi. Up until now not one of the four has the slightest idea where they're headed. If chance had willed it, Tamara wouldn't have picked up the phone and would still be lying on her bed reading. A frustrated Frauke would have ended up staying over with one of her three lovers, and Wolf would have spent the day outside the university and gone to the cinema with Kris in the evening. If chance had willed it, none of any of this would have happened.

But today chance doesn't come into it.

"I have to piss," says Kris, and goes off to the bathroom.

Wolf passes the joint to Tamara. She shakes her head and says her eyes are too dry, she can't smoke any more, then she creeps on all fours to the stereo to change the CD. Wolf tries to slap her on the bum, and misses by a foot and a half. Frauke nestles her head on his thigh. Tamara puts on Elbow. Guy Garvey sings, *I haven't been myself lately, I haven't slept for several days.* Wolf thinks the guy knows what he's talking about. Tamara says the last time she had an orgasm she smelled flowers. She doesn't say that when she was having her last orgasm she was by herself in the shower thinking about a film star. Wolf doesn't want to know the details, either. He feels Frauke's breath on his thigh and tries to suppress an erection. There's a sound of flushing. Kris comes out of the bathroom and stops in the doorway. He looks at his friends as if he hasn't seen them for days. Then he says:

"Do you know what people out there lack?"

"I know what you lack," says Tamara.

"No, seriously. What do people lack?"

"Which people?"

"Business types, for example. What are they short of?"

"Good taste?" Wolf suggests.

"Dammit, take me seriously here, people. Just for a minute, okay?"

"Okay, then, tell us," says Frauke. "What do people lack?"

Frauke can do that. She can switch from one moment to the next, while Wolf takes a bit longer. Tamara, on the other hand, doesn't react at all. She tosses around in her head the memory of the flowers that she smelled when she had her last orgasm, and suddenly bursts out laughing. Frauke nudges her. Tamara stops laughing. Kris raises his index finger, every inch the teacher.

"There's one thing," he says, "that bosses and action men lack, and which they can't get by without. There's one thing that hangs over their lives like a dark shadow and pisses in their macchiato every day. No wealth protects them against it, it doesn't even help if they make donations to charity or take out *Greenpeace* magazine subscriptions for their employees. This one little thing makes their lives so incredibly difficult that you can see it in their faces."

Kris looks at them one by one. It's plain that none of them has the faintest idea what he's talking about. So Kris stretches out his right hand, palm upwards, like an offering.

"They can't apologize," he says. "And that's exactly what we're going to offer them. Apologies galore, at a damned good price."

FRAUKE

KRIS TALKS ABOUT HIS morning at the Urbanhafen and how he apologized to the woman. He said he knew exactly what was going on with her.

"And she believed me. She accepted my apology without hesitation. No doubt, nothing."

"You couldn't have done that with me," says Frauke.

"With me you could," says Tamara.

They talk for a while, and one idea chases the next. They anticipate each other's sentences, they are moving on a single wavelength, so that Frauke can't shake the feeling of floating above the ground.

It's the dope, she thinks, *we're just a bit high, it's nothing more than that.*

But it isn't the dope or the wine. It's a particular string of circumstances that brings particular people together at particular times. And anyone who finds that puzzling has never been influenced by such a concatenation.

At three in the morning Wolf gets up and announces that he's going to butter some rolls.

"I'm incredibly hungry, aren't you?"

They watch him go, then Tamara explodes with laughter and says, "He's not really going to do rolls, is he?"

"Of course I'm doing rolls!" come the words from the kitchen.

They laugh, tears run down their faces, they gasp for air. The last time they got so hysterical was at the end of school. All the senior grades went to the Teufelsberg to celebrate their goodbyes. Kris wore a suit, Frauke and Tamara came in dresses. Black and white. They all felt inviolable, and Frauke can still remember what she whispered in Tamara's ear: *I'm immortal, what about you?* Tamara had grinned and said she was with them. *Of course I'm with you, do you think I'd leave you in the lurch?*

They thought the whole world was at their feet. First university, then the big job, then masses of cash. They particularly agreed on the last point. They planned to meet up again in a few years and celebrate their successes appropriately. Even today Frauke can't get her head round how naïve they were back then. They talked about going abroad, as if abroad were right on their doorstep waiting for them. England, Spain, Australia, China. They wanted to go everywhere. *We thought no one could touch us. We thought we could get everything that could be—*

"Frauke, are you still there?"

Tamara snaps her fingers in front of her face.

"Where else would I be?" Frauke asks back.

She has no idea how long she was thinking about the party on the Teufelsberg. No one is laughing now. Kris rolls the next joint, Wolf goes on busying himself in the kitchen, and Tamara sits with a ballpoint in her hand, bent over a notepad.

"One minute," she says.

Frauke is amazed at what it is that has brought her and Tamara together and held them together for so long. There was one falling-out during their school days. Tamara had met a new clique of girls, and Frauke didn't fit in with them at all. It was a bad month, and then all of a sudden Tamara sat next to Frauke during break and said it had been a really bad idea. Frauke never told her that she could almost have cried with relief. She felt incomplete without her best friend. She knows exactly what her life would be without Tamara. Like an endless winter's day. Like no sun ever again.

"I've got it."

Tamara holds the notepad out to Frauke. Frauke reads, and the grin vanishes from her face.

"What's up?"

Kris crouches down and joins them. He and Frauke freeze. Wolf comes out of the kitchen with the rolls.

"What's wrong with you guys?"

Tamara blushes.

"Nothing in particular. It's just what Kris said," she explains, and is about to set the notepad aside when Kris grabs it.

"You've *just* written this?" he asks.

Tamara shrugs.

"I could try and do it a different way, if you . . ."

She gets no further, Kris has passed the pad on to Wolf, and put his hands on Tamara's cheeks.

"You bloody genius," he says and kisses her.

When Frauke comes back into the room at half past four, her answering machine is flashing. Three messages, three times the same voice.

How are you . . .

What are you doing . . .

When are we seeing each other . . .

Frauke deletes the messages without listening to them all the way through, and pins Tamara's text to the corkboard beside the monitor. Kris said she should take her time, Wolf would really want to do it himself, and Tamara had no opinion, because she'd gone to sleep on the floor.

Frauke promised to set about designing the text right away the following morning. But she's so uneasy that she doesn't know if she can even get to sleep. To calm herself down she takes a shower. Her brain is intoxicated with the ideas that they all had last night. It feels a bit as if they had traveled into the past together to bring their youthful immortality into the present.

I'm immortal, what about you?

I'm not tired, Frauke thinks and gets out of the shower to switch her computer on.

Two and a half hours later Frauke pushes herself up from her desk. She has turned Tamara's text into an advertisement, and is now so amped that she can't sit still. Work as a pick-me-up. Her muscles are tense, her thoughts a bright flame. In a few minutes Frauke has put on her running things and is out the door.

The Tiergarten is deserted at this time of day, the morning light is like underwater photographs on a rainy day. Colorless and crisp. Frauke runs three times around the little lake, her body has found its rhythm, her breathing adapts to her footsteps. *As if I could slow down time, as if the minutes were collapsing into one another and the clock hands slowing down.* Frauke likes the idea. The faster she runs, the harder it gets for time to advance. Time becomes material. Frauke has the feeling that she can stretch, compress, or tear that material. Time has torn so often for her before that Frauke finds herself wondering how it is that time still exists at all.

When she gets back from her run, he's waiting for her by the door to her apartment. She often wonders how he manages to get up the stairs. The tenants are very suspicious and even discuss on the intercom with the man from the parcel service because they think he's delivering some sort of junk mail.

He's sitting on the floor, his back resting against the door of the apartment, chin on his chest, hands clasped in his lap. Once a neighbor found him like that and called an ambulance. Frauke knows he isn't asleep, he's in more of a twilight state. Or as he once explained: *Half the time I'm on standby.*

She shakes him by the shoulder. He stirs, opens his eyes, grins.

"Hi, sweetie."

"You shouldn't do that," says Frauke.

"What? And what am I supposed to do in *your* opinion, if you don't call back?"

He sits up and she helps him; even though she doesn't really want to, she helps him. He gets to his feet, groans and sighs, then tries to hug her. Frauke shrinks back.

"Let's go in," she says.

Frauke's flat isn't big, and with him inside it shrinks by half. Space and time. It all comes back to her father.

"Have you been running again?"

"What does it look like?"

He takes his shoes off and marches into the living room as if he does this every day. Frauke hears him sigh again, then he falls silent. Even though she knows he expects coffee, she puts on water for tea. Green tea that tastes like hay, which she drinks when she wants to punish herself with health.

"What's that supposed to be?" he asks when she comes into the living room with the tray. He holds up one of the printouts. Black text on a white background. Frauke sets the tray down and takes the printout from his hand.

"Since when have you been doing obituaries?"

Frauke is glad she used a dummy text, otherwise she would have had to give her father answers that she doesn't want to give him. She sets the printout back on the desk. Her life is none of his business.

"New job?" he asks.

"New girlfriend?" she asks back.

"First some coffee," her father says to change the subject and walks over to the tray. For a few seconds he stares at the teapot and the two cups as if he can't work out what their function might be. Frauke can tell from his back that he is repelled. His shoulders are slightly hunched, he looks ridiculous. He looks like all the fathers over the age of fifty that she meets in the street. Preposterous and old.

"What's this?" he asked, sniffing at the tea. "Cow piss?"

Frauke pushes him away, takes one of the cups and sits down on the sofa. She can't help grinning, even though she doesn't want to. Her father sniffs at the tea again and leaves his cup where it is.

"Sweetie," he says, and walks over to her. His head settles in her lap and his eyes close contentedly. He always uses the same tactic. As if his life ran only on a single track. The gestures, the words.

"I miss you both," he murmurs.

Frauke feels like crying. It's been her ritual since she moved out ten years ago. And she always gives her father the same answer, because whether she likes it or not, she's part of the ritual.

"Your own fault," she says, although she knows it isn't his fault.

Frauke drinks her tea, as her father's head lies heavy in her lap and time seems to stretch out comfortably again.

Gerd Lewin owns a construction company and various plots of land in the north of Berlin, occupied by apartment blocks. He owns shares in two big hotels, and twice a year he changes his girlfriend, who is supposed to replace Frauke's mother and can't.

Every two weeks it's visiting time.

Frauke takes the train down to Potsdam and waits outside the clinic while her father smokes one last cigarette. Always frantically, with one eye on the street, as if he can only accept the presence of the clinic at the very last minute. It's only when he drops the cigarette on the pavement and crushes it with his shoe that the brick building, with its park and its grandiose entrance, becomes real for him. By now Frauke wants a cigarette as well, but she quells her craving because she doesn't want to be like her father.

Tanja Lewin has been living in a private clinic for fourteen years. Her life there is barely any different from the life she led at home. From outside everything looks normal, if it weren't for the times when Frauke's mother would climb the walls, throw up her dinner, and hide in the wardrobe. Times when she saw the devil everywhere.

If you ask Frauke's father, he claims he should have seen it coming. He often says he should have seen something coming. The crisis in the building trades, the chlamydia one of his girlfriends gave him, the bad weather, and of course the misunderstandings between him and his daughter.

*   *   *

Frauke's mother first ran away on her forty-third birthday. The police caught up with her just before Nuremberg. Tanja Lewin had locked herself in a gas station bathroom, and was endlessly calling out her own name. Questioned later, Frauke's mother didn't know exactly what had happened. She remembered feeling a sudden urge to get out of Berlin. Then she had a blackout and woke up in the gas station bathroom—her throat was sore from shouting, and two men lifted her into an ambulance.

Frauke's mother entered psychiatric treatment for two months. The next blackout came a few days after her release. This time Frauke's mother stayed in Berlin, and was arrested in the bedding department of a furniture store. All she remembered was waiting for the bus on Nollendorfplatz. A man told her the bus was going to be late. A moment later the bus stop had disappeared, and Tanja was naked in the bedding department, clutching a pillow, asking what all the people were doing in her bedroom.

It was in the furniture store that the devil first appeared to Tanja Lewin. He came in the form of a policeman and told everyone to move on. He gathered up Frauke's mother's clothes from the floor, and handed them to her under the covers. He was nice. He only spoke when she was dressed. He said, *I'll always be with you now. I will come to you with different faces, but you will always recognize me.*

Tanja Lewin would never forget those words.

The doctors studied the Lewin case at length. They questioned Frauke's mother and gave her medication; they spoke to Frauke's father and advised him to have his wife put in a clinic. The medication worked to some extent, but round-the-clock care was recommended.

A week later Gerd Lewin signed the papers and put his wife in an exclusive private clinic in Potsdam. The same day Frauke's father stopped sleeping. He lay in bed at night staring at the ceiling as if waiting for the everyday to return to his life. Incredibly, he went on working, brought money into the house, and did what he had to do to protect the lives of his wife and daughter. Only his eyes gave him away—dark, burned-out hollows that scared Frauke. For over six months Gerd Lewin survived this state, and then one evening he stood by Frauke's bed.

"Tanja," he said, "my Tanja."

Frauke didn't know whether he thought she was her mother or was only asking after her. She brought him back to his bedroom, covered him with a blanket, and was about to go when he reached for her hand.

"Stay."

"I'm not Mama," said Frauke.

"I know," said her father. "I do know."

He pulled Frauke onto the bed so that she was lying on her mother's side.

"Sleep," he said, and fell asleep immediately.

It was his first sleep in seven months and sixteen days. The next morning he woke up next to Frauke, looked around in surprise, and started crying. He howled until the snot poured unhindered from his nose and mouth.

That was how the rituals between father and daughter began. Gerd Lewin couldn't get to sleep alone, so for the next few years they shared a bed.

Since Frauke has had her own flat, her father's insomnia has returned. That's why he comes to her place from time to time. Because of the calm she gives him, because of the pathetic illusion that his wife is with him again and he can sleep. Love can be cruel. It won't let you go, it wants to be noticed day and night. Gerd Lewin could write a book about it.

Frauke pushes a pillow under her father's head and gets up. She is so exhausted that she can no longer think clearly. Nonetheless she sits down for a moment at her Mac, converts the advertisement into a PDF file, and e-mails it to Kris. Now everything's right. Her work is done. Sleep.

When Frauke wakes up ten hours later, her father has vanished from the sofa, and Kris has left a message on the answering machine:

That's brilliant! See you later! We've got to celebrate!

Frauke plays the message through four times, leaning against the wall, one foot over the other and a hand pressed to her mouth so that the laughter doesn't explode from her. She is happy. She is really happy.

A week later the advertisement appears in *Die Zeit* and *Der Tagesspiegel*. It is set in the style of a high-class obituary, the death of a head of state or something. Eye-catching. The text is literally as Tamara wrote it during the night. It embodies Kris's idea perfectly.

SORRY

WE ENSURE THAT NOTHING
EMBARRASSES YOU ANY MORE.
SLIPS, MISUNDERSTANDINGS,
DISMISSALS, ARGUMENTS, AND ERRORS.

WE KNOW WHAT YOU SHOULD SAY.
WE SAY WHAT YOU WANT TO HEAR.
PROFESSIONAL AND DISCREET.

Under the advertisement there is no homepage or e-mail address. They unanimously decided against it. Frauke only put in Kris's landline number. It's a gag. She wanted to see who would call, whether anyone would call, and what he would have to say.

The first day nothing happens.

The second day nothing happens.

The third day they get four calls.
By the weekend it's nineteen.
Without understanding how it's possible, they're in business.

PART II

After

THE CLICK OF THE NOZZLE wakes me. I'm standing next to the car, leaning over, arms on the roof. I must have gone to sleep. My calves are trembling, it's a wonder that I haven't fallen over.

I walk into the gas station shop and get coffee from a machine. It's eleven in the morning, it's the second day, and I feel like a pinball that's being bounced noisily from one cushion to another, never coming to rest. An hour ago I drove past Munich and set my course for Nuremberg. I'm thinking from one city to the next. I don't know where I'll go after Nuremberg. Only Berlin is out of the question. As soon as I see the next exit, I'll switch on the indicator and look for a destination. Life can be reduced to the most elementary things. Filling up, drinking, sleeping, eating, peeing, and driving. Driving, time and again.

"Will there be anything else?"

The cashier has an eyelash on her cheek. I tell her. She laughs and wipes the eyelash away. She could've made a wish, but she doesn't look like someone who believes in wishes. She hands me my change. I look outside. A man wearing blue dungarees and holding a bucket stops by my car. He sets the bucket down and starts cleaning my windshield.

"Wait, your coffee!"

I'm already on my way outside and turn round. The cashier holds up my paper cup. I take the coffee and thank her. When I leave the gas station shop the man has finished the windshield and is on his way to the back window.

"No!" I shout.

"It's free," the man says, setting the bucket down on the ground.

"Even so . . ."

I put the coffee on the car roof, rummage for change in my trouser pocket, and press two euros into his hand.

"No offense," I say and wait until he goes. Then I get into the car and drive off. Fifty yards away from the gas station I stop in the car park. My hands are trembling. I look in the rearview mirror. The window behind me is brown, I left the coffee on the car roof. I burst out laughing. I just sit in the car for a few minutes and try to calm myself down. My hands are trembling, and although I've just been to the bathroom I feel pressure on my bladder.

"It'll all be fine," I repeat, resting my hand on the tailgate and enjoying the silence beneath it.

Before

TAMARA

"TAMARA, I don't think that's funny."

"It's a surprise."

"I hate surprises. It's far too cold for surprises."

"Take the blanket."

"You think the blanket will help? What's it even made of? That's not wool. That's barbed wire!"

The day is gray and overcast. Tamara has picked her sister up from the jetty at the Ronnebypromenade. It was only when she appeared behind her that Astrid noticed her and clutched her heart in alarm.

"I thought you were going to pick me up?"

"I *am* picking you up."

"Tammi, it's winter, and that's a bloody rowboat!"

Tamara pointed to the seat opposite. A blanket and seat cushion lie there waiting.

"Come on," Tamara said, tapping the cushion. "Get in, before your makeup runs."

"My makeup won't run, it's far too cold, in case you haven't noticed," Astrid replied, and got into the boat. She sat down opposite Tamara and pulled the blanket around her shoulders. Since then they've been on the water, and Astrid's mood isn't improving.

"I hate open water," she says.

"It's the Wannsee, not the open sea."

"Still."

They drift under the Wannsee Bridge. There's a hint of rain in the air. It's the mildest winter for ages. Tamara likes the feeling in her hands when the oars part the water. She looks very contented.

"What are you looking so pleased about?"

"I'm happy to see you."

"That could have happened ages ago, if you'd bothered to give me a call. I'm your big sister, can't you imagine how worried I've been about you?"

"I was going to call you . . ."

"You *didn't*, though. You disappear for six months and no one knows where you are, and then all this . . ."

She points across the Wannsee as if the lake belongs to Tamara. Tamara goes on rowing and grins. Astrid doesn't find that at all funny and kicks Tamara's leg.

"Ouch!"

"Did that hurt?"

"Of course it hurt."

"Good. So what was up?"

"I was busy."

"Busybusybusy."

"You could say that."

Astrid lights a cigarette and looks at Tamara through narrowed eyes. They drift past the tram depot and approach the brightly lit hospital.

"Do I have to worm it out of you?"

"I was working."

"Aha."

"I've made some money, Astrid. A lot of money."

Astrid's mouth opens.

"You haven't robbed a bank or something, have you?"

"Nothing like that," Tamara says, holding the oars in the water to stop the boat, then points to the shore.

"Look, over there."

The house is overgrown with ivy, and looks unassailable. The garden seems like a botanic experiment, but that's just the first impression. If you look more closely you can see the paths and the plan behind them. The garden is thought-out down to the last details, even the terrace is part of it. There is a wooden table and two chairs covered with a plastic sheet.

"That's where the Belzens live," Tamara goes on. "They're both about seventy and very nice. Once a week they walk along the promenade, take the ferry, and have a coffee on the Pfaueninsel. That's what I'm going to do when I'm that age."

Astrid tilts her head.

"Tamara, what's going on?"

Tamara points to the opposite shore.

"And that's where we live."

The opposite shore is a good fifty yards away. Through the dense trees an old villa can be seen. It's two stories high, and there's a tower on the left-hand side. There are lights on in three windows.

If fireworks went off now, Tamara would find that very suitable. The view always reminds her of the beginning of winter, and what it was like going down to the shore late at night and looking back at the villa. As if it were all just a dream and the villa could disappear at any moment. Tamara has the deep and certain feeling of having arrived.

"You're joking, aren't you?"

"Shall we go ashore?"

Astrid puts a hand on Tamara's arm to stop her rowing any further.

"Tell me you're joking.",

"I'm not joking."

Astrid looks across at the villa, then back at her sister.

"Who have you landed for yourself?"

"Nobody."

"Nobody with loads of money? Just stop right now."

"No, really," says Tamara and can tell by her voice that even she herself hasn't really quite understood. Six months have passed since they founded the agency, and she still finds it hard to believe that they've come this far.

"Kris had an idea," she begins, and tells her sister what has happened.

At first they were contacted only by companies with internal problems. Next came companies that wanted to apologize to other companies. There were also private requests, but they were quickly excluded. The agency has no interest in patching marriages together or apologizing on behalf of people who had accidentally run over a cat. At first they were limited to Berlin, but over the weeks that followed requests from the south and west of Germany started piling up, Kris said.

"Either we go beyond Berlin or someone else will do it."

Thus Wolf became a representative of forgiveness and traveled all around Germany. He likes the change and the anonymity that goes with it—night after night another hotel room, day after day another town.

The brothers are responsible for the apologizing. Tamara tried and failed. She makes everything personal, and if she's honest she doesn't think much of apologizing for somebody she finds unsympathetic. Kris said:

"You don't take sides; you do your job, that's the only way it works."

And because it only works like that, Tamara let it go. Apologies were out of the question for Frauke as well. She opted for office work, putting timetables together, coordinating commissions, writing bills, things like that. That's her world, while Tamara sits by the phone and is responsible for the requests. Because anyone who doesn't get along with Tamara can go hang as far as the agency's concerned.

*   *   *

"Why haven't you told me any of this?" Astrid wants to know.

"We didn't want anyone else muscling in on us. We wanted to be able to go our own way. We had no idea how it would go."

The machinery was set in motion without any help from them. Apart from the advertisement in two big newspapers there was no other promotion. Frauke said it would be tacky. The companies heard about them and reacted. Guilt-stricken company directors phoned up; managers explaining their problems in the third person, and secretaries who, pushed forward by their bosses, wanted to find out how the thing actually worked.

Often it's endless phone conversations with embarrassing confessions, and of course there are also customers who don't want to talk at all and send their ideas by post. They are Tamara's favorites. Cool and matter-of-fact, they ask for the agency's help. Tamara's job is to separate the serious from the non-serious cases. Of every ten commissions three are usually a waste of time.

Of course there are complaints, too. Customers who can't get their heads around how the agency works. It goes too far for them, and it's not how the customer would have imagined it. Kris insists that there's no such thing as "too far."

"If they don't know what that means," he explained to Tamara, "tell them forgiveness knows no bounds, that always sounds good."

Many people see this as a Bible quotation. Frauke has taken it as a motto and incorporated it into the questionnaire.

Forgiveness knows no bounds.

There were some imitators too, for a while, but they didn't worry the agency. It's not just about an idea, it's about a philosophy. Kris quickly revealed himself as a master of forgiveness. His philosophy is the motor that drives the agency onward.

"Of course people can imitate our idea," he says, "but our concept will remain a mystery to them."

And if anyone were to ask what their concept was, all four of them would have to act mysterious, because the truth is that they have no idea of concepts. Kris has taught Wolf everything—the right words, the right gestures, when you have to be silent, when you have to talk. The rest is experience, that's why it's no wonder that the imitators had to shut up shop. They simply had no reasonable concept.

"Why didn't you stay in Berlin?"

"Astrid, this is Berlin."

"Wannsee isn't Berlin, Tammi, it's the East."

Astrid flicks her cigarette butt into the water, as if to demonstrate to her sister what she thinks of the Wannsee. Tamara doesn't want to contradict her; Astrid's never been a star in geography. Instead Tamara says:

"We were getting cramped. The commissions were pouring in, and we were still in Kris's apartment, coordinating everything from a single room. One evening Wolf had had enough."

"I hate the fact that we're still hanging around at Kris's apartment," he said. "I mean, commune or not, we're really too old for this. We should stop behaving like amateurs. With every commission we're making more than any of us has ever made in six months. Shouldn't we do something with the money?"

They found a dilapidated villa on the Kleine Wannsee. Tamara couldn't believe such things still existed. Except in films, of course. Every few minutes you heard the train running quietly in the background, and from the conservatory you could look out on to the shore of the Kleine Wannsee over breakfast. Of course there were a few reservations. Who in their late twenties moves to the edge of Berlin to renovate a villa? Either some kind of prehistoric hippies who inherited money from their parents, or crisply tanned film producers who have to invest their profits somewhere. But them?

They couldn't have cared less.

The villa turned out to be a dream, a dilapidated dream admittedly, but they were living out that dream. Tamara still can't grasp how quickly it all happened. The real estate agent took his cut, the bank waved them through, and the villa was theirs. Frauke's father arrived with a gang of workmen, and together they knocked down walls, scraped off old wallpaper, improved the floors, and put in new pipes, so that the villa was ready to be occupied by the beginning of January.

For the first week they walked speechlessly through the rooms. Everywhere there were freshly sanded floors, freshly whitened walls, rooms full of light. The stench of their youth lay behind them. All of a sudden everything was stylish and authentic; all at once they felt grown-up.

On the first floor are the living room, a library, and the kitchen; on the second floor Frauke and Tamara's studies and bedrooms. The brothers take the top floor.

It's perfect, it works so well that Tamara can imagine this arrangement going on to the end of her life. Out here on the Kleine Wannsee with a view of the water and access to a jetty.

Their very own paradise.

"It's just perfect," Tamara concludes. "That's all. Nothing else has happened."

Astrid is about to say something, when she hears someone calling behind her.

"Yoohoo, Tamara!"

The sisters turn round. Helena Belzen stands waving on the shore. She is seventy-four and wears a pullover that makes her look like the Michelin man. She has wrapped scarves around her hips and her neck, on her head she wears a woollen cap. In her right hand she has a shovel, in her left a bucket.

"Helena, this is my sister Astrid," Tamara explains.

"Pleased to meet you," says Helena, pointing with her

spade to the dinghy. "Isn't it a bit cold to be rowing about on the lake?"

"Tell that to my sister," says Astrid.

"How are you two?" asks Tamara.

"Joachim's taking his radio apart again, and I can't keep out of the garden," Helena replies, shaking the bucket. "I could spend the whole day burrowing about in the earth. Are we seeing each other on Sunday?"

"I'll bring cake."

"Wonderful!"

Helena waves goodbye and disappears into the undergrowth of her garden.

"Are you having a kaffeeklatsch with the old girl?" Astrid whispers.

"She's invited me four times, it gets embarrassing eventually. And I like the Belzens. Wait till you see her husband. They're a dream couple. The day we moved in, they moored on our side and brought us a bag of salt and fresh bread."

"What do you need parents for?" Astrid says and looks back at the villa. "I still can't believe it. If you weren't my little sister, I'd push you in the water right now, is that clear? Shit, why doesn't stuff like this happen to me? Have you any idea how many guys I've picked up in the faint hope that one of them might have enough money to buy me something like this? I hate you, do you know that?"

"I know."

"So what are you grinning about?"

"Maybe because it's so cold?"

"Very funny, Tammi."

They grin at each other.

"Can I at least see the joint from inside, before you banish me back to my pathetic little life?"

Tamara lowers the oars into the water and sets course for their pad.

KRIS

IT WAS HALF A day before they managed to track down Julia Lambert.

The job center plays its cards close to the vest, so Kris tries to find her new workplace indirectly. Frauke helps him with that. It takes them fifteen minutes to log on to the employment agency.

"How illegal have you just been?" Kris wondered.

Frauke held her thumb and index finger a millimeter apart.

Julia Lambert has been with the company for a week. The office with a view of the parking lot is like a waiting room. Cardboard boxes in the corner, electric cables temporarily installed, a dusty plant by the window. Probably Julia Lambert isn't entirely sure whether it's worth making this workplace entirely her own. Her hesitation is like the one of the four prints on the wall that hangs at an angle.

"You must have heard that we've split up."

Kris nods, Hessmann's secretary told him everything. The boss himself didn't want to say anything on the subject.

"I was amazed you didn't lodge a complaint," says Kris.

Julia laughs briefly.

"How do you take action against someone like Hessmann? He has more lawyers than employees. And who would believe me? What proof do I have? For a while I thought about burning down the office building, but can you imagine where that would have got me?"

In jail, Kris thinks, and agrees, she did the right thing.

"I'm here to apologize to you," he says.

"You?"

"Me."

"Why you?"

"My agency represents Hessmann. Since we took on the

commission, it's a personal thing for me if my client makes mistakes. I'm something like his conscience. And you can bet that someone like Hessmann wants to have a clean conscience."

She doesn't react, she looks at the card.

"Hence Sorry?"

"Because we apologize."

"For other people?"

"For other people, yes. Do you want to tell me what happened in your own words?"

"I don't think so."

"Are you sure?"

Julia Lambert nods and clasps her hands. The card is in front of her on the table. Kris shouldn't force it now. Her gestures are unambiguous. But it's a good sign that she set the visiting card down on the table faceup. Kris can see the logo, he's very pleased with the logo. They look at one another. Kris will keep his mouth shut until Julia Lambert speaks first. She needs time to think about his words.

Her history is typical. Since Sorry took on its first commission, there have been several such cases. Her boss had an affair with her and fired her when he craved fresh meat. You could call that the end of a career. The secretary, of course, put it differently.

Julia Lambert is someone who learns from her mistakes. Kris can see that she will get back on her own two feet all by herself. But he also sees that she's still preoccupied by her humiliation. Not being able to defend herself, being totally subject to the word of someone who was first her boss, then her lover, and finally her boss again.

Where the emotions are concerned, we all cave in sooner or later, Kris thinks, and is glad to keep the thought to himself.

"You don't have to apologize," Julia Lambert says after a minute.

"No one said anything about *having to,*" Kris replies. "Hessmann knows he made a mistake. And you know that he would never personally admit it to you. People like Hessmann make things easy for themselves. He changes his women as often as he changes his tie."

Her eyebrows contract, Kris could bite his tongue. *How can I be such an idiot? What is this? A chat over a glass of beer?* He has universalized Julia Lambert, and made a crude mistake.

"I'm sorry. The image was inappropriate."

"Keep talking."

"I'm not here to offer you money," says Kris, although that's exactly why he's here. "Money is comfortable, and I think you're concerned about more than comfort."

Bull's-eye. She doesn't nod, she doesn't shake her head, her right hand has found the business card again, and is turning it around in her fingers. She waits for more.

"As you know, Hessmann has contacts. The business listens to him. And when I see where the job center has sent you . . ."

Kris sums up her office with a wave of his hand.

" . . . then I think you deserve better."

"You do?"

"I do."

"I like it here."

"No, you don't."

She stops turning the business card around. She doesn't contradict him.

Thank God.

"Where do you want to go?" Kris asks.

"Simple as that?" she asks back.

"Simple as that. I'll find you a better position in a different company, in return you accept Hessmann's apology and leave the fury and hurt behind you; that's my offer."

Kris knows it's never that easy to leave fury and hurt behind. But he thinks Julia Lambert ought to hear that the possibility exists, and that a better job than the last one represents a good kind of revenge.

The phone rings. Julia Lambert lets it ring and presses two buttons so that they can have some peace. The phone falls silent.

"From when?" she asks.

"Hessmann gave me carte blanche where you're concerned. That is to say, whenever you like. No one wants to live with guilt. Not even Hessmann."

Julia Lambert laughs for the second time since Kris has been with her. It's a restrained laugh, but it's still a laugh that comes from deep down.

Good.

"He's been able to live with it pretty well for the last six months," she says. "I doubt he had any sleepless nights."

The sarcasm is clearly audible. Kris is still not on safe terrain. It's the way Julia Lambert sits there. Tense, suspicious.

The whole thing could be one big joke.

"Here's my suggestion," Kris says and gets to his feet. "I invite you out to dinner now, and while we're eating, you tell me which companies you're interested in, what position you think you could do or would like to have, and what an appropriate wage might be."

Kris stretches out his hands so that she can see he isn't hiding anything, that he's on her side. No tricks.

"What do you think?"

Her nostrils flare, her mouth has opened a crack, not a word comes out. Enough sarcasm. She's excited, she's understood. Kris can see that Julia Lambert likes his offer. It has happened. She belongs to him.

"You did *what*?" Wolf asks in the evening when they're sitting in the villa's conservatory.

"I had dinner with her."

"No, no, no, I mean that carte blanche . . ."

Wolf leans forward and taps his brother twice on the forehead.

". . . what kind of an idea is that?"

"I thought it would be appropriate."

"And what did Hessmann say?"

"What do you think he said?"

"You did *what?*"

Hessmann's voice was shrill, then there was a faint crackle on the line and Kris knew that someone was listening in. Ten minutes before, Kris had said goodbye to Julia Lambert and promised to call the next day. Then he had phoned Hessmann from his car.

"How do you think that's going to work?"

Kris heard the panic in Hessmann's voice. Panic isn't good. Panic can lead to short-circuited reactions. Kris was relieved that he wasn't talking to Hessmann alone. Whoever else was listening at the other end, it meant that Hessmann had to restrain himself. Kris cleared his throat and said how he imagined the solution to the problem:

"You get Miss Lambert a job at one of the two companies she named. You know you can do that. Then you and Miss Lambert will be quits. Peace."

Again there was that faint crackle on the line; Kris listened into the silence that followed. For a few seconds he was sure that the connection had been broken, then he heard a loud intake of breath and Hessmann said his thank-you, and that it had been a pleasure working with the agency.

"How could you be so sure it would work?" Wolf wants to know. "Guys like Hessmann eat you for breakfast, what were you thinking of?"

Kris is surprised by Wolf's reaction.

"I had nothing to lose," he replies. "And I think it's a good thing for him to bleed a bit."

Wolf lets that idea run through his head for a moment.

"I have the feeling that all this apologizing is turning into something personal for you."

"A bit personal can't hurt," Kris admits. "Be honest, it isn't just a question of apologizing. It's about understanding. What's the point of apologizing if the other person doesn't sense that you're serious about it?"

"You say understanding, Kris, but you mean empathy."

"No, with empathy you're private, while we stay detached. We can't afford empathy, which is why Tamara's unsuited for the job. You fit in much better. You have a superficiality about you that's emotionally cool, relatively speaking."

"Hey, how convenient."

"You know what I mean."

Wolf nods. Kris can get away with saying things like that.

"So you're sticking with understanding?"

"Understanding with a hint of sympathy."

Wolf rubs his neck.

"It's still a hard job for me. I'm pursued by ghosts. Before and after each commission. Often for hours."

Kris thinks about how it is for him. He doesn't see ghosts, and if he's perfectly honest, the commission ends there and then. But he doesn't want to rub it in.

"No one said it would be easy to apologize on other people's behalf. If it was easy, someone would have thought of it ages ago. I reckon we'll soon be condemned by the church. We deliver absolution and bring light to dark souls."

"And we're more expensive."

"Yes, we're more expensive, but that doesn't mean anyone has to fall on their knees and thank us in the evening. And think about how many people we've brought happiness to already. On both sides. Perpetrators and victims. We're the good guys. Look at our commissions. If we weren't the good guys, we wouldn't be booked up for months in advance. Guilt seeps from people's pores. Wolf, we're the new forgiveness. Forget religion. We mediate between guilt and remorse. You can bet your ass that we're the good guys."

*   *   *

Four days after the Hessmann commission, Julia Lambert gets the job and sends Kris a thank-you card. A week later there's a check from Hessmann in the mailbox. He's added a bonus to the fee. Wolf kisses the check over and over again, until Frauke tells him to stop or the bank won't accept it.

And at this point we leave Wolf and Frauke briefly. We leave Tamara, reading on the sofa, and Kris, in the shower a floor above. It's time for you to enter this story. Through a back door. Like a ghost rising out of the floor and taking the stage.

Welcome.

YOU

You FIRST LEARN ABOUT the agency over lunch. You're sitting with your boss and three other colleagues in a restaurant on Potsdamer Platz. The restaurant isn't to your taste. Too loud and too chic. Once a week your boss plans a lunch for you, it's a quirk he has. He thinks a bit of foodie culture can't hurt.

You've just ordered when your boss mentions the agency. For a few seconds a high-pitched noise rings in your ears and you have the feeling that reality is trembling; it lurches for a moment before coming to a standstill again with a scraping sound. You study the frozen faces around you and wonder what would happen if your heart stopped at a moment like that and you died. Would you really be dead? Would you have disappeared from reality? Then someone laughs, then someone says it's all nonsense, and time is time again, and you're sitting with your colleagues at the table and you raise your water glass to your lips even though it's empty. Your colleagues don't notice a thing. You quickly set your glass back down again, a waiter leans toward you and pours you some water. You ignore him and laugh with the others. It sounds like a joke. An agency that apologizes. You say something now too, you say:

"Oh, come off it."

"No, no, it isn't a joke," your boss assures you, passing you the bread. "It's the latest thing. A lot of big companies are working with them already. I've heard it firsthand. I wouldn't even be surprised if we used them one day."

You all shake your heads in disbelief; the idea is ridiculous, unimaginable; all the things people come up with. You spread butter on your bread, sit still and look like someone spreading butter on some bread. Inside you're in turmoil. *What if it's true?*

you wonder. *What then?* Your boss surprises you by reading your thoughts and says:

"Look on the internet. They must even have a homepage."

A search on Google brings up 1,288 entries. The agency's name is Sorry. Their homepage is only one page long. A short text, e-mail address, and phone number. You run your eyes over the comments on the agency but don't click on them, because you don't need the opinion of outsiders.

An agency that apologizes . . .

All those months, days, hours, minutes. Every second is a weight around your neck. Resistance is difficult. How many times have you wanted to fall on your knees? Always resisting, always bracing yourself. It's understandable that you're tired. Anyone else would be tired too, many would have given up, but you're stubborn, and well on the way to freeing yourself of your guilt. You've found a way. You've only just figured out what needs to be done, and that same day in the restaurant you hear about an agency that apologizes in return for payment. Isn't that ironic? Would we talk about coincidence or synchronicity? Do you want to enter into a discussion about the elements of fate?

No.

Your fingers tremble as you dial the number. It took you four days to accept the agency's existence. Four days of stomach pains. Four days when you wanted to pummel the walls with your fists. You're so nervous that you hang up after a single ring. You laugh. You're aware that you're overreacting. You're not sixteen years old and calling the love of your life. You calm down and press redial.

"This is Sorry, Tamara Berger speaking. How can I help?"

"My name is Lars Meybach, I wanted to ask exactly how you operate," you say, pressing your hand to your mouth to suppress a nervous giggle.

"The procedure's very simple," Tamara tells you. "We listen to what you want to apologize for, who it's to, and what's to be said. After this detailed discussion, we send one of our colleagues to see you. He fulfills the commission and—"

"How do I know that your colleague will fulfill the commission to my satisfaction?" you interrupt.

"Trust," she replies without a moment's hesitation. "Of course you can also ask for a report, then we put the conversation in writing and send you the report."

"Sounds interesting. What's the catch?"

"The only catch is that we don't take personal requests. Is it a private or a business problem?"

"Business," you lie. "Definitely business."

"Wonderful. Should I mail you a copy of our standard business terms?"

You weren't prepared for that. It's all happening very quickly. Too quickly.

Don't hang up!

You switch the receiver to your other hand and ask:

"Is everyone at the agency as nice as you?"

"No, just me, unfortunately. If you heard the others you'd never call us again."

She laughs; you like her laugh.

"Miss Berger—"

"Tamara," she says.

"Okay, Tamara, I've got a really pressing problem, and I'm not sure whether you can really help me. How fast is your agency?"

"How pressing is it?"

"Very."

"Then we're very fast," she promises.

Minutes later you've printed out and read the business terms and the application form. You log on to your bank and transfer the advance payment to the agency's account. The pace of it all takes your breath away. It's going to happen in ten days' time. You still can't get your head around it.

To concentrate on your text, you sit down on the balcony and take a deep breath. You think of the mirrors hanging in your flat. You think about how long it's been since you could look yourself in the eye. Two months, twenty-six days, eleven hours.

You pick up the pen and fill out the form.

The words have to be right.

Every sentence is important.

WOLF

HIS ROOM IS AT the end of the corridor. His name is in brightly colored wooden letters on the door. Frank. He lives in his mother's flat. On the walls there are pictures of guardian angels. Pink little fatties, lowering their heads in prayer; stormy angels, bathed in light. Soft filters and kitsch. The whole flat smells of air freshener, all the curtains are drawn, and a budgerigar sings from a tiny cage.

The mother adjusts her skirt, she can't look Wolf in the eye. Her son is single, thirty-six years old, and a failure. She doesn't know what she did wrong. Her hand trembles slightly as she pours out the coffee. Cups with floral patterns and gold rims. One of the cups has a crack at the top, and a dark lipstick stain can be seen in the crack. Wolf is glad it isn't his cup. A glass of powdered milk is pushed in front of him. Wolf pushes it back. At last the mother starts talking. Her son is working at Lidl now, stacking shelves. He hopes to make it to cashier this year. Wolf isn't learning anything new here. There isn't a photograph of the son anywhere in the living room.

"It was all different in the old days," says the mother and touches the coffeepot with the back of her hand to check that it's really hot enough.

Wolf knows how different it was. Her son's decline occurred incredibly quickly. There are still idiots who think they can surf the internet and download sex clips without anyone finding out. And then there are idiots who go in search of child pornography during their lunch break. The company sacked Frank Löffler without hesitation. Until September his monthly income was 3,377 euros before tax, a week later he was clearing the shelves at the discount supermarket for 9 euros an hour.

"He works till eight," his mother says, "but he should soon have a break."

By the door she clutches Wolf's arm for a second.

"Luckily there wasn't a scandal. I wouldn't have survived a scandal under any circumstances."

Frank Löffler looks exactly as you would imagine. Widow's peak, belly hanging over his belt, greasy hair. His eyes are never still, his handshake is slack. After Wolf introduces himself, Löffler says he hasn't got a break for twenty minutes and could they meet outside.

"The management doesn't like us talking to the customers."

"I'll be over there," Wolf says, crossing the street to a laundromat. He's always liked laundromats. They're like waiting rooms for people who never travel. Wolf gets a hot chocolate from the machine. Around him the washing swirls in the drums. A woman is sleeping on two chairs, she looks uncomfortable. Wolf wishes he'd brought something to read. He wonders when he was last in a place like this. Once he and a friend tried to break into a vending machine in the laundromat on the Kaiserdamm. Screwdriver and jimmy. They gave up after a quarter of an hour, when the screwdriver got stuck in the metal and wouldn't come out again. They shared a hot chocolate and then cleared off. Sixteen years later Wolf is sitting in a laundromat on an uncomfortable plastic chair, checking his e-mails on his cell phone. Life is plainly treating him well.

Frank Löffler arrives on the dot. He steps outside the supermarket and looks up and down the street as if he doesn't know what to do next. Wolf can understand why the company fired him. Frank Löffler is a born victim.

They walk around the block and past a playground. The children are screeching and throwing sand at a dog. Löffler tries not to look. He says he's received threatening letters. One night a stone came through his car windshield. The neighbors saw nothing; they say it's what you get.

"This is a respectable area," Löffler explains, as if he understands people's reaction. It makes things even worse because he's innocent.

"I'm here because with that conversation your file will have vanished," Wolf says. "You're clean, or cleansed, or whatever you want to call it."

Löffler doesn't react; he probably didn't understand. Wolf wants to shake him.

"The world's your oyster again," he says instead, as if Löffler had spent the last year in jail.

Löffler's face flickers for a second, his hands move in his trouser pockets as if they wanted to come out. Wolf waits to be asked what happened. It takes a whole minute, then Löffler clears his throat:

"What happened?"

Four months after his dismissal the same download was discovered on another PC. The perpetrator wasn't revealed, because he was a clever co-worker who sat down at his colleagues' desks at lunchtime and scoured the internet as he saw fit. The company didn't know what to do and installed blockers. No one mentioned Frank Löffler. It was as if he had never existed. For six months the head of the company lived with the fact that he had fired the wrong man and reported him to the police. Then his conscience got the better of him. He dropped the accusation and turned to the agency.

"And they don't know who it was?" asks Löffler.

"One of your colleagues, that's all we know."

"It doesn't matter anyway."

Wolf agrees.

"How much?" Frank Löffler wants to know.

"Eighty thousand."

He stops.

"As an apology?"

"As an apology."

They're a few yards away from the supermarket entrance. Wolf knows what Frank Löffler is thinking now. He's wondering if he should take it to court. If he asked, Wolf would advise him against it. They aren't in America. The company would say it was a mistake and apologize. There would be a headline in the *Berliner Zeitung* and *Bild* would just wearily wave it away. Everyone's allowed to make mistakes. And anyway, who's to say that Frank Löffler wasn't one of those people?

"My mother mustn't find out anything about this," he begs Wolf, suddenly leans against the wall of the house and gasps for air, like someone who's just emerged from the water.

"Not a word to my mother, you hear?"

Wolf has no idea why his mother mustn't know about it. Perhaps he wants to punish her. He promises.

Löffler clutches his chest, takes a deep breath, and looks at Wolf properly for the first time.

"Who are you?"

"A protecting angel," Wolf replies, and regrets it. As soon as he said it he saw kitschy pictures of guardian angels in his mind's eye.

"No, really, who are you?" Löffler won't let it go. "You're not from the company, that much is certain."

Wolf tells him about the agency and gives him a card.

"We do good," he explains.

Frank Löffler stares at the card.

"You *apologize* for other people?"

His voice sounds slightly shrill when he says it. *If he's going to go all moralistic on me, I'll have to smack him,* Wolf thinks, taking the card back.

"Isn't that unethical?" Frank Löffler asks.

"Depends on your point of view. The church does it one way, television another. We have ours."

Löffler suddenly bursts out laughing. It's okay. He isn't

laughing at Wolf or the agency. He's laughing at life. Wolf knows that laugh. Drunks have it, and hysterical toddlers, enjoying themselves so much that they can't calm down. Frank Löffler is a mess. He leaves Wolf where he is, without saying another word. He walks past the supermarket and crosses to the other side of the street. One thing is certain, Lidl won't be seeing him again. Even though Wolf didn't think him capable of it, for someone like Frank Löffler that's a very good exit.

Five minutes later Wolf tells the head of the company that Frank Löffler has refused the offer and is threatening to take him to court.

"But . . ."

The company head falls silent. He senses that Wolf has more to say. Kris taught his brother how to stay quiet. Tell the customer what you have to tell him, then give him silence. Heighten the tension. Keep the client in suspense.

"We talked for a long time," Wolf goes on. "Mr. Löffler would agree to a higher settlement. He would like to have the payment in installments, I'm sure you still have the bank details."

Yes, he has them. Wolf tells the boss the amount. The boss clears his throat. Wolf smiles. He wishes all commissions were like this. It feels bloody great to be an angel.

He has just an hour before his next appointment, and goes to an Indian restaurant by the Schlesisches Tor. There are a few grains of rice on his chair, he brushes them off and sits down. He isn't hungry, he needs people around him. Restaurants are perfect for that.

The midday tide has ebbed, only five tables are occupied, there are candles burning in the windows, the flames quiver in the warmth that rises from the heaters. Wolf orders soup, tea, and a glass of water. He turns his phone off for the next hour and rests his hands on the tabletop.

Calm.

Once it was a flock of birds that swirled in the air and made Wolf think of her eyes. Once it was the way a woman knocked her spoon against the edge of her cup. The world is full of triggers. Little tripping hazards for the memory. In his quiet moments Wolf seeks them out carefully.

The tea comes, the waiter puts a plate of poppadoms down on the table and says something about the weather. Wolf thanks him for the tea and waits until the waiter has gone. He smells, he tastes. The flavor of cardamom and the sweetness of honey make him sigh.

Erin.

Wolf knows that memories fade and undergo a transformation over the years, until in the end no one can tell whether they are memory or imagination. And because Wolf knows all that, he clings to every memory, no matter how insignificant, that leads him to Erin.

His second appointment is on Wiener Strasse opposite the Görlitzer Park. There's no doorbell plate by the entrance to the building. The door is ajar and looks as if it's been kicked open at least ten times a day. Next to the front door a gate leads to the rear courtyard. The gate is open too.

Wolf walks past bicycles, rubbish bins, and a sleeping cat lying on the stones. He glances at his watch. His appointment is at four; he still has a few minutes and taps a cigarette from the pack.

"Want one?" he asks the cat.

The cat's belly rises and falls as if it feels completely safe. Wolf wishes he had the cat's confidence. He looks up. A square of sky floats overhead. No clouds. In the distance the rustle of traffic, a slamming door, someone coughing. Right now Wolf doesn't want to be anywhere else. It's only in Berlin that cigarettes taste so good to him.

*   *   *

At the back of the building the air is stuffy. It smells of fried onions and boiled meat. The smell reminds Wolf of the jellied meat that his aunt always made. Her hands smelled like the house. Jellied meat was her speciality. Wolf tries to remember his aunt's name. A woman in a headscarf comes toward him.

"Hi," he says.

The woman lowers her eyes and presses herself against the wall so that he can pass. Her footsteps are barely audible on the steps. Wolf climbs further up the stairs. On the fourth floor he gasps for air, his armpits are steaming. He urgently needs a shower and he would really like to light the next cigarette.

A nameplate is missing; but as it's the only door on this floor, Wolf has no choice. He rings. He waits. He knocks. The door swings inward.

Not good, not good at all.

There's a light on in the hall. There's a sound of music. Loads of bad films start exactly like this.

"Hello? Mrs. Haneff?"

Wolf pushes the apartment door a little further open.

"Hello? I'm from the agency. We e-mailed each other yesterday."

No reaction.

If that was Mrs. Haneff coming down the stairs toward me, then . . .

Wolf thinks about simply leaving again.

Maybe Frauke got the dates mixed up.

"Hello?"

The hall floor is dirty. There are scratches along the wallpaper, on one wall there's a water stain in the shape of a Christmas tree. Wolf doesn't want to have come to Kreuzberg in vain.

"I'm coming in, okay?" he says and goes in.

It's not just the hall that looks as if a renovation is overdue. Wolf expects to see a ladder, tools, and decorators in one of the rooms, hiding their beer bottles behind their backs and smiling awkwardly.

The first room is the kitchen. A beat-up stove stands in the middle of the room, otherwise there's no furniture. The windows are dirty, there's a smell of drains in the air. If anyone's out of place here, it's Wolf.

"Mrs. Haneff?"

He follows the music and finds the woman in the room with the radio in it. One side of the wall is entirely covered with a photomural. It must have been recently applied, because it still glistens with damp and is coming away at one corner. The photo wall shows mountains in the background, and in the foreground an autumn forest with a lake. A stag stands on the shore and drinks. Mrs. Haneff is floating above the water of the lake as if she wants to rise to heaven. Her arms are stretched upwards and placed together, her feet hang inches above the floor, her open eyes are fixed on the opposite wall. The head of a nail protrudes from her forehead, a second nail holds her hands above her head. She is barefoot, a puddle of blood has formed beneath her feet. Her shoes are placed neatly beside the radio. Wolf sees another drop of blood dripping from the tip of the woman's foot. If the radio were off, he would be able to hear the drop landing in the puddle.

Wolf's first thought is: *Where would you get such long nails?* His second: *This isn't real, it's . . .* He doesn't have a third thought, because his stomach heaves, and he runs retching from the room.

Minutes later Wolf is leaning against the filthy wall of the hallway, smoking. The cigarette trembles between his fingers. Every now and again he glances at the open door of the room. The radio goes on tirelessly playing. Wolf's thoughts are in chaos. He stares at the ceiling of the hallway and tries to concentrate. Still more water stains. His hands won't stop trembling. *Damn it, calm down, please.* He feels as if he's about to shit himself. Then he starts thinking. Finally.

Kris. I've got to call Kris . . .

No, I've got to call the police. I've got to . . .

Get out of here, I've got to get out of here as quickly as possible. And then call Kris and—

Wolf gives a start when his phone rings.

If that's Kris, then . . .

"Yes?"

"How's she looking?"

"What?"

"How's she looking? Has she slipped? Have the nails come out?"

Wolf feels a twitch in his face and looks at the display.

The number has been blocked.

He holds the phone back to his ear.

"Still there?" the voice asks.

"I'm still there."

"So?"

Wolf stands up. He staggers, needs to cough, coughs. He walks on quivering legs through the kitchen to the window. A bitter taste rises in his gullet. Wolf suppresses another retch and looks out at the courtyard.

Where is he? Where is he hiding?

"Who are you?" asks Wolf.

"Wrong question," the voice replies. "The question is, have you done your job?"

"What job?"

"Tell me, are you an idiot?"

Wolf says nothing, he hears the man at the other end breathing, and there's no one to be seen even in the windows opposite.

"What am I paying you for, eh? Do your job. And do it properly."

The man hangs up. Wolf is still pressing the phone to his ear. There's no one running down the stairs. Everything is still.

Do your job.

Wolf runs to the front door.

I've got to get out of here. Quick. Before all hell breaks loose and the police turn up. I've got to phone Kris, because Kris will know what to do—

There's a paper bag outside the door.

Wolf stands motionless in the doorway and stares at the bag.

Jump over it and get away, just do it.

After Wolf has glanced into the bag, he shuts the door from inside and taps in Kris's number.

FRAUKE

KRIS SAID ON THE PHONE that he had to meet them immediately. Frauke and Tamara set off for Kreuzberg at once. They crossed the courtyard, walked into the back of the house, and climbed the four flights of stairs. Now they're standing in the doorway of the living room, not daring to enter. There's a radio on the floor, playing a song by America. The nailed-up woman stares at the opposite wall.

"Is she dead?" asks Tamara.

"Of course she's dead," says Wolf.

"Have you checked?" Kris wants to know.

Wolf shakes his head. Kris walks into the room and turns the radio off. He stops in front of the woman, stretches and touches her neck. For a minute he just stands there, before lowering his arm. All four turn away at the same time.

Tamara is leaning against the wall beside the kitchen window. She says she doesn't know if she can stand up all by herself. Frauke hands her a cigarette, Tamara shakes her head. Wolf talks about the phone call and what the man said. Then he shows them the paper bag that was outside the door to the apartment.

"I don't know what you think, but we should get away from here. As fast as possible."

Kris shakes his head.

"No one leaves this place until we know what this guy's playing at."

"What do you mean?" Wolf yells at him, pointing into the corridor. "Does that thing out there look like a game?"

"Come on, Wolf, pull yourself together."

"I have no intention of pulling myself together, I just want to get out of here!"

"Wolf's right," says Frauke. "We should call the police."

"I didn't say anything about the police!"

Kris turns to Frauke.

"Do you really want to call the police? What do you think will happen then? Do you think they'll take the corpse off the wall, shake our hands, and send us on our way?"

"I don't care what they do."

"Yes, you do, Frauke," says Kris, looking back at Wolf. "And you think we should get out of here as quickly as possible and hope that no one saw us coming and going? And what about this?"

Kris holds up the paper bag.

"How do you explain this? Are you going to forget it too?"

In the paper bag there are three photographs, a digital recorder, and a computer printout with a message.

I KNOW WHERE YOU LIVE, I KNOW WHO YOU ARE.

I AM VERY GRATEFUL TO YOU.

YOU MADE ALL THIS POSSIBLE.

YOU AREN'T GOING TO PANIC.

YOU WILL GO ON LIVING AS BEFORE.

BECAUSE OTHERWISE I WILL VISIT YOUR FAMILIES.

YOUR FRIENDS.

YOU.

One of the photographs shows Kris and Wolf's father. Lutger Marrer is filling up his car. He has one hand in his trouser pocket, and he is looking at the gas pump. The second photograph shows Tanja Lewin. Frauke's mother is in bed, smiling at the camera. Frauke recognizes the background. The murderer has sought out her mother in the clinic. The third picture shows Jenni tying her shoelaces.

Tamara picks it up and says, "How does he know about Jenni?"

They look at her. It's the first time in three years that Tamara has mentioned her daughter by name to them.

Don't break down on me now, kiddo, Frauke thinks.

"And how does he know about us?" Tamara goes on.

Silence. No one has any idea.

"We're about to find out," says Kris, turning to Frauke. "Did you remember to bring the folder?"

Frauke takes the rucksack off her shoulder and wipes a space on the floor clean. She opens the folder and looks for a moment before taking out the right file.

"His name is Lars Meybach. He called ten days ago and—"

Tamara gives a start. Everyone looks at her.

"It was me. Oh, my God, it was me."

"What was you?"

"He . . . he phoned me. He said it was urgent and—"

There is a dull thud. Wolf has thumped the wall with his fist. He looks with surprise at his right hand, as if it has developed a life of its own. Blood drips to the floor from his scraped knuckles.

"That wasn't intelligent," says Kris. "But if it makes you feel better . . ."

While Tamara binds Wolf's hand with her scarf, Kris and Frauke look at Meybach's file. There isn't much to read. Meybach didn't apply in writing. A short summary of the situation, nothing more. He was a colleague of Jens Haneff, he said, and the company wanted to apologize to the widow for the fact that her husband died on a business trip.

"He lured us with a sob story," Frauke said. "Plane crash, widow, guilt."

"I don't get it," says Kris. "What does he want from us?"

"I don't care what the guy wants," says Wolf. "Let's get out of here."

Kris nods as if he understands, then takes out his phone.

"What are you doing?" Frauke asks.

"Calling him," Kris replies, holding the folder out to her. "Lars Meybach was kind enough to leave us his cell phone number."

KRIS

IT'S RINGING AT THE other end. Kris switches the phone from one ear to the other. His mouth is dry, and he feels cold sweat under his armpits. After the fourth ring the call is answered.

"Problems?"

"No problems," says Kris, "just a question. What's this all about?"

"Ah, that sounds like Kris Marrer, the big brother. I'm very glad we have the chance to speak to each other. I bet you're the driving force behind the agency."

"There's four of us—"

"Yes, but one of you must be the brains behind the operation. Four heads never think alike, one head must be in charge."

Kris says nothing.

"I cleaned her up," Meybach goes on. "All that blood and saliva would have destroyed the picture. And cleanliness has always been important to her. I didn't want to break with tradition. Did you get a good look at her? You can look everywhere, but the answer is always right in front of your eyes. If you look long enough you see everything. Stupidly, people never look properly. But if you really do look, you'll be amazed at how you could have overlooked the truth."

Kris has no idea what the guy's talking about.

"What have we got to do with it?" he asks.

Meybach tells him what they have to do with it. He says it once and repeats it a second time as if Kris had learning difficulties. Kris has to grip his phone harder so that it doesn't slip from his sweaty hand. At last he hears a click; Meybach has put the phone down. Kris has to force himself to keep holding his phone to his ear. He knows that if he brings it down now he will hurl it to the floor. *Wolf did the right thing when he thumped the wall.* For a whole minute Kris goes on looking out of the window as if Meybach were still on the other end. He doesn't want to turn round.

How can I tell them?

Kris gulps, switches his phone off, and turns round. They don't ask, they just look at him.

"He says we should do our job."

Wolf wipes his mouth and turns away. Tamara frowns as if she doesn't understand what's going on. Frauke is the only one who reacts.

"Forget it, you can leave me out of this," she says and runs out of the kitchen. Her footsteps echo down the corridor, then the door slams behind her.

No one expected that.

"What exactly did he say?" Tamara asks. "Kris, damn it, what exactly did he say?"

"He says we're to apologize for him," Kris replies, pointing over her shoulder, "to her."

They look at him as if he has just walked into the room. He wishes Frauke was still there. Tamara shrinks back into the wall behind her, while Wolf just stands there opening and closing his injured hand as if he had a cramp.

"Say that again," he says to Kris.

"We're to apologize to her. For him. He wants us to take on the apology. He wants a recording. Hence the digital recorder. He says he took us on so that we'll . . ."

Kris falls silent.

"So that we'll what?" Wolf presses.

"Take his guilt from him."

"But . . . but that's not how it works," says Tamara.

"Tell me about it," says Kris.

Wolf presses the balls of his hands against his eyes. The scarf around his hand looks ridiculous. He reminds Kris of football fans who walk bellowing through the streets on the weekend.

"It's *my* commission," says Wolf, lowering his hands, "so I'll go in. But I'm not doing it for that bastard, okay?"

"Okay," says Kris.

"What shall I say?"

Kris tells him about the piece of paper in the woman's pocket. He takes the digital recorder from the paper bag and hands it to Wolf.

"After this we will talk," says Wolf, stepping into the living room.

Tamara and Kris don't move. They hear Wolf's footsteps, the crunching of dirt under his shoes. The rustling of paper. A throat being cleared. Silence. And then:

"I need forgiveness, I beg forgiveness for what I had to do," Wolf says at last. "The pain and the fury are paid for now. It . . ."

Silence. Tamara looks at Kris, Kris shrugs helplessly, Wolf goes on reading:

"It's over. Past and present are cleansed. You . . ."

Wolf breaks off. Tamara wants to go to him. Kris tries to hold her back, she dodges him. Her footsteps echo through the hall.

"STAY OUTSIDE!" come the words from the living room.

Tamara stops in the corridor. Wolf goes on talking.

"Past and present are cleansed. You've made me what I am. So I will take from you what you took from me. Lars Meybach. PS: Of course—"

A long silence follows, then Wolf comes out of the room. He holds the letter out to Tamara and Kris like a manifesto. A PS is added at the end of the page:

> OF COURSE I'M ASSUMING
> THAT YOU WILL TAKE CARE OF THE CORPSE.

Tamara suddenly explodes with laughter, then she bites her bottom lip and falls silent. Wolf and Kris look at one another. Tamara says quietly:

"We're not going to do that, are we?"

"Of course we aren't," Wolf says, crushing the piece of paper. "We'll get out of here and find Frauke and ... What's going on? Why are you looking at me like that?"

Kris thinks about the photographs in the paper bag. He can't stop thinking about how innocently Jenni is kneeling there and tying her shoelaces. *How close did Meybach get to her?* He thinks about his father, about Frauke's mother. And then there are all the clues that they've left here. The blood from Wolf's wound. The fingerprints.

We can't simply get out of here. Meybach knows who we are.

"Kris, please say something," Tamara pleads.

Kris says what he's thinking.

THE MAN WHO WASN'T THERE

HE KNOWS HOW DANGEROUS it is to be here, but he goes into the house anyway. He crosses the courtyard to the rear and looks up for a moment. Above his head the rectangle of sky glows like a window into the void. He lowers his gaze again, his eyes are uneasy. He knows how dangerous it is to be here, and still he goes up the stairs. Hastily, because he's in a hurry. He is familiar with each individual step. The worn wood of the banister slides away under his hand. He walks to the top floor, and stops by the door. He knows that if the door is locked he will go back down again. He won't try anything. He will go and—

The door is open.

He steps inside. He walks down the corridor. He looks into the kitchen. How many times has he stood in this kitchen? *Squalid, it's all squalid.* He walks on down the corridor and steps into the living room and stops. He sees her. On the wall. He sees her and bursts into tears. He walks over to her and touches her face. *Too late.* He is suffering. He feels the pain. He can't stop touching her face. His heart contracts. His heart pauses, then starts beating again. He turns away, takes a deep breath and looks at her again. The way she hangs there. Her staring eyes. He wants to close them, he must close them. So he steps forward and stretches. Her eyelids feel like parchment.

He leaves the apartment. He feels ancient. He walks through the courtyard and stops in front of the building. Ancient and burned out. He crosses the street. The traffic flows around him, he hears no car horns, he sees no danger. He considers what he should do. He can't just let it happen. He can't. He bears responsibility. So he decides to wait till they come back. How does he know they will come back? He just does. He can feel that they aren't finished with her yet. So he will wait and hope for an answer. Every question has an answer. That's how it has always been, that's how it always will be.

PART III

After

HE TRIES TO TALK TO ME. He tries to explain himself.

At irregular intervals I turn on the hazards and only stop if the rest area is really deserted. I open the trunk and see him lying there. He can't see me, I've taped his eyes shut. His eyes, his mouth. I don't want him to look at me; I don't want to hear his voice. The trunk smells of burnt skin, urine and sweat. It's a repellent mixture, but I can bear it. I can bear a lot of things.

All he gets from me is water. I explained the rules to him. At first he didn't listen. I pulled the tape from his mouth, and at once he started screaming. He couldn't have known where we were. He couldn't have known that a truck would go thundering past us every ten seconds. But I made good on my threat, taped his mouth back up, shut the trunk, and drove on. For the next three hours he stayed thirsty.

Next time he was silent. I poured water into his mouth. He coughed, he stayed silent, and then he tried to talk to me. I poured in some more water and taped his mouth up again. He tried to move. He has no room to move. He's wedged in between pillows and blankets. His feet are taped together, his knees, his arms too. He's a trussed parcel. He can't even move his head. He no longer really exists.

Before

TAMARA

WOLF HAS BOTH HANDS on the steering wheel. His jaw muscles are tense, his eyes fixed on the road. Kris keeps looking back at Tamara, as if to check that she's still there. Tamara ignores him and looks outside without really seeing anything. When they left the building, she could have sworn that Frauke was sitting waiting for her, smoking impatiently, outside the door. Nothing. Even her car had vanished from the parking lot.

Where on earth are you?

They've already tried a few times to reach Frauke on her cell phone. All they get is her voicemail. Nothing makes sense. Tamara feels numb. The noises reach her through a filter, while the daylight is clear and harsh. She closes her eyes, drifts off, and gives a start when Kris opens the door on her side.

"We're here."

In the DIY superstore they buy buckets and cleaning materials, a pair of pliers, trash bags, spatulas, and a black plastic tarpaulin. They put a flashlight and three spades in the shopping cart, so that the handles stick out like palisades. They don't say a word to one another, and look like three strangers walking together through a DIY superstore. Finally Kris puts a sleeping bag in the cart. No one asks what the sleeping bag is for.

Back to the apartment. Up four floors. Through the door, down the corridor. The woman is still hanging on the wall. Everything is unchanged.

And I thought, if we come back . . .

Tamara starts whimpering quietly.

"Tammi, pull yourself together," says Kris.

"Her eyes are shut," says Wolf.

For a few seconds they stare at the dead woman's closed eyelids.

"Who cares," says Kris. "Let's get started."

They start with the hands. Wolf holds the woman's body around the hips and lifts her slightly so that some of her weight is taken off her hands. Kris stretches up and applies the pliers. The brothers are pale and look absent, as if far away.

I want to go there too, Tamara thinks and flinches when the nail is pulled from the palms with a sucking noise. Kris loses his balance and curses. The nail falls to the ground with a clunk and rolls around on the floor in a semicircle. The corpse's arms fall and come to rest on Wolf's back.

"Get a move on," says Wolf.

The pulling of the second nail sounds like a cork being twisted out of a wine bottle. The dead woman's head slumps forward, its chin falls on its chest.

"Okay," says Kris, taking a step back.

Wolf lets the corpse slip down until it is sitting with its back against the wall.

"Tammi, could you please give me a hand here?"

They put the woman in the sleeping bag and close it. The zipper sticks twice. Tamara wonders whether she should leave an air hole. Kris asks what she's doing.

"Nothing," says Tamara, pulling the zipper all the way.

They lift the sleeping bag. It rustles, and Tamara wishes the radio was on again. They carry the corpse into the corridor and lay it next to the wall so that it isn't in anyone's way. Kris and Wolf go back into the living room, spread the plastic sheet, and start scraping off the wallpaper with the spatulas. Tamara is responsible for the kitchen. She wipes Wolf's blood from the floor and polishes the door handles and everything they've touched. She pauses a few times while working and looks into the corridor as if she has heard something.

Tamara doesn't know how many hours have passed. It's night. Her legs are stiff, her neck is one big cramp. Her hands hurt, and her fingertips are puckered from the wet cloths.

The brothers carry the sleeping bag downstairs, while Tamara drives Wolf's car into the courtyard. She doesn't worry that anyone might see her. She simply functions. When the sleeping bag is stowed in the trunk, Kris and Wolf take the rubbish and the cleaning materials out of the apartment and distribute them among the trash cans.

"Let's get out of here," says Kris.

Wolf drives out of the courtyard and asks a question. Kris replies. Wolf asks again. Kris replies. Tamara is sitting in the back seat, and has no idea what they're talking about. She does understand the words, but the words produce no meaning. There's a dull thump behind her temples, there's a desire to shout at the brothers to shut their mouths. Tamara presses her forehead against the glass of the window and shuts her eyes. Her thoughts keep returning to a single point. *Jenni.* The photograph is in her trouser pocket. Tamara wants to call David. Tamara doesn't want panic. Tamara *is* panic.

"Everything okay with you?" asks Kris.

Tamara nods as if she understands what he says.

They drive north along the autobahn and leave the Berliner Ring. Ten minutes later they take the first exit into a forest path. Wolf turns the headlights off and carries on at a walking pace. Tamara lowers the window. The distant hum of the autobahn fills the car. Wolf stops in a clearing. The engine ticks on. They have left Kris's car in Kreuzberg, and plan to pick it up on the way back. They think they've planned everything thoroughly.

Ten minutes pass. Tamara knows that one of them has to give the sign or else nothing will happen.

"Fine, then let's get going," says Kris.

They get out and walk to the trunk. They stare at the sleeping bag.

"I don't want to," says Tamara.

"Who does?" says Kris wearily, pulling out one of the spades. He walks a few yards from the car and starts digging. Wolf hands Tamara the flashlight.

"What am I supposed to do with this?"

"Someone has to light what we're doing," says Wolf, taking one of the spades. "Or don't you want to do that either?"

KRIS

THEY'RE BUSY DIGGING THE grave when Wolf suddenly realizes it's not right. They are working back to back, the earth is rich and heavy, they're sweating as they've never sweated before.

"It's not right."

For a moment Kris thinks Wolf was talking to Tamara, who is crouching on the edge of the hole and illuminating them with the flashlight. Then Wolf stops digging. Kris turns around and sees Wolf's face in the beam. Dirt sticks to his sweaty skin, and for a few seconds Kris thinks he can see fear in his brother's pupils. Wolf raises his free hand to shield himself against the glare and asks Tamara to lower the flashlight. Tamara directs the light toward the hole. Wolf stares at the handle of the spade and repeats that it isn't right.

One part of Kris knows exactly what he means, another part doesn't want to know, because it's clearly too late for that now. They've been digging in that damned soil for over an hour, and have already disappeared up to their necks in the hole. Kris insisted that they dig the grave at least six feet deep, because otherwise animals could catch the scent and dig up the corpse.

You can't just stop halfway, Kris thinks and says, "It's really a bit late for that now."

"She isn't even in the ground yet," Wolf observes.

Kris really wants to thump his little brother. Wolf senses it and quickly goes on:

"We have no idea who this woman is and why she had to die. And if you're entirely honest, we have no idea what we're doing here either. If we bury her now, then . . ."

His hands move helplessly through the air.

" . . . then she'll just disappear, and that's not right."

"It's fine by me," says Tamara. "I don't want to put Jenni in danger."

"And what about you?" Wolf asks his brother.

Kris feels no moral impulse. A woman has died, none of them knew her, none of them is responsible for her death. He doesn't think the woman died because they set up the agency, that's just silly. This grave here in the forest is the solution to a problem that could screw up their whole lives. As soon as the corpse has disappeared, this problem will disappear from their lives as well. At least that's what Kris hopes.

"We shouldn't be doing this," says Wolf, looking over at the car as if the corpse could hear every word. "It's unethical."

Kris walks over to him.

"Wolf, this killer took a photograph of Father."

"I know."

"He took one of Jenni as well. He was near her, do you under-stand? And then we've still got Frauke's mother. He's threatening us, doesn't that make you think?"

"Yes, but—"

"Wolf, whatever we do, this woman stays dead, and we're still alive. We're the ones who are being threatened. If we don't do what he tells us, we'll put other people in danger. Those are the simple facts. We're just reacting."

"That's exactly it," says Wolf. "I think we're reacting wrongly."

"And how should we be reacting, in your opinion?"

Wolf sticks the spade in the earth, twice.

"Not like this."

Not like this isn't the kind of answer that puts your mind at rest, when you're standing in a freshly dug grave with a corpse in your trunk. Kris is glad that he and Wolf aren't alone right now. Tamara acts as a buffer.

"Do me a favor, little brother," says Kris. "Pull yourself together and let's get this over with. As soon as we're home we can talk about everything. Your whining isn't going to get us anywhere right now."

Wolf doesn't react, he just looks at Kris. Tamara steps in.

"Wolf?" she says, nearly in a whisper, as if she didn't want to startle them with her voice. "Hey, Wolf, who's the corpse?"

"No idea, how should I know?"

"Have you taken a good look at her?"

"Of course I did. Why do you ask?"

"Does she remind you of anyone?"

"Tamara, stop it."

"I'm just asking."

"And I'm asking you to stop."

"Then say it."

"That's silly."

"Even if it's silly, I want to hear it from you, please."

"She isn't Erin, okay. I know that."

"And you still think we should behave ethically and not bury her here?"

Wolf maintains eye contact until Tamara looks away. Kris knows how much his brother hates rhetorical questions. Particularly when they come from Tamara. It reveals what she thinks of Wolf, and thinks he's capable of.

"I don't know what you want to hear," he says, "but I know that whatever's happening, it has nothing to do with Erin."

With these words he leans the spade on the edge of the trench and climbs out. Kris can't believe it. He remains behind like an idiot set on pause, holding his spade in his hand. Wolf sits down in the car. For a few seconds he is lit by the inside light, then the driver's door slams shut and his face disappears once more in darkness.

"Shit," says Tamara.

Kris tightens his grip on the handle, the pressure's too much, he doesn't know what to do with his anger; he wants to slough it off and shovel it out of the grave. Of course he can't do that, so he climbs out of the trench and follows Wolf to the car. He wrenches the driver's door open and sees Wolf's shocked face. Kris grabs him by the T-shirt and drags him out like a disobedient dog. The blows come automatically. Kris can't control them, and if he's honest he doesn't want to. His arm goes up, his arm comes down, Wolf hasn't a chance. He tries to stay on his feet, and staggers, he slips on some leaves and falls over. Kris drags Wolf behind him to the grave.

The weird thing is that the brothers don't exchange a word. It all happens in a scary silence, as if it were a flashback of a flashback, from which all sound had been erased over time. At least that's how it feels to Kris. He doesn't hear the wheezing and the dull blows. Everything seems to be wrapped in thick cotton wool. Later Kris will learn that Wolf was trying to talk to him the whole time, and that Tamara was screaming at him to stop.

Later isn't now.

Kris hauls his brother to the trench to make him get back to work; that's all he's concerned about. He is so gripped by fury that he doesn't see the shadow until it's too late. The spade hits him on the back of the head, and the explosion makes his consciousness vanish in a blinding void.

TAMARA

IT'S A FEW MINUTES before midnight when they turn into the driveway of the villa. Kris is still unsteady on his feet, Tamara and Wolf help him out, and support him as he climbs the steps. Wolf's nose has stopped bleeding, his left eye is swollen, and dark stains can be seen on the front of his T-shirt.

Frauke's car is in its place, and there's a light somewhere on the ground floor. Although Tamara is furious with her best friend, she can't deny a feeling of relief at the sight of the car. Kris expresses it:

"At least we know where she is now."

Frauke is sitting on the sofa in the living room, and looks up when they come in. Tamara meets her eye and asks herself where her strong friend has disappeared to. Frauke looks small and fragile, but her voice has stayed the same, demanding and precise.

"Where have you been?"

Tamara is about to ask her the same question when she sees that Frauke isn't alone. A man is sitting opposite her.

"This is Gerald," Frauke says. "He's from the criminal investigations department."

That's all it takes. Just a few drops, but Tamara feels them dripping down her thigh. CID. Tamara's voice sounds crushed as she says she urgently needs to go to the bathroom. Before anyone can object, Tamara has disappeared upstairs, even though there's a bathroom on the ground floor as well.

"What?"

David's voice sounds as if he were thousands of miles away. Tamara thinks how curious it is that someone who was so close can be so far away.

"I said—"

"I heard you. Where are you?"

Tamara doesn't want to tell him she's locked herself in the bathroom. And she doesn't want to tell him that she's sitting in the dark on the closed toilet seat, knees at her chest, arms wrapped around them.

"At home," she says.

"Tamara, we agreed—"

"I wanted to know if Jenni was okay."

"She's fine, why shouldn't she be?"

"Please go and look."

"What?"

"Just very quickly, David. Will you please go upstairs and check if she's really okay? I'll stay on the line."

David says nothing. Tamara hears him breathing in, then there's a rustling sound and footsteps fading away. She waits. She stares at the mirror over the basin, which stares back like a black stain.

If I creep over and peer in, maybe I'll see myself sitting on the toilet with the receiver pressed to my ear. Maybe I can leave this Tamara behind and start all over again somewhere else.

"She's asleep," David says at the other end.

"Thank you, thank you, thank you."

Tamara takes a deep breath, aware that tears are spilling from her eyes.

"Tamara, tell me what on earth's going on?"

"Couldn't the two of you go away for a while?"

"What? What do you want?"

"Just go away for a while. A few weeks or something. The weather's fine and—"

"Tamara, the weather's awful. It's the middle of February. Are you on something?"

The tears are flowing now, Tamara sobs. David tries to calm her down, Tamara doesn't want him to hear her crying. She sniffs and tries to steady herself.

"Fear," she finally forces herself to say.

"What?"

"I'm frightened, David."

"What of?"

"There's so much evil out there."

"Tamara—"

"Promise me you'll pay special attention to Jenni over the next few days, promise me that."

"It's a promise," says David, and then there's a pause that sounds to Tamara like longing and hope, but David destroys the moment by asking her to pull herself together.

"Do you hear me?" he insists.

"I hear you," says Tamara and tries to imagine the light in David's house. Light and smells and the knowledge that someone is always there. Before she can ask David what he thinks, what he feels, he's hung up.

WOLF

WOLF IS IN A bad way. His nose hurts, and his right eye is almost closed. He knows Kris is even worse. The brothers can hardly stand. It doesn't exactly help that Frauke has dragged a criminal investigator into their house.

"What happened to you?" she asks.

Kris says that isn't important now.

"I'd be interested to know what someone from CID is doing in our villa."

Frauke and Gerald glance at one another, as if to agree on what they're going to say, then Gerald says Frauke called him in.

"I'm not on duty, so relax."

Wolf really wants to ask how Gerald imagines that happening. Who could relax when he comes home after removing a corpse from the scene of the crime, and finds a cop sitting on the living room sofa. Wolf is torn between flight and fight. He doesn't know what good it would do him to attack a criminal investigations officer, but at any rate it's better than putting his tail between his legs and running out of the villa. He's also surprised that a cop can simply go marching into their house and demand answers. *He isn't even on duty.* Before Wolf can ask a question, Frauke says:

"Gerald and I know each other from a computer-programming seminar that I ran two years ago."

"A little hobby of mine," Gerald explains, waggling his fingers about as if working on a keyboard.

Kris isn't having any of it.

"I'm getting my wires crossed a bit here, Frauke," he says. "What *exactly* is Gerald doing in our house?"

"I asked him for help."

"With what?"

"You know very well with what."

Gerald rubs the back of his head as if he's embarrassed to find himself in the firing line.

"Why doesn't one of you tell me what's going on here?" he says, and doesn't make it sound like a question.

No one replies. Frauke looks at her hands while Kris takes off his jacket. He lays it over the back of the chair and sits down. Wolf admires his calm. Kris must be completely exhausted. He can see that his brother's shirt is drenched with sweat at the back. *How on earth can he control himself like this?* The sound of flushing can be heard from the second floor, then Tamara comes back downstairs. Wolf knows how he must react before Tamara comes into the living room and opens her mouth.

"Frauke, could the two of us talk alone?"

His words sound calm and resolute, as if he knows. Wolf has no idea what he wants to tell Frauke. He sees her hesitate. Her eye wanders from Gerald to Kris as if Wolf weren't there.

"Please, just for a moment," he adds.

She'll never come, she'll talk about the dead woman, and that'll be that. The cop will never understand why we wiped away the traces. And why should he? He'll suspect us, he'll . . .

Frauke gets to her feet, walks past Wolf and goes outside. Wolf is so surprised that he just looks after her for a few seconds before he works out that it might not be such a stupid idea to follow her.

Frauke is waiting for him on the veranda. She has lit a cigarette, and is looking at the driveway. Wolf goes and stands next to her. He finds it unsettling that Frauke still can't look at him.

"Why won't you look at me?"

Frauke blows smoke out through her nose. She turns her head and looks at Wolf, *finally*, then looks away again. Wolf takes her by the shoulders and turns her around; the cigarette falls from her fingers and rolls over the veranda. Wolf feels Frauke's warm breath on his face. Cigarettes and mint. *Where does the mint come from?* He hasn't been so close to Frauke for ages, and wishes the situation were different. He would like to hug her and erase everything around them with his hug. Sex as medicine.

"What are you doing dragging a cop into our house?"

"Wolf, pull yourself together. Gerald is a friend—"

"He might be *your* friend, but as far as we're concerned he's a cop. I want you to get rid of him, or I'll throw him out myself."

The corners of her mouth turn down slightly.

"What sort of a face is that?" Wolf says.

"Even if you wanted to, you couldn't."

"Couldn't what?"

"Wolf, you can hardly stand upright, and you want to start a fight with Gerald? Have you completely lost it? He'll wipe the floor with you. Give me that."

She takes the handkerchief from his hand and dabs fresh blood from his top lip.

"What happened to you?"

Wolf steps back, leaving her hand floating suddenly in the air. The exhaustion makes each of his movements a torture. He doesn't know what he should say to Frauke.

"We had an argument," he says at last, and picks the abandoned cigarette up from the floor, takes a drag on it, looks back at the villa. "But that isn't the problem. What in God's name have you started here? If the killer learns that you've gone to the police, then . . ."

He looks at the cigarette and doesn't know what to do next.

"Why did you clear out?"

"Did you take a closer look at the photographs?" Frauke asks back.

"Are you fucking with me? Of course I took a good look at the photographs."

"Did you notice that every photograph was taken outside? Your father and Jenni. Only the picture of my mother is from the clinic. He was with her, do you understand that? The bastard visited my mother. They were eye to eye. That's why I'm sorry if I overreacted a bit, but it was too much for me."

Wolf nods, he understands, he doesn't know how he would have reacted in her position, but he understands that. Still. *You put your mother in danger,* he wants to say, and instead says:

"We could have talked."

"I didn't want to talk," says Frauke. "What good would it have done? Don't you see what's happening here? We wouldn't be able to sort it out. A gun's being held to our head. We aren't capable of sorting it out. That's why Gerald has to know everything."

Frauke walks over to Wolf, her hands rest on his chest, it's such an intimate moment that Wolf is filled with longing.

So near.

"Please, Wolf, go in and persuade the others that this is the best way."

"It's too late for that."

"Nonsense, we'll take Gerald to the apartment and—"

"Frauke, I said it's too late. If you don't want us all to go down together, then talk to your cop friend and get rid of him. After that we can talk."

Wolf turns away, leaving Frauke alone on the veranda.

Tamara sits next to Kris on the lounge chair. Kris hands her a glass of red wine and refills Gerald's glass. The atmosphere is relaxed, even if Wolf has no idea how that's possible. He sees the swelling on his brother's knuckles and instinctively touches his own eye. Later he will discover that Kris has sprained his hand.

Kris asks if Wolf would like a glass of wine as well. Wolf nods. Gerald observes that it's a nice place they have here. He looks at his watch, he crosses his legs, then he points at his own face and says, "Whose path did you cross?"

"Family argument," says Kris.

"Ah," says Gerald.

Wolf takes a sip of his wine and tastes nothing. At last Frauke

· 114 ·

comes in from outside. Wolf doesn't turn around. Frauke stops next to him and says she's sorry, but she has to apologize to Gerald.

FRAUKE

GERALD HAS PARKED HIS car outside the property. He and Frauke stop by the gate. Gerald has no idea what just happened in there. He does know that he shouldn't just leave like that. He's always found it hard to interpret silence or sit opposite a complicated woman who stares straight ahead and doesn't say a word. Frauke isn't one of those complicated women, so it's all the more alarming to Gerald that she's keeping her mouth shut now.

"And you're sure that I—"

"I'm sure," she cuts him off.

Gerald looks over at the villa.

"I don't like his face."

"Wolf's okay, he's just very sensitive."

Frauke stands on tiptoe and kisses Gerald on the cheek. As she does so, she thinks: *When we women say goodbye, we're very clear about it.* Gerald nods as if he's understood. Frauke sees more than she wants to in his eyes. Three times they have slept together, three times they have told each other it wasn't a good idea. Frauke finally ended the affair when Gerald started saying he wanted a steady relationship. After that they saw each other less, they remained friends, everything seemed to be sorted out, even if Gerald's expression now suggests more.

"Give me a call. Any time, promise?"

"Promise."

Gerald leaves Frauke at the gate and gets into his car. One last wave, then he drives off. Frauke breathes out with relief and doesn't move from the spot. She's afraid to go back into the villa. She knows it wasn't a particularly brilliant move just to run away from the Kreuzberg flat like that. For a while she had simply stood in the street hoping they would follow her. Then she drove to Gerald's place.

After Frauke has closed the gate, she turns toward the villa and to her surprise sees Kris sitting on the top step of the veranda. Tamara is leaning against the banister next to him, Wolf has put his arm around her shoulders.

They just want to see that Gerald's really leaving.

But perhaps they also want to see whether I'm really coming back.

Frauke makes an effort and walks toward them.

"How did you get rid of him?" is the first thing Kris asks.

Frauke points to Wolf with a tilt of her chin.

"I said he hit me."

"You're kidding me," says Wolf.

"What else was I supposed to say, after you put on that show on the veranda? It was the best I could think of. Now would you please tell me what you've done?"

"We've done what was demanded of us, and what you should have done too," Tamara replies. "But you had to clear out and put us all in danger. Not just us, but Jenni, too."

Frauke feels as if someone has kicked her feet out from under her. She expected all kinds of things, but not Tamara's disappointment. She wants to react, she wants to explain herself, as she finally comes back to what Tamara said at the start.

"What do you mean? What should I have done?"

"He wanted us to get rid of the corpse," says Kris.

"He wanted you to do *what*?"

"He demanded that, Frauke, he—"

"Kris, *he* is a bloody murderer. How can you listen to a murderer?"

Her friends look at her in silence. Their eyes look tired and burned out. No one gives Frauke an answer, so she goes on:

"We have to end this here and now, and talk to the police. Do you get that? We have to stop him before he looks for his next victim."

"And what are you going to tell the police?"

"What happened."

"And *what* happened, Frauke? Are you going to tell them how Wolf marched into a deserted apartment to apologize to a woman who was nailed to a wall? Are you going to show them the proof? What proof is there? A letter, an e-mail address, and a cell phone number that probably doesn't even work any more. What do you think your cop friend will say then? Do you think he'll make a quick call and the killer will say, *Hey, great to hear from you.* Hasn't it occurred to you for a second that this guy might be watching us?"

Frauke can't help bursting out laughing. Artificial laughter that she remembers from her school days, when embarrassing moments were covered over with hysterical laughter.

"You've seen too many movies. Are you trying to tell me that you've really apologized on behalf of this pervert? What next? Are you going to give him a discount next time? I could design a new advertisement. *Murder your neighbors, friends, and enemies. We'll find the right apology.* I simply don't believe it, you've all lost your minds. A woman was nailed to a wall, and you give me shit like this. What have you done? Have you chopped the corpse into little pieces and flushed it down the toilet?"

Kris looks away, Tamara looks at the floor, only Wolf doesn't take his eyes off Frauke.

"Wolf, what did you do with the corpse?"

Wolf reaches into his trouser pocket, pulls his hand back out, and looks at it before he throws Frauke the keys. A flash in the air, a tinkle when she catches them. Frauke has no idea what's going on. Wolf nods toward his car, which is standing next to hers in the driveway, and says:

"She's lying in the trunk."

Something in Frauke tears. It's almost a relief. The ropes that have been holding her upright until now have been snipped. The cramp in her stomach disappears. Frauke leans forward and throws up on the gravel path.

KRIS

THEY AREN'T STANDING IN front of the villa any more, they're sitting in the kitchen. It's just after one in the morning, and Kris has a throbbing headache. Tamara is wrapped in a blanket, shivering as if the heating weren't working. Next to Wolf there's a bowl of water into which he dips a tea towel from time to time, before holding it up to his swollen eye. Frauke is the only one not sitting down; she stands instead with her back resting against the wall. She has been listening to them, and hasn't interrupted them once. Kris knows Frauke too well. She regrets sending Gerald away.

"So it was your idea not to bury the woman?" she says, turning to Wolf.

"I wouldn't call it an idea, exactly, but I'm sure you would have done the same if you'd been with us in the forest. But then you just had to clear out like that."

"I've already said I'm sorry. I was in a panic."

Wolf sticks up his thumb.

"Good excuse. Luckily the three of us weren't in a panic. Not at all, we were relaxed, and laughing cheerfully away."

"You're such an asshole."

"Wolf isn't an asshole," Tamara joins in.

"Then what do you call what he's doing? I apologize and he makes jokes. Tell me, what d'you call something like that?"

"He doesn't mean it that way."

They look at Wolf. It's quite plain that that's exactly how he means it. Kris knows his brother is about to say something stupid. Wolf has never had a good sense of when to stop.

"Hasn't it occurred to you that each one of us bears some of the responsibility?" he asks.

"What are you talking about?"

"Come on, people, calm down now," says Kris. "It won't get us anywhere—"

"Stay out of this," says Frauke, props her hands on the table, and leans forward as if she needs to be closer to Wolf for her next few words.

"What did you just say about responsibility?"

"You heard me."

"Do you mean there might not have been a murder if our agency hadn't existed?"

Wolf leans back and folds his arms.

"You know that's nonsense," Frauke goes on, looking at Kris and Tamara. "Could one of you please tell him?"

"He knows," says Kris.

"That's not the message I'm getting."

"You'll have to live with that."

"Thanks, Wolf."

"You're welcome, Frauke."

Kris has always known that the two of them should never have slept together. Wolf is subordinate to Frauke, and always feels it keenly in conflict situations.

"You three seem to have planned everything down to the last detail," says Frauke. "Where do we go from here?"

"We thought we'd listen to what you have to offer," says Wolf. "Like me, you're just full of good ideas. You and the CID, me and my ethics. We should pool our resources."

Yesterday they'd have laughed at that, they'd have looked at each other and exploded with laughter, Kris thinks and says, "We'll send Meybach the file and put an end to it."

"And that'll be that?"

"That'll be that."

"Great plan," says Frauke. "So let's forget the corpse. We can leave it in the trunk until no one remembers where it went."

"That's not funny," says Tamara.

"Tammi, I'm not trying to be funny. I don't know whether to laugh or cry. And if I can't tell it's time for me to go to bed. As soon as you have a sensible plan that also includes dead bodies in trunks, we can talk about it. Until then, please leave me alone. I've had enough for today."

Her last glance is meant for Wolf. Perhaps she hopes he'll contradict her.

"Good night," says Wolf, without a trace of sarcasm.

"Night," says Frauke, and goes upstairs.

The silence that falls is calming. They're sitting in the kitchen, all three so tired that for a while they just stare straight ahead and enjoy the peace.

"You look bad," Tamara observes eventually.

Kris tries to make a fist of his right hand, but can't do it, his knuckles are too swollen. Tamara gets a tube of gel from the bathroom and rubs it in. Kris sighs.

"That feels good," he says.

"And how's your head?"

Kris shrugs and pulls a face. Wolf says that someone with a skull like his can't get concussions. Kris thanks him for his remark.

"I didn't mean to hit you so hard," says Tamara.

"It was just a joke," Kris says in a conciliatory voice. "I have a steel plate up there, so don't worry."

Wolf points to his eye.

"Can you do something for this, too?"

Tamara fetches ice cubes from the freezer, wraps them in a tea towel, and runs water over it for a moment. Wolf thanks her and presses the ice to the swelling. Tamara leans against the oven and yawns.

"You look tired," says Kris. "Go lie down, we'll talk in peace tomorrow."

"I don't want to leave you all in the lurch," says Tamara, and as she says it, Kris really wants to get up and hug her. He has the feeling she's the only one who really seems to be in control of her faculties. *Who'd have thought it, our gentle Tamara has the heart of a lioness.* Kris doesn't know if he's just making a mistake and his own exhaustion is making him see things that aren't there. Tamara strikes him as resolute and single-minded.

"Go lie down," Wolf agrees. "We'll think of something."

"Perhaps that's exactly what's worrying me," Tamara says, bundling herself up in the blanket. She kisses first Kris and then Wolf on the cheek. For a few seconds she looks Wolf in his good eye, and something happens even if Kris can't put his finger on exactly what, but something happens between the two of them.

"Even if I hate you because you didn't simply want to get rid of the corpse," she says to Wolf, "I think you made the right choice."

"Thanks."

They hear Tamara going upstairs, they hear the familiar creak of the floorboards and the sound of her bedroom door closing.

"She's great," says Wolf.

"You're just saying that because she agreed with you."

They say nothing, they don't look at each other.

"I'm sorry," says Kris after a pause, "I shouldn't have hit you."

"Forget it, I deserved it."

"No one deserves this kind of crap."

"You can say that again."

Wolf grins.

"So what do we do now, big brother?"

Kris looks at his swollen hand.

"We could have a family therapy session."

"I told you, it's fine."

"No, it's not fine. I saw red, and if Tamara hadn't been there—"

"If you don't shut up, I'm going to bed and then you can see what you can do with the rest of this brilliant evening."

Kris raises a dismissive hand.

"Okay, I'll be quiet."

"Thanks, because I certainly couldn't sleep now."

"Suggestions?"

"We could get drunk, then it won't hurt so much."

Kris laughs.

"Be honest, you've got a headache, and my eye's practically falling out, can you think of a better medicine?"

Kris shakes his head, no, he can't think of a better medicine.

They're sitting in the conservatory looking out on the Kleine Wannsee. Outside it's windy, every now and again moonlight wanders across the property and catches on the bushes and rubs over the bark of the trees before the clouds close again, plunging the garden back into darkness. They have vodka and tequila on the table, a few flickering candles stand between them, giving off a light that makes the brothers feel like they're in a cave. They drink and toss their two big problems around. One of them is in the trunk, the other is a lunatic who's waiting for them to send him a file with an apology.

"Maybe you were right before," says Kris.

"I've been right so many times today, you'll have to be more precise."

"Meybach wrote that he's grateful. And that we made it all possible. What if it's true? What if he only killed because we opened the agency?"

"That's nonsense. I don't think we tempted a lunatic out from behind the fireplace. We might have been the trigger, but anything can be a trigger. Whatever the reason he killed that woman, I don't think we were involved."

"So why did you say we were?"

"To get Frauke's goat."

"What a jerk you are."

"Thanks. Keep my seat warm."

Wolf goes indoors to get an ice cube for his eye.

"Chips or nachos!" Kris calls after him.

Wolf comes back with the ice cubes and a bag of nachos.

"Do you think Meybach will disappear?"

"I hope so."

"And what if he doesn't?"

Kris doesn't react.

"I mean, do we want to take that risk?"

"What risk?"

"Well, the risk of getting a new commission from him every other week."

"Oh, stop."

"I'm just saying."

Kris looks into his empty glass.

"You know, I'm constantly asking myself what the guy expects from this. Does he really think everything will be made good just because we've apologized for him?"

"No idea," says Wolf, refilling their glasses. They clink them together and drink, then open the bag of nachos. It's a while before one of them speaks again.

"And what do we do with her?" Kris asks.

"If only I knew."

Wolf lights a cigarette and looks at the glowing tip as he draws on it twice.

"We could put her in the cellar."

"Forget it."

"At least it's cool in there."

"Yeah, great. And how long will that go on?"

"Until we've got a better plan."

Kris doesn't think much of the idea. He knows very well that Frauke would freak out.

"We should have buried her in the forest," he says.

"Ethics," says Wolf.

"Asshole," says Kris.

"I can't sleep," says Tamara.

They give a start, the vodka sloshes out of their glasses, they both turn red in the face. They look like two boys who've been caught with a porn magazine under the covers. Kris doesn't know why they find the situation embarrassing.

"I can't get her out of my head," says Tamara. "I'm so sorry she's in the trunk."

"You're not the only one."

Wolf hands Tamara a glass. She takes a sip, then swallows the vodka down. Kris can see the gooseflesh running down her arms. Tamara rubs her eyes.

"What are we doing?" she asks, and it's as if her question closes a circle. No one has a sensible answer. Wolf taps his knee, Tamara sits down and rests her head on his shoulder. It's a gentle image. They look into the dark garden and at the lake, the lake looks back, the night is quiet, five minutes pass, then there's the sound of quiet snoring.

"Wolf?"

"I'm still awake."

"Give her to me."

Kris picks Tamara up, he feels her breath on his neck, she's light as a feather. Kris has no trouble carrying her up to her room. He lays her on the bed and wraps the blanket tightly around her. *If she hadn't been there today, who knows what I would have done to Wolf.* Kris leans forward and kisses Tamara on the cheek. She opens her eyes and doesn't give a start, even though he's inches away from her face. She doesn't even look surprised.

"Hi," she whispers.

"Hi."

"How did I get to bed?"

"I carried you upstairs."

"You look sad."

Her hand comes out from under the blanket and touches his cheek.

"I'm fine. Go to sleep now."

Tamara closes her eyes again. Kris goes on sitting beside her for a moment, and can't shake the feeling of having infected himself with his brother's melancholy.

*   *   *

When he comes back down, Wolf is no longer sitting in the conservatory. Kris finds him in the kitchen with his head under the tap. He reaches past him and turns it off.

"That felt good," says Wolf.

Kris hands him a dish towel. Wolf dries himself, touches his swollen eye and quickly pulls his hand back, then looks at the dish towel and says, "We should do it. Here and now."

"Forget it. I don't want to have a corpse in the cellar."

"I'm not talking about the cellar."

Wolf looks out of the window.

"It would be ideal. And it would be safe."

Kris follows his gaze. Outside is the night, the Kleine Wannsee and . . .

"You can't throw her in the Wannsee. What would be safe about that, you idiot?"

"Who's talking about the Wannsee! I want to keep her nearby, because if we keep her nearby it's dignified . . ."

Wolf is struck silent. In the silence Kris suddenly hears the ticking of the kitchen clock, clearly and distinctly. He can't know that the ticking will pursue him for a long time to come. Dry and calculating, it will sound repeatedly, every time he thinks back to this night. Then Kris bursts out laughing and walks to the fridge. He suddenly craves some ice-cold milk. The silence breaks at the edges, the ticking hurts inside his head.

"You're so drunk, you can't even believe it," he says after the first swig.

Wolf says nothing. Kris puts the milk carton back to his mouth. Wolf doesn't take his eyes off his brother, and says that Frauke and Tamara must never find out.

They open the second bottle of vodka, sit back down in the conservatory, and go on talking. For two hours. Eventually they are standing in front of the villa and have no idea how they got there. The air is piercingly cold and wakes them up. *Drunk and alert is worse than just drunk,* Kris thinks, holding on to his brother's shoulder. They are clearly drunk and alert and determined and stand by Wolf's car and watch with fascination as the tailgate silently opens.

"Technology," says Wolf, proudly holding up his car key.

In front of them is the sleeping bag. There are no excuses now. They agree that no one should end up like that. No one. Wolf presses the button on his car key, the tailgate closes again and they nod contentedly and rest their bottoms against it and try to act sober. It's cold, it's colder than cold.

"I thought we were going to have the mildest winter in years," says Kris.

"Fuck the weather report!"

"Fuck the weather!" Kris agrees.

They fall silent, they ignore the cold for a while, then they go on talking.

At half past four they get to work and dig the grave a few yards away from the shed, between the villa and the lakeshore. The garden is protected from the street by a six-foot wall. The neighbors would have to set up a ladder to see them. The ground is drier than it was in the forest, which makes their work harder. They ram their spades into the earth, press them in hard with their heels, furious with death. The stars hide behind the cloud cover. Two days ago everything was different. Then the sky was a nightly celebration. They sat on the terrace, wrapped in blankets, staring into the night, and Frauke saw her first shooting star.

Two days like two years like two decades and more.

When they can no longer see over the edge of the trench, they lift the corpse from the trunk. They don't think of taking her out of the sleeping bag. Tired, exhausted, and still drunk, they stagger toward the grave. The sleeping bag falls with a rustling sigh into the depths. They're pleased as they look down at it, but after even a few seconds they regret not having taken the corpse out of the sleeping bag. The rattle of earth on nylon. They wish they had no ears. They start shoveling faster. The handles of the spades are slippery with sweat and the burst blisters on their hands. The rattle finally falls silent. They go on shoveling and try not to think, they want to finish this work and then forget. And if anyone appeared now and asked them if they actually knew what they were doing, their honest answer would be that they know exactly what they're doing. No alibis, no excuses. The alcohol has nothing to do with it. Their plan is perfect. Over breakfast they will say they brought the corpse back to the forest. Kris will say: *Luckily my little brother had a different idea of ethics.* And the little brother will grin with embarrassment and apologize to Frauke and Tamara for talking such crap.

As they are smoothing the earth over the grave, the first raindrops fall. It's the best thing that could happen to them. They look up and smile. Minutes later there's no sign of anything that looks like a grave. Mud splashes up, and a deep rumble of thunder rolls wearily through the dawn.

They fetch the wheelbarrow from the shed and carry the surplus earth down to the lakeshore. As they tip two wheelbarrows full into the Kleine Wannsee, their eyes dart repeatedly to the opposite shore. Everyone knows that old people don't sleep much, but even if the Belzens were awake it would be hard for them to make anything out through the dense rain. No, they're sure of it.

After the last of the earth has ended up in the Kleine Wannsee, they rinse off their spades and wheelbarrow on the shore and put them in the shed. Side by side, they walk back to the villa. They're completely drenched, they're no longer drunk, they're just tired now. Sweat and rain, the twitching of muscles, the sore palms. And then the cold. It has nothing to do with the cold around them. This cold is deep within them, like a pain radiating in all directions.

They take off their wet clothes just inside the front door

and leave them there because they don't want to drag the dirt all through the villa. They don't speak, because there's nothing to say. They run upstairs naked and disappear into their rooms. They're too exhausted to wash. When Wolf reaches his bed, he creeps under the covers and falls into a deep sleep. Kris takes a bit longer. He pulls the covers up around him and just lies there exhausted for a few minutes. And listens to the rain and watches the lightning twitch across the ceiling and hears the gusts of wind rattling the windows and thinks it's all over at last.

At last.

YOU

WIND. STORM. THE NARROW gap of the clouds on the horizon, the rumble of thunder and then the gentle fall of rain. You are standing at the open window, a flash lights up your face and makes you think about the boys. *Butch Cassidy and the Sundance Kid.* They were nine when they first saw the film. There was never an argument about which was which. They watched the film eight times and afterwards they knew the gestures and the lines by heart.

In the months that followed they did justice to their names and robbed every bank that crossed their paths. They avoided bullets, jumped on any speeding trains that happened to be passing, and whipped their horses on. When they fell into a cowardly trap, they hid from the Mexican police on a building site near the sports ground. They knew no one would look for them there.

It was Sunday, there was no sign of a builder, the site belonged to them alone. It was also the last day of the summer holidays, it was time to say farewell to a golden age. The boys explored the building site and stopped by a concrete pipe. The pipe became their place of refuge, it too belonged to them now, because they were best friends and shared everything. Butch and Sundance, in fact. They never wanted to part, they had so many plans, and they even wanted to walk together into their enemy's hail of bullets. *Together.* You can still remember how their faces lit up. As if there was a light in their heads, as if their friendship were an energy all its own.

Each boy sat at one end of the pipe. They spoke to each other in a whisper, and the echo carried their voices and made them sound weird.

When they come creeping, give me a sign.
Sure thing.

Do you have enough ammo?
When my gun's empty I'll start throwing rocks.
Butch, what can you do with rocks?
Wait and see, Sundance, just wait and see.

The rain came unexpectedly. No clouds, it came pelting down as if from nowhere. A summer storm in Berlin had always been a small miracle as far as the boys were concerned. For a while they just looked into the sky and couldn't believe it. They stepped out of the pipe, stood shoulder to shoulder and laughed. The rain came whispering down on them. Their clothes clung to their bodies like a cocoon, their bony joints shining through. Even now, when you close your eyes, you can feel that warm rain. Summer rain. Unexpected and mild and in the midst of it two boys laughing as they stretch their arms into the air.

Eventually they sought refuge in the pipe again, and sat down together at one end. They pressed their sneakers against the inside wall and spat outside into the rain. They were so unsuspecting.

Butch heard the noise of the engine first. Shortly afterwards came the squelch of tires in mud. A car parked by the building-site fence. The boys ducked down in the pipe. Maybe it was a security guard, maybe they'd been seen. But it wasn't a security guard. A man and a woman were sitting in the car. The man had a cigarette between his lips, the woman had flipped the mirror down and was doing her makeup. They could only be made out vaguely through the pouring rain. After a while the man got out, stood by the fence and peed.

Butch laughed out loud when he saw that. His laughter echoed down the pipe like the sound of someone quickly clapping. Sundance hissed a warning at him, and they retreated further down the pipe, but it was no good, Butch had lost control of himself.

"So what have we here?"

The man's face had appeared at the entrance. Like a moon

breaking through cloud cover. The boys didn't run away. They were so young and naïve that they thought the man couldn't touch them. There were two of them, after all. And the pipe had another end. The boys stayed in the middle, they were safe there.

"Aren't you going to come out?" asked the man.

Sundance shook his head, Butch really wanted to run away. He wished he hadn't laughed. You still clearly remember the way his hands pressed against the inside of the pipe. As if he could break the pipe open and fly away.

"Come on now," said the man.

A knocking sound gave the boys a start. They turned round. A second moon had risen. The woman's face was looking in at them from the other side of the pipe.

"What have we here?" said the woman, and Sundance thought, how funny that the woman should ask exactly the same question as the man.

"Funny, isn't it?" he whispered to Butch.

"What?" Butch whispered back.

"The two of them."

"Two pups," said the woman and disappeared again.

The man stayed where he was and asked their names. How old they were. What they were doing here. If they wouldn't come out.

"If you don't come out I'll have to come in," he said, ducking into the pipe.

The boys ran to the other end and stopped. The woman's shadow could be seen in the pelting rain. She was waiting for them.

"Will you come to me?" the boys heard the woman saying.

"Or will you come to me?" the man's voice rang out down the pipe.

The boys looked at each other. They made up their minds and went to the woman. They trusted her more. They were like stalks of grass in a field that had never seen a lawnmower.

*   *   *

"One of you can go, the other has to stay. Who's going to go?"

Simple as that. A question, an answer. Nothing more. The boys looked at each other. They had been crying, but the rain washed their tears away. They had told the man and the woman their names. Their real names, as if it would change things. As if reality would suddenly become reasonable if they acknowledged that they weren't two desperados who attacked trains and blew up bank vaults. The boys had explained that they were only there to play. They wanted to go home, to which the man said it wasn't so simple.

"Isn't that right, Fanni?"

The woman told the boys that of course she wasn't really called Fanni. Her real name was Franziska, but who wanted to be called Franziska? The man said he was Karl. Just plain Karl.

Butch tried to run away, past the woman, because he thought it would be easier to escape her. She kicked his legs out from under him. It was all so quick that Butch didn't know what was happening. Suddenly he was lying with his face in the dirt, someone pulled him up and he was standing next to Sundance again. His knees trembled, blood ran from his nose, his face was smeared with mud.

"You're bleeding," Sundance whispered to him.

Butch wanted to wipe the blood away with the back of his hand, the woman was quicker. Her arm was like a snake. She grabbed the boy's chin and said, "Shut your eyes, pup."

Butch shut his eyes. His whole body trembled. Blood and snot ran from his nose as he stood there and didn't dare to move, to look, to be. The woman wiped the mud from Butch's face with her fingers, then licked the blood away and kissed his trembling mouth, ran her tongue over his cheeks, licked his tears.

Sundance wanted to shout at her. He wanted to draw his two revolvers and shoot the man with his left hand and the woman with his right. His mouth remained closed, and the revolvers were far away in Mexico.

When the woman stood up again she said that one of them could go now and the other had to stay.

"Who wants to go?"

The boys looked at each other, and one of them was about to say that he wanted to go, that he really wanted to go, when the other one got in first. He was just a second faster and turned round and walked away. It was just a small betrayal; in that situation the boys wouldn't have given each other anything anyway. One went, the other stayed. That was how it was. But Sundance didn't really go. He hid behind a stack of tiles. He knew he owed it to Butch. To be there. For a while at least. Then he would get help. Then.

You remember everything. How Butch became a pup. How the boy turned from a human being into a dog. What the man did to him. What the woman did to him. How the pup had to crouch on all fours in the rain after they had undressed him. How he trembled and how his wails rang out beyond the pouring rain. Thin, lost, lonely. And how Sundance threw up. Out of fear and helplessness.

When the man and the woman disappeared, Butch became a human being again and lay in the rain. He tried to stand up and simply fell over. Too weak. No one can describe that pain. No one should. Not even you, even though you're always trying to find words for it.

TAMARA

THERE'S THE SOUND OF thunder. Tamara suddenly sits up in bed. Her mouth feels as if it's full of cotton. She remembers waking in a panic once before. An eternity ago, in her sister's apartment. That time she had danced through the night with Frauke and had to go to the job center in the morning. This time is the night after the worst day of her life, and it had taken a glass of vodka to calm her down yesterday.

The clock says half past nine. Rain hammers against the window, lightning flashes vertically in the sky, illuminating a cloud front that looks like a waving banner.

Tamara waits for the thunder and counts the seconds.

On the ground floor she sees the clothes scattered by the front door. Two piles, trails of mud, dirty shoes. Tamara touches one of the piles with her foot. Wet. It looks as if Kris and Wolf had crumpled on the spot.

Tamara leaves the clothes where they are and goes into the kitchen. The smell there reminds her of parties with spilled cocktails and overflowing ashtrays. Tamara yawns. She knows it was a mistake to get up. She hates being awake before the others. *Who would willingly be the first to get up on a day like this?*

She turns on the espresso machine, and as she waits for it to warm up, she drinks a glass of water and looks out at the Kleine Wannsee. The rain is being driven by the wind, making furrows in the lake. The markings by the jetty tell Tamara that the water level has risen. She is surprised that the Belzens' lights aren't on. At that moment she would have given a lot to see Helena and Joachim having breakfast through the panoramic window. The same place every morning. It would be normal, it would be like the old life. They would wave to her, Tamara would wave back, and the day would be a day like any other.

They probably had had breakfast ages ago.

To give the place a good airing, Tamara opens the kitchen window that looks into their neighbors' property. Cold air blows in and makes her shiver. Tamara holds her face into the rain. She sees the shed and the roof of their neighbors' house. The rain leaves silver streaks in the air that make Tamara think of scratches on glass. When she is about to shut the window again, she notices a bright glimmer on the soil. She leans out again, stands there motionlessly and stares and waits for the glimmer to repeat. Her hair goes wet, she shivers and wipes the rain from her eyes. She doesn't have to wait long. A gust of wind runs over the land, and the glimmer is visible again. Now Tamara recognizes it clearly. Something white is waving to her from the mud.

"Wolf, what have you done?"
    "What?"
    "Wolf, what the hell have you done?"
    Tamara pulls the covers off him.
    "What are you talking about?"
    "Why are there flowers in the garden?"
    Tamara hits him on the back with the palm of her hand.
    "Wolf, wake up, damn it!"
    Wolf turns round and swings his legs out of the bed. Tamara can see that he has an erection.
    "What sort of flowers?" he asks.
    "White flowers. In the middle of the garden. What have you done?"
    Wolf rubs his face.
    "I have no idea what you're talking about. I swear."
    Tamara goes to wake Kris.

Five minutes later. The three of them lean out of the kitchen window, stare into the rain and watch the wind stirring the flowers on the muddy earth.
    "Lilies," says Kris. "I think they're lilies."

"And what does that mean?" asks Tamara.

Kris and Wolf look at each other quickly. Tamara knows them both too well, their exchange of glances amounts to an admission of guilt. They both have bloodshot eyes, and their hands are dirty. Tamara remembers the wet clothes in the hall. Her head is working slowly this morning, but it's still fast enough.

"What have you done?"

"We got drunk," says Kris.

"I can smell that, what else have you done?"

Rather than answering, the brothers look out the window again. Footsteps can be heard from upstairs, footsteps on the stairs. Tamara turns round and sees Frauke coming into the kitchen.

At last, she thinks, *at last I'm not alone with them any more.*

KRIS

THE HEADACHE DOESN'T EXACTLY help him think. He feels as if someone's hitting the back of his head every ten seconds. He knows what's about to happen. There are these moments that can't be stopped.

Frauke doesn't walk over to the fridge or put a cup under the espresso machine. She glances at her friends and says, "What are you doing?"

Only now does Kris notice that he's standing with his bare feet in a puddle.

"There are flowers in the garden," says Tamara.

Frauke joins them. Wolf makes room for her. Tamara points outside.

"You see?"

Frauke doesn't take as long as Tamara. She looks from Wolf to Kris, and for a moment Kris has the panicky thought that she can read his mind.

I've got to start thinking about something else, I've got to—

"You've buried her?" says Frauke. "On our land?"

It sounds like a question, but it's a statement. The emphasis is on *our land*. As if *that* were the greatest affront, rather than the fact that they have buried the woman.

Wolf shrugs.

"Still better than putting her in the cellar. We thought."

Frauke pushes Wolf in the chest with both hands. He staggers backward.

"Are you guys perverted or something?"

"I can explain," Kris butts in, without knowing what he wants to explain here. Wolf looks at him with surprise and Kris thinks: *What am I supposed to explain, for heaven's sake? It's a bit late to make up something about going to the woods for a second time, isn't it?* Wolf's surprised expression makes Kris grin. He feels hysteria

· 138 ·

mounting within him. *How can I grin now?* The corners of his mouth twitch, his head aches, he doesn't know what to say in their defense.

"Do you think this is funny?" Frauke asks.

"No, I—"

"So why are you grinning like an idiot?"

"Please calm down."

"Shit, I *am* calm."

"We can dig her back up again," Wolf says lamely.

Frauke has him in her sights again. *Why can't Wolf just keep his mouth shut?* Kris thinks, and is about to interrupt, when everything goes in a different direction. As if someone has pulled the plug, Frauke turns away from Wolf and leaves the kitchen without a word. The front door bangs against the wall and falls shut again with a crash. They wait and then see Frauke running through the garden. She's barefoot, her feet gleam brightly against the mud as she leaves the paved path and runs diagonally across the plot. She's wearing her knickers and a T-shirt. The rain soaks her in seconds. There's a flash of lightning, followed wearily by thunder. Frauke appears as a negative for a moment.

"I hope she isn't going mad," says Wolf.

Frauke freezes. The flowers are at her feet. The white is smeared with dirt, the wind has fanned the lilies out like playing cards. Frauke crouches down and picks them up.

"How on earth could you do that?" says Tamara.

"You'd never have found out," says Wolf. "We wanted to tell you we'd taken her back to the woods and—"

"I'm talking about the flowers, you idiot," Tamara cuts him off. "How could you leave flowers on her grave? Nobody could be as drunk as that."

"It wasn't us," says Kris.

"Sure, and you didn't bury her either."

"Tamara, hang on, it wasn't us," Kris repeats, wishing it was all a film. Because in a film the main characters would look at each other in surprise, and then the camera would show the garden again, and then there would be a merciful cut to the next scene, and Wolf wouldn't say, "Maybe Meybach was watching us and followed us first to the woods and then back here. Maybe that's why there are flowers there. They're like . . ."

"A visiting card?" Tamara finishes his sentence for him.

They fall silent. They watch as Frauke stuffs the lilies in the trash can. When she turns back toward the house, all three turn quickly away from the window so that Frauke won't think they were watching her.

They're sitting at the table again. It's like the night before, except that they're all waiting for Frauke to speak at last. Frauke goes on ignoring them. The rain drips from the tips of her hair, her breasts are clearly visible through her thin T-shirt. Frauke takes some mineral water from the fridge and drinks it from the bottle.

"Frauke?" Tamara says at last.

Frauke puts the bottle back in the fridge. When she speaks, the fury has gone from her voice, which makes the situation much more threatening.

"I don't know you any more," says Frauke. "You're alien to me. I don't want to know why you did it. And I'm not interested in how you could put flowers on her grave."

"We have no—"

"It doesn't matter, Wolf. I don't want to hear any explanations from you, I've had it up to here with explanations. I'm going to get my things and get out of here now. I need some space away from you. That thing out there should never have been allowed to happen."

That was it. Frauke leaves the kitchen, and it strikes Kris that Frauke has walked out on them for the third time in twenty-four hours. Wolf mumbles a curse and stubs out his cigarette in the ashtray. Tamara doesn't react at all. She just looks at the door as if Frauke were going to come back in at any moment.

"I could run after her," she offers at last.

"I'd be very grateful," says Kris.

TAMARA

TAMARA HASN'T A CHANCE. She stands in the door frame like someone who was looking for their own room and opened the wrong door.

"But that's nonsense," she says. "You can't just run away like that."

"I can do what I want. Look at me. I'm packing, I'm going, I'm gone."

Frauke puts the rucksack over her shoulder, then walks so close to her best friend that she has to force herself not to flinch.

"Tammi, finish it, draw a line. Kris and Wolf don't know what they're doing any more. They'll make it even worse if you don't put the brakes on them. I brought in Gerald, and you kicked me in the ass for that. I'm out of here."

She pushes past Tamara and leaves the room. Tamara wants to burst into tears. *Draw a line.* She wishes she knew how. She's disappointed in her friend and runs to the window to call after Frauke. Tamara can't even open the window. *What am I supposed to say? It's all been said.* So Tamara watches helplessly as Frauke opens the door, gets into her car and drives off. The gate stays open, the day is the day it has been since Tamara woke up. She has achieved nothing. *How do you draw a line in a situation like this?* She feels she's been left in the lurch. Her vision is blurred. *Frustration and panic, I'm going blind out of frustration and panic.* She wipes the tears from her eyes. *Frauke is right, I have to pull on the brake, and I haven't the faintest idea where the damned brake is.*

Tamara's thoughts falter; suddenly she understands, it's an inspiration, she knows where to find the brake.

When Tamara comes into the kitchen a quarter of an hour later, Wolf is sitting at his opened laptop. Kris is standing next to him, holding a bag of ice cubes against the back of his head.

"What are you doing?"

"Sit down, we have to talk," says Kris.

Tamara sits down facing them.

"How exactly did Meybach contact us?" Kris asks.

"I think we've got a very different problem."

"Frauke will be back, don't worry."

"It didn't look like that to me."

"Tamara, try to stay on the ball. How did Meybach contact us?"

"He called up and asked us to tell him how we work. His application came in writing. You've read it. He asked us to arrange a meeting with Dorothea Haneff by mail. I wrote to her and received a reply the same day."

"Did you speak to her personally?"

Tamara shakes her head.

"She told me by e-mail what date would work. She also asked for Wolf's cell phone number, in case she got stuck in some traffic jam somewhere. That was all the contact we had."

"At least we know now how that bastard got hold of my number," says Wolf.

Tamara still has no idea what's going on. Kris explains it to her:

"Wolf and I think we have more information on Meybach than we think. We've got an e-mail address *and* a cell phone number that worked until yesterday."

"So?"

"Tamara, tell me, are we talking in riddles? We want to get that killer, that's what this is about."

"You want to do WHAT?!"

Tamara gets up from the table.

"You're completely crazy."

She can see that the brothers are quite serious. *Guilt. They want to make up for the shit they've unleashed, by going on the offensive. And I've pulled the brake.* As calmly as possible she says:

"Do you really think he'd give us so much as a clue about where to find him? How can you even think something like that? You're like two show-offs waving their arms around with nothing to say. Frauke was right, you haven't got anything under control. Think about it. Anyone can set up an e-mail address in a few minutes and make it disappear again. It's even easier to get hold of a prepaid cell phone."

The brothers look at her.

"You could have a point about the two show-offs," Wolf says.

"Idiot," says Tamara, unable to keep herself from laughing.

"Even if anyone can set up a new e-mail address or buy a new prepaid phone," says Kris, "how about we assume that Meybach doesn't *need* to hide. What would that tell you?"

Tamara doesn't know how she's supposed to take that.

"Either he's a half-wit," Kris goes on, "or he isn't afraid of us. And why should he be afraid? We've erased his clues, and we've taken care of the corpse. So let's find out who Dorothea Haneff is. You see what I mean? We have to rummage through her past. That's always the way, you find the perpetrator in the victim's past. Sooner or later we'll bump into Meybach, or whatever his real name is. Something in her past will lead us to him. Meybach told me he didn't want to break with tradition. He talked about the dead woman as if he knew her."

The brothers look expectantly at Tamara.

"So?" she says. "That doesn't change anything. Maybe you don't understand the danger, but the guy scares the living shit out of me."

"What's that supposed to mean?" says Wolf, surprised. "Do you want to let him get away with it?"

"Wolf, please, take a look at us. We're just a bunch of friends who run an agency. We're not cops, we're not secret agents, we're just completely normal people who've crossed paths with a lunatic. The police ought to take care of him. We can't do it. And I don't want us to be able to do it. I don't want that danger."

"If you're worried about Jenni—"

"Of course I'm worried about Jenni," Tamara says, annoyed. "Even though I may not be the mother I should be, I'm concerned about my daughter, okay? Is that appropriate?"

"So what do you suggest?" Kris asks her. "Do you want to run away like Frauke, or wait until the killer phones again and tells us what to do next?"

"Neither, you know that," Tamara replies.

"What, then?" Kris continues.

She had actually planned to come into the kitchen and put her decision on the table right away. She feels like a traitor.

They'll never understand.

Tamara makes an effort and tells them, and with every word the guilt in her voice is clearly audible.

The brothers react simultaneously:

"YOU DID WHAT?!"

Kris throws the bag of ice cubes in the sink and runs from the kitchen. Tamara hears him rumbling about in the corridor, and a few moments later he's standing in the kitchen again.

"Where's the mini-disk player?"

"Upstairs, I told you I'd sent him the file."

"How could you do that?"

"Somebody had to put a stop to things."

Somebody had to put on the brakes.

Wolf gets up from the table.

"If you weren't Tamara, I'd punch you in the face."

He walks past her to the door.

"Where are you going?" asks Kris.

Wolf disappears outside without replying. Tamara looks at her hands.

"We could have talked about that," says Kris.

"The way we talked about where we were going to bury the corpse?"

Kris sits back down. He rubs the back of his neck. Tamara watches him flinch and goes to stand behind him. She tells him to move his head forward. The swelling on the back of his head is purple and the size of a chicken's egg.

"You should take that to the emergency room, a doctor needs to have a look at it."

Kris waves his hand dismissively.

"It's just a bump."

Tamara takes the bag out of the sink and fills it with fresh ice cubes. Then they sit facing each other again and wait for Wolf to come back. Tamara has the feeling that she hasn't achieved anything.

WOLF

WOLF CLOSES THE SHED door behind him and leans against it for a moment before clenching his fists and going ballistic. Planks and canisters go flying through the air, the wheelbarrow takes so many kicks that it tips over in a dented heap, Tamara's bike loses its rear tire.

How the hell could we fuck it up so badly?

For a quarter of an hour Wolf rages, then leaves the shed with an armful of wood. He's out of breath, but he feels better. When he comes into the kitchen, Kris is sitting alone at the table.

"Where's Tammi?"

"In the living room. She's researching Haneff and Meybach on the internet."

"How did you persuade her to do that?"

"We had a quiet talk, that's all it took."

Wolf sits down.

"We've fucked up, haven't we?"

"We have."

"We could dig her up again . . ."

"And then?"

Kris shakes his head.

"Forget it, let's leave her in peace and wait and see what Tamara comes up with."

"And Frauke? I'm worried about her."

"Frauke is Frauke, she'll calm down in good time. You know her. She runs away quickly, but she comes back just as fast."

Not exactly my experience, Wolf thinks and says, "She was so cold. She even packed a rucksack."

"And didn't even say bye, I know."

The brothers look at each other.

"She'll be back," Kris says confidently, "believe me."

Wolf nods and believes him. At that moment no one can know that Kris will soon regret his confidence.

Tamara is sitting on the sofa when the brothers come into the living room.

"Did Meybach reply to your e-mail?" Kris asks.

Tamara shakes her head.

"I put the names through two search engines. No hits for Lars Meybach, but I now know who Dorothea Haneff was. She was never a widow, because she's never been married. She's never lived in Berlin, either. Some classmate of Haneff's has a homepage, and listed all his fellow pupils with their biographies. Dorothea Haneff was born in Hanover, she graduated from high school and then worked for a construction company there."

"That's something," says Kris. "Let's check her background."

"I don't think so," says Tamara.

"Why don't you think so?"

"Because Dorothea Haneff died of a brain tumor three years ago."

"What?"

Wolf walks around the sofa and looks at the screen.

"Perhaps there's another Haneff."

"Wolf, please, a name like that—"

"But why would he give us a false name?"

"Why would he give us anything at all?"

They look at each other; the brothers' theories have been thrown into disarray. A new question has arisen, and Tamara finally voices it:

"Who's the woman in our garden?"

YOU

YOU'VE NEVER THOUGHT OF giving away her real name. Not out of fear, you have no reason to be afraid. Without a name she's erased, as if she had never existed, and that was the idea behind it. You made her vanish from reality, and Dorothea Haneff had to act as her stand-in. If your father knew, he wouldn't be very pleased. Dorothea Haneff was the love of his youth. Three years ago your father drove all the way from Berlin to Munich just for the funeral. More than four hundred miles, to say goodbye to a woman who rejected him when he was young. Very dramatic.

The agency's e-mail reaches you at eleven in the morning. You download the message plus attachment and play it. First there's nothing, then a rustling sound, then you hear Wolf Marrer's voice. The seriousness, the fury. You suppress a laugh and erase the file.

Even though it might look to an outsider as if this were all just a game for you, you know better. You're not a player, you're a debtor. And because it's not a game for you, there are no rules. Everything is possible. We're talking about life here. We're being a bit metaphorical, but it suits the way you're thinking. Anyone who's aware that there are no rules has taken a step forward. You understood that very early on, but it didn't really help you sort out your own life. You made mistakes, you made the wrong decisions. Wrong decisions can't be avoided. Not when you're twenty-six, and certainly not when you run home through the rain when you're nine years old, after being raped.

Sundance helped Butch out of the mud, took off his own T-shirt, and used it to wipe away the dirt from Butch's body.

Blood. Sperm. Soil. The rain helped, while Butch let him get on with it as if he were anesthetized. He stood there motionless, breathed, blinked, and was both present and a long way away. Sundance picked his clothes out of the mud, rinsed them in a puddle and helped Butch put them on.

On the way home they didn't exchange a word, they kept a yard's distance apart. The city ignored them completely, its noise continued regardless. There was the rattle of rain on the asphalt, as it hit the puddles, there was the whoosh of the passing cars and their dazzling headlights. Nothing could interrupt that rhythm.

When they got to Butch's house, Sundance waited till his friend had disappeared through the door, and then continued on his way home. That same night he was woken by his walkie-talkie, which was under the bed and always set to receive.

"Yes?"

There was a crackle on the line, Sundance heard Butch's breathing as if he weren't four streets away, but right beside him.

"They're here," said Butch.

Sundance didn't hesitate for a moment. He put his clothes on and crept outside. He crossed the street and took the shortest way across the gardens. Butch was waiting for him. He was standing up on the second floor by his bedroom window, still as a ghost behind glass. Sundance waved to him. Butch disappeared from the window, and a few moments later the terrace door swung open.

"Where are they?" Sundance whispered.

"Outside the house."

"Are you sure?"

"They said they'd be back. As a warning. So that I'd keep my mouth shut."

Butch's words sounded rehearsed, as if he'd recited them mechanically several times before. The mantra of a boy who wants to drive evil away. Sundance asked how they knew where Butch lived.

He wished he hadn't asked.

"*They know!*" Butch hissed, grabbing Sundance by the wrist. He pulled him into the kitchen, and then onto the floor. They crouched down behind the sink and carefully got up to look outside through the window. There was a car parked on the opposite side of the street. Sundance thought it could have been any old car; he was about to say so, when he saw the glow from the tip of a cigarette inside the car. Shadows. Two. Sundance put his hand over his mouth. Midnight struck inside the house. The car doors opened, the man and the woman got out.

"Midnight," whispered Butch. "They..."

His breath came in hectic bursts.

"...said they'd come...to...If I tell...They..."

He gasped for air, he tugged on Sundance's arm.

"...said...They'll slice my parents open and I...I'll have to watch and...and they asked if I wanted them to prove it...Said I believed them...I swear! You know...what...they said...next..."

Sundance went on looking outside. The man and the woman were standing in the middle of the road, looking up at the house. Their faces looked blurred, as if somebody had set the focus wrong. The street at their feet was still glistening with the rain that had stopped hours before.

"...said at midnight," Butch stammered. "And now...You see, now they're here."

He was crying. His head was touching his chest. Sundance bit his upper lip to hold back his own tears.

"Let's run away," he said quickly, dragging Butch back down to the kitchen floor. "Let's just run away, do you hear me? Then they'll look for us and leave your parents in peace because they can't find us."

Butch looked at Sundance with surprise. The idea made his face light up. Hope. When you think back on it, you can't help smiling at the naïveté of the two boys. They thought life was fair. They believed in equilibrium, and the good guys winning in the end and the bad guys losing mercilessly and shamefully. You're aware that life is anything but equilibrium. It's the purest chaos. Darkness lurks behind every door. Shadows live behind every window.

"Run away?" Butch asked.

"Run away," said Sundance, and meant it.

They listened to the silence. A car engine started. Butch and Sundance stood back up and saw that the car had disappeared from the opposite side of the street. The boys exploded with hysterical laughter, they pressed their hands to their mouths and laughed. They high-fived each other and believed in magic, as if their decision had banished the demons. Simple as that.

"They've fucked off now," said Butch.

"They really have fucked off," Sundance agreed.

They were relieved, they hadn't really planned to run away from home. They had wished so hard for the two demons to disappear from their lives, and the demons had obliged. They were gone.

For a year.

To the day.

Then they came back.

Butch and Sundance never mentioned abuse. If you could go back to that time, you would whisper that word in their ears. You would write it in their school exercise books, you would go from one class to another and fill the blackboards with that one word.

Abuse.

Only a single sentence was ever uttered about it. That sentence still resounds for you like an unpleasantly high note that summons up all the memories at once. Even though it only ever left Butch's mouth in a whisper, it held more power than a scream.

"I never want to be a dog again."

Butch was the first to see the woman and the man a year later. The car was parked in the driveway opposite the school gate. The couple didn't seem to have changed, as they sat behind the windshield and waited.

Butch saw them, they saw Butch.

He turned round and went back into the school. He sat down on the floor next to the vending machine and waited till Sundance came in from games. He just sat there on the floor for two hours without moving. He knew they would never dare set foot in the school. He thought he was safe and stared at the entrance. He tried not to blink, because if he kept his eyes open all the time, they might stay away.

Sundance nearly walked past him.

"Hey, what are you doing here?"

Butch couldn't answer him. His eyes were dry, his mouth felt like a trap that had snapped shut and wouldn't open again. *They're here again!* he wanted to shout. *I saw them!* Not a word came out, it was only when Sundance helped him up that the trap suddenly snapped open, and the words came tumbling out of his mouth like prisoners who hadn't seen daylight for a year.

"It's starting again."

He didn't need to say anything more than that.

The same day they planned their escape.

At the time it had seemed there were rules in life. The boys woke up in the morning and went to sleep in the evening. They ate several times a day and listened to their parents; they behaved at school and stood at the crossing and waited when the light was red. That regulated world began to break down on the day of the rape.

The boys didn't think of telling anyone about what had happened at the building site. The fear of punishment was too great, because what if Fanni and Karl found out? And then of course there was the fear that people would point at them and think it was their own fault. *What did we do wrong? What could we have done differently?* You can understand it, down to the tiniest detail. There are books on the subject, the power of the perpetrator over the victim. Children are so easy to manipulate, they only know the simplest rules. If you throw them a ball they catch it. Everything changes when the light turns away from them and the darkness touches them.

Butch and Sundance allowed themselves two days to prepare. They wanted to be inconspicuous. During those two days they kept a lookout for the car and saw it several times outside the school, at the bus stop, at a crossing. Once the man was sitting alone in the car, and Butch and Sundance got in such a panic that the woman might suddenly appear behind them that they got into the wrong bus. Just to keep moving. Six stops.

On the evening of the second day they decided to spend the night at Butch's, before disappearing during the night. They had two addresses. Butch had an uncle in Bochum. He said his uncle was okay, they could tell him anything. The second address was Sundance's sister. She lived in Stuttgart. If worse came to worst they could go there. That was their plan.

You remember the smell of fear that rose from the scalps of the two boys when they said goodnight to Butch's parents. They lay down in bed, fully dressed, and waited for the lights in the house to go out. They had hidden their rucksacks behind the trash cans, and their bikes were ready beside the garage. They had also thought of taking money out of their parents' wallets, and knew the times of the first trains.

Until two in the morning they lay sweating and nervous in the dark and pretended to sleep, in case Butch's parents looked in on them unexpectedly. At exactly two o'clock the alarm clock under Butch's pillow went off. They got up and crept downstairs in their socks. It was silent, it felt as if the house were watching their every single footstep and holding its breath.

The woman was waiting for them in the living room. She was sitting in one of the armchairs with her legs drawn up, so that it looked for a moment as if she were floating. She was a shadow in the shadows. When Sundance spotted her, he stopped on the last stair. Butch bumped into him and was about to say something when he saw the woman, too. Butch immediately started breathing faster, and that was probably the signal for the house. Suddenly everything clicked and started moving again, suddenly the living room was filled with sounds—the clock on the wall ticked, the wooden floor creaked, and the fridge came on in the kitchen. The woman put her forefinger to her lips. The hissing of a snake.

"Shhh."

Butch wet himself. His teeth chattered. He was ready to die on the spot. You can still hear that noise. One row of teeth against the other. Wherever you happen to be, in the quietest moments of your life, that sound is hiding everywhere. Sundance, on the other hand, didn't shiver, he didn't make a sound, tears just ran down his cheeks.

"Where do you think Karl is now?" Fanni asked.

The boys didn't answer. Fanni pointed upstairs.

"He's checking to see if everyone's really asleep. Why aren't you asleep?"

Sundance knew at once that the woman was lying. How was Karl supposed to have crept past them? Never in a million years was he upstairs. Butch, on the other hand, believed the woman's every word. He wanted to, because he thought that everything would be all right if he did.

"Please," he whimpered.

"Shhh," said Fanni. "Otherwise your parents will wake up, and you don't want them to see that you've wet yourself."

It was only at that moment that Sundance noticed the smell

of warm urine. He didn't look at Butch. He wondered whether he could make it to the veranda door.

"We don't see each other for a year, and you want to go off on a journey," said Fanni. "How very rude of you."

Butch tried to deny it, the woman shook her head, she didn't want to hear any explanations.

"You've hidden your rucksacks behind the trash cans. Your bikes are ready. Where are you off to?"

There were footsteps on the stairs behind them. Butch nearly burst out laughing. His parents had woken up, and were coming downstairs, and once they got there—

"I'm sure they want to go to our place," said Karl. "Isn't that right, lads?"

Butch and Sundance turned round. The world collapsed, all rules vanished.

It was only years later that you thought seriously about how that could have happened. Books. Statistics. You've studied everything. About child behavior. Men and women who move around as couples, murdering people. America. There was something like that in America. But here in Germany? You weren't aware how transparent children are. Butch and Sundance thought they were being secretive, but they carried their plans in front of them like a neon sign. Clearly visible to everyone who looked closely. Fanni and Karl had looked closely.

They said they would take Butch with them now.

They said they'd developed a taste for him.

"We like you," said Fanni.

And Butch cried. Silently. And Butch looked at Sundance. And Sundance was brave and told them to let Butch go. Quietly.

Please.

"Take me."

Fanni and Karl thought for a moment and then shook their

heads. No. They liked Butch better. You should have thought of that. You had your chance at the building site.

Karl ran his hand over Sundance's head.

"Maybe we'll come back to your offer one day."

Then Butch sobbed. Once, loudly. Karl immediately drew a knife from his belt. Butch fell silent. Karl tapped the tip against Butch's nose. He ran it over his cheek and wiped the tears away with the blade.

"Would you like me to pop upstairs to your parents and cut their lousy hearts out?" he asked softly. "Would you like that?"

Butch gasped for breath again, he felt dizzy, he swayed and began to fall. Fanni jumped from her chair and caught him. She pressed Butch to her chest and whispered in his ear: "Okay, it's okay. Breathe, my little one, breathe."

Karl ordered Sundance to fetch the rucksacks from outside. Then Sundance was to go upstairs and get into bed.

"If you don't listen to us I'll open up your face to see if there's a brain hidden behind there. Like this, you see?"

Karl came closer to him, he showed Sundance a scar that ran from his left ear to his chin.

"I survived," Karl said. "Who knows if you will. And don't worry about your friend, he'll be back soon. Do you believe me?"

Karl smiled, he put his forefinger to Sundance's lips as if asking him to be quiet. Sundance was silent, he was a master of silence.

"Lick my finger if you believe me," said Karl.

Sundance licked his finger. Salty. Sharp. Karl brought his hand back down and put the damp fingers in his mouth.

"Mmmmm," he said.

Then they left. With Butch in Fanni's arms. Through the veranda door into the night. And Sundance remained behind. Trembling, silent. He just stood in the living room for ten minutes, before wiping his mouth, again and again, spitting and spitting, before he crept into the bathroom and washed his mouth out until the taste of soap made him retch. Then he did as Karl had told him. He brought the rucksacks in and took them to Butch's room. He didn't get into bed, though, but came back downstairs. He sat down on the floor and waited for Butch to come through the door. He was being disobedient. He knew it. He struggled with himself, but he had no option, he had to wait for Butch. As he did so he thought of the knife, and he thought again and again: *I will survive I will I will I will survive I will wait and I will survive when Butch is with me again we will survive together we will survive we will . . .*

At first there was just a shadow.

Sundance heard the waking birds. The gray of the sky over the garden dissolved only hesitantly and became a dull blue. Sundance leaned his back against an armchair, his bottom hurt, the carpet under him was as hard as concrete. Sundance felt as if his spine was completely twisted.

And then there was a shadow.

Sundance rubbed the sleep from his eyes and closed them tight a few times to see better. The shadow was on the lawn. Like a pile of earth or an animal that didn't want to be discovered.

Sundance stepped outside through the veranda door. The grass was wet with dew. Butch looked like a clenched fist. His head was on his knees, his legs were pulled up, his arms wrapped around them. Sundance heard him breathing. Heavily and quickly. He put his hand on his back. Butch immediately started trembling.

"They've gone," said Sundance.

Slowly, very slowly, Butch freed himself from his cramped posture. His face glistened with tears, his hair was damp with sweat. A bird shrilled down at the boys. A new day had broken. Sundance helped Butch to his feet. He supported him as they walked upstairs together. Butch didn't want to go to his room, he wanted to go to the bathroom. Sundance led him to the bathroom, where Butch locked himself in. Sundance stood by the door and heard the shower being turned on. He didn't know what to do. He waited for five minutes, the thunder of the shower didn't stop. Sundance waited another five minutes. He thought of the bird that had shrieked down at them. He wished he'd thrown a stone at it. Sundance knocked quietly on the door. The shower went on running. When Butch's parents started stirring in their bed, Sundance fetched his rucksack, went downstairs, and ran home.

You still ask yourself, how is it possible for two friends to lose each other so easily? Is nothing sacred in this world? Butch and Sundance were like brothers back then, they had stuck together since kindergarten, they were meant for each other. For a while the rape at the building site brought them even closer together. But the night they wanted to run away from home, the night they failed completely, drove a wedge between them.

You don't know whether it had something to do with Butch feeling betrayed for a second time, or whether Sundance couldn't deal with his feelings of helplessness. Whatever the reasons, it's too late now to figure it out. At the time all that mattered was the result, and the result was fatal.

Over the next few weeks Butch stayed away from school. Sundance didn't dare check in on him or call him up. Every evening he turned his walkie-talkie on. Butch didn't call.

On the ninth day Sundance paid him a visit. He expected Butch's parents to turn him away, he expected all kinds of things, but not that Butch would open the door to him.

"Everything all right with you?" Sundance asked, as if they'd only seen each other the day before.

"Everything's all right," said Butch.

His left eye twitched once, then he looked past Sundance as if he were waiting for someone.

"Are you ill?" Sundance asked.

"A bit," Butch murmured.

Sundance leaned forward. He had to ask.

"What did they do to you?"

He expected Butch to say he didn't know who Sundance was talking about. He expected Butch to start crying. Anything. But Butch just said, "They're gone. Forever."

Sundance nearly burst out laughing.

"No," he said.

"Yes."

"But—"

"I have to go inside," said Butch. "And I want you to believe they're gone. Because that's what I believe. And if I believe it, then . . ."

He fell silent and looked at Sundance in surprise, as if someone had stolen the words out of his mouth. Sundance grew nervous.

"We're still friends, aren't we?" he said.

"Of course we're still friends," Butch replied and closed the door.

TAMARA

ON THE AFTERNOON of the same day that Frauke leaves the villa with a rucksack, two patrol cars drive up to the property. Three policemen jump out of the first car and stand next to it. In the second car nothing happens for a minute, then the side door opens and Gerald gets out.

"I hate that," he says to no one in particular and walks toward the villa.

Tamara isn't aware of any of it. She's on the second floor making a phone call when Wolf calls her downstairs. On the ground floor she bumps into two policemen. The younger of the two asks her to sit down. He seems friendly, but his friendliness can't hide the tension that he's feeling. Tamara hasn't a clue what's going on, and anyway she finds it hard to take policemen seriously when they're younger than she is.

"I'd rather stand," she says, and asks Wolf if he knows what's happening here.

"Look out the window."

Tamara walks past the policemen and stands by the window. She sees the patrol cars in the yard and next to them Frauke, who's talking to Gerald and pointing at the water.

"Could you please sit down?" the policeman asks her again.

Tamara stays standing. Outside two policemen are busy digging up the grave with spades. A third policeman has a German shepherd on a leash. The dog sits at his feet with its tongue hanging out. Tamara can clearly make out his breath in the icy air. Wolf comes and stands next to her.

"Frauke is serious about this," he says.

Tamara has no idea what to say. *It's like this morning,* she thinks, *we're standing at the window, we're looking out, and the world outside is changing while nothing is happening to us.* She knows she's lying to herself. Since they found the dead woman on the wall, many more things have happened to them than they're willing to admit. Everything's collapsing, everything's losing its value.

"Where's Kris?" Tamara asks.

"He took your advice," Wolf replies, "and went to the Immanuel Hospital a quarter of an hour ago with that horrible bump."

They see Gerald taking cigarettes out of his jacket and handing one to Frauke. Frauke lets him light it, then looks up and sees Wolf and Tamara standing at the window.

Tamara hasn't the strength to raise her hand. Wolf turns away.

Half an hour later the policemen are standing in silence around the excavated grave. Frauke and Gerald have joined them. They look over at the villa, then back into the grave. Tamara can't tear herself away from the window. She feels as if she's dropped something valuable, and no one can put the shattered pieces back together.

And if I turn away, it's all over. I'll miss the moment, which will put Frauke and me back together. How can she betray us like this? How on earth?

Two policemen climb down into the grave. Tamara sees them lifting out the sleeping bag and turns away.

Enough's enough.

That is why Tamara doesn't see Frauke storming toward the villa with Gerald at her side. In the kitchen one of the policemen blocks her path, she shoves him aside and heads for Wolf.

"What have you done with her?"

Wolf just looks at Frauke.

"What have you done with her, Wolf? Damn it all, where is she now?"

"Who are you talking about?"

"You know very well who I'm talking about. Damn it, where's the corpse?"

Tamara is surprised that Frauke can't remember the dead

woman's name. *Perhaps she doesn't want to say her name out loud, because if she does—*

At that moment Frauke's words finally reach her.

"I have no idea what this is all about," says Wolf. "But you can be sure that I don't want to see your face for a while."

Gerald clears his throat and sends the two policemen out. Tamara thinks his voice is friendly for someone who works for the criminal investigation agency, and has to do house visits on two successive days.

"There's a sleeping bag in the hole," he says. "Frauke suspected it was a body—"

"I didn't *suspect*," Frauke interrupts him. "She was there."

Gerald is about to go on, but Frauke ignores him.

"Where have you hidden her?" she demands of Wolf. "Please, tell me, so that it'll all be over."

"I don't know what's up with you," Wolf says calmly. "First of all your performance last night, then all this. I mean, how could you tell Gerald I'd hit you?"

Frauke blushes. Tamara guesses what's going to happen next. It's like that distant roll of thunder this morning, and the nervous wait for the lightning after it. *I could run out,* thinks Tamara. But it's too late for that. Frauke has already turned around, and fixed her eyes on her.

"Don't look at me like that," says Tamara. "I have no idea what's up with you either."

Frauke's mouth hangs open. Tamara is so relieved at her quick reaction that she immediately wants to apologize to Frauke. Gerald says:

"We'd like to search the house, if you have no objection."

"Be our guest," says Wolf. "Frauke can guide you around, she knows her way around."

An hour later the two patrol cars have disappeared from the property, and the police have spread dirt all around the house. They've discovered a stash of marijuana in Wolf's room, but not wasted a word on the subject. Gerald is the only one who stays behind. He asks them to sign a form declaring their agreement with the search of the house and the plot of land.

"And what if we don't sign?" Wolf asks.

"Then I could get into trouble," Gerald says honestly.

They sign.

Wolf wants to talk to Frauke alone. Gerald says that's not such a great idea. Wolf curses and tries to get hold of Kris on his cell phone, while Tamara walks Gerald to the door. Frauke stands smoking outside the front door, looking pitiful. Gerald walks across the gravel to her. *It's like the end of a sad film,* Tamara thinks, and waits unconsciously for Frauke to glance at her. Gerald and Frauke step into the street and are gone.

Tamara wearily shuts her eyes and wishes she could wake up in her bed and give the day a second chance. When she opens her eyes again, snowflakes are floating past her face. The first flakes are light and delicate, the ones that follow thick and heavy. It's late February, and snow is falling for the first time that winter. Tamara looks into the sky for a while, there's a smile, a few tears too, then she shuts the door and walks into the kitchen, where Wolf is waiting for her.

"Is it snowing?" he says and runs his hand over her hair.

"It's just starting."

Wolf hands her a mug. They stand side by side at the window as if there were no other room in the kitchen. They look at the falling snow and the ravaged garden. Their arms touch. Tamara sips at her tea and hands the mug back to Wolf. The two of them can't be furious yet, because they don't yet really understand what Frauke has done to them.

"It wasn't you," says Tamara.

"It wasn't us," Wolf assures her.

Tamara rests her head on his shoulder. She thinks of the Belzens, and how early they wake up every morning. *Maybe they saw something. Maybe they saw who dug up the corpse from the other side.*

· 164 ·

She keeps her thoughts to herself, because if she's being perfectly honest, she doesn't want to know who did it.

"Kris will go mad," says Wolf.

One of the phones rings upstairs. They don't move, and they don't want to part either. The snow covers the churned-up soil that was still a grave not long ago. They stand at the window until all traces have disappeared under the white.

"What sort of sick fuck fetches himself a corpse and leaves lilies behind?" says Wolf.

Tamara doesn't react. Her thoughts are somewhere else entirely, and she's wondering how she'll behave next time she sees Frauke. *Will she simply apologize, and everything will be like before?* Even if it's what Tamara wishes, it's not what she believes.

THE MAN WHO WASN'T THERE

HE DOESN'T UNDERSTAND WHAT'S happening. It feels as if time is advancing at the wrong tempo. The rhythm is unpredictable, and the pauses feel as if they're in the wrong place. He keeps losing the beat and stumbling along behind, clumsy and uncertain. He suspected it would be like this one day. Anyone who doesn't have his life under control lets everything slip and gets left behind, empty-handed.

He doesn't know who they are. He doesn't know where to start. And that used to be his special talent. He was able to find anyone's weak points and exploit them. He doesn't know how much of that he's been left with. It's so long ago. He just knows that he'd like to wake from this rigidity as soon as possible. Like someone sitting up in bed in the middle of the night, glad that the dream was just a dream and he's part of reality again.

He waits more than two hours for them to leave the apartment building. He drives after them. Out of Berlin and onto the highway. When they turn in to a forest path, he switches off his headlights and follows their taillights. He sees the two men digging a grave, while the woman lights their work with a flashlight. Then an argument breaks out, and the woman knocks one of the men down. He can't work it out any more. Five minutes later the three drive off, without putting the corpse in the grave.

And there he is now, watching the locked gate to the property. Shortly after midnight a man and a woman leave the villa. He's never seen these two before. The man says goodbye and drives off, the woman goes back into the villa.

How many more are there? he wonders and goes on waiting. When he starts feeling cold he explores the area and walks down the side streets. It's important to be familiar with the surroundings. He has studied the roads on the map. He's bothered that he can't acquaint himself better with the plot of land. As he looks around the area, slowly, very slowly, he gets closer to his element. Hunting instinct. It's been so long. It torments him to feel like an amateur.

He quickly realizes that he isn't going to get anything done on foot. He gets into his car and drives back down Bismarckstrasse to Königstrasse. He parks on the other side of the Kleine Wannsee and gets to work.

His first choice is wrong. He knows as soon as he's rung the bell. It's almost impossible to get a view of the properties from outside. In the past he would only have rung if he'd felt a hundred percent certain.

A woman opens the door, holding a cat. He apologizes for disturbing her so late, and leaves without giving her any further explanation for his visit. Two houses along a man opens the door to him. His instinct tells him this is the place, but he has to convince himself.

"Sorry to disturb you so late," he says. "My car broke down. I'm just over there and I was hoping to call ADAC and have it towed."

"Anyone who hates cell phones is a friend of mine," Joachim Belzen replies and invites him in.

His mother raved about this talent of his when he was still a child. He always found the right words, he had the right smile.

"Nice place you've got here," he says.

Joachim Belzen calls up to his wife, who comes downstairs. Her hand is small and strong. She doesn't show the slightest trace of suspicion either. Whatever he does, people always see the good in him.

"You're chilled to the bone," says Helena Belzen.

He rubs his arms and shrugs. A minute later she has disappeared into the kitchen to make him some tea. In the meantime he phones the weather information service, reads a fake customer number off a parking ticket, and thanks them for their quick service.

"ADAC will be here in three quarters of an hour," he says, and looks through the terrace window into the garden, discovering the villa's illuminated window.

"I always thought it took longer," he adds.

"ADAC never has much to do at night," says Joachim Belzen, and asks his guest to sit down. Helena comes in with a cup of tea. She tells him to forget about sitting outside waiting in the cold. And the Belzens start talking. It only takes him four questions to cut to the chase. He talks about their wonderful property and asks as if in passing who could afford that ostentatious villa opposite.

They tell him everything. How nice the new owners are, what their names are and how successful they are in their work.

"So it's an agency," he says at last.

"We think they do something with insurance," says Helena, "although they really don't look that way."

"At any rate they have more money than they can earn," Joachim cuts in, and all three of them laugh at the ambiguity of his remark.

The Belzens talk about their house and the many years of work that they've put into it. They give him a guided tour, and his suspicion that they don't often have visitors is confirmed. They're the sort of couple where if one of them dies the other one quickly loses the will to live.

"I could make you another cup of tea if you like," Helena offers.

He glances at his watch and shakes his head. It's time to go, the tow truck is probably waiting already. He thanks them for their hospitality, and for letting him use their phone. The Belzens walk him to the door. He shakes them by the hand. He's always found it important to keep physical contact for a few seconds. As he's about to turn away, the cell phone rings in his coat pocket.

Fifteen minutes later he washes his hands in the guest bathroom and sits down on the Belzens' terrace. He should have turned off his cell phone. He doesn't understand how it's possible for him simply to forget the most important things.

"Karl?" he says. "Now we can—"

"I don't know where she is," a voice says before he can finish. "It's been two days and—"

"Karl, try to be calm."

Karl sounds flustered. That can't be right, he's never flustered.

"But she always calls me when she—"

"When I say calm, I mean calm, do you hear me?"

It's an order, and Karl shuts up immediately. It's the only way.

"I am calm," Karl says quietly after a few seconds, and when the man hears that he gets a warm feeling in his heart. And after the warmth comes grief. *I know where Fanni is, Karl.* He wonders how to tell him. They were like brother and sister. *My children.*

"I know where she is, Karl," he says carefully and starts telling the story. Soon all that can be heard is Karl's weeping. He doesn't want to tell him off, but he doesn't want that wailing noise in his ear either.

"Karl, pull yourself together."

And then he warns Karl, telling him that whoever murdered Fanni could be after him as well.

"You're in danger, Karl. You've got to be careful." With these words he leaves him alone. Full of fear and full of insecurities. Because anyone who's scared and insecure is also sensitive to the dangers around him. And he demands all that from his children. It's the least they can give him back for his love.

The place on the terrace is ideal. He has taken the plastic sheets off the chairs, and is sitting in the shade of a porch, with the darkness of the house behind him. The villa is in front of him, and he has a clear view of a shed and part of the drive. It couldn't be better.

He knows all he can do now is wait. *The correct action is rooted in patience, patience consists of waiting. He who doesn't wait shows no patience and misses the correct action.* He can't remember where he got that quote. He probably read it on the page of a calendar; he hasn't been interested in books for ages. Life is already complicated enough without other people's thoughts.

It's cold, he fetches a blanket from the house. He wouldn't have been so cold before. Everything's different now. He voluntarily spent the last few years in exile. A house in the west of Berlin, an anonymity that makes him smaller and more insignificant. But it had been his decision. No more contact. His heart was too weak. After the operations and the weeks and months in the hospital he changed his life and disappeared. He became a character in a fairy tale who voluntarily fell asleep for years. Until her phone call woke him.

"You won't believe who's sitting in my bathroom right now," were her words.

He replied with a silence. Her call was unexpected. They had had contact by mail, but the contact was one-sided. He didn't want to live for his children any more. They had outgrown him. Although they couldn't know it, their very existence showed him what life was denying him now. So he said nothing and heard their breath in his ear and felt a shudder running through his body. It was as if he was trying to hold back an orgasm. Without success, his body was trembling. Grateful. Happy. Relieved. *Fanni.* She was family. Even though he would never show it, he really missed his family.

"He's got so big," said Fanni.

"Who?" he said at last.

"Little Lars. Our little Lars is back. He's—"

He put the phone down. He was so nervous that he let out a little trickle of urine, which slid down his leg. All the years of silence, and then this message. One of his sons had come back. *Lars.* Why couldn't it have happened when he was still healthy? Why now? Now he was history.

He reacted spontaneously and drove to Fanni's. He had her new address, he knew where all his children lived. On the way he was surprised that the hunger could be so intense, that he threw all his principles overboard. He laughed. He felt young and reckless again. *Our little Lars is back.* As if the pieces of the jigsaw all suddenly fit. And he was part of it.

Yes.

But he was too late. By a mere matter of minutes. Today for the first time he was aware that time was out of joint. It had never been too late before, he would have punished himself severely for such inattention.

In the hallway he met a man who was coming down the stairs carrying a black trash bag, and who stepped aside respectfully to let him pass. They nodded to each other. He couldn't see the connection, he was too excited and hungry. Too many feelings, too many memories raged in him. Comprehension came only when he was standing at the door to Fanni's apartment, ringing for the fourth time. His instincts kicked in, and he dashed down the steps and into the street. Of course the man was long gone. He stood there with his fists clenched. He concentrated. *Where to?* And with every passing second he started becoming the man he had once been.

He replayed Fanni's call again and again in his head. He sat down in a café and thought. The pieces didn't fit. *What does Lars want from Fanni?* He drank his first coffee in four years. His body spoiled his enjoyment, his stomach started rumbling, he started to fart and rushed to the bathroom. When he was back sitting at his table, he ordered a large cappuccino. He didn't plan to be ruled by his body. The coffee also helped him think. And he had a lot of thinking to do. In the end he drove back to Fanni's apartment. It took him less than a minute to crack the lock. His suspicions were correct, Fanni was gone.

The sofa cover had bright stains in two places, and the sofa itself had been shifted. He could see where the feet had been, and knew that Fanni would never have left it like that. Fanni was well brought up, and he had been the one who had brought her up. He bent over the discolored patches on the sofa and sniffed. The smell was familiar to him. Bitter and sharp, CS gas. And now that he looked more closely, there were clues everywhere. Under the coffee table he discovered a hole burned into the carpet and bits of ash beside it. The woollen fibers could have caught fire, but someone had stamped out the cigarette butt and then put it in the ashtray. A few fibers still stuck to the filter. Fanni would have emptied the ashtray immediately and wiped it out.

He imagined himself as little Lars, who was now a man. He saw him in front of him. He opened himself up to memory, as if pulling the boards away from an abandoned well. The silence, the chill that rose from down below. He laughed. It was so easy when he relied on his instincts. There was only one place Lars would take his Fanni.

He drove to Kreuzberg. He found a parking space on the opposite side of the street, got out, and waited for a gap in the traffic before crossing. And as he was waiting, he saw them coming out of the house. Two men and a woman. Something in their faces made him stop on the pavement. He took his cell phone out of his coat and pretended to read a message. They crossed the street and walked past him. The woman brushed his shoulder slightly. He turned round and saw them getting into a car. They pulled out and drove off, and he understood what he had seen in their faces. *They had met death.* Without hesitating, he crossed the street, got honked at, pushed the front door open, walked through the courtyard and up the stairs.

But once again he was too late.

Hours later, when he is sitting on the Belzens' terrace watching the opposite shore, watching the same men whom he met on the street, who are also the ones who dug the grave in the forest, he knows their names and he knows they are brothers. Kris and Wolf, the Belzens didn't know their surnames. The brothers are sitting in the winter garden, getting drunk. They suspect nothing, they sense nothing. He doesn't take his eyes off them for a second. The longer he watches them, the bigger the mystery becomes. *What do these people have to do with Fanni? What's the connection?* The mystery is like a house with walled-up windows and only one locked door. There's only one way into the house, and he knows that Lars Meybach is the key.

At about four o'clock in the morning he sees the brothers digging another grave. There's no argument this time. They lay Fanni's corpse in the hole. It starts raining. An ice-cold rain that pelts down, accompanied by a storm. The brothers take the soil to the water in a wheelbarrow and tip it into the Kleine Wannsee. He can't sit still any longer. He ignores the rain and goes and stands by the shore. He's fifty meters away, and hears the brothers' wheezing breath over the rain. They look up once, they can't see him, because he doesn't want to be seen. He hasn't forgotten everything he learned. He disappears into the shadow. He could call out to them, and they wouldn't see him.

Here, I'm over here.

The brothers go back into the villa, the lights go out. He stands there motionless, listening to the silence. He isn't cold in spite of the wind, an inner fire keeps him warm, his soul is in flames.

The rain is the only sound. Rain, wind, and in the midst of it, him. His heart has found the rhythm, he senses it, he breathes it.

The Belzens have told him about the boat that they use to row to the Pfaueninsel. The boat is on the other side of the house. He pulls the tarpaulin down, the oars are fastened at the sides. He goes back to the house and fetches an oilskin jacket that he pulls on over his wet clothes. He also finds a baseball cap and puts it on so that the rain doesn't get in his eyes as he works. He's about to go outside when he's struck by the flowers in the corridor. They're just beautiful, pure, white. They are life itself. He picks up the bunch of lilies and takes it with him.

As he slides the boat into the water, he imagines his doctor's worried face. For a few minutes an uneasy flickering sensation runs through his chest, but with each stroke of the oars it gets weaker and weaker. The current is hardly noticeable. He covers the fifty meters to the opposite bank without any trouble, ties the rope to the jetty, and goes ashore. He knows where the brothers have put the wheelbarrow and the spades. He takes one of the spades and finishes his work.

At dawn he goes back to the Belzens' house. He left the sleeping bag in the hole, the grave has been filled again. After making Fanni comfortable on the sofa, he beaches the boat and puts it back in its regular place. He is tired, but the euphoria is stronger. He hangs the oilskin jacket in the wardrobe and puts the baseball cap on the shelf next to it.

Everything is as it was before.

He looks down at himself. His clothes are smeared with dirt, his trouser legs covered with a crust of mud. He stuffs his clothes in the washing machine and switches it to the quick-wash cycle. He goes to the cellar wearing only his underpants. The fire inside him has calmed down, he doesn't plan to freeze. The cellar is a big workshop with a long work surface. Model airplanes hang on wires, there's a worn-out sofa, a rattling fridge, and in one corner an old pinball machine. After he's set the heat to twenty-five degrees, he discovers a pair of binoculars in a leather case hanging from one of the struts.

In the shower he presses Fanni to him and yields to grief. It's like a reunion. He washes her, kisses the wound on her forehead. He looks at what's become of her. His own Fanni. She's aged. He touches her lips, he lifts her breasts and lets them fall again. He rubs the blood from the wounds in her hands until only the clean, open flesh can be seen. He washes her hair and feels aroused. His penis lies full and heavy against his thigh. He rinses the foam from her hair, dries her, and carries her upstairs. He lays her on a sofa in the next room because he doesn't want her to share a room with the Belzens. Fanni was special. He pulls the blankets over her, and leaves her alone.

He spends the night in the living room with a view of the villa. When he hears the beep, he takes the clothes out of the washing machine and puts them in the dryer next to it. A short while later he slips into his clothes, still warm, and feels great. His tiredness is behind him.

He makes some coffee, fills a cup, and sits down in his chair in the sitting room. The thin curtains hide him, but give him a clear view of the villa.

And that's how he spends the morning, and that's how he sees the police coming and digging up the grave. He doesn't know who called the police or what's going on over there. But he smiles at their perplexity when all they salvage is the sleeping bag. And then he sees him and can't believe that he sees him. He sits up and presses the binoculars to his eyes till it hurts. He's got a very good memory. Even without the suit or the trash bag in his arms he recognizes him right away.

There you are, he thinks and says quietly:

"Lars. What on earth are you doing? What are you doing, son?"

Only after the police have driven away from the property does he lower the binoculars and leans back, puzzled. He doesn't know what's going on here, but he's gradually starting to enjoy the mystery. He feels excited. He's breathing too quickly, his blood pressure is rising, a flicker runs through his chest like an electrical impulse. He tries to stand up, twinges race up and down his left arm. All his muscles tense with a spasm, and long before he can get to his feet his heart convulses. He slumps to one side and stops breathing. He's gone.

PART IV

After

I'm woken by a dull knocking, and for a moment I'm completely disoriented. Everything around me is gray; at irregular intervals floodlights cut through the darkness and fray the fog. The memory rushes in at me, so that I have to shut my eyes and breathe deeply in and out. My blackouts last longer and longer these days. I really need to sleep for twelve hours, the short pauses aren't enough.

The knocking again.

A man appears out of the fog. Yellow flat cap, green army jacket, and an orange tracksuit. Flip-flops on his feet. He stops by one of the rubbish bins and throws in a bag. After that he pees in the meager grass next to it, as if my car and I didn't exist. Perhaps he thinks I'm asleep, perhaps he doesn't care. When he's finished, he scratches his backside and disappears back into the fog.

I take my cramped hand off the ignition key, I was prepared for anything. Two taillights glow red in the darkness, a minivan pulls out of the rest area, and again there's that knocking from the trunk. It lasts for exactly twenty-four seconds. When it's quiet again I get out and take a look.

His forehead is covered with blood. Somehow he's managed to get his head free. I leave the trunk open for a few minutes so the stench can escape, then duct-tape his head to the spot. It's the third day. He isn't getting any water from me, he hasn't earned it.

Before

A DAY HAS PASSED since the police dug up the empty grave by the villa. Within that short time winter crept out of its hiding place and rolled over the country. Within a few hours the temperature fell below zero, snow settled over the land like a whispering sheet and produced a disconcerting silence—the noise of traffic has disappeared, there's no sound of birds, people talk to each other more quietly.

There's a state of emergency in southern Germany, the railway has stopped, all flights have been canceled, and the schools are closed. In the north and west there are hurricane-force winds, while a new ice age is spreading across the east. Berlin has turned overnight into a suffocating dream in white. The traffic drags itself through the city like a wounded animal. The pavements are deserted, hardly anyone risks going outside, and in the morning hours the streetlights are just shimmering yellow smears that can't hold their own against the gloom.

Frauke isn't very interested in this disastrous state of affairs. She sits shivering on a fallen tree trunk with a newspaper under her bottom. Krumme Lanke lies frozen at her feet, covered with a layer of snow in which there are no tracks to be seen. The only movements in the snowed-in landscape are ravens flapping silently from one branch to another.

Frauke feels as if the weather is reflecting her inner state. She flicks her cigarette away and stamps her feet on the spot a few times. Her watch says a quarter to ten. Frauke is slowly getting nervous. *I probably just want to go home,* she lies to herself, and takes the next cigarette from the pack. She spent last night in a hotel, although Gerald told her she could stay over at his place. Frauke had thanked him, no. She has enough complications on her plate without adding Gerald to the mix.

After the police withdrew from the villa site on Saturday morning, at Frauke's request Gerald went with her to a café. Frauke could sense how irritated he was. First of all she'd turned up on his doorstep in a complete state the previous evening asking for help, then a few hours later she threw him out of the villa in front of her friends, before turning up again at his office the following morning and pouring it all out—about some dead woman who'd been nailed to a wall, and the murderer, who had bought an apology for himself.

"He wanted what?"

"He wanted us to apologize for him, to the dead woman."

"And then?"

"Then he wanted us to get rid of the evidence."

"And you couldn't tell me that last night?"

"I wanted you to hear it from us all. I thought if they got to know you they'd find it easier to talk about it. But that's not what happened."

"I know, I was there."

"If I'd known that Kris and Wolf were burying the corpse in our garden, I'd have—"

"They did what?"

"The corpse is in our garden now, that's why I'm here."

Gerald was confused. He let Frauke know that she was putting some very serious accusations on the table here. Frauke waved a dismissive hand.

"We have nothing to do with the murder. You have to understand that, Gerald, he threatened us all, what were we supposed to do?"

Gerald leans forward.

"Frauke, you realize this all sounds a bit—"

"Crazy?" Frauke finished his sentence for him. "I know. But I can show you everything."

Gerald drove to Kreuzberg with Frauke to look at the apartment where Wolf had supposedly found the dead woman. Gerald never actually said the word *supposedly*, but Frauke heard it in his voice.

The apartment was deserted, there wasn't even any dirt on the floor, and there was no photomural on the wall either. When Frauke pointed out the two holes, Gerald was unimpressed and said there wasn't much he could do with that. Outwardly Gerald looked interested, but Frauke saw that he was getting annoyed.

He probably has the stories I told him about my mother running through his head, and is wondering if I've got a screw loose too.

"There's nothing here," Gerald observed. "All we've got is a deserted apartment. You've got to give me more than that."

"The dead woman's in our garden now, is that enough for you?" Frauke shot back testily.

She was aware that Gerald would already have waved anyone else away long ago and told them not to take so many drugs next time. Frauke wasn't just anyone else.

"What do you want from me?" said Gerald.

"I want you to dig up the body."

"Frauke, I can't do that without a crime scene."

"Then I'll report a crime. I'll turn myself in if you want."

Gerald sighed. He looked around the deserted flat.

"Are you sure?"

"I'm sure."

Gerald drummed up two squad cars and relayed Frauke's self-denunciation. If he had taken the correct legal course, he would have had to talk to the relevant investigating judge to obtain an approved search warrant of the house and property. It would have taken too long. Gerald wanted to put the whole business behind him as soon as possible, so he deliberately did without the support of other agencies. He only wanted to have his own team along because he wouldn't have to explain anything to his men. They didn't ask questions.

They had found nothing but a sleeping bag in the grave. Gerald was relieved when Wolf signed the search agreement without a moment's hesitation. Frauke's housemates could've legally made things extremely unpleasant for him.

"I want to apologize to you," said Frauke to Gerald when they were sitting in the café half an hour later. "I was sure the woman was in the grave."

"Your friends struck me as very convincing."

"Gerald, they're lying."

"Yes, perhaps, but they are your friends."

Frauke pressed her lips together as if to force herself to be silent. She avoided Gerald's eyes. She had no idea how to convince him.

The snow blew against the window in horizontal gusts, the rattle sounded like tiny fingers drumming against the glass. But Frauke couldn't see or hear any of it. Her thoughts tumbled over each other. *Concentrate, convince him.* She wanted to suggest that Gerald should take a closer look at the trunk of Wolf's car. *And what about the sleeping bag? Why did Gerald leave it behind?* So many ideas came to Frauke in retrospect.

They could test the holes in the walls for traces of blood . . .

They could do a lie detector test . . .

"I don't get any of this, I just don't get it."

"If you like I could talk to your friends again."

"No, it's fine."

"Really, I can—"

"You don't believe me, Gerald, be honest."

He stared into his coffee and said nothing. Frauke dug around in her pocket, then set a photograph down on the table. Until a minute before she hadn't planned to bring her mother into this.

I've got to protect her.

"I've still got this," she said.

"Who's that?"

"My mother. There were three photographs in the paper bag. One of them shows Tamara's daughter, sitting on a step outside the kindergarten, the other photograph is a picture of Lutger, he's Kris and Wolf's father. He's filling up his car. But this one . . ."

Frauke tapped the photograph.

" . . .this one the killer took at my mother's house."

"Doesn't your mother live in that clinic in Spandau?"

"In Potsdam. She has a two-room apartment there. Do you get what I'm trying to say? Meybach sat opposite my mother, he must have talked to her. He was there."

Gerald didn't pick up the photograph, he touched it with his index finger, that was all.

"Why didn't he send you a picture of your father?" he asked.

Frauke looked at him as if he'd made a joke.

"Are you kidding me?"

"No, no, I'm quite serious, why did he take the trouble to seek out your mother?"

"How should I know?"

Gerald pushed the photograph over to her. A small gesture, but Frauke nearly recoiled. *I've only known him for two years, and I can still read him like a book.* The gesture told her everything.

He thinks anyone could have taken the picture. Even me.

"My mother is the only one who knows what Meybach looks like," Frauke said, and couldn't help the fact that her voice sounded furious. "My mother sat opposite this murderer, Gerald, she'll remember. If you talk to her and do a composite, then—"

Gerald suddenly slammed his hand down on the table, and Frauke immediately shut up.

"Listen to me," he said quietly, "just so that we really understand each other. I really like you, I'm entirely on your side, but I've already gone too far out on a limb. Things could get pretty complicated for me. I was at your house, and you threw me out; I looked at an abandoned flat with you, and then sent my men to your garden without a warrant, so that they could dig up a damned hole. And now you want me to go to a clinic and question a woman who's been mentally disturbed for more than a decade?"

Silence had suddenly fallen around them. Gerald hadn't noticed that his voice was getting loud toward the end. He hadn't planned to let himself go. Frauke's face told him everything. He had lost her. The people went on with their conversations. Frauke picked the photograph off the table and put it in her pocket.

"Frauke, I didn't mean—"

"You're right," she said and got to her feet. "You're far enough out on a limb."

"Don't be ridiculous, where are you going?"

"Where do you think I'm going? I'm going to see my mentally disturbed mother and ask her who took that picture of her," Frauke replied, buttoning up her overcoat and leaving the café.

It's a quarter past ten, and Frauke can't feel her legs any more. The floor at her feet is scattered with cigarette butts. She knows that if she smokes another one she'll throw up. One of the ravens lands a few yards away from her in a cloud of snow on the Krumme Lanke. It hacks twice at the ice, ducks down and flies away again. Frauke sees it disappearing, and the landscape is motionless and silent once more.

As a child she thought all ravens were guardian angels in disguise. When she thinks about it now she doesn't know where she got that idea from. But she does remember how good it made her feel. Every time she saw a raven she felt protected and safe.

Her right hand grips the wooden handle in her coat so tightly that it hurts. She bought the knife early this morning in a household supply store on Schlossstrasse. It has a double blade and sits nicely in the hand. *No raven will protect me today.*

Today I'll protect myself. Frauke looks at her watch again. In the distance she hears the roar of an engine. Road maintenance is on its way and will soon drive past her. Frauke takes the pack of cigarettes out of her coat. The first drag makes her retch, after that it's better. *One more cigarette can't hurt,* she thinks and stares so intently across the ice that the landscape melts and flickers before her eyes like a misty dream.

After leaving Gerald sitting in the café, Frauke drove to Potsdam through the snow, registered as a visitor, and walked into the rear wing of the clinic where her mother had her apartment. She felt as if she were in a waking dream. In all those years she hadn't been alone here once. It would have seemed wrong.

"Where's your dear father?"

Frauke gave a start when she heard Mrs. Sanders's voice behind her. She didn't turn around, she could clearly imagine Mrs. Sanders standing in the doorway of the apartment—on tiptoes, careful not to cross an invisible line.

"He's not coming today," said Frauke.

"Aha, but they're going in and out of your dear mother's apartment. Whoremongering, I dare say. Is she pregnant again? You can't turn on a light, your head stays in the dark."

Frauke ignored Mrs. Sanders and stopped outside her mother's door. Number 17. She laid one ear against the wood. She was nervous, but then anyone would probably be nervous if they hadn't spoken to their mother for eleven years.

Tanja Lewin started seeing the evil in her daughter after her husband had had her committed to the private clinic. One day—they had been in the garden at visiting time, and her father had nipped off to the bathroom—Tanja Lewin took her fifteen-year-old daughter aside and said, "I know who you are and who's hiding behind your face. And I know what you've done. Look at me, or is that so hard to do? It's because of you that I'm here. It's because of you that it all happened."

That was how it began.

The phone rang at night, and when her father picked up the receiver the line went dead, but when Frauke got the phone her mother hissed in her ear: "How's my whore-child? You know I'm locked up in here while you share a bed with your father? How much must you hate me to do such a thing?"

Her mother's doctor asked Frauke time and again how she felt and how she was dealing with her mother's illness. She wanted to know if her mother had made any accusations against her, and repeatedly explained that Tanja Lewin was non compos mentis and confused people and situations. *If that's the case,* Frauke wanted to say, *why is she accusing just me and not my father too?* Frauke kept her mouth shut. To the doctor and also to her father. She didn't want anyone to learn about her mother's threats because she was afraid that the doctors would increase her mother's medication or worse. Buried deep inside Frauke was the hope that if everyone thought her mother was normal she would soon be able to come home and resume her old life.

So during visiting times Frauke always stayed in the background and avoided looking at her mother. The worst thing about it was that there were also lucid moments in her mother's life, when she was warm and affectionate and called Frauke over to her. This emotional roller coaster increasingly threatened to tear Frauke in two.

The big split came the year Frauke finished school and went to Italy for two months. Her mother was so disappointed by her absence that she stopped talking to Frauke when she came back. And that is how it has stayed until today.

Frauke took a deep breath, knocked and lowered the handle. The apartment was deserted, and her mother wasn't in the adjoining bathroom either. Frauke looked at the back of the door where the weekly schedule was kept. It was macaroni cheese today, with rocket salad. Under the word *Saturday* was a big letter S with a circle around it.

Now Frauke knew where she could find her mother.

She had to push aside the curtain over the narrow window in the room to see her mother sitting on a bench. She was naked and alone. Frauke tapped against the glass, but her mother didn't react. Frauke opened the door and stepped inside. The heat struck her in the face.

"Mama?"

Her mother looked up, startled. The doctors didn't care for spontaneous visits. They said patients had to prepare themselves for visits. *Perhaps I don't exist for her, because I didn't register in advance,* Frauke thought and tried to smile.

"I didn't think you were coming so soon," said her mother. "Birgitt was going to massage me after the sauna and—"

"I've got to talk to you," Frauke interrupted her and stopped in the door. It felt as if her lungs were refusing to inhale the sultry air. Her mother tapped on the bench next to her.

"Then sit down."

"Couldn't you—"

"Shut the door and talk to me here," her mother snapped and slid aside to make room for her daughter.

Frauke shut the door and sat down. She was nervous, and wished she could light a cigarette, but she had no idea whether that was even possible in a sauna.

"I knew you'd come," said her mother. "I felt it here."

She lifted her left breast and let it fall again.

Nice gesture, thought Frauke, and nodded as if she understood exactly what her mother meant. Her body was drenched in sweat, but she didn't think of taking off her coat. *It's my armor, it's staying on.* Her mother's hand settled on her knee, and Frauke flinched.

"Calm now," said her mother.

"I am calm."

Her mother patted the knee.

"He was here," she said. "He talked to me. He likes you. I think that was why he sought me out. He wanted to know more about you. He asked me why you suffer so. You can imagine how surprised I was. I didn't know you suffered. That's why I had to speak to you. I wanted you to know that you're blameless. Do you understand?"

Frauke tried to react. *Order, bring order into this chaos.* She cleared her throat and wiped the sweat from her eyes.

"Mama, who was here?"

"The devil, who else would I be talking about?"

"How do you know he was the devil?"

"Do you think I wouldn't recognize the devil when he's standing by my bed?"

Her mother laughed, at Frauke, and Frauke did something she would never have thought possible: she slapped her mother in the face.

"I'm twenty-nine," she said and had to repeat it. "I'm twenty-nine, I'm not fifteen any more. I've got enough shit on my plate. You've got to stop telling me such crap, do you hear me? Enough now."

Mother and daughter looked at one another. Was there any recognition in the mother's eyes? Something about her expression confused Frauke. Then Tanja Lewin raised her hand and rested it on her daughter's cheek, gently, as if Frauke had taken the blow rather than her mother.

"Don't cry," said her mother. "I know how hard it is for you."

"You don't know anything."

"I do, I know, and if you knew all the things I know, you'd be locked up in here with me. We crazy people just know too much."

She smiled as if she had made a joke. Frauke wanted to get away. She imagined herself running out of the sauna, she saw herself leaning against the wall, breathing heavily, and tasted the cigarette, and then she was in the street and then in the car, and then she was gone.

"What did you tell the devil," she asked quietly, and her voice sounded almost brittle. Painfully, she understood what she was doing here. She was getting involved with her mother. *Again.*

Tanja Lewin has seen the devil so many times that she's no longer deceived. The devil has sung for her and recited poetry for her; he has gripped her heart, thus proving to her that she belongs to him. Frauke's mother knows what the devil smells like, his preferences and his dislikes. Once he came to her as a child. He crept into the clinic, stood by the side of her bed and said he'd gotten lost. Tanja Lewin laughed at him. Another time he visited her as her doppelgänger, and that time she screamed until not a sound issued from her mouth.

After an absence of several years, five days ago the devil came back to Tanja Lewin. He was wearing a thick jacket, boots, and a woollen cap. He was young, he was friendly.

"The devil doesn't get cold," she said by way of greeting.

"I didn't want to stand out," he said and pulled up a chair. The devil had no rings on his fingers, his eyes were brown, his face clean-shaven.

"So they know you're here?"

"Of course, they let me in. Look what I've brought you."

The devil held up a camera.

"You want my soul?"

"I want to remember you."

The devil asked her to smile. Frauke's mother smiled, the devil took a picture, then another.

"Tell me about your daughter," he said.

"I'm not telling you anything," said Tanja Lewin and laughed anxiously. Even if she spent day and night waiting for the devil, it didn't mean he didn't scare her. The devil shook his head and said that wasn't what he'd understood. He folded his hands. He plainly had time. They looked at each other. They looked at each other for a long time. It hurts when the devil is silent. It's a bit as if the energy is being sucked out of the room. The air. The life.

"What do you want to hear?" asked Tanja Lewin after a while.

"Tell me what you did to her," the devil said.

Tanja Lewin wanted to scream. She wanted to jump out of bed and drag her fingernails across his face. The devil didn't let it come to that. He pushed Frauke's mother onto the bed with one hand, and with the other he held her mouth shut.

"Everything," he said and leaned over her. "Tell me everything."

Tanja Lewin bit into the heel of his hand. She was so filled with fear that the fear gave her courage. The devil kept his hand resting on her mouth. His eyes closed for a moment. The blood from the wound flowed into her mouth, making her swallow and choke. The devil didn't flinch. His eyes were a question.

Tell me everything, okay?

Tanja Lewin nodded, the hand detached itself from her mouth, Tanja Lewin spat blood on the floor, she choked and nearly vomited. The devil handed her tissues from the bedside table. Tanja Lewin heard the blood dripping from his hand onto the floor.

"I'm bleeding for you," he said and smiled.

Tanja Lewin started to cry. As she later explained to Frauke, it wasn't out of fear, it was pure relief that the devil wasn't furious with her. He was acting sympathetic. He ran his uninjured hand over her forehead and told her to calm down. Now.

She calmed down.

He told her to look at him. Now.

She looked at him, and again the devil asked her to tell him everything.

Tanja Lewin shook her head.

*   *   *

"You didn't tell him anything?" Frauke said with surprise.

"Nothing. Not a word."

"And he was satisfied with that?"

"He was satisfied with that. The devil is a gentleman. That's why I have to talk to you. I don't trust him. The devil says he likes you, but beware. The devil lies, he always lies. And what he likes, he hates; and what he hates, he calls love. That's why I gave nothing away. He isn't to know who you are. You're my daughter. That's all he's going to get. There's nothing more to say. Do you know what tired means?"

Tanja Lewin didn't wait for the answer, but laid her head in Frauke's lap. Like her father. As if her mother knew how he had behaved toward his daughter. Frauke got goosebumps in spite of the heat.

"Let me sleep just for a day," said her mother. "Or for a week, okay?"

She closed her eyes, one hand still resting on Frauke's knee and the other clenched in a fist in front of her mouth. Tanja Lewin went to sleep like that, and Frauke sat there and sweated her soul out of her body and didn't dare wake her mother.

She protected me.

The thought was like ice in the heat.

Frauke withstood it for twenty minutes, then she carefully lifted her mother's head and rested it on a tissue. The air outside the sauna was the loveliest that Frauke had ever known. Relief came over her in sobs. She slumped onto a chair in the corridor and breathed greedily.

He was here, he wanted to know more about me.

On the way out Frauke asked the nurses if her mother had had any visitors over the last few days. No one knew anything; they explained that her mother wasn't in a high-security prison.

What does he want from me?

The snow came as a relief. All the white, the cold, the silence.

Frauke went to her car and was just tapping a cigarette out of the pack with trembling hands when her phone rang.

The display showed Tamara's number.

"Yes?"

In the silence that followed Frauke expected all kinds of things. Insults and questions. She wouldn't have been surprised if Tamara had simply been mucking about.

Do you still know me?

"Could you come, please," said Tamara. "Your father's lying outside the door."

Frauke gives a start. She doesn't know how long she's been staring straight in front of her. *How could I be so careless?* The noise of the passing snowplow pulled her from her thoughts. *How did Meybach know I felt guilty? How did he know that?* Her right hand hurts, she loosens her grip and stares at the knife. It's twenty past ten, and Frauke wonders if she's really capable of killing. She used to believe that if she ran up a hill fast enough she would get to the top and go flying off. It was the run-up that mattered.

Killing might be like that, I need a proper run-up and I have to believe in it, then it'll happen all by itself.

Frauke tries to imagine her life afterward. Starting work again, ordering a plate of tabouleh at the Arab restaurant, browsing in the bookshop or talking to Kris, making a date with this man and that one and knowing exactly whether she would or whether she wouldn't have sex with him; talking to Wolf, holding Tamara in her arms, everything being as it should be and she just being who she is and no one else after she's killed a human being.

"Where are you?" she says in a whisper and listens to the departing snowplow and wishes she was back in the villa.

Normally it doesn't take Frauke ten minutes to get to the villa from Potsdam, but yesterday the journey through the snowstorm took half an hour. Arriving in front of the villa, she didn't dare drive up to the property and parked like a stranger on the pavement outside.

What if they don't let me in?

Frauke checked her face in the rearview mirror. The black hair, the center part, perhaps a bit too much makeup around the eyes. She brushed her hair behind her ears and got out.

Her father was sitting on the veranda, wrapped in a blanket. He held a cup in his hands and reminded Frauke of a black-and-white photograph that she'd once seen at an exhibition. When her father saw her coming toward him, he quickly took the blanket off his shoulders. *He doesn't want to look old and weak.*

"I thought there was no one there," he said by way of greeting, and pointed behind him with his thumb, "so I waited outside."

"You could have frozen to death," said Frauke, glancing at the kitchen window. There was no one to be seen.

"People like me don't freeze that easily," her father replied and tapped his chest with his left hand. "Premium steel, you know?"

He folded up his blanket and laid it on the bench.

"That was a joke."

He tried to hug her. Frauke recoiled. She had had more than enough affection from one parent already.

"I know it was a joke," she said. "Why didn't you call me?"

Her father pretended he hadn't heard her.

"Tamara's heart probably stopped when she found me outside the door. My, you should have seen her face. She probably thought I was dead. But this air makes you tired, too."

"Dad, why didn't you call me?"

"Your car wasn't there. I thought you were bound to be back soon. I'm used to waiting. Tamara made me coffee, but I wouldn't go in. Trouble brewing, right?"

He took one last sip from the cup and tipped the rest in the snow before setting the cup on the bench. It left an ugly brown stain in the immaculate white.

"What's up?" asked her father. "Are you two fighting or not? You can tell me. I—"

"It's got nothing to do with you."

He raised his hands defensively.

"Fine, fine. That's not why I'm here anyway. Your mother rang, she wants to talk to you."

"I know, I just paid her a visit."

"But how did you know . . ."

Her father fell silent and rubbed his hand over his face, he was tired as always, his eyes bloodshot.

"You two are a mystery to me," he said. "I don't understand you. Your mother called me this morning, she phoned me from one of the pay phones in the common room. I was to find you and tell you that she . . ."

He broke off mid-sentence. Frauke saw the tears and wondered how he could love her mother like that. After all those years. *No human being should love another human being like that.*

"What did she tell you?" he wanted to know.

She told him. She told him everything she had learned from her mother, and saw him switching from joy to grief. Joy that his wife's mind had been clear for a few moments and that she had phoned him; and grief because she talked of the devil as if he were a welcome guest.

"Come on," she said, "let's go."

In the street outside the villa she let go of her father's arm and sat down in the car. She closed the driver's door, started the engine, and turned on the heating. She breathed deeply in and out. She didn't want to look at her father standing there on the edge of the street watching her. It wasn't one of her best days. First she had dragged the police into the house in front of her friends, then she had got involved with her mother, and now this. *Maybe he'll just go, maybe he'll forget me, and we'll never see each other again.* The passenger door opened, and her father slumped into the seat with a sigh.

"I'd just like to go to sleep," he said. "Will you stay at my place tonight?"

"And what about your car?"

"I'll collect it another time."

His hand pressed her leg.

"Please, Frauke, I beg you."

Frauke didn't want to go back to her father's and meet his new flame. No one should see her like that. Her father said he understood. So she took a room in a little hotel on Mommsenstrasse. No sooner had they walked into the room than her father lay down on one side of the bed and was asleep within minutes. Frauke sat by the open window and smoked. Her thoughts circled, they were like birds of prey waiting for a rash movement.

How could Meybach do that?

At around midnight she took a bath and had a pizza delivered. The question didn't go away, the question wanted an answer. Meybach had made a crucial mistake. He had got too close to Frauke. He should have stayed away from her mother. Now things were personal, and Frauke couldn't cope with that.

How could he? Just tell me, how?

For a while she watched her sleeping father, who had been passive all his life, and had always lived with the weary hope that his wife would be well again one day. As Frauke heard his steady breathing, she understood that she could never allow herself to be like that. No passivity, no weary hopes. She decided to aim straight for her goal. No nervous dancing around. Enough waiting. She hated being helpless.

She ate the pizza and waited to see if she would change her mind. But with every passing minute her confidence grew. The only snag was that she didn't want to leave too early, which was ridiculous, because there was no wrong or right time to visit one's own house.

Unless you want to be caught.

She washed her face with cold water and looked at herself in the mirror.

Now or never.

She wrote a note for her father, pulled on her coat and went out into the snow.

Half an hour later she closed the front door. It was quiet, a pleasant, familiar darkness filled the rooms, and the smell of a wood fire lay in the air. Frauke took off her boots and left them by the front door. *No traces.* She laid her hand on the radiator in the hall. The warmth was still there, it would only fade at dawn. Frauke knew how chilly the villa felt after you woke up. The luxury of a shower, the boiler working to pump warmth through the house, a new day.

Without me.

Frauke left the front door open a crack and stepped inside.

Please be where you always are, please.

She stopped by the wardrobe and looked through the jacket.

Nothing.

She reached for the coat.

Nothing.

And now? What do I do now? I can hardly go upstairs and ask Kris if he could help me for a moment.

Frauke thought for a moment, then took out her phone and tapped in Kris's number in the dark.

Please don't let it—

The sound of a ringing cell phone came from the kitchen. Frauke immediately hung up, the ringing noise stopped, and Frauke crept across the floorboards in her socks. Her footsteps were barely audible; the floor just creaked a little in the kitchen.

The phone was on a pile of magazines. She put it in her coat pocket and crept back out of the kitchen. As she stepped into the corridor, she was suddenly standing in front of herself. Her heart stopped painfully for a moment, then Frauke looked away from her reflection and stepped outside. Boots on, shut the door carefully, down the steps to the gate. The crunch of her footsteps in the snow was frighteningly noisy. She didn't look back. She knew that no one was watching after her. She was confident that just as she was vanishing now, her footsteps would vanish over the next hour.

Her father hadn't moved from the spot. *He could be dead,* Frauke thought, and rested her hand on his back. Warmth, the rhythm of his breathing. Frauke shut herself in the bathroom. She found the right number after a few seconds. Kris had given her not a name, but a sign: #.

Frauke pressed CALL.

Meybach picked up after the fourth ring.

"I was wondering when you would call. I wanted to thank you for the file, that was good work."

"You are one sick fucker," Frauke hissed.

Silence.

"Hello?"

She looked at the display. Meybach had hung up. She pressed REDIAL. He kept her waiting and only picked up after the eleventh ring.

"Let's start again from the beginning," he said.

Frauke breathed deeply in and out.

"That sounds better, you're relaxing."

"How the hell could you go and see my mother?"

"Oh, it's you, Frauke Lewin, lovely to hear from you. It must have struck you that I have a spot for you. From the very first day I knew we had a particular connection, you and I."

"There is no connection between us. How dare you visit my mother?"

"She's an interesting case. Other people's pasts haven't given me much, but your mother is a special case."

"If you ever go back and—"

· 198 ·

"Come on, Frauke, this isn't about your mother."

He fell silent. She didn't want to ask, she asked.

"So what is it about?"

"About guilt, of course, what else? Don't you get the irony behind this? You have an agency that apologizes, but there's lots that you can't forgive yourselves."

"What do you know about us? You don't know us. You know nothing about us."

"I don't know much. I'm being honest. But what do you know about guilt? What do you know about forgiveness?"

Frauke was confused, she had no idea what he was talking about.

"We are doing a job," she said.

"Maybe that's the problem. You were *just* doing a job. Perhaps we should leave it there. Do your job. I just need one more apology from you and then it's quits, the job is over."

"QUITS? WHAT DO YOU MEAN QUITS?" Frauke exploded. "NO ONE'S GOING TO APOLOGIZE FOR YOU EVER AGAIN, YOU SICK—"

Again that silence at the other end. Frauke hoped her yelling hadn't woken her father up. She stared at the display and marched up and down the bathroom a few times. She could have called Meybach from the street, but she wanted to be near her father. As if he could offer her protection.

Seven rings later.

"It's always a question of sympathy," Meybach said.

"You won't get any sympathy from me. You're a murderer. Murderers don't deserve sympathy. And don't think I don't know who you are. My mother gave a precise description of you. The police know all about it."

"Frauke, you insult me. I know your every footstep, so stop bluffing. And anyway no one's going to listen to a woman who's been living in a closed institution for fourteen years, and who gets visits from the devil from time to time. But that isn't the point either. I can tell you what I look like. You *know* what I look like. But what good will a description do you? Are you looking for me or something?"

She couldn't get her head around it. She felt so furious that the pressure in her head nearly tore her in two.

He's fucking with me, this sick fucker is fucking with me.

"I want us to meet," she said urgently.

"Say that again."

"I want us to sort this business out between us. Whatever your plan is, you'll get it from me as long as you leave my friends out of it."

"How do you know you can give me what I need?"

Let me do it, cried a voice in Frauke's head, *let me take the burden off my friends, just let me do it.*

She went on speaking as quietly as possible.

"I have no idea what this woman did to you, but it seems plain to me that it's a matter of revenge."

No reaction. Frauke heard his breathing. Meybach didn't agree with her, but he didn't deny it either. Frauke went on.

"I can help you. I can give you what you're looking for."

"And that might be?"

"Absolution."

She knew he was smiling.

"Perhaps we should meet, then," he said.

Frauke tried to sound normal, but the words came too fast.

"Where and when?"

Meybach laughed.

"You're under pressure, aren't you?"

Now it was Frauke who came close to hanging up. *I've betrayed my friends, I have nowhere to live now, you bastard, and you're asking me if I'm under pressure!*

"Maybe I'm the one who can grant absolution," Meybach went on.

"Yes, maybe," Frauke lied.

After that he told her where she could find him; then he hung up, and Frauke stared with surprise at the display on Kris's phone for a few moments, before she kissed it.

I've got you, she thought, *now I've got you.*

Which is why six hours later Frauke is sitting on a fallen tree trunk on the shore of the Krumme Lanke, shivering pitifully. So far there hasn't been a single stroller or jogger. Only the ravens switch from one tree to another, as if they were impatient too.

It's 10:33. Meybach said he would be there at ten. Frauke looks around, the forest is a dark wall behind her. She doesn't think Meybach will come from there. The snow would give him away after only a few steps.

He'll come along one of the gritted paths, and then I'll sort everything out and I'll—

Kris's cell phone rings in her coat. She takes it out. The display shows #.

"So there we are," Meybach says by way of greeting.

"I'm here, where are you?"

"To be perfectly honest, I found it rather difficult to trust you. Who's to say that you wouldn't turn up with another police unit?"

"I'd never—"

"I know you would if you could. But you've probably taken your toll on the policeman's nerves, am I correct?"

Frauke looks behind her.

"You were watching us?"

"I always had an eye on you all. It was very daring of you to call on your old friend in the criminal investigation department."

Frauke starts sweating.

"I did all that on my own," she says quickly. "I'm . . . I'm losing it. The others had nothing to do with it. I'll make up for it."

"We'll see."

"I thought we were going to meet."

"We *are* meeting," says Meybach, and a moment later there's a whistle. The ravens rise up out of the trees. Frauke sees a man standing on the opposite shore. A hundred meters away. Perhaps less.

"That's not fair," she says.

"What's not fair? Did you want to shake my hand?"

No, I wanted to slit your fucking throat, Frauke wants to answer. She narrows her eyes slightly and sees that he's wearing jeans, a black jacket, a cap, and has his phone pressed to his right ear.

Frauke walks closer to the shore of the Krumme Lanke. Her eyes hurt, she's concentrating so hard on seeing Meybach. But however hard she tries, he stays a blur, as if he were a mirage that could dissolve into nothing at any moment.

"Why didn't you bury the body in some forest or other?"

"Scruples," says Frauke, "and respect for the dead woman. We didn't just want to chuck her in any old place. Everyone deserves a decent funeral."

"So you buried her in the garden?"

Frauke says nothing.

"Not everyone deserves a funeral, Frauke. Some people should just be chucked."

"Is that why you came and got her from our property?"

The figure on the opposite shore doesn't move.

"Who says I came and got her?" asks Meybach after a long pause.

Frauke breathes in with a hiss.

"What are you doing?" asks Meybach.

Frauke looks down at herself with surprise. She has stepped on the ice of the Krumme Lanke.

"Don't be ridiculous. The ice won't hold you. Do you think I'd be so stupid as to stand here if it held you?"

Frauke doesn't answer him. Her right hand grips the handle of the knife in her coat pocket. In spite of the cold she feels sweat on her back. *Like yesterday in the sauna, everything's repeating itself.*

"Did you really think I'd go to the trouble of getting the

corpse out of your garden? I thought you were smarter than that. I probably shouldn't spend any more time on you, now that you're out of the game."

"Who says I'm out of the game?"

Meybach laughs, and Frauke could kill him for that laugh alone.

"You mean your friends forgive you and are glad to see you again after you brought the police into their house? I wish we'd met under different circumstances, I think we would have gotten along. Whatever you have to do with the agency, you aren't really a part of it. You should forgive yourself, Frauke, that's the first step, and no one else can—"

"HOW DARE YOU MEDDLE IN MY LIFE!"

Frauke's words ring out over the ice. She wasn't speaking into the phone, she leaned forward and yelled the words straight at him. When she puts her phone back to her ear, Meybach says softly, "So I've touched a raw nerve, then."

She can't look at him any more. It's over. She's finished. *I'm not going to beg,* she thinks and snaps her phone shut. She puts it in her coat pocket and looks across to Meybach as if waiting for a starting flag, then she starts running.

YOU

FRAUKE LEWIN WAS the only one you were really taken by. When you took a closer look at the agency, she stood out right away. Something about her fascinated you. She seemed different from Tamara Berger, who struck you as fragile and anxious, too weak for real life. She was different from Kris Marrer, who seemed to consist entirely of corners and edges. And she was different from his little brother Wolf, who might have looked predictable, but you knew it was only an illusion. Those of us with feelings of guilt are the most unpredictable of creatures.

You concentrated on Frauke Lewin. For two days you were so close to her that in retrospect you wonder why she didn't notice you. There was a closeness there, there was a connection, there was . . . You still can't quite grasp it. You only know that you wanted to find out more about her.

You disliked her father right off. But you were fascinated by her mother. Her medical report, her life before and after she was admitted to the clinic, her relationship with Frauke. You saw where the guilt came from and decided to pay her mother a visit. It was a stupid idea. It was irresponsible and dangerous of you. And then she turned you away and didn't tell you anything. Nonetheless your visit was worth it. You not only came a bit closer to Frauke, no, she phoned you and wanted to see you. And now that Krumme Lanke is the only thing separating you, you really regret that there's this problem between you. You wish you'd met her in normal life. You also wish she'd think about everything in peace. With a cool head. She would understand you. With more sympathy she would understand you. But like this . . .

"You aren't really a part of it," you say and try to read her facial expression in the distance. "You should forgive yourself, Frauke, that's the first step, and no one else can—"

"HOW DARE YOU MEDDLE IN MY LIFE!" her voice rings out across the ice.

For a moment you're speechless, then you say carefully, "So I've touched a raw nerve, then."

They're the wrong words, the conversation is over. Frauke puts her phone away, ducks down, and suddenly comes running toward you. *How can she be so brave?* After ten meters her woollen cap flies off her head and falls on the ice, her coat opens like a black flower. You can make out her determined expression, her arms pump away in the rhythm of her footsteps, something metallic glitters in her hand.

She's attacking me, you think and can't believe it, *she's really attacking me.* The big question now is, what are you going to do if she makes it across to your side? Are you going to have a fight with her? Look at her face, she's a Fury. You could run away and—

I'm not going to make a fool of myself.

Frauke has crossed the middle of the lake. She shows no hesitation, she has only one goal in mind. Meter after meter she's getting closer, her footsteps echoing dully across the surface of the ice, you think you can hear her loud breathing, then there's a sharp crack and the surface beneath Frauke collapses. The knife falls from her hand and skitters across the ice to you. Frauke tries to grip the edge of the hole, the edge comes away, water slops out and turns the snow gray before making it transparent. You stand there and watch. You can't deny it, you're relieved. Something like pity, something like disappointment rises up in you. You wonder how she could've been so stupid.

Not stupid, brave.

Fine, as you wish. But I hope you know that the brave almost always die first, don't you?

FRAUKE

THE SHOCK ISN'T just the cold of the water, the shock of failing's much worse.

I was so sure I'd make it.

Frauke knows instinctively that she has to hold her head above the surface or it's all over. She reaches for the edge of the ice, which breaks away under her fingers. She kicks out with her feet, a ring of iron settles around her ribcage and cuts off her breathing.

Calm, stay calm, I'll get out of this and then . . .

For several seconds she forgets to tread water. She sees Meybach clearly and distinctly standing on the shore. He hasn't backed away. He hasn't tried to run off. The mirage has a face.

I . . . I know him, I . . .

Frauke disappears under water, re-emerges, her fingernails scratch across the edge of the ice. She manages to brace her left arm. *Tired.* The cold is slowly making her tired. The back of her neck feels as if it's in a bear trap. The pain is paralyzing and flows down her back, one vertebra at a time. The tiredness is everywhere now, it slows her movements and makes the pain fade into the background, while her waterlogged coat drags her down. Now Frauke gets her right arm out of the water as well, and supports herself on the edge.

The ice holds.

Rest, just rest for a moment . . .

Then she sees Meybach turning away.

"Hey, where do you think you're going?"

He doesn't reply, he doesn't listen to her, he goes back up the embankment.

"Stop, you . . . Are you scared? Have I—"

The ice breaks, Frauke was careless for a moment and supported all her weight on the edge. Her head disappears under water, her nose fills up, she emerges coughing and gasping for air. Something sharp moves in her head and splits her nerves. Everything becomes dull and numb. The water freezes on her face, and when she reaches around, the edge of the ice isn't there any more. Her hands meet the water and send it splashing into the air. The ravens start screeching. The lake pulls hungrily at Frauke, the tiredness is everywhere, the heaviness, the cold and the numbness that settles like a cocoon around her body and her whole being.

Calm, here is the calm.

No one is standing on the shore now. No footsteps can be heard on the ice. Only the sun looks through the clouds, making the ice glitter. It looks like hope.

Soon . . .

Warmth settles on Frauke's face. Her hands reach into the void, her movements slow.

Soon . . .

A wall of clouds pushes in front of the sun, the wind comes back, the ravens fall mute. It is silent. It is silent. Slowly the hole in the ice closes up again.

PART V

After

HANOVER IS BEHIND ME, and I'm heading for Osnabrück. Only silence coming from the trunk. I stink. I'm lonely. I wish a tire would burst, the car would overturn, and everything would come to an end. I'm lonely, and I'm also cowardly. I don't know what I'm really doing here. It's up to me. It's all up to me. Too much responsibility, too many decisions. I would only have to drive to the edge of the road. I could hold his nose shut. I could soak him in gasoline. I could throttle him or drop the jack on his head until he stopped moving. I've played it all out in my mind. Dragged him out of the car and pushed him into the highway. Thrown him from bridges. Laid him down in front of the car. Extinguished him.

I already let him talk to me. Even though I thought I was immune to it, I want to hear his story. He speaks, I listen, and as soon as I've had enough, he gets the tape back over his mouth and I drive on. I recognize the lies. But I don't know. He's told me four stories so far. He's everything, he's nothing, in his fear he reinvents. I'm waiting for the moment when it clicks and I can see through him. I don't want all the things that have happened to look like a big coincidence. I hate coincidences. But that's exactly what he makes it look like. One great big damned coincidence. I don't want my friends' lives to be left to chance. I'd rather kill a handful of gods. Or the one God, if he dared to antagonize me.

Before

TAMARA

THE FUNERAL TAKES PLACE four days later on a Thursday morning. The birds are clamoring in the trees, and a smell rises from the earth that is almost shaming in its intensity. Winter hurled itself over the land, and has withdrawn just as quickly. No snow now, no ice. Spring is triumphant, and the sun is a flickering, pulsing disk that makes Tamara lower her eyes.

Why can't it rain?

Tamara feels awful. The air is too lush for her, the light too bright. Kris once said that nobody should say goodbye when the sun is shining.

Nobody.

Tamara has the feeling of not being a part of it. She is standing at the edge of the playing field, waiting for the final whistle. The feeling reminds her of the summer afternoons she spent with Frauke at the sports ground. Two fourteen-year-olds watching a boys' team training. They were the most boring hours of her life, and all just because she and Frauke wanted to show the boys that they were there.

Frauke, where are you?

Tamara wishes her thoughts could switch off for a while. She wishes the earth would tremble and the world take notice of the fact that she has lost her best friend. *After an argument, after a goddamn argument.* Tamara now thinks she knows how Wolf must have felt when he found Erin dead in the bathroom stall. After that, nothing can be resolved any more. No discussions, no apologies.

Gone.

Tamara lacks the courage to step forward. She wants to lay her hands on the coffin and say so many things, but she stays right where she is and straightens her legs.

An anonymous caller told the police that a woman had fallen through the ice on the Krumme Lanke. Within twenty minutes a rescue team with water search dogs was on the spot and getting to work. The Krumme Lanke is a stretch of flowing water, and normally location within fifteen meters would have been possible, but the water temperature and the ice made the search difficult. The dogs couldn't find a trail, so the rescue team broke the ice at two spots in the direction of the current. They sent two divers down to follow the flow of the water. Frauke was found at the mouth of the stream, just before the bridge. She had been underwater for three hours.

The same afternoon, Frauke's father called the villa, after he had identified his daughter's body. Wolf took the call, listened, asked no questions, and put the phone down when Frauke's father asked him if he had understood everything. For several minutes Wolf just stood in the corridor staring at the telephone, then he went upstairs to Tamara, who was sitting behind her desk.

"Come here for a minute, Tammi."

Tamara sat where she was. She didn't like the way he stood in the doorway and looked at her.

"What is it?"

"Please, Tammi, come here."

Tamara got up and walked over to him. He hugged her, he held her tight, and then he spoke. When he had said everything, he closed his eyes and tolerated Tamara's fingernails in his back, but he didn't let go whatever she did, he held her tight.

It was good that he held me, thinks Tamara and reaches for Wolf's hand. Behind her she hears a whisper, someone sniffs, a raven settles on the mausoleum opposite. They're standing among Frauke's schoolmates and fellow students. Tamara has recognized some faces, the rest are strangers. *What do they remember when they remember Frauke?* The raven rubs its beak against the wall of the mausoleum, then flies off again and disappears over the cemetery. In the distance the traffic murmurs along Onkel-Tom-Strasse. Life doesn't take a break, it just goes on.

And afterwards we'll start exactly where we left off.

Tamara wishes for an earthquake.

On the phone, Frauke's father spoke of an accident, and the police wrote it off as an accident as well. Still, the next day Gerald turned up at their place to ask if Frauke had been a suicide risk.

"Did she ever talk about it? I mean, she might have had guilty feelings about . . ."

He made a gesture that was supposed to take in everything—the villa, her friendship with them, the supposed corpse in the garden.

"Frauke would never have killed herself," said Kris, and gave Gerald a challenging look. *Come on, contradict me,* his eyes said. When he learned of Frauke's death, Tamara saw him crying for the first time. The tears didn't last long, then the armor went up again, but they had been there, Tamara had seen them and was relieved that Kris became Kris again afterwards. Someone had to keep a clear head. Someone had to tell them what they had to do.

"And in any case it's a really stupid way of killing yourself," Kris added.

"Then that leaves us with an accident—"

"Accident my ass," said Wolf. "Frauke wasn't as stupid as that, she wouldn't go running out on the ice."

Gerald waited for a better explanation. Wolf didn't think of giving him any kind of explanation at all. Gerald expected something at least from Tamara. She sat on the sofa, hidden under a blanket, unreachable. So he turned back to Kris.

"I brought you the things we found in her coat."

He set a transparent plastic bag down on the table. House keys, wallet, two phones, odds and ends. The plastic bag had condensation on the inside, as if Frauke's things were breathing. Tamara emerged from under the blanket, Wolf leaned over the table.

"And this was on the ice," said Gerald, setting a second plastic bag down next to it. "Do you recognize the knife?"

Kris shook his head. Wolf picked it up.

"Never seen it," he said.

"Tamara?"

Tamara shook her head too. She couldn't take her eyes off the two phones in the other plastic bag.

"The knife isn't ours," she said.

"It was near the hole in the ice. Frauke's fingerprints are on the handle and the blade. Even if it wasn't her knife, she definitely held it in her hand."

Gerald looked from one to the other.

"So if you have something to say to me, please do it now."

Pause, silence.

"Are you being threatened?"

"No one's threatening us," Kris replied.

"And what about that corpse?"

"Which corpse?" Kris asked.

"And what about the killer who wants you to apologize on his behalf?"

Gerald wouldn't let go.

"I mean, did that really all come from Frauke's imagination?"

Kris laid his head on one side. Tamara was glad that Gerald hadn't homed in on her.

"Do you believe her now that she's dead?" asked Kris.

Gerald just looked at him, then lowered his eyes and changed the subject.

"Why did she have two cell phones?"

"One is private," said Kris, "the other is business. We all have two phones."

"I see."

He got to his feet. Tamara saw that there was more he wanted to say. Gerald changed his mind and left the villa without saying goodbye to them. *That's not a good sign,* thought Tamara. The front door clicked shut. Wolf took the phones out of the plastic bag.

"She must have been here in the night," he said. "She must have sneaked in and grabbed your damned phone."

Wolf handed the blue cell phone to Kris. It was wet, and when Kris flipped it open, a few drops of water fell on the table.

"Why would she do that?" he asked.

"Some subtle form of revenge," Wolf supposed. "Don't ask me, that woman was always a mystery to me."

"All women are mysteries to you," said Tamara.

They looked at each other for a moment. And everything was there, pain was there, and the past, and despair.

Is it really true?

It's really true.

Kris tried to turn on the phone. Nothing happened. He set it down on the table and rubbed his face with both hands.

"Frauke would never have avenged herself," he said. "It wasn't her style."

"Just as it wasn't her style to run out on a frozen lake and drown in it," Tamara added. "That was never an accident. I don't believe it."

She looked at Wolf.

"You said yourself a moment ago that she'd never have been so stupid."

"Yes, but she was dumb enough to rat on us," Wolf objected.

Tamara nudged him in the shoulder.

"Don't say that. Frauke wasn't dumb."

"I don't understand why she stole it," says Kris, tapping his phone as if the phone could give him an answer. "I really haven't the faintest clue."

Tamara sees the radiant blue sky in the black paint of the coffin lid. She thinks that if she leans far enough forward and looks down at the coffin, it would be like something in a fairy tale. It wouldn't be her reflection looking back, but Frauke, and then they could talk to one another as if nothing had happened.

Frauke's father stands at the head of the coffin, and beside him is her mother, who was allowed to leave the private hospital for the funeral. Tamara shook her hand when she said hello. *I knew Frauke better than you,* she wanted to say.

Frauke's mother ignored her. She avoids any eye contact. She either looks pointedly over her shoulder or stares at the coffin as if she could see her dead daughter through the wood.

What we're doing here is wrong, Tamara thinks, *Kris was right.*

As teenagers they had sworn they would never end up six feet under. They wanted to have their ashes scattered on the Lietzensee, so that they would always be together, even in death. Frauke's father wasn't interested in any of that. He insisted that Frauke was to be buried in the City Cemetery in Zehlendorf. And when Kris started arguing with him, Gerd Lewin said, "I need a place where I know my daughter is safe and where I can always go and visit her, don't you understand that?"

Tamara understood. Whatever connection there might have been between the two, Frauke's father wasn't going to let his daughter go that easily. Kris didn't want to understand. He refused to come to the funeral, and went off to the shed after breakfast, then came into the sitting room with several loads of wood and stacked them next to the fireplace. Wolf remarked that it wasn't all that cold any more, to which Kris replied that they should go to the funeral, and in the meantime he would keep the fire going.

Perhaps that's the best way of saying goodbye, Tamara thinks and looks at her hand, which is solidly and securely in Wolf's. She misses Wolf, even though he's standing next to her. She misses Kris. And Frauke. Right now she would like to have everyone who has ever been close to her right next to her, and hold them tight. She also wishes she had stayed with Kris in the villa. She wishes so many things, but none of them happens. No one speaks. No one leaves the cemetery. The minutes drag on. No one thinks of fulfilling a single one of her wishes. Tamara starts to cry. She thought there were no tears left. Wolf puts an arm around her shoulders. Someone hands her a tissue. It's going to be a long morning.

KRIS

KRIS WAS ON HIS WAY back from jogging when he found out. He walked into the villa and was surprised by the silence. First he looked in the kitchen, then in the living room. On the way upstairs he heard crying.

Tamara and Wolf were on the floor in the corridor. Wolf was sitting down, Tamara had rolled herself up in a ball, her head in Wolf's lap. Kris didn't say a word. A floorboard creaked under his foot. Wolf looked up and looked at him. *Don't,* Kris wanted to say to him, *please, whatever you want to say, keep it to yourself.*

"She's dead," said Wolf.

Kris wanted to turn around and go, but he couldn't move from the spot. Wolf shrugged as if he was perplexed, and repeated, "She's dead, Kris, she's just dead."

Tamara's weeping sounded like an insect that's caught in a jar, looking in vain for a way out.

Now Kris is sitting by the fire wearing his shorts, feeding the flames as if his life depended on it. His hair sticks to his head. Sweat drips on to the carpet and leaves dark trails. His back is wet. To his right is a bottle of water, little bubbles have formed on the inside of it, the water is piss-warm.

Kris is glad he said no to the funeral. He knows it's wrong.

Every few minutes he leans forward and puts on another log. The fire is almost silent, it only crackles every now and then, sending up white sparks. *If only everything were as simple as a fire that needs to be fed, we'd all sit by fires and sink into a state of bliss,* Kris thinks and takes a sip from the bottle of water.

He knows what he's doing here.

When they were children, he and Wolf spent their summer holidays with their grandparents on Lake Starnberg. In the summer when Kris was eight and Wolf was six, their grandfather died in a car accident. It was their first contact with death. They experienced their grandmother's grief, they saw their parents crying and later stood forlornly beside all the other mourners in the cemetery and had no idea how to behave. At the time, Kris swore he would never go to another funeral.

The same night their grandmother came into the spare bedroom that he and Wolf shared during the holidays. She had two candles and explained that even the dead need light to guide them.

"If your grandfather sees the light, he won't be afraid, and he'll know how much you love him."

The brothers watched wide-eyed as their grandmother handed each of them a candle, lit it, and then left the room again.

Years later they laughed about that night, but at the time they had been baffled, and each of them sat on their bed with a candle, not daring to move. How would they sleep now? What if the candles went out? Would their grandfather get lost in the dark?

Their grandmother was so immersed in her grief that she had forgotten to give them candle holders. So they spent the night with their backs against the wall and their eyes fixed on the candles in their hands. They talked about their grandfather for a while, until they grew tired. Wolf nodded off and was woken by the hot wax running over his hands. Kris, on the other hand, barely dared to blink and stared at the candle flame as if it were his grandfather's life-light. He thought that if he kept the flame alive overnight, their grandfather would be back at the breakfast table tomorrow morning.

At about three o'clock Wolf gave up, blew out the candle, and lay down to sleep.

Kris kept going. At dawn he heard their grandmother getting out of bed. He heard the waking birds, the sounds of the first tram from the nearby stop, and the rush of the blood in his ears. When his candle was no more than a tiny stump, and about to burn his fingers, their grandmother called to them. They were to get up, breakfast was ready.

Wolf started awake and saw Kris sitting on the bed with the flickering candle stump in the palm of his hand. Kris still remembers his little brother staring at the snuffed candle on his bedside table and wondering whether he should quickly light it again. Of course at that moment their grandmother came in.

Wolf admitted, sobbing, that he was sorry but he couldn't, he just couldn't stay awake. His grandmother reassured him and told him it hadn't been intended that way. She was about to say more, when Kris screamed. It was both a cry of pain and of relief. The candle in his hand had burned down, the wick had settled like a red-hot needle on the palm of his hand. Kris had persevered.

Although their grandfather wasn't at the breakfast table the next day, Kris was proud of himself. He felt like a protector. And that's why he's sitting by the fire this Thursday. A candle isn't enough. Frauke should be sent on her way with a roaring fire. That's why Kris is keeping the fire alive. To be with Frauke, to give her protection, wherever she is now.

The days before the funeral were a vacuum. Since they found the dead woman on the wall, all their commissions have been postponed. So far no one has thought of going back to work. They have hoisted their drawbridges and disappeared into themselves. Wolf sank into melancholy, and Kris wasn't sure who his brother was grieving for more—for Frauke or for himself and the misfortune that seemed to follow him like a shadow. Tamara did what Tamara always does when there's a crisis. She set up her base on the sofa and read one novel after the other, as if the outside world had been reduced to printer's ink and white paper.

They barely spoke, they lived past one another.

Kris was the only one to move forward. The fact that Frauke had been in the villa to take his cell phone the night before her death wouldn't leave him in peace. As his phone had stopped working, the next day Kris drove to Charlottenburg to the head office of his provider, to find out about his incoming and outgoing calls.

The area depressed him. Five years ago the Ernst-Reuter-Platz had still been really lively, when the Kiepert bookstore still occupied the whole corner. Now the place is like a playground for yuppies and *flâneurs* having their frappuccinos and chocolate chip cookies before popping in to Manufaktum to buy overpriced presents that look as if they'd been cobbled together before the Second World War.

The provider's offices are on the top floor. A member of the staff kept Kris waiting for ten minutes before sitting down at his notebook and printing out a list of all incoming and outgoing calls over the last thirty days. Then he asked Kris if there was anything else he could do for him.

"Just one little thing," said Kris, getting stonewalled. The staff member absolutely refused to track Meybach's number.

"I'm sorry, I can't do that. I'd end up in a hell of a mess. And anyway he's with another network."

Kris thanked him for the list and left. His suspicion had been confirmed. Frauke had taken his phone to get Meybach's number. Of course Frauke could have gotten it from the files in her office upstairs, but in that case she would probably have risked bumping into one of the others.

We could have talked.

Frauke had done exactly what Kris should have done long ago. She had gone on the attack. She had called Meybach at 11:45 on Saturday night, and he had called her back at 10:23 the next morning. Shortly afterwards she drowned. But that wasn't nearly enough information for Kris.

On Gneisenaustrasse he headed straight for the office of his former boss, ignoring everyone's *excuse me*s.

"What are you doing here?" said Bernd Jost-Degen when he saw him.

"We need to talk," said Kris and closed the door behind him. Before his ex-boss could protest, Kris said, "I know you need five minutes to talk to your friend from the press office. It'll take him three minutes to get through to his man in the police, and he won't need more than a minute to find out what name this phone number is registered to."

Kris put the piece of paper with the number on the desk.

"Bernd, I need the address, and I know that you've got the contacts to find it for me. It wouldn't be the first time that you've used your contacts. Please, do it for me."

He did it for Kris. He didn't do it because Kris was a nice guy, or because he'd still been working for him six months previously. It takes other arguments to persuade someone like Bernd Jost-Degen. This argument was very subtle. Kris emanated an unsettling sense of danger. Bernd Jost-Degen didn't know what had happened to Kris. He only saw that his former employee wanted to have this information at any price. Even though Bernd Jost-Degen had probably never had to suffer physical violence, he could see a blow coming when a fist was clenched.

The knuckles stood out white on Kris's fists.

It took Bernd Jost-Degen eight minutes.

Afterwards Kris was breathless. He sat down in a café on Savigny Platz and stared at the street through the window. In his pocket was Lars Meybach's address. It was Tuesday morning, Frauke was to be buried on Thursday morning, and Kris didn't know what his next step was going to be. For a while he considered talking to Gerald. But he rejected it because he didn't think Gerald would jump on the idea that Meybach had spoken to Frauke shortly before her death. What did that tell him? There was no solid proof, there were only her statements and of course the corpse, but even that had disappeared. Gerald would laugh at him.

Over the next two hours Kris phoned once and waited. He ate three brownies, and with each brownie he had a milky coffee. Afterwards he had a sugar rush, and his stomach was rumbling. At five to three he sat down in his car and drove to Nollendorfplatz.

His name is Marco M. Even when he was at school he called himself Marco M and corrected the teachers when they only said Marco. Marco M belonged to the group of computer freaks who did everything for bytes and graphics cards in those days: burglaries, shoplifting, nothing violent, just the easy way of getting hold of quick cash. His style has changed since then, he never burgles anywhere any more, his hands are clean; these days other people do it for him.

When Kris was finishing his studies, Marco M lived at his place for a while. Marco M kept Kris supplied with grass and uppers, they spent various evenings zonked in front of the television. After university they lost touch with one another, because Marco M came up with the idea of selling his stuff in the wrong area. He was ratted out, spent two years in jail, and showed up on Kris's doorstep a week after his release. He showed him a scar on his neck, displayed a homemade tattoo on his ankle, and asked if Kris knew who was currently dealing drugs in his old area. Kris told him what he knew. Marco M addressed the problem. Since then he controls the area around Nollendorfplatz again, and that's where Kris arranged to meet him.

Marco M is like one of those dogs that have to lift their legs on every street corner, without managing a stream of urine. If you see him, you don't inevitably think of a pit bull or a boxer. Marco M has the elegance and alertness of a greyhound. Although it's hard to imagine a greyhound with a gold chain and a tracksuit.

Every day Marco M strolls through his territory at the same time. He calls it surveillance. He wants to know what's going on, and he wants people to see him.

On this particular day Marco M was sitting on a bar stool outside the comics shop. He had a glass of Coke in front of him, and was rolling two qigong balls around his right hand.

"New hobby?" Kris asked and stopped beside him.

"It helps me relax. Ever tried it?"

Marco M handed Kris the balls. They were warm. Kris rolled them around, it felt good.

"Not bad."

"Gives you muscles," said Marco M, and opened a velvet-lined box. Kris put the balls into it. When Marco M got up, he left the box on the bar stool.

"What belongs to Marco M doesn't get stolen," he said and put an arm around Kris's shoulders.

"Let's go for a walk around the block."

They walked down Motzstrasse and took a stroll around Winterfeldplatz. Kris offered to buy Marco M falafels and they sat on the park bench in front of the stand and watched the roller-skaters. They talked about the area and how Schöneberg had changed since Kris moved away in the autumn. They didn't talk about Frauke. Kris didn't want Marco M to express his sympathy. He tried to think about Frauke as little as possible, which was of course ridiculous in that it was because of Frauke that he was sitting on Winterfeldplatz. After ten minutes Marco M's phone rang.

"Normally I don't let people disturb me when I'm eating," he said apologetically, and took the call. He listened for a moment before hanging up.

"That's it, then," said Marco M, and they shook hands.

Kris left him sitting on the park bench. He walked up Maassenstrasse, past cafés and people sitting outside drinking overpriced macchiatos. They didn't look good, they were pallid, yearning for sunlight, and had no idea what trend they were supposed to be following right now. It felt good not to be one of them.

Kris sat down in his car and drove toward Potsdamer Strasse. He was calm, he didn't look too often in the rearview mirror. At the first lights he took a CD out of the glove compartment. Hardkandy. The music brought a bit of light into his day. Kris drove home.

It was only after he had parked outside the villa that he noticed his tension slowly fading away. He glanced in the mirror and saw the open front gate. He glanced at the villa. There was no one to be seen.

Kris reached under the front seat and pulled out the two packages. The automatic had scratches and dents, but it sat nicely in his hand. Kris couldn't help thinking of Frauke's gas pistol. He had once held it in his hand, and the automatic had a very different weight. It was more real. Kris opened the second package. Marco M had told him that there would only really be any noise after the sixth shot.

"I only need two shots," Kris had replied.

The silencer fitted the barrel perfectly. Kris unscrewed it again and checked the safety catch before shoving the gun and the silencer back under the front seat and getting out.

In the evening they had dinner together. Kris asked Tamara to pass him the bread and wondered how Meybach could be so stupid as to use a registered cell phone. Wolf said he wanted to disappear for a few days after the funeral, to the country or maybe the sea, he didn't know exactly, and Kris nodded and wondered what he would do when Meybach was standing face-to-face with him. *Could I? Would I?* He wasn't one for heroism, but he had the feeling that if he did nothing, nothing would happen. It was a metaphysical law.

Could I hold the gun to Meybach's head and put an end to it all?
It was the only question that Kris refused to think about.

After Tamara and Wolf set off for the cemetery that morning, Kris lit the fire. Three hours later he's still sitting in front of it. He knows he's deliberately drawing out the moment of decision. He's afraid of himself. His thoughts revolve around the life that all four of them lived in the villa before that lunatic went and nailed a woman to the wall of a room.

Kris thinks that if he sits here long enough, he'll sweat out all his anxieties. His eyes hurt, his lungs are struggling to process the oxygen. He nods off for a moment and wakes with a start. He saw himself. With the gun in his hand. He wasn't holding the gun, the gun was holding him. In his dream he couldn't shake it off. As if the gun were stuck to his hand.

Kris gets to his feet. He has worked out that he would never have the guts. The combination gun plus Kris is ludicrous. He's no hero. Who was he actually trying to convince?

You go off and buy yourself a gun and what then?
Kris stretches, he spits in the fire, then he pulls the window open. The fresh air is so good that for a moment Kris just stands there in the draft, enjoying the cold on his skin. Spring and the sound of birds. *How could I imagine I was capable of it?* He leaves the window open and is about to get in the shower when the ringing of the telephone from the corridor stops him. Kris picks up the receiver. It's Meybach. He hopes it isn't a bad time. He has one last job for them.

YOU

TWO PIGEONS STRUT TO the middle of the road and wait for the lights to change. When the cars start moving, the pigeons fly up and land on a windowsill. As soon as the light turns red, they land on the pavement, strut back to the middle of the road, and the game starts all over again. You watch them for four phases of the lights and wonder if pigeons have a sense of humor.

A bell rings as you walk into the bakery. The smell of warm bread and fresh-brewed coffee makes your stomach rumble. You say good morning and pretend to study the display. There's a radio on in the background, somewhere in Berlin mattresses are now so cheap that no one can believe it. The man behind the counter wraps the baguette and puts a plastic lid on your coffee. You round up the total, giving him a thirty-five-cent tip, and you say goodbye to each other.

The pigeons have gone, although the light is red. You cross the street and sit down in your car. You hold the coffee cup in both hands and put the plastic lid on your right knee. It surprises you that you're so calm. The coffee in the cup isn't trembling.

His name is Karl Fichtner. He owns four bakeries in the north of Berlin. In this particular one he helps out between five and seven in the morning, before delivering the bread to the other bakeries. His work ends at two o'clock in the afternoon. He doesn't know that today is his last working day.

You wait in the restaurant where he has his lunch. You sit at his table, but not in his seat. You have drunk some mineral water and studied the street through the window. He only sees you after he's shaken the waiter's hand. You nod to him, he hesitates, you smile. You're good at smiling.

Fichtner is someone who only speaks after he's thought about what he wants to say. Someone who doesn't like to take his words back. He joins you, opens his jacket, and rests his forearms on the tabletop. As he does so he watches you, his hands folded. He has a small tattoo on his forearm. It's an edelweiss.

You say nothing, you've learned to wait. After a pause Fichtner clears his throat and asks if he knows you. He seems tired, but you'd probably be tired too if you shoved rolls into the oven at 5:00 a.m. every day. You like the fact that Fichtner asks you the same question as Fanni did a week ago.

"We know each other from before," you reply, pushing the photograph toward him.

Fichtner picks it up. He doesn't blink, he seems to stop breathing. The waiter comes, Fichtner ignores him, the waiter turns on his heel. Fichtner holds the photograph at a slight angle, so that it catches the light, then he sets it back down on the tabletop and says, "It's so long ago."

"An eternity," you agree.

His eyes seem to settle on your eyes. That's how it feels. As if his gaze were touching you. The scar on his cheek stands out white.

"You were still a child," says Fichtner. "You were—"

And then he starts crying, his chin sinks to his chest, it's humiliating. He doesn't even put his hands in front of his face. No dignity, just violent sobbing. And then the tears. You look around. You hope that everyone is taking in this embarrassing moment.

As so often over the last few days you wonder what Butch and Sundance would do now. *What if?* It's a silly game, because Butch and Sundance don't exist any more. They've been wiped from the memory of time, and it is that loss you can't forgive. Not yourself, and not society, and if there's a god anywhere, then he's the last one you would forgive for it. But whatever way you twist and turn it, we keep returning to the insight that there are people who do not deserve forgiveness. People you have met.

One of them is dead, the other is sitting opposite you, crying.

Out of shame, perhaps? Perhaps he's weeping over the loss? All vanished innocence is a loss. Butch and Sundance vanished the day they met Karl and Fanni for the second time. The first time they came out of it only with injuries. Butch in particular. Wounds that would turn into scars. But nothing more than that. The second time they were pushed over an invisible barrier and disappeared forever into the void. Darkness, emptiness. It was an insignificant day in the history of the world, and nothing and no one can give you back that day.

After they took Butch away the second time, the friends went on seeing each other at school, in the street, or in the supermarket, but *seeing each other* wasn't enough. They lost one another, even though they were both within sight.

Sundance has never understood how that could happen. At the time he needed some advice, he needed to talk to someone. Whenever his parents asked about Butch, he changed the subject. In his helplessness, Sundance moved further and further away from his best friend.

On the other hand, Butch repressed so much that Sundance became irrelevant. For most of his teenage years he kept to himself and became a crab that disappeared backward from the screen of life, until everyone had forgotten that he had ever existed. His parents, his friends, and, to a large extent, himself. That was how the friendship between Butch and Sundance broke down, as the friendships of youth often do—without words, without much point.

They lost sight of each other for twelve whole years.

Imagine you're on a train that's traveling along a distance that consists of days and weeks speeding past. The train doesn't stop.

Months whistle by, and becomes the thunder of years. You sense the echo in your head. There's a draft in your face, and the speed makes all movement difficult, because time commands your attention. Sundance learned very early how long even a short span of time can be when you miss someone. He was there, he lived there. Yes, he found new friends, but in his memory there was always a room reserved for him and Butch alone. That room grew dusty, and no light entered it.

After finishing high school, Butch moved to Charlottenburg, while Sundance stayed in Zehlendorf and went on living with his parents. Over the next few years their paths never crossed. Every now and again they heard about one another via friends, but nothing happened. Until that Saturday evening when both of them went to a district of Berlin that they hadn't gone to before. Köpenick.

They were going to a party. Butch had promised to take a girlfriend, while Sundance was doing a mate a favor and picking him up. There were so many circumstances that day which didn't tally, and still they led to Butch and Sundance meeting up again. Probably it's one of the many rules that life has come up with to knock us off balance.

It happened in the corridor. Music was racketing in the background, a neighbor in flip-flops asked them to be quiet, and a few screeching girls passed a wig around, while the boys sat on the steps calling out to the girls to tell them how ugly they looked. Amid this chaos Sundance was coming upstairs just as Butch was going downstairs. They recognized each other immediately. As if twelve years were a gap that could be covered in a few footsteps.

Butch was scrawny and tall, looming a few inches over Sundance. But his face, Sundance would never forget that face. As if Butch never got enough sleep. Sundance, on the other hand, looked the way he always had, but Butch saw the difference right away. If Sundance had still had the same naïveté as his friend during their childhood, it had completely vanished. Sundance seemed driven, he wanted something from life.

"Wassup," said Butch.

And Sundance burst out laughing.

The evening ended in a bar in Schöneberg, where they drank cocktails and couldn't get over the coincidence. They talked about everything that had happened before their encounter with Karl and Fanni. In their stories the memory of their childhood ended with the day at the building site. Time after that was a void. It belonged to a different Butch and a different Sundance. There was only one afterward—after school, after passing the driving test. They moaned about community service and asked each other how so-and-so was doing.

Fanni and Karl were not even mentioned.

This façade survived until dawn. Until Butch said he couldn't drink any more, his bladder was about to burst. Sundance remained alone at the table, while Butch went to the bathroom. Sundance was pleasantly drunk. He leaned forward slightly to get a better glimpse of the morning sky through the window. And as he was nostalgically watching the new day, he suddenly had a curious feeling. It was one of those premonitions that can be prompted by anything—by the silence between two songs, the sound of a waiter clearing his throat, scraping chair legs, or the silence after someone has lit a cigarette and exhaled the smoke.

Sundance went to the bathroom. He knew that Butch wouldn't be there any more. Vanished through a window or a back door. Forever.

"Are you still there?"

Silence. Above the silence the hum of the air conditioning, a cough from the bar, then quietly, from one of the stalls:

"I'll be out in a minute."

"Is everything okay?"

"I . . ."

Butch fell silent, Sundance looked under the door of the stall and saw Butch's shoes. He waited for Butch to go on talking.

"I can't go on any more," Butch said at last. "It's been such a long time . . . and I . . . I missed you so much . . . and I . . . I can't . . . I can't look at you any more . . ."

Sundance suddenly felt an emptiness in his head. Reality had arrived. With billowing banners and an army of clamoring warriors it had marched in and taken him, here in the bathroom of a bar in the middle of Berlin, on a day like any other. He leaned his back against the stall door and squatted down. For a while they didn't speak, then Sundance asked the question he'd been trying to squeeze out of himself. For years. *What happened next? How did we lose each other?* And Butch began to tell the story, well hidden and with a door between him and Sundance.

They came to get him once a month. Twelve times a year.

"At first they picked me up from the street. You know, like someone who doesn't know where he wants to go, and then someone who does know comes along and picks him up. That's exactly how I felt every time."

He talked of the drive through Berlin. Over time he became familiar with every crossing and the phasing of every traffic light. He counted the seconds, he counted the passers-by, he counted his breaths. They never talked to him. They drove through the city center to Kreuzberg, where they stopped outside an old apartment building. A park opposite. Butch never found out what the park was called. Through the building into the courtyard. No sun, only shade, a row of garbage cans, neighbors behind curtains, a cat that darted away, the fourth floor, the stairs and then the door to the apartment. No nameplate, no bell. Corridor. Kitchen. Bathroom. Everything rundown and dirty, except for one room. The floor mopped, the windowpane washed and with a view of a façade. That was where they brought him.

" . . . always had to walk in first, then they closed the door behind them and talked to each other, as if I wasn't there, as if I was a ghost."

He remembers the smell in the apartment, the stench of fried onions and meat, along with the chemical smell of detergents and stale cigarette smoke, as if the building were sending its breath up through the parquet into this room. And he remembers the photomural. An autumn landscape with a forest and a lake. On the shore of the lake was a stag. The first time Butch saw that mural, the woman ran her hand over his head and said, If I were a good boy . . .

" . . . If I'm a good boy and stretch really high, I too will certainly get to heaven. On the same wall there was a hook. They stripped me to the waist. Then they tied my hands together and told me to stretch up. They hung me from the hook like that. I could only stand on tiptoes, my feet just touched the floor, and I remember thinking, how do they know how tall I am? They took photographs of me. *Before and after,* they said, and took off the rest of my clothes as I hung there. They said: *We don't want your parents to think badly of us.* That was one of their jokes. They said that often. As if my parents knew what was happening to me. Then, when I was naked, they washed me, because I had to be clean. They washed me before and after. They took warm water that they heated in a kettle. As they did so they played around with me and told me to watch, because that was how they were going to do it, but I tried to look away . . ."

The stucco on the ceiling of the room had been painted over so many times that its outlines had dissolved. The stucco was like a tumor growing white and pale out of the walls. Butch knew every crack and every spot where the rain had come through the roof. He had counted the fishbone pattern on the floor.

" . . . hit me on the shoulder till I cried. It was important to him that I cried. He said: *If I see no tears, I see no repentance.* I didn't know what he meant by that, I would have cried anyway, but he struck me and I could see that he himself had tears in his eyes, as if I was the one hitting him rather than the other way around . . ."

In the winter the heat was on full, and it was stuffy in the room. In the summer, on the other hand, it was consistently cool, as the sun never reached the façade. Butch never knew how long they kept him prisoner. He got used to the smell, he got used to the light. He got used to everything. As soon as he was in the room, he lost his sense of time. In retrospect he understood that it was better that way. If he had been able to impose a framework on time, it would have become as real as a timetable. Butch didn't want reality.

" . . . outside and left us alone. Then the woman stuck her fingers into me. Into my mouth, my ass. She stuck her fingers into my nose, holding my mouth closed so that I nearly suffocated. Then she asked me if I wanted to see her naked, and I wasn't allowed to say *no*, that was important, I had to say *yes*. The first time I shook my head, and she squeezed my throat shut until I could hear it cracking, as if my neck was a dry branch. So I said *yes*. Always *yes*. Then she took my foot and rubbed herself against it and asked if I could feel how wet she was. As she did so she looked into my face, and I had to smile, I had to have fun. It was so hard. It was so terribly hard, because my face—"

The bathroom door flew open, and a drunk staggered in. He saw Sundance sitting on the floor and recoiled. Sundance told him to clear off, the toilets were broken. The drunk murmured an apology and went on his way. Sundance got up and bolted the door.

"Are you still there?" Butch asked.

"I'm still here."

Sundance sat back down and waited. Butch spoke of his feeling of shame, of the fury and the hope of just sticking it out, because if he stuck it out everything would be good again, and his parents would be safe and the nightmare would finally be over.

" . . . the man came back, and she told him what to do. She sat

down on a chair and said: *Turn him around and fuck him till he faints.*
Then he turned me around. I saw the photomural, I looked
straight into the forest. Then there was the cold of the lubricant
and the hands on my shoulders pulling me down till I thought
my arms would tear at any moment . . ."

Butch plunged into the photomural. He stood beside the stag
on the lakeshore and heard it drinking. The slurping noise, the
splashing of the water, the murmur of the forest, and as Butch
looked across the lake into the green he saw himself far away
in a room in Kreuzberg standing with his face to the wall. He
saw what the man was doing to him, and it didn't touch him.
He couldn't even have described the man's face. Even when they
demanded that he look at them, he looked through them. He
wanted to forget who they were. His whole existence had shrunk
to a tiny moment. The moment he left that room and returned
to real life. Butch saw what he wanted to see, and wanted to see
so little that he could even have been blind.

" . . . I came to again, they lifted me down and washed and
dressed me. That's how it was every time. Sometimes they said,
*If you don't scream, if you're very quiet, we'll let you go right now this time,
and you'll never see us again.* And I believed it, you know, I really
believed it. So I tried not to scream, but have you ever tried not
to scream when someone's holding a cigarette to the sole of your
foot? It's impossible, however hard you clench your teeth, it just
doesn't work. I couldn't even press my hands over my mouth
because I was hanging on that hook. So I screamed. And the
woman shoved . . ."

One day a month, twelve days a year. In between, Butch
worked like clockwork. He didn't cause any trouble, he seemed
to be a self-sufficient boy. He waited by the fountain for the
car once a month. In retrospect he was surprised that no one
noticed him regularly getting into a car at an intersection in the
middle of Zehlendorf. The same ritual for years. Maybe it was
something to do with the place, maybe too many things were

happening at the same time. And maybe in his shame he just didn't want to be seen.

Being in darkness while everyone else was in the light. Being helpless, defenseless. Being furious and not showing it. Alone in society. Constantly hungry, thirsty, weary, exhausted. Feeling the life around him and not being able to touch it. Not thinking about that one day a month. Thinking about that one day a month all the time. Subconscious. Traveling on a distant track. Far away. Invisible.

Butch thought he would bore them sooner or later. He bet on it. He turned thirteen, he turned fourteen. Sometimes he wished they would leave him hanging on the hook. For thirty days. And then when they came back he would have died of hunger and thirst, and it would all be over. But whatever he wished, he also knew somehow, deep inside, that one day it would all be over. He knew it for sure. He turned fifteen and he turned sixteen.

" . . . and then they disappeared."

Butch was seventeen years old, he was standing at the curb, and the woman and the man didn't come. Out of fear, he went back to the intersection every day that month. The red Ford never came. It never occurred to Butch that he had grown too old for them. Young Butch wasn't a boy anymore. His seventeenth birthday made him an adult and no longer significant to them.

Butch repeated the ritual over the months that followed. At night he looked out the window and waited for them to come and get him. He was sure he had done something wrong. He feared for his parents. Month after month. And then he was the one who didn't come.

" . . . Nights got worse, even though it was what I had wanted, I couldn't believe it was over. I think that if you've been pursued by a nightmare for seven years, however often you wake up, you don't trust the whole thing. The nightmare becomes reality, and why should reality suddenly disappear?"

Butch fell silent. Suddenly the sounds came back. The music

from the bar, the splashing of the water, the fluorescent light humming quietly. Butch remained quiet for a long time. Sundance looked at his watch. He felt tired, he was cold.

"Are you coming out?" he asked.

"I can't."

"Just open the door."

"I said I can't!"

Butch's voice sounded panic-stricken. Sundance walked into the next stall. He stood on the toilet and looked over the partition. Butch had drawn up his legs and wrapped his arms around them. He was sitting on the lid of the toilet, his face hidden between his knees, rocking back and forth.

Sundance heaved himself up. The partition wobbled, but held. Sundance climbed into the stall and put his arms around Butch. It was like hugging a stone. It took Butch ten minutes to relax. They left the bar, and from that day on they were inseparable again.

WOLF

"LET'S GET OUT OF HERE," says Tamara.

Wolf gives a start, he's been so locked away in his thoughts and feelings that the sounds around him have faded out. He didn't talk to anyone during the ceremony, he stayed by Tamara's side and gave her support, he wasn't capable of anything more than that. Now Tamara tugs on his arm. They break away from the mourners, but don't head for the exit from the cemetery, the way Wolf had hoped. Instead, Tamara crouches by the coffin, and when she gets back up to her feet she is holding a rose in her hand.

"I think everyone saw that," says Wolf.

"I don't care."

Tamara takes his arm, they don't say goodbye to anyone, they just go. When they get to Wolf's car, Tamara stops on the driver's side. Wolf doesn't ask, he throws her the key and gets in.

"I haven't been here for ages."

As it's a weekday, there are only a few mothers with strollers walking around. Two old men sit on a bench with a box of red wine between them. Wolf has the feeling that the park hasn't changed since his youth.

They walk past the playground and the newsstand and head for the war memorial. Just before they get there, they turn off onto a path that leads straight down to the water.

"In there."

Tamara points to the dense bushes by a weeping willow and plunges into the undergrowth. Behind the bushes there is a tiny patch of grass that leads to the water and offers just enough room for two people. The grass is screened from the path by bushes. A row of old residential buildings and the hotel can be seen on the opposite shore.

Tamara crouches on the shore as she crouched by the coffin, and lays the rose on the water. For a moment it bobs up and down, then it moves out toward the middle of the lake. Wolf squats down next to Tamara.

"Good plan."

"Thanks."

A duck swims toward the rose, bumps it once with its beak, and swims on. Wolf and Tamara stand up at the same time, bump into each other, and almost fall into the lake. Wolf puts an arm around Tamara. He's surprised when she presses herself against him. He feels her breath on his neck, smells that scent that has always been a mystery to him. *How can she smell so good?* In her scent he finds the whole day. The grief, the weariness, and the fury. He pulls Tamara closer to him and buries his face in her hair. For a second she flinches, his breath in her ear. *Hungry, he's hungry.* His lower body presses against hers, Tamara doesn't flinch, even when she feels his erection she stays close to him. Her lips wander over his neck, his hand runs through her hair and pulls her head back so that she's forced to look at him. They are both breathing heavily, both waiting for the next step.

"Here?"

"Here."

He lies on the damp grass with the Lietzensee at his feet. He doesn't care who's watching from the houses opposite, he doesn't care if the hotel is selling tickets to the show. He only has eyes for Tamara, who is moving above him and looking down on him as if it were something she did every day. They aren't in despair any more, their grief is drifting like the rose on the surface of the Lietzensee, and moving further and further away from them. It's pure pleasure. Her hands on his chest, her eyes closed, and whenever she looks at him he smiles, and she closes her eyes again to hold on to this moment for as long as possible.

"Come whenever you want."

He doesn't think about it. He too wants to hold on to this moment and wishes Frauke could see him now. *For you,* he wants to say, *whatever else we have done wrong, we're doing this right, and hope you understand, I really do.* Tamara's movements become more demanding, Wolf tries to stay calm, his left hand grips the back of her neck, his right is on her bottom. Someone somewhere whistles. Tamara laughs, her lips on his mouth, her moaning in his mouth, his moaning in hers, and then she holds still. *Deep.* Deep, so deep inside her that there's no going forward or backward. *There.* They look at each other. Tamara tenses her muscles and smiles. *As if she knows very well who I am and why I'm here.* Wolf loses himself in this smile. They've both arrived, they're both there.

YOU

"And, how are you?"

Karl has regained his composure. He has ordered a beer from the waiter, and drained the glass and actually regained his composure. From the way he asks you the question you understand that he has no idea who you really are. Yes, he has seen the photograph, and you're sitting in front of him, but he doesn't know who you really are. It was the same with Fanni. It's a mystery how these two people could be so cruel and mechanical, without seriously engaging with the children they destroyed.

"I'm not so great," you say.

Fichtner nods as if he understands. He says you haven't changed.

"You've grown, but . . ."

He falls silent, his chin quivers.

"I'm so sorry. I . . . I don't know what I . . ."

Again that silence, interrupted only by the clattering of plates and the murmur of voices in the restaurant. Your stomach is churning, your hands are so damp that you have to wipe them on your trouser legs. All this isn't right, it shouldn't be like this. *Repentance?* You don't want to see this man collapse, you don't want his pity. It's all wrong.

Fichtner says he has to go to the bathroom.

"I don't want anyone to see me like this," he explains with a weary smile, pointing at his eyes. You resist sympathy, you resist the desire to follow him to the bathroom.

When Fichtner comes back to the table a few minutes later, he suggests going somewhere else. It's almost as if he can read your thoughts. If he could do that, he'd run away right now.

You pay, Fichtner waits for you outside the restaurant.

"Have you got a car?"

You shake your head, you're relieved it's so easy. All those days that you spent on research have paid off. You should have tracked Fichtner down earlier, but you wanted to be quite sure. As far as you're concerned there's nothing worse than amateurish work.

The two of you stop by Fichtner's car, it's a different make, and the paint isn't red. You get in and fasten your seat belts. Fichtner sets off without telling you where you're going.

A new closeness emerged from the remains of the old friendship. When the flat below Butch's came free at the end of the year, Sundance moved to Charlottenburg. They finished their studies, took a month to travel through Asia, and spent more and more time together over the years that followed. It was almost too perfect.

You're aware that it's hard to sum up two people's lives. Years don't count, everything depends on events. The bad days and the good. If you look back on the lives of Butch and Sundance, you can say for certain that the years they spent together were the best ones. No distance between them, a wonderful kind of closeness.

Of course they also went through crises, they argued and insulted each other, but those were superficial rows which didn't last longer than a day, and for which they always found a solution. If anyone had asked Sundance at the time, he couldn't have said what could ever have come between him and Butch. Friends had become brothers. There were no secrets between them. That was why Sundance was completely unprepared

Butch called one morning from his office. He needed some important papers, he was stuck in a meeting and couldn't get away.

"If you're anywhere near the apartment."

Sundance promised to drop the papers off around lunchtime. An hour later he opened the door to Butch's flat and hesitated for a moment when he realized he was stepping inside his friend's apartment on his own for the first time. Everything looked as it always did. Butch lived in a meticulously orderly fashion. His socks were sorted in drawers, nothing was at an awkward angle on the clothes rails, and even the toiletries in the bathroom were arranged according to a system.

If you think about it today, you put everything that happened next down to curiosity and forget that bad timing was also a significant factor in this. If Sundance hadn't had time to spare that day, if Butch hadn't gotten through to him, if Butch hadn't forgotten his papers . . .

Sundance found the papers on the living room table and noticed the chaos in front of the television. A wineglass had tipped over and left a stain on the carpet, and there were lots of crumpled tissues next to it. One of the drawers in the chest was half pulled out. Sundance pulled it all the way out and saw narrow DVD cases. They were facing downwards and had no titles. Sundance opened one of the cases. The DVD inside had no title either.

I'll go now, he thought, *I won't look at my best friend's porn collection, let's be clear about that.*

But that was exactly what he did. He took the DVD out of its case, put it in the player, and turned on the television. With a feeling of guilt, against his own better instincts, but also with a lot of curiosity.

Butch was new to the advertising agency and wanted to prove himself, which was why he didn't leave work before eight every day. Today was to be no exception, although Butch was confused. Sundance hadn't just failed to bring him the papers, he hadn't replied to his repeated calls, either. Butch was worried. Even at Sundance's work no one knew where he was.

At ten past eight Butch left his office and took the elevator to the underground garage. He pulled out from his parking space and was about to drive off when the passenger door was yanked open and Sundance got in. Butch braked. Sundance told him to drive on, so Butch took his foot off the brake and drove on. At the first lights he looked at Sundance. His friend was freezing, it had been a rainy day, his hair stuck to his head like a helmet, spittle had dried to white crumbs at the corners of his mouth. Butch was aware of a sour, bitter smell.

"What's up with—"

He got no further, because Sundance grabbed him by the back of the head, his fingers clawing at his hair.

"Hey, slow down, what's—"

"Shut your mouth," said Sundance. "Just keep your mouth shut, okay?"

It was only when Butch nodded that Sundance let go of him. For the rest of the journey no one spoke. Sundance drummed his feet on the floor, he stared at the road and looked as if he were supercharged. When Butch found a parking place by the law court, he thought for a few seconds about running away. But who runs away from his best friend?

"We're going to my place," said Sundance.

They walked into Sundance's apartment. In the kitchen Butch had to sit down on a chair.

"Can I talk again now?" he asked.

"You can."

"What's all this shit about?"

Sundance reached under the table and took out a plastic bag.

"Open it," he said.

Butch looked into the plastic bag and closed his eyes.

It turned out to be a long night. The DVDs lay between them the whole time like a sacrificial offering, while Butch talked about his addiction. He repeated himself. He kept calling it his addiction, and Sundance felt ill every time he heard those words. As if it were an illness, as if anyone could be infected and develop it. Butch insisted that he couldn't shake it off, he'd tried everything, but there was still this hunger.

"I'm hungry for it. Without it my life is empty, without it I don't work properly."

"But they're children," said Sundance.

"I know they're children, but I—"

"THEY'RE CHILDREN!" Sundance suddenly yelled at him. "CAN'T YOU SEE THAT?"

Butch started crying, it was pitiful, it was the saddest thing that Sundance had ever experienced. And there was nothing he could do. He could shout his head off, he could hammer the table, it wouldn't help.

Butch made one promise after another. He would change. He saw things clearly now. He admitted that it had always scared him, but he couldn't shake it. He was addicted now, and hungry and—

Sundance wanted to know where he got the films.

"I stumbled on them by chance. On the internet. You can find this kind of thing everywhere if you look hard enough."

"Since when?"

"A year or two."

"Since when?" Sundance interrupted.

"Three years, I swear, no more than three years. Maybe four. I can't remember exactly."

"You can't *remember*? How can you lie to me? And what do you mean, *stumbled on them by chance*? You find child pornography if you really look for it, you don't just stumble over it by *chance*! I want to know where you got this filth. I want the addresses. I want the exact addresses!"

Butch lowered his head, he was ashamed, and Sundance couldn't stand the sight of him any more. He swept the DVDs onto the floor. He was about to knock the table over, but whatever he did, the images had taken root in his memory and wouldn't go away.

He had looked at two of the DVDs, there were thirty-four

of them in all. Short films. Children having sex with children. Adults having sex with children. Adults having sex and children watching them and then having to join in. Sundance didn't know what to do with himself. He knew what needed to be done, and he knew he couldn't do it. And of course that was the very question Butch asked.

"You're not going to turn me in, are you?"

"How can you even ask me that?"

"I only mean that if you turn me in, then—"

Butch stopped talking. He leaned forward as if he had stomach pains. Sundance felt the need to put his hand on his shoulder and reassure him, but at the same time he resisted it. He didn't want to be soft and indulgent at any price. He didn't want to forgive. He wasn't ready for that yet.

This business needs to be sorted out, he thought, *this business can't just be apologized away.*

"You really jerk off while you watch them?" he said.

Butch looked up, his face pale, pearls of sweat on his forehead, his lips almost drained of blood.

"Of course I jerk off, it turns me on."

"And what about the blood?"

After Sundance had looked at the DVDs, he picked up the tissues from the floor and expected them to be stuck together with sperm. There was more than sperm.

"What's with the blood?" Sundance probed.

Butch got up; Sundance could see that his knees were trembling. Butch pulled his jeans down. There were cuts on the inside of his thighs. Two of the wounds were fresh.

"It's part of it," he said and stood there pitifully with his trousers down. "It's just part of it."

You keep wondering whether there might not have been a chance to change the course of events at that point. As a child you often tried making the rain in the garden flow in different directions. You could dig as many trenches as you liked and divert the rain streams, but as soon as your attention wavered for a moment the rain went its own way again. You don't know what would have happened if Sundance had been tougher that day. What if he'd turned Butch in? Would it all have been different? Sundance knew what Butch had been through. He would have been inhuman not to have shown some understanding of Butch's situation. He couldn't turn him in. So he tried to take control.

And that was the beginning of the time of trust, the time of therapy, the time of cleansing. Sundance fought for his best friend, he didn't want to lose him for a second time. When they were children, he hadn't been able to protect him against Fanni and Karl, so it was only just that he try to protect Butch from himself now. They agreed that it was an illness. Sundance started reading books on the subject, he wanted to understand his friend's psyche.

The new year began, and it looked good. Spring became summer, and it looked good. They took a holiday, and went to Sweden for five weeks to visit old school friends. Butch was relaxed, he had asked his therapist to put him on a course of antidepressants, his unease faded, he seemed to be at peace with himself. And then came the autumn, and the autumn was like a shadow that put all the lights out. Pure darkness.

Fichtner parks the car in front of the block. He sits there for a moment with his hands on the steering wheel, as if there's something to see there.

"I don't know if I can go up there," he says. "It's so long ago."

You doubtless want to know what kind of face you made when he told you on the journey that he couldn't throw the key away, and asked you if you wanted to see the apartment again. At that moment your face was as open as a book, and it was good that

Fichtner had to concentrate on driving. When you asked him who paid for the flat, he said he didn't know. You knew he was lying. You checked. The rent is taken out of Fichtner's account every month.

"I'd really like to see the flat again," you said, and added after a pause, "to exorcise the ghosts."

You had expected Fichtner to ask what ghosts you mean, but he had said nothing, and you park in front of the building, and Fichtner goes on staring straight ahead, so you stir yourself and get out first.

Nothing about Fichtner reminds you of the man who walked into the restaurant half an hour ago and looked at you disdainfully. He doesn't look broken. He just reminds you more of those pensioners in the supermarket who stand for far too long in front of the shelves.

You go into the house.

The courtyard, the steps, the door, the key, the lock.

Fichtner steps in and holds the door open for you, you walk past him, the door closes behind you with a click, and the blow strikes the back of your neck and throws you forward. You try to find a grip on the wall, Fichtner kicks your legs away and grabs you by the hair.

"You little scumbag!" he hisses in your ear, trying to smash your face against the parquet floor. You manage to hold an arm in front of your face, but the tip of your nose scrapes over the wood.

"What do you think you're doing here? We treated you like a family member. We took you in and showed you what you were worth, and you, you filthy fucking little rat, you come after us?"

Fichtner tries to crush your face against the wood, your arm finds no purchase, you avert your head at the last moment, your ear slaps against the wood. Once, twice. He knees you in the crotch. You can't get out from under him, come on, dammit, move.

Fichtner breathes on the back of your neck.

"We were better to you than your lousy parents, and this is the thanks we get? Give me an answer, you miserable fuck. What did you do to Fanni?"

You hear him sobbing above you. How could you be so stupid? It was all just a farce—the repentance, the feelings of guilt, the tears. *Now* he's suffering, *now* he's grieving. How could you get suckered like that? What kind of a sap are you? All these years and you haven't learned a thing!

Your foot finds the wall. Fury wakes you, hatred gives you strength. You push yourself up and Fichtner loses his balance. He falls over you, lands on your back, and his fingers loosen their grip on your hair. He tries to get to his feet. The back of your head slams back and hits his nose. There's a cracking sound. The weight disappears from your back. Fichtner rolls into the corridor and lies there. He has one hand over his face and the other raised in self-defense, as if he could stop you.

You get to your feet, you suddenly feel very light, and stop in front of Fichtner. He reaches out for you, you break his outstretched arm with a single blow. Before he can cry out, you ram your fist into the bridge of his nose. The only sound coming from him now is a groan, his mouth is full of blood, there's no strength left in him now, he lies on the ground trembling, his good arm sweeping back and forth on the floor. You grab him by his jacket collar and drag him behind you into the room.

Then the quiet, then the silence.

You sit opposite Fichtner on the floor and look up at him. His gaze is fixed on the wall above your head, he has stopped breathing. You're filled with a pleasant contentment. You have paid your tribute and you take the phone from your jacket pocket to dial the number of the agency.

"Hello?"

"It's me, Meybach. I hope this isn't a bad time."

Silence, then the sound of Kris Marrer's voice. Quiet, threatening.

"She's dead, you know that?"

For a moment you have no idea who he's talking about. *Of course she's dead,* you want to say, then you realize he doesn't mean Fanni.

"It's no fun cleaning up after you," Kris Marrer goes on, "but I've been able to live with it up till now. What I can no longer live with is Frauke's death."

"It was an accident."

"And that means?"

You tell him what happened. You tell him you called the fire department. And you admit that you're sorry. Perhaps you should never have arranged to meet her. But it was the only way.

You feel as if you've said too much. Why are you actually explaining yourself? A few minutes ago this meditative peace settled upon you, does that mean you're suddenly becoming talkative?

Kris Marrer is silent. You expected fury and disbelief. Something about him has changed. You think you can sense his thoughts. They aren't good thoughts. And it's the wrong moment, and you're the wrong person for him to talk to about his girlfriend.

You had a reason for calling. Get it over with.

You tell Kris Marrer that this business is your last job for them and you expect the same procedure. You apologize for the fact that it had to happen on the day of the funeral, but it is the only way. You say it twice. *It's the only way.* Kris Marrer asks you if your sense of humor has always been as perverse as this. He also asks you why he should believe you when you say you're not to blame for Frauke's death. That's enough for you. You hang up, switch off the phone, and study Fichtner's corpse. This time you won't clean it up as you did with Fanni. They'll see what you're capable of. It'll certainly win you a bit of respect. You didn't like Kris Marrer's tone one bit.

After a while you get up and go and wash your face in the bathroom. Your left ear is swollen, and there's a small cut on your forehead. You take off your pullover and your T-shirt and use your T-shirt as a towel. Then you feel better.

Do it.

You look up. Nervous, almost feverish. For a moment your eyes dart sideways, then you meet your own gaze, and it's like a reunion. You're you again. *Thank you.* It feels so good, it's wonderful. You missed yourself. *Thank you.* You didn't know how you would find yourself again. *That was the way.* You're even glad of the tears, tears of relief. For a few minutes you lean against the basin and watch yourself crying. Tears of joy. *Thank you.* Then you leave the flat without closing the door behind you. It's over. There's no connection left, the bridges have been blown up, the guilt is gone.

PART VI

After

I REMEMBER HOW WE thought it was over. I still have a clear memory of the relief we felt. Behind all the rage and perplexity there still lay a faith in goodness. We were so naïve. We were so damned naïve.

I have now left the Ruhr behind me, and am driving past Saarbrücken on the way to Singen. Years ago we went to Lake Constance because there was supposed to be a big party there and a friend of Frauke's had promised us a vacation cottage. The party never took place, the cottage was a shack without a bathroom, but we still stayed for ten days, played at being a commune, and spent a great summer together. Perhaps I'll find that shack again. Perhaps I'll lie down on one of the moldy mattresses and catch up on my sleep.

It's the morning of the fourth day. I don't know if they're after me yet. When do the police ever notice a properly parked car? I've thought of everything. I have the papers, I have the explanations, I've even got the first aid kit on the back seat in case anyone wants to see it. No one will look in the trunk. I feel safe, even if it sounds ridiculous, I feel completely safe. As if a protecting hand were floating above me. Justice. I only wish it wasn't simply protecting me, but showing me what direction to go in.

At a rest stop bathroom I wash my armpits, my torso, and my arms. I do a few stretching exercises by the car. The back of my neck and my back hurt the most. What I miss is a bed. I miss the grief. I miss a long break. I don't know when I'll have all those things. Rage and despair predominate. I don't want to call anyone, because this is something I've got to do on my own. My only contact is with the people at the cash registers in the gas station shops. That thing in the trunk isn't a person. I'm all alone in the world with him and know that if grief fights its way up and gets the upper hand, I will kill him. I think that's what'll happen. I'll just kill him.

And maybe I'll get a bit lucky and find that shack.

Before

TAMARA

TAMARA AND WOLF FIND a sweaty Kris, sitting in the living room wearing only his shorts, drinking mineral water from a bottle. The entire ground floor is boiling hot, even though the windows are wide open. Kris doesn't ask what the funeral was like. He looks at them as if he's surprised they're back.

"Is everything all right?" says Wolf.

"Everything's all right." Kris asks back.

Wolf goes upstairs to change. When he has left the living room, Kris points to the door with his chin.

"Close it."

Tamara shuts the door and leans her back against it. *He knows we had sex,* she thinks, *he can see it in our faces, and he probably knew all along that something was going to happen between Wolf and me.*

"I need your help," says Kris, "and Wolf can't find out about it."

"But—"

"Tamara, please, I'll explain as soon as we're alone, until then you've got to keep your trap shut. We eat together in the evening, we behave quite normally, then the phone will ring, and it'll be Lutger."

"Why should your father—"

"Because I've asked him to call. Lutger will ask if Wolf could come by for a few hours. Wolf won't say no, he'll go and see Lutger."

"And then?"

"And then we'll both go away."

"And I bet you won't tell me where to?"

"And I won't tell you where to."

The phone rings at nine exactly, and Tamara passes the receiver to Wolf. He's so surprised by the call that he asks his father several times if everything is really all right, before he says goodbye and drives to his place.

Five minutes later Kris and Tamara are sitting in the car as well.

"So?"

"Not yet."

"What do you mean, not yet? Wolf's gone, we're alone."

Kris doesn't look at her, drives through the gate and stops outside.

"Will you close the gate?"

"Only when you give me an answer."

Tamara looks at him expectantly, Kris sighs, undoes his seat-belt, and gets out of the car. After he has closed the gate he comes back to the car and fastens his belt again.

"I know why you don't want to tell me," says Tamara. "Because if you do I won't come, right?"

"Right. Happy now?"

"Kris, what are you up to?"

"Trust me, you'll understand afterwards."

"You think?"

"I *know.*"

Kris drives; at the Wannsee junction he stops at the lights, looks in the rearview mirror, and then straight ahead again. Tamara doesn't take her eyes off him for a second.

"Could you please stop staring at me?"

"I'm not staring."

"Tamara, please."

"I wasn't staring," Tamara repeats and stops staring at him.

* * *

Ten minutes later Kris asks, "How bad was it?"

"We missed you."

Kris doesn't react.

"Frauke would have wanted you to be there."

"Tammi, she wanted to be cremated and scattered over the Lietzensee. *That's* what she wanted. So tell me what you really want to say."

"I'd have liked you to be there."

"Thanks."

They fall silent. The dusk has made way for deep black night, and the lights over Berlin look like a constant lightning flash. Tamara knows from stories that the whole of this section of highway, the Avus, was once fully lit, and that car races were held there. The lights remain, but they haven't been turned on for over twenty years. The stands have fallen into disrepair and have the sadness of dilapidated houses. Behind the stands the Funkturm juts into the darkness, a glittering streak; its tip is surrounded by a pall of smog, and looks like the tip of a lighthouse. Tamara slides lower into her seat and feels exhausted. Ten hours ago she was standing by Frauke's grave, then she had sex with Wolf on the shore of the Lietzensee, and now she's in the car with Kris and doesn't know where they're going. Tamara wishes Wolf were here.

"How long now?" she asks.

"A quarter of an hour."

Kris turns off the Avus onto the city highway.

Tamara shuts her eyes.

"Tammi, wake up."

She sits up with a jolt, for a moment she is disoriented, then she narrows her eyes slightly to work out where she is.

"You should get a pair of glasses."

"I've got a pair of glasses. For reading. That's enough."

Tamara looks behind her. A wall, trees.

"Where are we?"

They get out, and Tamara recognizes where Kris has brought her.

"You're joking, aren't you?"

"Let's go upstairs."

"Kris, I'm not budging from the spot until you've told me what we're doing here."

"Please, come upstairs with me, then—"

"Look, are you deaf or what?" Tamara breaks in, glancing at her watch. "I'll give you two minutes, then I'm taking the tram home."

Kris just looks at her. His expression scares Tamara. She doesn't know what he's thinking, or if indeed he's thinking. She finds herself imagining a fish in an aquarium with its fixed, un-approachable expression. *I've slept with your brother!* she wants to yell at him. Kris nods once, very slightly, as if he's made a decision, and goes to the trunk. He waits till Tamara is standing next to him. For one cruel moment she's sure that the woman's corpse is back in the trunk. *Sorry, all that to-ing and fro-ing,* Kris would say, *but we've got to hang her back up on the wall.*

In the trunk there's a blanket, under the blanket there's a pair of pliers, a flashlight, the dirty sleeping bag that they transported the corpse in, and the two shovels from the shed. Kris's voice reaches her ears as if from a long way off.

"Meybach called. We've got a new job."

It's her fourth cigarette, it's her last cigarette. Tamara lets it fall to the ground and grinds it into the concrete.

"Did you know I only smoked if Frauke offered me a cigarette?"

"Everybody knows it."

She studies the remains of the cigarette at her feet. Ash. Tobacco. A flattened filter. She rests her bottom against the passenger door. Kris sits facing her on a doorstep.

"I loved her, did you know that?"

Kris nods, he knows that. Tamara regrets opening her mouth. *We all loved her,* she thinks, and wants Kris to say it. Just once. She can clearly read the traces of the last few days on his face. His cheekbones stand out starkly, and in the lamplight his short hair looks as if it's been cropped to the scalp.

"We all loved her," he says. "But it has nothing to do with this business here, Tammi."

"Why won't you talk about Frauke?"

"What is there to say? She's dead, and there's nothing to be done about that. Of course I'm sad, of course I could cry, but our problem up there . . ."

He points to the apartment building.

" . . . is more important. We can talk about Frauke later, but I want to get through this quickly without starting any new ethical discussions about where and how the corpse is buried. That's why you're here and Wolf isn't. And anyway I'm not sure how Wolf would react to a second corpse."

"You don't know how I'm going to react either."

"You're stronger than Wolf, you're better equipped to deal with it."

Tamara laughs.

"That's a compliment."

"You're welcome."

Kris stands up and knocks the dust off his backside. He walks around the car, gets the sleeping bag out of the trunk, puts the pliers in his jacket pocket, and shuts the trunk again.

"Whatever you decide," he says. "I'm going upstairs now."

Tamara puts out her hand and Kris gives her the sleeping bag. They cross the street side by side and walk into the building.

The door to the apartment is open, and the smell of cleaning stuff still hangs in the air. They glance into the kitchen and the bathroom before stepping into the living room. There is a man hanging on the wall. His feet float inches above the floor. His face has been beaten bloody.

"Relax," says Kris.

"I am relaxed."

"You're not relaxed, Tammi, you're breaking my arm."

Tamara looks down; her hand is gripping his forearm. She lets go and shakes her fingers as if they've gone to sleep.

Please, Kris, don't say anything now.

Kris walks over to the corpse and takes a piece of paper out of the dead man's jacket pocket. He looks him in the face. The blood isn't just coming from the wound in his forehead. The man's nose has been smashed in, and his lower lip has burst. Kris unfolds the piece of paper; the words are the same as they were on the one found on the woman.

"That mural again," Tamara says and touches the wall, which is still damp.

"Let's get started," says Kris. "We'll take the corpse down and . . ."

He stops and glances at the dead man.

"What is it?" asks Tamara.

"Don't you think it's strange that his eyes are open? The woman's eyes were, too, do you remember?"

Tamara remembers how weird she found it that the woman's eyes were closed later, when they came back from the hardware store. She also remembers what she thought: *Perhaps she got tired waiting for us to come back.*

Kris goes and stands right in front of the corpse, with his head on one side as if he was trying to find the right angle of vision.

"If someone hammered a nail through my forehead, I'd close my eyes tight, believe me."

Kris leans closer to the dead man's face.

"Look at this."

"Kris, I—"

"Please, Tamara, look at this."

Tamara comes and stands beside him. She sees the dried blood, which has followed the folds and wrinkles in the skin and is flaking off in places, she sees the dust on the dead man's eyelashes, the little veins in the open eyes, and the look that disappears into nothingness.

"When I spoke to Meybach the first time, he asked me if we'd taken a good look at the corpse. He said we could look all over anywhere, but the answer would still be in the eyes."

"You mean something along the lines of *the eyes are the windows of the soul?*"

"Something like that."

Tamara shrinks back. "Sorry. I don't see anything."

"Because there's nothing to see, we're dealing with a dead person here. Wherever his soul has gone, his eyes aren't going to help us much . . ."

Kris stops talking and turns around as if someone had tapped him on the shoulder. He stares at the opposite wall as if he'd never seen a wall before. Now Tamara sees it too. A little photo is pinned to the wallpaper at eye level. It shows two boys on a street; they're balancing on one bicycle without their feet touching the ground.

Kris crosses the room and pulls the pin out of the wall. He holds the photo with outstretched fingers as if he didn't want to dirty it. Tamara goes over to join him.

"How could we not have noticed that?" she says.

"We had other things on our plate."

Kris points at the dead man's head.

"Look at the height. It's a line. Meybach wanted his victim to see the photograph even in death."

Kris holds the photograph at a distance, as if he could recognize the boys in it better that way. He turns it over. The other side is blank. He looks back at the two boys and says, "Who are you? And what are you doing here?"

*   *   *

After Kris has put the photograph in his wallet, he takes the pliers out of his jacket. Tamara turns away.

"I'll wait outside."

"Hey, what are you doing?"

"I said, I—"

"Tammi, you can't go, I won't be able to do this on my own. If I could do it on my own I wouldn't have brought you along. Someone has to hold him up so that the weight . . ."

He taps the pliers against his forehead.

". . . is taken off the nail."

"You want me to touch him?"

Tamara can hear that her voice sounds shrill.

"As far as I'm concerned you can pull the nails out as well if you feel like it."

"Kris, stop it."

"Come on, Tammi, it won't take long. It's just two nails. Please, don't leave me hanging here."

"Kris, that's not funny."

"It wasn't meant to be. Please grab his hips and lift him up, I'll do the rest."

Tamara walks over to the dead man. She puts her hands on his hips, feels his belly and grips harder. The man's fat shifts and there's a gurgling sound.

"Don't let go," says Kris.

Tamara feels as if she's going to throw up.

"Just don't lose it on me."

She can see him closing the dead man's eyes.

"Can you get it a bit higher?"

She supports the corpse with her shoulder as well.

"That's fine."

Kris tries to use the pliers and swears. The nail is deep in the forehead. He can't find the head of the nail, he pushes the pliers further into the flesh and is relieved that no blood comes out. The pliers hit something hard and grip the head of the nail.

"Okay, I've got it."

There's a sucking sound, then a jerk, and the corpse slips down a bit. Panicking, Tamara wraps her arms around the dead man's hips and feels that his trousers are wet. Kris supports the corpse with his free hand.

"He's just slipped a bit," he says. "Now I'm going to get—"

"Please, stop blabbering and get this over with."

Kris drops the nail on the floor and stands on tiptoe to reach the hands, which are positioned one on top of the other. Tamara stares at a spot in the photomural and disappears into it. The good old bourgeois dream Germany of the 1960s. Forest with stag, lake with mountains all around it. *Why this ugly photomural? What's going on in this lunatic's head? And how long is Kris going to spend fumbling around up there? Please, let it be over soon, please.*

Tamara stands by the kitchen window, greedily breathing in the night air. The corpse is in the sleeping bag, the sleeping bag is in the corridor. Tamara can hear Kris's voice from the living room. She has an image in front of her eyes that she has never seen and never will see: Kris leaning forward, with the digital recorder to his lips, apologizing to the dead man. Tamara is surprised at how calm she is now. Kris was right, she's strong. This time once again she had no problem pulling the zipper of the sleeping bag right up to the top.

I'm getting apathetic, I'm burning on both sides, I—

Kris joins Tamara at the window. They both look into the dark courtyard. Lights are on in only two apartments.

"Are you cold?"

"A bit."

Kris puts his arm around her shoulders. It doesn't warm her, but it's pleasant.

"Will you get the car?"

It's like a week ago. Tamara goes down the steps, opens both halves of the gate, gets into the car, and reverses into the courtyard. *It's exactly like a week ago. Except that Wolf isn't here and Frauke isn't alive and I'm no longer the person I once was.* She gets out of the car and looks up at the façade of the building. Kris's face appears as a pale patch in the darkness. They look at one another across a vertical distance of four stories. A man and a woman dealing with a dead man.

They aren't stupid, they go to find the same spot in the forest. One side of the grave has caved in, and the ground is water-logged in places. It takes them half an hour to get six feet down.

The corpse slides into the hole with a soft rustle, a dull thump, then silence. Kris and Tamara look at one another for a moment, then start filling in the grave. They don't say a word, and both hope they will never see that sleeping bag again. When they leave the clearing, it looks as if they'd never been there.

WOLF

THE HOUSE WELCOMES him like an old friend. Every visit is a journey into the past. As soon as the door opens, Wolf is enveloped in an aroma of wood and apples, even though no one has stored apples in the larder for more than a decade. Along with the smell there are the noises, and the way they sound in the various rooms. The creaking of the floorboards, the clanking of the radiators or the echoing silence as soon as the doors are closed and peace settles again. Smells, light, space, and all the traces that people leave over the years in a place where they've grown up. Every time he visits, Wolf deliberately looks for these traces. He calls it nostalgia, Kris calls it frustration. In his opinion Wolf has never gotten over their mother's disappearance.

"Be honest. You're waiting for her to come back to the house one day and call you down to breakfast."

Wolf knows his brother is right, but he would never admit it. Especially not in front of Lutger. Since their mother left them, their father insists that his sons call him by his first name, explaining that Father was too formal for him.

Kris and Wolf heard from their mother for the last time after the divorce was final. She said goodbye in a marvelously colorful postcard, and wished them all the best for their lives. The card had also been signed by someone called Eddie. When the brothers wanted to know who this Eddie was, Lutger changed the subject.

That was sixteen years ago, and since then they haven't spoken about their mother. But although Wolf never mentions her, she still lives like a ghost in the house. Whenever he visits his father, he thinks he hears her movements, her quiet humming in the bathroom, the whisper of the curtains closing as she passes from room to room on the ground floor at night, or the gentle drumming of her fingertips as she waits impatiently for the coffee to percolate. Her constant presence is another reason why he likes going back to his childhood home.

"Man, am I glad you're here."

Lutger behaves as if he hasn't seen Wolf for ages, though this morning they were standing six feet apart at Frauke's funeral. Wolf knows what his father means. *As if Frauke's death had separated us and brought us back together again.* They hug and hold each other tight. The smell of fresh-baked bread and chili comes from the kitchen.

"You're hungry, aren't you?"

They go into the kitchen, and Lutger points at the stove. Wolf leans forward and sees two loaves of bread.

"I couldn't help it. I was just making chili when I had the idea of making some bread dough, and in the end I suddenly fancied some noodles. Fresh homemade noodles, you remember how delicious they are? So, what'll you have?"

"I'll take the chili."

"Chili it is, then."

Wolf sets the table as Lutger puts the dishes on mats, talking constantly as he does so. It's always been like this. As if he had to fill their mother's place with words. Wolf wonders, not for the first time, what it would be like if Lutger had left the house rather than their mother.

Where would I be now? Who would I be?

After dinner he goes upstairs to his old room to look for photographs. Tamara had asked him to. In the mid-nineties Wolf went through a phase of recording every day. He developed the films himself, and they fill countless albums that Lutger keeps in one of the cupboards.

Nothing in the room reminds Wolf of the fact that he grew up here. The posters have disappeared from the walls, even the stickers have been scratched from the inside of the door. Not a single piece of furniture is left from those days, and even the color of the walls is different. The room could be anyone's.

In one of the cupboards there are stacks of cardboard boxes containing his old belongings. Books, comics, cassette tapes. The bottom row is devoted to the photograph albums, and on top of the albums there's a box filled to the brim with film canisters. Wolf's photographic phase lasted two years, and afterwards he sold his darkroom and never picked up a camera again. More than thirty undeveloped films are left over from those times. Wolf doesn't know how durable films like that are. He should have thrown the box away a long time ago.

The dates on the albums were written with a silver marker. Pictures of the clique, pictures from school, and even a handful of nude shots of a girl who went to America shortly afterwards and didn't want him to forget her.

Wolf piles up the albums chronologically, then he hesitates and puts them back in the cupboard. He doesn't know what he's doing there. He only knows that right now he doesn't want to look back.

Lutger finds him lying on the bed in the spare room, his face buried in a pillow. Lutger sits down on the edge of the bed and waits a minute before he says, "Take your head out of the pillow, or you won't be able to breathe and you'll suffocate. And where will that leave me?"

Wolf laughs involuntarily. He lifts his head and sees his father's face as a pale patch in the darkness.

"You're a good father," he says.

"I know."

Wolf turns onto his back. He wishes he could cry. Since Erin's death he has shed no more tears. He would so love to weep for Frauke, but there's nothing.

"I slept with Tamara after the funeral," he says, "and I don't regret a second of it."

Lutger says nothing for a moment, then says, "I'm glad. After all those years you're almost like brother and sister, but they say love between brother and sister has its charms as well."

"Lutger, that's not funny. I've known Tamara for more than ten years, and I never thought it would come to anything. And suddenly Frauke dies, and Tamara and I . . . Does that make any kind of sense? I can't see it. But it's good, it's right. So I don't need to see any sense in it."

"Wolf, it's fine."

"Of course it's fine."

Wolf falls silent and a few seconds later he adds, "It really is fine, isn't it?"

"What are you really worried about?"

"Nothing."

"Come on, what is it?"

How does he know? He can't even see my face in the dark, am I that transparent? Wolf imagines giving his father a brief summary of the nightmare that invaded their lives just a week ago. *By the way, the killer took a picture of you, Lutger, what do you have to say about that?*

"I feel like everybody's disappearing," he says instead, and even as he says it he realizes that he's more concerned about that disappearance than he is about a lunatic who gave them the job of getting rid of a corpse.

"They all disappear, and I'm left behind," he says.

Lutger shrugs.

"I stayed behind when your mother left us. Kris did the same. You're exaggerating a little. And besides, Frauke and Erin didn't just disappear. No one did that to *you*."

Wolf stares at the ceiling and is glad they're sitting in the dark. Of course no one did it to him, but it still feels as if there's an invisible weight lying on him. Loss, and more loss, time and again. Wolf doesn't want to say it, he guesses that it's going to sound like the ravings of an idiot, and yet he says it anyway.

"It seems not to matter so much to all of you. You're strong, you keep going the way you were, but take a look at me."

"You're whining."

"Yes, I'm whining."

"And we don't just keep going the way we did before, we're just good at bluffing, believe me."

Lutger stands up.

"Come on, let's the two of us go downstairs now, and I'll open the expensive wine that you and your brother gave me last year. Let's raise a glass to Frauke. To Frauke and Tamara."

"Just like that?"

"Just like that. And because I'm glad you're here. Kris was right. It was time for us to talk to one another again. The house missed you too, I could tell. If you must, you can stay the night here—"

"What do you mean, *Kris was right*?" Wolf breaks in.

"You know what he's like. He asked me to invite you to dinner so that we can spend a bit more time together."

Wolf reaches for the bedside light and turns it on. Dazzled, father and son screw up their eyes.

"*When* did he ask you?" Wolf demands.

"It was right after the funeral. He called and said you could use a break and . . . Hey, where are you going?"

"I've got to go."

"But . . ."

"We'll catch up later."

Lutger is left alone in the room. He hears the front door closing and wonders what has just happened.

Two hours and fifty-six minutes after he left the villa, Wolf turns back into the drive and is surprised that only his car is missing from the parking area. He's even more surprised by the picture that presents itself to him in the kitchen. It's past midnight. Tamara and Kris are sitting at the kitchen table drinking tea. They've put out a mug for him.

"What's going on here?" asks Wolf.

"Sit down," says Kris.

"Why did you ask Lutger to invite me?"

"Wolf, please, sit down."

Wolf sits down at the table. When Tamara is about to pour him some tea, he holds his hand over the mug.

"We've got to talk," says Tamara, "so take your stupid hand away and have some tea with us."

Wolf withdraws his hand, Tamara pours the tea, the brothers look at each other.

"We had to get rid of you," Kris starts to say.

"I worked that one out for myself, but an explanation would be nice."

And so Wolf learns of Meybach's final job and hears what Kris and Tamara have done.

"You'd have been in our way," Kris explains.

Wolf digests the news, then he says, "Does that mean it's over now?"

Wolf and Tamara look at Kris at the same time, as if he were the one to decide when it was over.

"It's over," Kris says resolutely. "I sent Meybach the file. We will never hear from him again. I promise you that."

Tamara nods. Wolf tilts his head slightly to one side as if to see Kris from a different angle. It's a short, bitter moment in which he understands with perfect clarity that his brother has just lied to them.

"What is it?" Kris asks.

"Nothing," Wolf replies. "I'm just glad it's over, that's all."

TAMARA

TEN MINUTES, FIFTEEN MINUTES. Tamara sits on the bed, and nothing happens. Frauke's room stays as it was before Tamara came in. Deserted and empty. Tamara doesn't know what she expected. She goes into the cellar and fetches cardboard boxes. She empties the shelves and starts packing Frauke's books in the boxes.

"What are you doing there?"

Wolf stands in the doorway.

"Cleaning up."

They look at each other.

"It's all fine," Tamara reassures him, "really."

Wolf nods, he doesn't come any closer, she can see that he wants to come closer. *It's time for us to tell Kris,* she thinks and says, "Why don't all three of us go out for dinner tomorrow night. We should get away from the villa for a few hours and . . ."

Words fail her, she doesn't know what's waiting for her out there.

Frauke will be everywhere.

" . . . celebrate Frauke," Wolf finishes her sentence.

"Exactly," says Tamara and smiles. "Celebrate Frauke."

And talk to Kris, she thinks and can't say it. *What am I scared of? They're brothers, not rivals. But we've known each other so long. We're like a constellation, and no one alters a constellation without producing chaos.*

Wolf wishes her good night and shuts the door behind him. Tamara regrets not asking him in. Suddenly she's alone again, with the emptiness that Frauke left behind.

She starts with the desk, clears up the papers, unplugs the computer and wraps up the cable. She takes the pictures and posters off the walls. She is very careful. She doesn't know which of her things Frauke's father will want to keep, and if she's quite honest she doesn't really care. This is her farewell.

She puts the cardboard boxes by one wall, the clothes by another. It takes her three hours and everything's cleared away. The only thing she's left untouched is the bed.

Tamara slumps back exhausted and there, between the sheet and the blanket, she finds Frauke and inhales her smell with relief. She buries her face in the pillows and cries herself to sleep as if she were a child with the weight of the whole world on her shoulders.

Tamara wakes up with no sense of where she is. It's seven o'clock in the morning. She opens the windows and feels as if by doing so she is freeing Frauke's smell. She looks around the room and is content. Afterwards she will ask the brothers to help her carry the boxes into the cellar. She'll think of a good restaurant tonight. She decides to stop grieving before midnight.

Tamara balances her breakfast on a tray and sets it down on the table in the conservatory. She steps out into the garden. The Belzens' house still looks abandoned. Tamara wonders where they could have gone.

Maybe there was a family emergency, or else they've gone off somewhere.
Yes, but why didn't they let us know?

And as she stands there, the rising sun bathes the house in light, and Tamara notices a movement behind the terrace window. She walks across the still damp lawn to the shore. The dew is cool under her bare feet. She stops by the low quay wall and now she can see that there is a man asleep in an armchair in the Belzens' living room. As she watches him, the man wakes up and looks at her. Motionless, as if he had only been pretending to be asleep. No surprise, nothing.

That isn't Joachim.

Tamara doesn't know how she's supposed to react. She tries to smile and raises her hand. The man gets to his feet and disappears for a moment from Tamara's field of vision, then the terrace door slides open and he steps out of the house and into the garden. He stops by the quay wall and calls over to her:

"Wonderful morning. You're from the villa, aren't you?"

"You got it," says Tamara.

"Helena and Joachim have told me about you."

The man puts a hand to his chest.

"I'm Samuel."

"Tamara."

Samuel points behind him with his thumb.

"I'm looking after the house while the two lovebirds are on the Baltic coast."

"I wondered where they were," Tamara says with relief.

Samuel sticks his hands in his trouser pockets and points to the water with his foot.

"I'm surprised they haven't built a bridge here yet. You're so close that you could almost touch."

Tamara doesn't think fifty yards is so close that you could almost touch, but she nods anyway and looks at the water as if she too is surprised that no one has thought of building a bridge.

"Okay, back to it."

Samuel waves goodbye, disappears into the house, and closes the terrace door behind him. Tamara turns around, and is about to get back to her breakfast when she sees Wolf in the conservatory doorway. The sight of him reminds her of him standing in Frauke's room yesterday. *He's still there, he's concerned.* Wolf is dressed only in shorts, and is holding Tamara's coffee cup.

"Old man Belzen's changed," he says.

"You should do something about your morning erection."

Wolf looks down.

"That's not an erection," he says. "I always look like that."

"Dream on."

Wolf hands her the cup.

"His name is Samuel," says Tamara. "He's looking after the house while the Belzens paint the Baltic red."

Wolf grins.

"Since yesterday I've only seen you grinning," says Tamara. "What's that all about?"

She kisses him before he can reply. Then she pushes her way past him and sits down at the table. Wolf stops in the doorway and looks down at himself.

"Now *that's* a morning erection," he says.

"Who's interested?" asks Tamara as she cuts open a bread roll.

KRIS

Not true.

Kris shuts his eyes tight, opens them again.

True.

He finds it hard to believe that the name appears just like that on the doorbell nameplate. He was sure the address was wrong.

Here I am in the middle of Charlottenburg, a few houses away there's an organic shop, there's a playground on the corner, and Meybach's damned name is right there on the nameplate. It's absurd.

The front door is open, three bikes lean against each other in the hall. Meybach lives in the front part of the building. Third floor. There is a sisal carpet on the stairs, and his footsteps barely make a sound. His finger settles on the doorbell. He doesn't know what he's going to say, but he'll know as soon as he sees Meybach, he'll know whether he finds himself facing the murderer or not. His face will give him away.

The gun lies heavy in his jacket. Kris has the feeling that everyone knows what he's hiding there. He saw himself in a shop window. He's so inconspicuous that it's almost embarrassing. A tall, scrawny guy with his hands dug into his jacket pockets. Nothing more.

He rings the bell again, and now there's a hint of relief. *Why should he be there?* Kris imagines Meybach on the other side, pressing his ear to the door and listening. *Why am I here?* Kris sees himself going down the stairs and driving off. No one needs to find out. Kris has made himself a hero unasked, and he could creep off unasked just as easily.

But not after the second job, everything was possible before, but now . . .

Since the second job Kris no longer believes that Meybach will stop murdering. *The lunatic has tasted blood, and if I don't stop him, what will he do next?*

"Hello, anyone there?" he calls, keeping his finger on the

doorbell. Then an idea comes to him, and he takes out his new cell phone. It takes him only a second to make a connection, and the cell phone in the apartment answers.

I knew it!

Kris knocks on the door. The ringing from the apartment comes like a shrill retort. *Here I am, what are you waiting for, come and get me.* It rings and rings, and Kris starts hammering on the door and gives a start when a voice downstairs says, "He isn't there."

Kris disconnects and leans over the banister. From the open apartment door a floor below, a man looks up at him.

"Hello," says Kris.

"Hello," says the man. "You're looking for Lars, right?"

"Right."

"He isn't there."

The man tilts his head on one side.

"Do we know each other?"

Kris shakes his head. He knows he has to explain himself now.

"It's complicated," he says. "Lars Meybach gave my agency a job, and there are some problems with it. I urgently need to speak to him."

"Have you tried his cell phone?"

Kris holds up his phone. The man laughs and says, "What kind of agency?"

"Dating."

"Typical Lars," says the man, and now Kris laughs too, although he doesn't know what he's laughing about.

"Any idea when he'll be back?"

"He's at work. If you leave him a message on his phone he'll . . .What is it?"

Kris points over his shoulder with his thumb at Meybach's door.

"His phone's ringing in the apartment."

"Oh," says the man. "Just wait a moment."

He disappears from the landing, and a moment later he comes upstairs.

"Lars isn't the type to leave his phone at home," he says, holding his hand out to Kris. "Jonas Kronauer."

"Kris, Kris Marrer."

Kronauer has a spare key. He says Meybach won't mind if he just looks in.

"Lars?" Kronauer stops in the doorway and just sticks his head inside.

"Hey, Lars, are you there?"

They listen, then look at each other, and Kronauer says, "Shall we?"

"Okay," says Kris, and they step inside the apartment.

He doesn't know what he expected. The apartment is normal, just normal and tidy. It smells of aftershave, there's a sweater over a chair; in the kitchen Kris sees an open newspaper next to a cup half full of milky coffee.

"Why are the mirrors covered?" he asks.

Kronauer lifts the cloth at one corner.

"No idea. In the Jewish faith you hang cloth over the mirrors in a house when someone's died."

"Has someone died?"

Kronauer shakes his head.

"Not that I know of. As far as I know, Lars isn't even Jewish."

They find the cell phone on the shelf in the bathroom. The mirror over the basin is covered with a cloth.

"He must have forgotten his phone," says Kronauer.

"Do you know where he works?"

"I'll write it down for you."

It's an advertising agency on Alexanderplatz. Kris says thanks and leaves the apartment with Kronauer. A floor below they part with a handshake. Kris can't believe how lucky he is.

When he comes out of the building, Wolf is leaning against the passenger side of his car, his arms folded in front of his chest. *There goes my luck,* Kris thinks, and tries not to show any signs of panic as he crosses the street and walks up to Wolf. His head is working, trying to find excuses.

"Are you shitting me or what?"

"What do you mean?"

"You think I don't know you? It's me, Wolf, your brother."

A couple turn to look at them.

"Keep walking," says Wolf to them.

"You followed me," says Kris, trying to change the subject.

"Of course I followed you. Just because Tamara fell for your act doesn't mean I'm going to do the same."

"What act? I haven't a clue what you're talking about."

"Where have you just been?"

"Visiting a client."

Wolf laughs.

"So one of our clients lives here?"

"That's right."

Wolf points to the building that Kris has just left.

"Over there? Don't you think it's a bit of a coincidence that Meybach's name is on the nameplate too?"

Kris blushes.

"Maybe Meybach and this client are one and the same person."

"Oh, shit," says Kris.

"Right," says Wolf. "Oh, shit."

They sit around the corner in the Leonhardt. The atmosphere is awful. Wolf wants to know what Kris thought he was doing, trying to go solo like that.

"Who are you? Dirty Kris or something?"

"I said I'd deal with it."

"This is what you call dealing with it? Going to the guy's house? Are you completely crazy? Isn't Frauke's drowning enough for you?"

Kris says nothing.

"How on earth did you get hold of his address?"

Kris tells him he found out why Frauke crept secretly into the villa the night before her death.

"Meybach's number was stored in my phone. Frauke phoned him twice. On Saturday night and then Sunday morning just before she drowned. I asked my former boss to use one of his contacts, and that's how I got hold of Meybach's address."

"And what was your plan?"

"I wanted to talk to him."

"Alone? You wanted to visit a guy who nails people to the wall? Are you completely insane? The guy's a murderer!"

Kris looks round, no one is listening to them.

"Do you think I don't know?" he says quietly, and unconsciously touches the gun in his jacket.

Wolf looks at him dubiously. Nothing that his brother is saying sounds properly thought through. And Wolf knows Kris would never do anything that wasn't thought through.

"So?"

"So what?"

"Was Meybach at home or not?"

"He's at work."

Wolf tilts his head.

"And before you ask me whether this Meybach is our Meybach: he is."

Kris tells him about the cell phone in the apartment.

"You were in *his* apartment?" Wolf laughs. "You're shitting me. So *if* the address is right and *if* this guy is our murderer, then he's a complete idiot."

"Or he's fearless."

Wolf stops laughing.

"Maybe he really is fearless," Kris goes on. "But maybe he also wants us to find him. Have you thought of that?"

From the way Wolf looks, he hasn't thought of that. Kris drinks from his coffee, which has grown cold. He wants the words to take effect. As he looks at Wolf, Kris wonders how he's going to get rid of him now. *I'm the big brother, protecting the little brother. That's how it's always been.*

"Don't think of getting rid of me," Wolf warns him.

"No one wants to get rid of you."

"Then trust me. Don't exclude me."

Kris hesitates, then he takes the piece of paper out of his trouser pocket and says, "If Meybach wants us to find him, let's do him the favor."

"What's that?" Wolf asks.

Kris sets the address down on the table and pushes it toward Wolf.

"Let's visit Meybach at work."

"Sorry," says the woman at reception, without taking her eyes off her monitor, "Meybach isn't with us any more. He resigned three months ago. Is there anything else I can help you with?"

"Are you quite sure?" asks Kris.

"Sure as I can be. His mother fell ill and Lars wanted to look after her. Only for a month at first, then he pulled out completely."

She looks up for the first time and smiles suddenly. It's the fakest smile that Kris has seen for ages. Pure business.

"What did you want to see him about?"

Kris doesn't know what to say. Wolf shoves him aside and takes over.

"We're old school friends. We're back in Berlin for the first time in years and we wanted to surprise him. Since he wasn't at home, we thought we'd come and meet him here. Any idea where we go from here?"

Bull's-eye. The woman has been challenged, they need her help. There are such people—people without a particular task to perform, who are almost lifeless in their dormant state, but full of energy as soon as you need them.

"Have you tried his cell phone?"

"He's not answering."

"Hm, let's take a look."

She bites her bottom lip between her teeth and leans forward on her chair. She no longer looks like a receptionist in her mid-twenties, now she's more of a teenager faced with a mystery.

"You could try his parents."

She slides back over to the keyboard, types and finds out that his parents live in Dahlem. She writes the address down and underlines the street twice as if Kris and Wolf were stupid. Her phone rings as she hands them the piece of paper. She picks up the receiver, her eyes drift across the room and past them. The brothers no longer exist for her.

"They probably breed women like that in a lab," Wolf says on the way outside.

"At least she's helped us."

Wolf looks at the piece of paper.

"What exactly do you expect to get from the parents?"

"Something," says Kris. "I'm happy with the crumbs from the table."

"How poetic."

No one answers when they ring the bell, but they can hear music from inside the house. Wolf walks to one of the windows and screens his eyes. After a few seconds he knocks against the pane. When he is standing next to Kris again the music falls silent and the front door opens. The woman is in her mid-fifties. She is holding a pair of scissors and a comb.

"How can I help you?"

"Mrs. Meybach?" asks Kris. "Lars Meybach's mother?"

Her mouth tightens and she nods. Wolf tells her the same story that he told in the advertising agency. The search for the missing friend continues. Meybach's mother asks them in. In the living room a poodle is sitting on a chair. There are hair clippings on the floor. When the poodle sees the brothers come in, it is about to jump off the chair, but its mistress snaps at it.

"Sit!"

The dog cowers and sits where it is.

"He hates it when I clip his hair," she explains and points to the sofa.

They sit down, and the poodle doesn't take its eyes off them. Mrs. Meybach scratches his head. She doesn't say anything, she just looks at the brothers, then clears her throat as if she had only just noticed that no one was speaking. She starts talking. She says she's sorry that they have to find out like this, but her son died three months ago, and it's a burden that the family still carries with it.

The brothers are back in the street. They don't understand a thing now. They sit in the car as if anesthetized and don't understand a thing. Wolf tries to introduce some kind of logic into the story. All that comes out is nonsense.

"You spoke to him on the phone. You found out his address, and you were in his apartment. I mean, his neighbor must know if the guy's dead or not."

"Maybe he's a different Lars Meybach," says Kris.

"Come on, Kris, that's just crap. It's *his* phone, ringing in *his* apartment. You saw the thing yourself."

It's four o'clock in the afternoon, the rush-hour traffic swells like a metallic tumor. They decide to drive back to Meybach's place and talk to the neighbors. Wolf says Kris should avoid the autobahn. Kris says the autobahn will be quicker. They spend the next half hour stuck in traffic, get off the autobahn, and onto the Kurfürstendamm, and five minutes later a series of side streets has delivered them to the Stuttgarter Platz. Jonas Kronauer is no longer at home, of course. They ring Meybach's bell again, and Wolf suggests breaking the door down. Kris has no idea what good that would do, and suggests going back to the advertising agency.

*   *   *

According to his mother, Lars Meybach had taken an overdose of sleeping pills and drowned in the bath. His neighbor and best friend Jonas was supposed to have found him. Mrs. Meybach had whispered the details in such a way that Kris and Wolf had had to sit leaning forward on the edge of the sofa to hear every word. She had said that her son was a depressive, so his suicide didn't surprise anyone.

"We didn't tell anyone outside the family that he's dead. We couldn't have stood the humiliation. You know how people talk. Lars was a source of shame to us all. His death was a relief. Please, don't talk to my husband about it. We have to go on living."

The woman at reception doesn't believe a word of it.

"Lars isn't dead, that's nonsense," she says, laughing a pearly laugh like sweet sparkling wine. "We're in regular contact with him, his last e-mail . . ."

She flips through her mailbox.

" . . . is dated 16th February. He wished André a happy birthday. André's our boss. He still hopes that Lars will come back and work here again one day. Who told you he was dead?"

"We went to see his mother," says Kris.

"Ah, mothers," says the woman and smiles ruefully.

The brothers stand on the Alexanderplatz, still confused.

"Why would his mother lie to us?" asks Wolf. "Did she seem crazy to you?"

"Did Frauke's mother seem crazy to you?" Kris asks back.

Before Wolf can answer, his cell phone rings. He takes the call, listens for a moment, and passes it to Kris.

"It's Meybach. He wants to know what the fuck we think we're doing."

YOU

YOU AREN'T REALLY surprised that they found the apartment. You expected that, it was what you wanted. But you didn't expect they'd actually turn up on your doorstep. You're glad it was Kris Marrer. He still remains a mystery to you. What he thinks, what he feels. You regret not having more time for him. His visit makes your life more real. Kris Marrer was in your apartment. Kris Marrer walked through your rooms, and Kris Marrer knows you're alive. *He knows.* Even if you're pleased, you shouldn't let him know on the phone. You're not an idiot. Let him have both barrels.

"What the fuck are you up to?" you ask again, after Wolf Marrer has passed the phone to his brother. "I thought we had a business agreement, and then I hear you've shown up at my house."

For a few seconds there isn't a sound at the other end, then Kris Marrer says, "It doesn't say in our agreement that we aren't allowed to visit clients to discuss problems with them."

You laugh.

"Very funny, Marrer, really funny. What sort of problems have we got?"

"There's this rumor going around that you took an overdose of sleeping pills and drowned in your bathtub."

The fun's over.

How could he . . .

You have no idea how that could have happened.

How dare he . . .

For a long, stubborn moment there's a red curtain in front of your eyes. The room disappears, the building dissolves, and the boundaries of reality blur as if it were all just an illusion. Your life, this world. You blink, the curtain dissolves again, and you ask quietly, "Do I sound dead to you?"

"No," Kris Marrer answers, "but—"

"DO I SOUND LIKE A DAMNED CORPSE?" you suddenly roar at him.

Silence, then out of the silence, cautiously:

"I said no."

"Thanks," you reply with self-control, trying to slow your breathing. You're alive.

Yes.

It's all okay.

I know.

Repeat it.

I'm alive. It's all okay.

Better?

Better.

"Why does your mother think you're dead?" asks Kris Marrer.

You sink back. It's getting worse and worse. You feel the sweat on the palms of your hands. As if someone had opened all the pores. Wet. Your voice is a hiss.

"You went to my mother's place?"

"The advertising agency gave us—"

"YOU WENT TO MY MOTHER'S PLACE? ARE YOU COMPLETELY INSANE?"

You can no longer sit still. You're aware of the irony of the fact that Frauke accused you of the same thing. How could you be so stupid? The brothers should never have gone to the advertising agency. You felt so secure. What an idiot you are! For a moment you're glad, the next moment you're crapping yourself.

Pull yourself together.

You get up and shut the door to your office.

You don't know what to do next.

You don't know.

"How could you go to my mother's place?" you ask again quietly.

Kris Marrer doesn't reply, there's a rustling sound, then the younger brother is back on the line.

"Listen, you sick fuck. Who do you think you're dealing with here?" he asks. "Be glad that we didn't find *you*, because if we do—"

"Wolf," Kris says, "give me the phone."

"I want to know what he did to Frauke."

"Wolf, give me the fucking phone!"

Rustling, cursing, then Kris Marrer is back on the line.

"Meybach? Are you still there? I'm sorry, we've all been a bit shattered since Frauke's death."

"It's over," you say. "Haven't you worked that out?"

"Yeah, but we—"

"You don't believe me. You think I'm just a sicko, wandering around the place killing people. That's your problem, not mine. You think what you like. I'm going to disappear now, and you're going to disappear. You won't think about Lars Meybach again. We no longer exist for one another."

Silence.

"Simple as that?"

"Simple as that. You've worked for me, I've paid you for it. There are no more jobs. That's why we're now parting in peace. If you so much as think about going on looking for me, if I see one of you anywhere near my parents, your families will pay for it. I mean it. What I've done so far had nothing to do with you. You don't want it to have anything to do with you. Say it."

"We don't want it to have anything to do with us."

"Now give me your brother."

Rustling, a deep intake of breath.

"What is it?"

"I want to tell you what I told your brother yesterday. I had nothing to do with your friend's death. It was an accident."

"And why should I believe a madman?"

"If I were a madman, none of you would be alive now. I'm

one of the good guys. Bear that in mind. And tell your brother I'm still waiting for the file."

You hang up and are very pleased with your last words. *I'm one of the good guys.* You still can't get your head around what these two brothers have done. *How on earth could that have happened?*

There's a knock at your door. One of your colleagues sticks his head in.

"Everything okay?" he asks.

"Everything's okay," you say and raise your thumb although there's sweat on your forehead and you're breathing far too fast.

The file comes by e-mail the same evening. You delete it without listening to it. It's over for good. You also delete the mail account before closing the notebook and looking around. The apartment has changed, as if it's leading a life of its own. The mirrors are unveiled, the darkness has made way for light. You walk through the rooms like a free man. Tomorrow you will close down the flat and sever all connections. You've paid your tribute; even if the brothers almost destroyed everything, you have stayed true to yourself and now it's over. You can't ask for more than that.

PART VII

After

HE TALKS ABOUT LOVE. He talks about the one, true love. And he talks about suffering. He says whatever he says has nothing to do with his past. He says he first encountered love as a child. He says a man took him on and chastised him. He says it with a smile. He has forgotten that the now has nothing to do with the past.

Lake Constance is like a bottomless mirror. I sit with my back against the rear tire and hear him talking. I hope he will simply die. That he will be consumed with hunger. But he's stubborn. He doesn't think of dying. He has plans for the future when this is all over.

He talks about pain and closeness and hunger and pleasure. He says that if you haven't discovered all of those things in your life you're not really living. And he waits for me to react. I sit where I am and say nothing. I'd really like to put my hand in his mouth and reach deep into his gullet until I get to his damned heart.

I didn't find the shack. There's a campsite in the place where we turned in to the forest more than six years ago. I didn't stop. Tears came into my eyes, I was so shocked that nothing remained of the past.

No shack, no memory, everything faded.

He says he sees no reason for apologies. He doesn't know what he's supposed to apologize for. Everything is based on instinct. Evil is the shadow of good, but no one thinks that good might be the shadow of evil. He coughs and wants some water. A gentle drizzle begins, I lift my face up and see a seagull. It lands on one of the rocks. Is it thinking? What is it thinking? I wish I were the seagull. I wouldn't think anything. I'd just be glad to be a seagull.

Before

THE MAN WHO WASN'T THERE

THE ROOM AROUND HIM shimmers white and black as if the shadows can't agree where they belong. Only after a few minutes does the shimmering subside, the sounds pierce through to him, and he recognizes his surroundings.

How stupid, how stupid, how—

He had a premonition and ignored it. There was a persistent pressure in his chest as he dug up Fanni and carried her to the row boat. He dismissed it as euphoria. He thought he had rested enough. Ignorance, sheer ignorance about his own body. Luckily the blackout didn't come until the Belzens' house, after he watched the police digging up the empty grave. When he saw Lars Meybach standing by the villa, the excitement was too much for him, and he had his second heart attack in four years. Except that this time his heart stopped. For more than two minutes he sat there lifelessly in the chair, his eyes wide open, his mouth an unbreathing slit.

Two minutes and forty-three seconds.

He had returned to his life with a sigh. The colors, the light, the air, time and again the air. He stayed in the chair for a whole hour and greedily absorbed the oxygen. Then he dragged himself laboriously to his car. He knew he should call a doctor right away and not move from the spot, but it was very important for him to put some distance between himself and the Belzens' house.

His car was two streets away. With every step he took he had the feeling that nothing inside him was working properly any more, and that a single false move could mean the end. His skin was as thin as clingwrap, his right eyelid was twitching uncontrollably, and he had to concentrate to ensure that his bladder didn't empty all by itself. When he was finally sitting in the car, he called his doctor from his cell phone and then mercifully lost consciousness. Now he's lying in a hospital bed pressing his hands to his chest as if they could hold everything together. His doctor stands at the foot of the bed and asks how he is. He also says: "We're going to run a few tests and keep you under observation. We don't know how long you spent without oxygen, so we don't want to take any risks. Give yourself two or three days' rest, then we'll be able to tell you more."

The two days turn into six. But he stays still. He undergoes the tests and stares at the ceiling as if there were a door behind it that he could escape through. His thoughts go on living in the Belzens' house. He wonders how many traces of himself he left behind. He feels used up and alone. Even though he's become familiar with this state in recent years, he doesn't want to take it for granted. Resignation doesn't suit him.

No one knows that he's back in the hospital, no one must find out. *There's such a thing as dignity,* he thinks, and can understand the old rites of the Eskimos, when they put their old people on an ice floe and pushed it out to sea.

Karl phones him on the sixth day.

"Where are you?"

"In the restaurant," says Karl, "in the bathroom. He's . . . he's here. He's sitting at my table, waiting. He's exactly like you said. He found me."

"Calm down, Karl."

"I'm going to kill that bastard, you understand? I'm going to do to him exactly what he did to Fanni—"

"I told you to calm down," the man cuts him off.

Karl breathes in deeply, Karl breathes out loudly.

"I am calm."

"Be calm and careful. And whatever you do to him, I want to see him. I want to hear what he has to say."

"When . . ."

Karl falls silent again. He controls himself, or tries to. His voice sounds different when he starts speaking again.

"When will we meet?"

Small, his voice is small, as if Karl were still ten years old and completely innocent. *When?* The man hesitates, no one should see him like this.

"You take care of Meybach," he says. "Then call me, and we'll see how it goes."

Karl sighs. The man grimaces. The sigh hurts his ear. Homesickness. He puts the phone down before the pain can get to his heart. He listens. He waits for an echo. A warning. Nothing comes back. The excitement is like a pulsing surge of electricity that flows down to his feet and ebbs away. Faint, but alive.

He waits.

He waits until the evening.

He waits until the evening for Karl's phone call, then he gets dressed and leaves the hospital.

The man has read that all human beings are interconnected. Whether mentally or genetically, he can't remember; he just knows that unfounded aversions and sympathies can be traced back to the fact. From birth, every human being has a past that goes with him all the way through his life. Regardless of where, regardless of who he is. And just as all human beings are connected to one another, so too are events. Nothing happens without a meaning.

He is aware that it's utter nonsense, and that the only things that happen are the things we cause to happen. That's why it's been so long since anything happened to him. He was absent for too long. As if he'd been living in a sealed tank. Absent. And although he dismisses it as nonsense, the questions roil around inside him. *What connects Lars Meybach and those people in the villa? Why did they bury Fanni on their land? What do they know?*

When he gets to the Belzens' house, the stench of putrefaction is so overwhelming that he staggers back. He shuts the front door behind him and stops in the hall. He retches and tries to breathe shallowly. He makes it to the bathroom on the ground floor, where he throws up.

He hasn't been in the house for a week, and he forgot to turn the heat down. A constant setting of twenty-five degrees has ensured that the putrefaction has advanced more quickly than he thought.

Once his stomach is empty, he lifts the ground floor windows and opens the door to the terrace to make a draft. In the upstairs bathroom he discovers a glass container of tiger balm. He rubs a thin film of it under his nose, steps into the garden, and takes a deep breath of the night air. On the other side he sees a single light burning in the villa. He checks his hands. They're calm. He looks at his cell phone again. He doesn't want to admit to himself what Karl's silence means. Karl would never keep him waiting.

Not Karl.

The Belzens are upstairs, where he left them. He seals the door with tape. He knows this won't contain the smell for long, but he doesn't plan to spend more than three days in the house. Three days should do it.

He stays by Fanni's side. Her smell doesn't bother him, it's a different smell. Sweeter, heavier. He sits by her bed and grieves for his family. Karl won't call again. Whatever has happened, Karl won't call again.

He admits the truth and goes on grieving.

After he has sealed up this room too, he goes downstairs to take his place at the window. He senses the caution in each of his movements. His hand wanders repeatedly back to his chest and feels for his heart. *Too cautious,* he thinks, but he can't do anything about that instinct. *You want to live,* he says to himself, *so behave accordingly.* He puts the binoculars to his eyes and looks across at the villa. He knows it's time to make amends for the mistakes of his children.

The cellar is the ideal place. In the Belzens' living room he finds a portable CD player and brings it downstairs. He puts on a CD of classical music, seeks and finds a passage when the whole orchestra is playing, and turns the volume up full. Upstairs in the corridor he can hear the music. He leaves the house. The cellar has two windows, one leading to the street side and the other to the neighboring plot. He leans forward and can hear the music.

During the course of the day he insulates the cellar. He buys some nylon tape and insulating material. Passing a florist's shop he spontaneously gets some white lilies. He hangs dark curtain material over the windows, and is glad to be doing something practical. It's very satisfying work. In the evening he turns the music back up and shuts the cellar door behind him. Nothing. Not a sound to be heard. Outside he leans forward and holds his ear close to the window.

Nothing.

That same night he sees them leaving the villa. He waits for two hours, watching the darkness behind the windows. After he has changed his clothes, he liberates the boat from the tarpaulin. He pulls it across the lawn to the jetty and is about to lower the boat into the water when a car turns into the entry opposite, and the trees light up for a few seconds in the headlights.

He curses. He hesitated for too long.

The man drags the boat back to its place and spreads the tarpaulin over it before going back to the Belzens' house to sit by the window.

That night the lights go out at 4:14. He shuts his eyes for a few moments. He knows he should lie down on the sofa. He knows his body needs peace. Perhaps it's stubbornness that makes him sit by the window. Later that's what he will think. Later he will curse himself for his stubbornness.

He goes to sleep . . .

. . . and is woken by the sun warming his legs. He is still sitting in the chair, it's a wonder that he hasn't slumped sideways. His body feels stiff. But it wasn't the sun, and it wasn't the stiffness of his limbs that woke him. He opens his eyes and sees the woman standing on the opposite shore. He's surprised how close she is to him, although they're separated by the water of the Kleine Wannsee. As if the distance had shrunk in the hours of morning.

In the night he felt safe in the darkness. Now he is clearly visible.

I should have closed the curtains. How could I just go to sleep like that?

He gets up and steps outside. It's the only way. He walks to the jetty and talks to the woman. It's only when he gets back to the Belzens' house that he allows himself to yield to the tension. His body trembles. He leans back against a wall and gasps for air.

WOLF

THEY GET THERE fifteen minutes late, and are stopped at the entrance by a woman holding out a welcome gift to them.

"What sort of nonsense is this?" asks Kris.

"It's sombrero night," says the woman.

"I don't care what it is," says Kris, "I'm not wearing a thing like that."

Wolf takes one of the sombreros and turns it around in his hands.

"They're made of paper."

"We're only allowed to give out paper sombreros," the woman explains. "Last time almost all the real ones got stolen. Sombrero night's very popular."

Wolf puts on his sombrero and poses. Kris shakes his head, he isn't about to dress up like an idiot. He tries to push his way past the woman.

"Sorry, but it's sombrero night," she repeats, and Wolf can hear that it isn't the first time she's had an argument with a guest.

"How old do I look?" Kris asks. "Do I look as if I'm six?"

"I'm sorry," the woman repeats, "I can't let you in without a sombrero."

Kris points at Wolf.

"You see my brother?"

The woman nods.

"You see how ridiculous he looks in that thing? Give me one reason why I'd want to look ridiculous."

"Because otherwise you won't get in," the woman replies quietly, making the sentence sound like a question.

Wolf bursts out laughing. Kris looks at him in surprise.

"What are you laughing at?"

"It's sombrero night!" says Wolf and taps his sombrero as if saluting a general.

"Forget it," says Kris, and starts to leave the restaurant. Wolf holds him back.

"Look," he says, "Tamara's here already."

Kris stands on tiptoe, now he can see her too.

"Give us a minute," Wolf says to the woman and pulls Kris to one side. "Come on, do it for Tamara. It's an important evening for her. Do it for her and Frauke."

"What has Frauke to do with it?"

"We're celebrating her this evening."

"Frauke is dead."

"Damn it, Kris, I know Frauke's dead, but we can still celebrate her. I'd celebrate you if you were dead."

Kris pulls a face.

"I hate Mexican food."

"I know."

"Why can't she find an Italian or an Indian restaurant? We've got over four hundred Indian restaurants in Berlin, and she has to want Mexican?"

"Our fajitas are great," the woman joins in, holding the sombrero out to Kris. "Please take it and I promise you won't have to join in the karaoke."

There's a cocktail in front of Tamara, the glass is full to the brim with crushed ice, slices of lime poking out of it here and there. In the middle of the table there's a second cocktail. There is a red paper sombrero on Tamara's head. It's plain that Tamara feels ill at ease. When she sees Kris and Wolf coming toward her, she jumps up from the table.

"Do you know how ridiculous the three of us look?" Kris says by way of greeting.

"I know," Tamara replies and points to the menu. "Who would guess that Metaxa is a Mexican restaurant? Can one of you explain that one to me? Metaxa's a Greek brandy, not a dive in Mexico."

"Maybe this place used to be Greek," says Kris, "and the new owner couldn't be bothered to change the neon sign."

"Yeah, maybe," Tamara agrees. "But I wanted to go to a Greek restaurant, not a Mexican one."

"Is that for me?"

Wolf points at the cocktail in the middle of the table.

"Hands off, that belongs to Frauke."

Kris and Wolf look at her.

"I know what Frauke would drink. We're here to celebrate her. So let's celebrate her properly."

"Not a problem," says Wolf and sits down. Kris hesitates for a moment before he too sits down. His sombrero is yellow, Wolf's is blue.

"Why are you so late?" Tamara asks. "It's half past six, we agreed to meet at six."

On the way there the brothers talked for a long time about what to tell Tamara. In the end they decided to say nothing.

"Something came up," says Wolf, and looks quickly at the menu.

"Brilliant excuse," says Tamara.

Kris points at Wolf.

"It's his fault, you don't have to look at me like that."

A waitress stops by their table. They give their orders. When the waitress is gone, Kris remarks that she wasn't wearing a sombrero.

"So?" says Tamara.

Kris takes off his sombrero and scrunches it up. He drops it on the floor, leans forward and does the same with his friends' sombreros.

"Hey, I wanted to keep mine," Wolf complains.

"You can get another one on the way out," says Kris. "At any rate I can't take you seriously if you're wearing these things."

As they wait for their food, they talk about Frauke. And at this point we'll look away and block our ears. Because it's private.

· 303 ·

We'll just wait till Wolf raises his glass and all three of them raise a toast to Frauke. And we'll also wait till the food comes and a portion of enchilada is set down for Frauke in the middle of the table. It's a good farewell. We don't need to learn any more than that.

Three hours later they're sitting in the villa, discovering that twenty-six new and seventeen old jobs are waiting to be dealt with. They sit together until after midnight, compare schedules and divide up the customers. At some point Kris goes upstairs and sends the file to Meybach.

Wolf is surprised at how quickly they fall back into their routine. *It's what Frauke would have wanted.* He senses her presence. In every room. During the funeral Wolf had decided that he would do everything to ensure that Frauke didn't simply vanish from their lives. Not like Erin. Two weeks partying, two weeks of happiness and that confidence, her incredible confidence.

How could she be so confident?

After Erin's death Wolf discovered almost nothing usable about her. Her parents weren't interested in talking to him. Two of her friends had coffee with him, but said they hadn't heard from her for a year. They passed a few snapshots across the table to him. Erin didn't look like Erin. Wolf left the photographs where they were. Even if Erin started haunting him in the form of other women, she remained a stranger to him, one who had fizzled out like a firework after a two-week guest appearance in his life. He doesn't want that to happen to him again.

"Wolf, is that okay with you?"

"What?"

"The boxes."

Wolf blinks and looks at Tamara. He doesn't know where Kris has got to. A moment ago the three of them were sitting around the living room table, and suddenly he's alone with Tamara. *I should tell her,* he thinks, and is a bit scared of her reaction. Tamara knows that Erin has met him time and again since her death, like a restless spirit. In the form of other women, in cafés, in the street. But Tamara doesn't know that Erin disappeared without a trace the day Tamara and Wolf made love on the shore of the Lietzensee.

Wolf looked for Erin. He kept an eye out for her because it was a little as if someone had stolen the memory of his great love from him. Wolf knows that he's lying to himself, but for a while it's been a good lie. However hard he looked, Erin was lost without a trace, and Wolf wondered how to tell Tamara.

You exorcised her ghost. Is that true love?

"Where were you?" asks Tamara.

"What?"

"In your thoughts, where were you?"

"Here and there," Wolf replies and rubs his face.

Tamara walks around the table and puts her arms around his chest. Her body to his back. Warm and safe.

"When are we going to tell Kris?" she whispers in his ear.

"I thought you'd never ask," Wolf whispers back and hears her breath as close as if she were sitting in the middle of his head.

"Tomorrow morning?"

"Tomorrow morning is good."

"You or me?"

"Me. Why are we whispering?"

"Because it's sexy, because I know that you can hardly sit still when I whisper in your ear."

Wolf shuts his eyes and touches her cheek over his shoulder. They sit like that for a moment as if the moment was made only for them—a man and a woman, touching one another.

THE MAN WHO WASN'T THERE

HE ISN'T INTERESTED in the girl, girls are alien to him. It's always been like that. Fanni was an exception. Boys are much closer to him. They are sons.

He shuts the door behind him and stands in the dark. He remembers the first time he saw Karl. How the boy's head felt under his hand. So firm and yet fragile. So easy to manipulate. There was this one gesture, when Karl laid his head on one side and looked at him. Affection. With the onset of age memories and yearnings are his life's only spice. He knows he thinks about family too much. He never wanted to end up an old man devoured by the past. And yet days accumulate when he is filled with yearning for those times and has to press the balls of his hands to his eyes to silence the thoughts.

After he has gotten used to the dark, he takes off his shoes and leaves them next to the door. He looks into the kitchen and curiously sniffs the air. He opens the fridge, looks in, shuts it again. For a few seconds he lets his hand rest on the tabletop and listens. On the wall next to the fridge there's a bulletin board. Bits of paper, stickers, mottos and notes. He takes one of the pieces of paper and turns it over. On its blank side he writes a message. He pins it to the board. No, no one will notice it there. He takes the piece of paper and looks for a spot above the sink between two concert posters. Lloyd Cole and the Commotions on the left and Madrugada on the right. He takes a step back. He likes what he sees. In the gloomy moonlight his paper sits perfectly between the posters.

He goes back to the hall and is about to climb the stairs when he meets his reflection. He holds his index finger to his lips for a second and walks on. The stairs don't creak, the hinges of the doors are oiled.

As if they were expecting me.

The girl is sleeping on her side. One hand beside her head, the other resting around a knee. He looks at her face, he sees her lips moving as she breathes. *Easy.* He turns away and feels a flush of confidence. He is who he is. A negative quantity.

Behind the next two doors he finds offices and finally an abandoned room with an unmade bed. The shelves are empty, by one wall there are suitcases, bags, boxes. It looks as if one of the four is about to move out.

On the next floor up he stops for a while by the older boy and admires the fragility of his sleep. The last room is at the end of the corridor. He shuts the door behind him and squats down beside the bed. He's surprised at how easy it all is. As if he'd been here many times before. His heart beats rhythmically, his muscles are supple, everything is in equilibrium. He wishes his doctor could see him now. Tonight he thinks he's capable of anything.

The pupils beneath the boy's eyelids are darting around. The man rests his hand on his forehead. There's so much sadness there. He senses it. The pupils come to a standstill. *A person can hide nothing in his sleep,* he thinks and whispers reassuringly:

"I'm here."

KRIS

THE NEXT MORNING Wolf has disappeared.

"What do you mean, *he's disappeared?*"

Tamara points up the stairs.

"Have a look for yourself."

Kris goes upstairs. The bedroom door is ajar, the sheets folded back, the bed made. Wolf never makes his bed. The previous day's clothes are draped over a chair, his cell phone and his watch on the bedside table next to it. Kris goes back downstairs. Wolf's shoes are in the corridor, his jacket is on the hook, and when Kris puts his hand in the pockets, he finds Wolf's keys.

He opens the front door. Wolf's car is still exactly where he parked it yesterday.

"Do you see what I mean now?" Tamara says behind him.

Kris doesn't turn around. He sees what she means.

Wolf has disappeared.

Anything is possible. Wolf has taken different shoes, Wolf doesn't need a jacket, it's mild outside, Wolf has forgotten everything, Wolf has had enough and is traveling around the world. Anything is possible.

But Wolf wouldn't just disappear like that. Not Wolf.

"I wish we'd argued," says Kris, rattling the gate to the property, which is still locked.

Tamara looks up.

"Do you think he climbed over it?"

"Perhaps. Or over the wall. A ten-year-old could do that without having to try too hard."

"But why should he?"

"Good question."

Tamara shakes her head.

"Wolf would never forget his keys."

They go back to the villa and look through every nook and cranny. But whatever they do, Wolf has still disappeared.

They wait till midday. They phone Lutger and they phone the people stored in Wolf's address book. They sit over his calendar. His next appointment would have been in Duisburg in two days. They phone Duisburg. They go on waiting. At four o'clock Kris locks himself in the bathroom and tries to contact Meybach on his cell phone. Tamara isn't supposed to know. No one answers, no mailbox, nothing. Meybach's words echo in his head: *I'm going to disappear now. We no longer exist for one another.* Kris has to keep himself from driving to Charlottenburg and camping in front of Meybach's door. He's in a panic, he doesn't know what to do.

"Where are you going?"

"To get some air, I might bump into Wolf."

Kris knows how lame that sounds. *No more solo gigs,* he thinks, and asks Tamara if she wants to come with him.

They walk to the suburban rail stop and stand around on the platform for a while as if Wolf might get out of one of the cars at any moment. A fine drizzle starts falling and floats irresolutely in the air. They don't know what to say. On the way back to the villa Kris wants to voice his suspicion. *Why should someone who nails people to a wall stick to the rules?* In the end he leaves it be, because Tamara doesn't even know that they tracked down Meybach.

He thinks of the gun. It's in his wardrobe, right at the back with his socks. At least that's where he put it yesterday evening.

"What's up?" asks Tamara.

"Nothing, I . . ."

Kris wants to run, he wants to leave Tamara standing there and run to the villa to look for the gun. Because if the gun isn't there, it's clear what's happened. Part of him wants the gun to be right where he left it, another part wishes that Wolf has found it and driven to Meybach's place.

Please.

The gun is still behind the socks.

Kris wanders restlessly through the villa looking for clues. He wishes he had a bloodhound. It feels as if Wolf is present, although he isn't present. *Where on earth are you?* For a moment Kris even puts an ear to the wall and listens. He knows he has to pull himself together.

"If Wolf hasn't rung by tomorrow morning, we'll go and see Gerald," he decides that evening. "We'll go and see Gerald and tell him everything. And forget the consequences. This is about Wolf."

Every unnecessary caller is ignored this evening. They go on waiting. Saturday becomes Sunday. They wait until one in the morning, they wait until two, then they can't keep going and collapse. The nervous tension overtakes them, and they fall exhausted on their beds. Total unease. Kris rolls from one side to the other and dreams about the patch of forest. They're burying the man, and suddenly he isn't dead any more. He lies in the sleeping bag and he starts talking and says he doesn't want to be buried alive.

Damn it, let me out!

Kris wakes up breathing heavily and turns on the light. It's ten to four. He stares at the ceiling, the ceiling stares back. His head is a hollow space. He gets up, fetches the television from his study and puts it by the bed. Again and again he dozes off, again and again he wakes and looks at the screen. When the morning light colors his room blue, he turns the television off and gets into the shower. Then the toothbrush, then his reflection. When he comes down, he isn't surprised that Tamara has been awake for ages. She's lying on the sofa. Book in hand, teapot and cup on a side table.

"How long?" he asks.

"Since four," she says.

The blue morning light has disappeared, the sunbeams whirl through the windows as if they were still drunk from the night before. Dust glitters in the air. Tamara and Kris sit down in the kitchen and have their breakfast. They don't want to go into the conservatory. There were three of them sitting in the conservatory the previous morning. Nothing is as it should be. They are so withdrawn that they don't even notice the piece of paper between the posters.

An unpleasant silence spreads. *It's sad when you can't bear silence with the people close to you,* Kris thinks and stands up.

"I'll put some music on."

In the sitting room he crouches down by the stereo, rummages among the CDs, and puts on Iron and Wine. The guitar, the voice. When he straightens up again he glances outside. It's unequivocally the wrong weather to miss his brother, just as three days ago it was the wrong weather to put a friend under the ground. Spring is exploding, Kris sees it everywhere. He wants to go back to Tamara and tell her they can phone Gerald, that the weather's getting on his nerves, that he's had enough of searching inside himself for explanations of Wolf's disappearance, when he notices a shimmering on the ground. It's like a déjà vu. Startled, he looks at his feet and expects them to be standing in a puddle. Then he looks to the right. Wolf isn't by his side, Tamara is still sitting in the kitchen, Kris is standing alone in the living room, and Iron and Wine are singing 'We Gladly Run in Circles,' and winking and nodding in the garden once again are the white heads of a bunch of lilies.

THE MAN WHO WASN'T THERE

THE MAN IS DRINKING his second coffee when the villa slowly comes to life. Light on the first floor, light on the ground floor. Kris and Tamara. Now he knows everything he wanted to know about the girl and the brother. Yesterday it took them two hours to notice the boy's disappearance. They scoured the whole area for him. The man watched it all. They stayed awake until late at night. Wolf. The boy insisted that he call him by his name. The man refused. He sips from the coffee and raises the binoculars again. He is a patient man. He knows they will discover the lilies in the garden at any moment.

Yesterday afternoon he saw the girl sitting smoking nervously under one of the chestnut trees and looking over at the Belzens' house. He wasn't concerned. He knew they couldn't see him. He focused the binoculars. He was so close to the girl that he could make out her face in detail. The sight was soothing. Fear and worry.

I see something that you don't see.

The girl went back into the villa. The man waited for the brother and was disappointed. After another five minutes he turned away from the window and went down into the cellar. He tried to be quiet as he did so.

The first time the man visited him was at nine in the morning. He bound him and pulled a pillowcase over his head. The boy had completely lost his bearings. The man could see that the boy was in a bad state. His heartbeat was irregular, and he had difficulty breathing. The man knows that the anesthetic was responsible for that. His doctor told him about the side effects of Isoflurane, but there's a big difference between theory and practice.

The man pushed the pillowcase up and held a bottle of water to the boy's mouth. The boy spat and cursed, he wouldn't drink. Then the man went back upstairs and went on watching the villa.

The second time the man stopped ten feet away from the boy before he spoke to him. He didn't curse him this time, just listened.

He doesn't know if I'm actually here.

The man tried to remember the feeling of being young and hungry and helpless. It was hard. Now he's hungry all the time, and his body is being consumed by that hunger. Before, hungry meant being strong. Today the hungry are helpless and weak. The justice of this world is a lie.

The boy sat naked on the chair. Muscles, sinews, the dark rivers of his veins. The nest between his legs was just a shadow, sweat covered his chest. It was hot in the cellar. The man stood motionless in front of the boy and admired his body. That morning he would have given a lot to wear the boy's skin.

Just for a day, even an hour.

The man sighed, giving himself away. The boy threw his head back and screamed for help. The man could hear that his breathing was improving. The gray color of his skin had vanished as well. His wrists and ankles were rubbed bloody, the nylon tape had sunk deep into his skin. The boy must be in pain.

The man endured the screams of help for a minute, then went back upstairs and washed his hands. He couldn't help it, he had to touch the boy. His trembling thighs, the softness of his hair.

It was the only way.

He turned the water off and listened. He wasn't worried. The house swallowed the screams as dry soil swallows a sudden fall of rain. The man looked at his watch. He would give the boy a few hours to calm down, then he would come and visit him again.

WOLF

WOLF TRIES TO REMEMBER. He sits in the dark and feels as if he's just come out of an operation. Spaced, zonked, and not really alive. There is something around his head, blocking his vision. He tenses his arms. His hands are on his back, he can't move his feet. Wolf tries to stand up, there's a jerk, something chokes him. He falls back on the chair and gasps for air. *Where am I?* Wolf tries to reconstruct what it was that brought him here.

Tamara?

Tamara came to him in the night. First there was the click of the door, and a moment later she was lying beside him, and he felt her nakedness. She felt familiar and alien at the same time.

His voice:

"How long are we going to do this?"

Her voice:

"Not long now. We'll tell Kris tomorrow."

Sex. They had made love, he still remembers that very clearly. Afterwards they lay there in the dark, and he felt as if he were glowing from inside. They were contented. Eventually Tamara sat up and wanted to go. His voice again.

"Stay."

He hadn't just meant that he wanted her to stay with him in bed. He had also meant: *Stay by my side for as long as you can.* He had meant: *Forever.*

She had kissed him, she hadn't wanted Kris to find everything out by some stupid accident. She had wanted him to hear it from them, so Wolf let her go. One last kiss. The footsteps, the closing of the door.

His eyes. His eyes had fallen shut. Contented, exhaustion. He had lain there and preserved the feeling of her still at his side. The impression on the mattress, her warmth. He had gone to sleep like that and dreamed of Erin. At last she was back. He remembers the relief.

They were lying on a hill. There was no city to be seen, no street, just flowing treetops. He sensed Erin beside him. There was the wind blowing over them as if they were both part of the landscape; there was a bird calling to another bird, and in between, clearly and distinctly, Erin's breathing. *Talk to me,* he thought, and Erin started talking and snuggled closely to his side, and her kisses covered his neck and wandered up to his cheek until he felt her lips on his, and then at last he saw her. *At last.* Her eyes, her hair. The way she watched him as if nothing else in the world existed, just her and him, and he closed his eyes happily and knew he couldn't tell her about Tamara, he could never let Erin go like that, because there was that familiar whisper when she took off her blouse, there was that stillness and the sunlight on her skin made everything fall silent. *Wake up,* said Erin. And he smiled and kept his eyes closed. *Please, wake up.* And he stopped smiling, because there was something in her tone that he didn't recognize. *Listen, wake up.* And he opened his eyes, and the hill and Erin had disappeared, the landscape was a room in a villa far from the reality of his dreams, and he saw an old man sitting on his chest, and the old man was nodding as if he was pleased that Wolf had woken up, and then the old man leaned forward and made Wolf disappear back into the darkness.

THE MAN WHO WASN'T THERE

"NOW THAT YOU'RE FEELING better, let's chat," said the man, and pulled the pillowcase off the boy's head. The man saw the boy closing his eyes tight, the ceiling light was blinding, the reaction was normal. Their eyes met, and the man curiously observed the sheer fury in the boy's eyes, and was not surprised. *Be furious if you want.* The boy looked down at himself, and his fury turned into panic. He was sitting naked on the chair, and his feet were tied to the chair legs. What he couldn't see were his hands behind his back. The man had bound them with nylon tape, he had pulled the nylon tape through a hook on the wall that led back to the boy and lay as a noose around his neck. The man didn't want to take any risks. He told the boy that. He also told him that education was an elementary part of life. And that applied to everybody, whether boys or girls.

"I'm not a boy!" said the boy. "My name is Wolf Marrer. I'm twenty-seven years old and I would like to know what the fuck's going on here."

Questions. The boy had so many questions. His eyes sought a means of escape. He tried to understand the room. He had no idea where he was.

"Where is this place?"

"Why am I naked?"

"Who are you?"

So many questions. And now:

"Are you Meybach? Are you that fucking asshole? I thought it was over. You said you'd disappear. What have we done now?"

A flood of questions. The man waited until the boy had fallen silent, then he cleared his throat and said:

"It doesn't matter where we are. It doesn't matter who I am. The rules are very simple. I will ask you questions, and you will give me the answers. If I don't like the answers, I will go away again and keep you waiting. I can do that all day long. I can keep it up for a whole week. If you like, I'll never come back. But you'll want me to come back. You will beg me to come back. That's how it has always been. You're all the same. You want to be free up there."

He tapped the boy on the forehead. Gently. The boy recoiled. They looked at each other. The boy who was a man, who didn't want to be a boy. And him. The man who wasn't there. He asked the first question.

"Why?"

"What?"

"Tell me why?"

"Why what?"

"Why did you kill her?"

The boy has jerked back as if the man had tried to hit him. It was like an answer. The man thinks it was an unambiguous answer.

Guilt.

"I have no idea who you're talking about."

"Good," said the man, "good. Let's start over again."

He looked at the boy, he waited, then he repeated:

"Why did you kill her?"

The boy looked down and spat. The man looked at the spit on the carpet. Suddenly the boy jumped up. The man sat where he was, he didn't flinch by so much as a millimeter. The noose dug into the boy's neck and pulled him back onto the chair. He sat still again, red in the face and breathing heavily.

"If you relax, the pressure will gradually ease."

The boy tried to relax.

"Poor boy."

"I'm ... I'm not a boy," came the tight-lipped reply.

"Poor, poor boy."

"I said, I'm ..."

The man stretched out his hand and wiped a tear from the

boy's cheek. The boy tried to turn his head away, and the noose made him grimace.

"Fanni."

"What?"

"Her name was Fanni."

"I don't know any Fanni."

"She was my daughter. First you drove into the forest with her corpse, but then something happened. You had an argument, didn't you? You changed your minds and buried her on your property. Why on earth?"

The boy tried to reply, but the man raised his hand.

"Don't try to deny it. I watched it all, you understand? I saw it. Her name was Fanni. She was my daughter, and now she's lying two floors above us."

The boy looked at the cellar ceiling; when he lowered his eyes again, the man was holding his hands out to him.

"I had to dig up Fanni with my own hands. It was very undignified, what you did to my girl. How could you bring yourselves to nail her to a wall? Tell me why you did that? Come on, talk to me. Why?"

The boy lowered his head, his voice was a murmur.

" . . . Shit, oh fucking shit, I knew we wouldn't get away with it. I knew, knew, knew it, I . . ."

The man made the boy talk, he was patient, he had nurtured lots of boys in his life, and could tell when they broke and when they healed again. This boy was no exception. The man waited and said not a single word. Then the boy began to tell his story.

That was yesterday, now a new day has dawned, it's Sunday, 9:21 in the morning, and the girl and the brother are running out of the villa. They're barefoot, they must just have woken up. The man imagines how one of them looked out the window and discovered the lilies on the ground. Now they're running. The man wishes he could see the expressions on their faces more clearly. Stop time and look at them from all sides. And if he could freeze-frame it, he would take the boat, row across, and stand next to them. He would like to smell their fear. Smell betrays so much. He doesn't know who he should focus the binoculars on, so he tries to keep them both in view. As they kneel on the ground and push the lilies aside and start digging. They're using their hands. They don't even think of the spades in the shed. *Not yet.* He watches them, their mouths move, then the girl jumps up and runs to the shed.

Clever girl, he thinks.

Yesterday the man learned the truth from the boy one piece at a time. He was amazed at what a story like this could mean, and was surprised when he heard that the second woman was dead. Frauke. How could so much happen in the short time that he was in the hospital?

"An agency that apologizes?"

"It was my brother's idea."

"Your brother must be pretty bright."

"Please, that's all I know. Can we bring this to an end now?"

The boy looked over at the cellar door.

"Can I go now? That's really all I know."

The man tilted his head, the boy went on talking hastily:

"I'm really sorry about what happened to your daughter. It wasn't us. We didn't do anything to—"

"And you never saw Meybach?" the man interrupted him.

"I never saw Meybach. How many more times do I have to say that?"

"And if Meybach were to come down the stairs now and claim the opposite, what would happen then?"

"Then he would be a liar."

"Tell me his address again."

The boy repeated it. The man nodded, he was content.

"And Karl?" he asked.

"Who's Karl?"

The man smiled.

"You know who I mean."

The man read in the boy's face that he knew who Karl was. But he read more than that. Karl was no more.

The man got to his feet, turned out the light, and went upstairs. He ignored the boy's screams and entreaties. *Karl*, he thought, *Fanni*, he thought and sat for a while in the living room and could think of nothing but his children.

Hours later the man came back. This time he didn't sit down.

"Can I believe you?"

"Why should I lie?"

"I bear the responsibility here, it wouldn't be a good idea to lie to me."

"Responsibility for what?"

"Responsibility for your life. For the lives of your friends. Do you know what that means? It's a burden. I'm an old man. I can't bear as much as I used to before. Before, none of this would have been a problem, but I have a weak heart. I'm cold and tired. Do you understand?"

The boy didn't understand.

The man said it didn't really matter. He put his hands on his knees and leaned forward as if talking to a five-year-old. In a quiet voice he said:

"Let's start all over again from the beginning. Tell me why you killed my children."

The boy started crying.

"What did you do to Karl? Where is he? What did you do to Fanni? And why? Speak to me, boy, speak to me."

The boy closed his eyes tight and said he'd told him everything already, he repeated it again and again.

"I've told you everything, I swear it."

The man just smiled.

Then the boy turned noisy.

"WE'RE A FUCKING AGENCY, OKAY? WE APOLOGIZE FOR PEOPLE WHO HAVEN'T THE BALLS TO DO IT THEMSELVES, DO YOU GET THAT? IS THAT WHY I'M HERE? ARE YOU SOME KIND OF RELIGIOUS FANATIC? DID THE CHURCH SEND YOU?"

"I'm here because of Fanni," the man said calmly. "I'm here because of Karl. No one sent me."

The boy's voice turned into a whisper, the rage was gone, giving way to resignation.

"I've said everything there is to say. He told us it was a normal job. I walked into that apartment, and there was the woman's corpse . . ."

"Fanni."

"Yes, for fuck's sake, Fanni! We just did what he wanted. He threatened us. All of us. And anyway she was dead."

"I know. I was in the apartment, I saw her."

The boy shook his head.

"There was no one there but us."

The man smiled again.

"I'm innocent," said the boy. "We're all innocent."

"No, that's not how I see it," said the man. "If you were innocent, you wouldn't be here. I am the punishment, do you understand? No? It's quite simple. Life has a balance of its own. Ask yourself the question again: How could I have managed to bring you here if you were innocent? Equilibrium is everything. You take something, you give something. You can't just take. Don't you believe in equilibrium? Don't you believe in good and evil? I'm good in this case, I know that, but I'm not sure what you are. Are you evil?"

The boy reared up. The nylon tape cut into his neck, it pulled itself tighter around his wrists. The boy didn't let that stop him. His words were poison.

"*I'M* FUCKING GOOD, YOU SICK FUCK. *YOU* TIED ME UP HERE, *YOU* DRAGGED ME HERE AND TIED ME UP. THEY WERE

ALREADY DEAD WHEN WE FOUND THEM. DON'T YOU GET
THAT? YOUR DAUGHTER AND YOUR SON *WERE ALREADY
DEAD.*"

The boy sank back into the chair. His face purple, his
breathing heavy. The man saw that this wasn't going to work
for much longer. He told him what he thought. That was how
it had always been.

"And how did that just sound? If you ask me, that didn't sound
like *good. Good* is like a song. It's melody. That wasn't a song, I
heard no melody. Tell me, do you feel guilty?"

Quiet, meek:

"Yes, of course, of course I feel guilty."

"Can I just let you go like that?"

"Please, I told you I was sorry."

"I asked. I can't let you go like that."

The boy nodded. There was hope in his face. The man went
to the workbench and picked up the pillowcase.

"That's not necessary," the boy said quickly and turned his
face away.

"It is very necessary, I don't want you to learn where you can
find me. How stupid do you think I am?"

He pulled the pillowcase over the boy's head. He put his hand
on the boy's shoulder. He told him everything would be fine. He
also told him not to worry.

"Stay calm," said the man, and injected the Isoflurane into
the boy's upper arm.

Less than two minutes have passed since the girl and the brother
ran out of the villa. The man feels as if he can control time.
Every time he holds his breath, everything outside freezes, and
only starts moving again when he breathes out.

The brother kneels on the earth and digs without interrup-
tion. When the girl comes out of the shed with no spades, he
ignores her and goes on digging. The man knows what the girl

is saying. He can read it on her lips. *The spades are gone.* He could call out to her where she would find the spades. The man has made sure it won't be easy for them. He wants them to go back to the source. He wants to see them kneeling on the ground and fighting against fate. He wants them to suffer the greatest doubts. And as he sees them digging there, he thinks: *It isn't the guilt that you're living with, it's your failure that makes you kneel in the dirt.* The man is pleased with this thought. Everything comes to a close. He lifts his hand and puts it to the windowpane as if waving to them. He notices the dirt under his fingernails and brings his hand back down. He shuts his eyes and wonders what it would be like to connect their pain with his. It would be the purest form of all emotions. It would be love.

TAMARA

TAMARA CAN'T BELIEVE THE spades have disappeared. She remembers exactly which wall they were leaning against. She rages through the shed, she overturns the wheelbarrow and is in such a panic that the room seems to quiver in front of her eyes. She looks in the corners, she looks behind the bicycles, she runs back outside.

"The spades are gone!"

Kris doesn't react, his hands shovel the soil aside. Sweat runs into his eyes, the breath leaves his mouth with a hiss. Tamara can see that he didn't even notice she had gone. She crouches down beside him. They go on digging.

With every movement her arms get heavier and heavier. Tamara can't go on. Her fingers are bleeding, her knees hurt. Kris, on the other hand, digs like a machine. He shovels the soil backward, rams his fingers into the dirt again, squats tirelessly in the excavated trench. And as Tamara watches him for a moment she understands what's wrong with this situation, and feels laughter rising up in her. Pure hysteria.

"He isn't here," she says.

Kris carries on. Tamara grabs him by the arm.

"Kris, he isn't here," she repeats emphatically. "It's a bad joke."

Kris looks at her. *At last,* Tamara thinks, wishing at the same time that he would go on digging. Something in his eyes. Blank, hard, strange.

"Let go of me."

"Wolf isn't here, Meybach's playing with us. It's nonsense, just think about it, why should he—"

"Tamara, let go of me, or I'll break your arm!"

She flinches and lets go of him. Kris goes on digging. He is no longer looking at her. His next words hurt.

"Go into the house if you can't keep at it."

Tamara hesitates. She wants to believe it's just a bad joke, she doesn't want Kris to take this hope away from her. Wolf walking through the gate and asking what they're doing. *Please.* Wolf, calling out from one of the windows to ask what they're up to. *Please, come.* In that case it would all be nothing but the black humor of a lunatic, who has made them bury two corpses over the past week.

Nothing more than that.

Tamara gouges her fingers into the earth again and goes on digging.

"Kris?"

"What?"

"Kris, I . . ."

The skin is like rubber. The skin is cold and not of this world. Tamara has found the right arm. It's the hand with the bandage. The hand feels alien and wrong. As if all its bones were broken. No resistance. The wrist looks as if cords have cut into the flesh. Tamara immediately wants to tend to the wound, she wants to wash it and put a bandage on it. Kris reaches for the hand. Tamara starts frantically shoving the soil away from around it. She doesn't want to but she looks up. Kris has pressed the hand to his face. Soil, dirt, two fingers covering his mouth. Tamara wants to scream, she chokes on the air and coughs, she stares down and keeps digging. A shoulder, she reveals a naked shoulder. She looks for his face, while Kris whimpers beside her, no words, just quiet whimpering.

There's a pillowcase around Wolf's head. The fabric is damp from the soil, a washed-out green with an embroidered lily. Kris tries to pull the fabric off Wolf's head and can't do it. Tamara leans forward and bites a hole in it with her teeth. She tastes detergent and soil. Kris enlarges the hole, the fabric rips and there is Wolf's face, and Wolf looks as if he's sleeping. Not a crumb of soil sullies his face, he is pale, his skin almost transparent. *As if he weren't there,* thinks Tamara, and turns away and weeps into her dirty hands and sinks sideways and lies doubled-up in the trench and hears Kris uttering noises that she's never heard before. Like a wounded animal forced to watch its young being murdered.

Kris carries him into the house. Kris carries him upstairs to the bathroom. He washes him in the tub. He dries him. Then he carries him back downstairs and lays him on the sofa. Kris covers him up. He turns round and looks at Tamara. He just looks at her.

"Kris?" says Tamara. "Kris?"

"I'm here," says Kris, "I can hear you."

They sit on the floor by the sofa holding each other tight. The day eats itself. It grows dark around them. For a while Tamara thinks it will stay like that. Forever. She and Kris in an embrace. Hours, days, weeks. *Make it years.* Wolf on the sofa behind them, inches away, and outside a world that turns and turns and couldn't care less what happens to them.

Tamara is woken by the noises from the kitchen. She is lying alone on the floor. It's light outside. When she sits up her eye falls on the sofa. Wolf is still covered up to his neck, eyes closed, motionless. Tamara puts her hand under the blanket, rests it on his bare chest, and feels nothing under it.

Kris stands in the kitchen by the espresso machine. He has dismantled it into its constituent parts. The surface is a chaos of bolts and gaskets.

"Kris?"

He turns around. There are blue shadows under his eyes. Tamara doesn't think he's slept.

"What are you doing?"

Kris looks at the machine as if to see what his hands are doing.

"I wanted to clean it, but then I couldn't stop. I wanted to really clean it. Every bit, you understand?"

Tamara goes and stands next to him.

"What's this?" she asks, holding up one of the gaskets.

"No idea," says Kris, setting down the screwdriver.

They drink tea. They sit at the kitchen table and drink tea in silence. Tamara doesn't want to ask, but she knows she must. She gives Kris five minutes, then another five, and then she says:

"What do we do now?"

Kris looks across to the living room.

"Kris, we have to do something. We have to go and see Gerald."

"I know."

"We have to tell him everything."

Kris looks at her.

"Do you think I don't know that?"

They hear the ticking of the clock.

"When?"

"When what?"

"When will we talk to Gerald?"

Kris looks past Tamara again.

"How on earth could he do that?"

For a moment Tamara thinks Kris means Wolf, then she shrugs. How can she answer that? How could anyone answer that?

"I don't know," she says.

"We didn't get in his way, and he broke his word even so . . ."

Kris says nothing, his hands grip the cup, his thumbs rub the ceramic rim.

"Shall I leave you alone with Wolf?" Tamara asks.

"Why would you do that?"

"I just thought you . . ."

She falls silent and realizes that she's projecting. She didn't have a single moment alone with Frauke. It all happened too quickly. She wishes she'd insisted on seeing Frauke one more time. Alone.

"Go on then," says Kris.

Tamara goes to Wolf and stays with him for a while.

Later, when she comes upstairs, Kris is standing at his study window looking through the window. Tamara taps against the door frame.

"Am I bothering you?"

"No, it's fine, come in," says Kris without turning around. "I was just talking to Gerald. We're meeting in his office at four."

"That's good."

"Yes."

For a moment they say nothing.

"Kris? Please look at me."

Kris turns around.

"If you like I'll stay with Wolf, you just have to say the word."

"Please," he says, "please, stay with Wolf. One of us should keep an eye on him."

Tamara nods and goes back downstairs. In the kitchen she puts on some water for tea, and her eye falls on the components of the espresso machine. She makes a bet with herself. *If I can put that thing back together before Kris comes back, everything will be fine.* She waits for the water to boil and studies the parts. As she is pouring the water, she hears Kris coming downstairs. He says he'll be back by six at the latest.

"I'll call you when I'm on my way."

Tamara looks at the clock above the door. It's three. She strains out the tea leaves and hears Kris driving away from the property. After she has filled a cup with tea, she puts the components of the espresso machine on a tray and takes everything into the living room. She adjusts one of the chairs in such a way that she can see Wolf on the sofa. Then she calmly begins to assemble the espresso machine.

KRIS

KRIS RUNS THROUGH the city until five o'clock, trying to clear his head. He's glad Tamara doesn't know how close he and Wolf got to Meybach two days ago. Shortly after five Kris sits down in a park and calls Tamara. He tells her everything's gone well with Gerald so far. He finds lying easy, it's always easier to lie when you have nothing to lose.

"He wants to come and see us tomorrow."

"And Wolf . . ."

"We'll take care of Wolf as well," Kris finishes her thought for her.

Tamara asks him when he's coming home.

"I need another moment to myself. Otherwise everything okay with you?"

"The espresso machine's working again."

"Brilliant."

"Kris?"

"What?"

"Please come back soon."

"I promise."

He hangs up. The second big lie of the day has been easy for him too. He turns off his cell phone. It's done. He's unreachable now.

It's nine in the evening, the restaurants are crowded and spring is a phony summer. Kris doesn't know what interests him less. He sits in his car opposite Meybach's apartment and looks at the building. Three hours is enough to find a parking space even on Leonardstrasse. The windows of Meybach's apartment are dark. Meybach's neighbor came home at eight. Kris has forgotten what his name is. Thomas or Theo. Kris wonders whether he should speak to him, but then thinks that in this state he'd rather not see anyone. The gun lies in his lap like an insistent erection. He doesn't know why he's holding on to it. And he doesn't know what he'll do when he's standing in front of Meybach.

At ten to nine the front door opens and Meybach's neighbor comes out. He is wearing a tracksuit, and does a few stretching exercises outside the building before jogging off toward the park. Kris knows what Wolf would say now. *What on earth are you doing? I thought you had a plan.* Kris rests his forehead against the steering wheel and shuts his eyes, then he stirs himself, picks up the gun and stuffs it into his jacket. He has a plan.

The front door isn't locked. Kris goes up the stairs, stops by the door to the apartment, and rings the bell. He knows Meybach isn't there. He rings again. Better safe than sorry. Five minutes later he sits down on the steps and calls the emergency key service. He has written down the number. The key service is around the corner in Kantstrasse. The man says he can be there in ten minutes. Kris tells him the front door is open and he should just come upstairs.

"Which floor?"

"The third. Meybach."

He comes in seven minutes. Kris tries to look guilty and depressed. The man takes a look at the lock and asks if Kris wants to keep it.

"Costs extra," he warns.

"Extra's okay."

The man takes less than five minutes to crack the lock and open the door.

"The key will stick a bit at first because of the metal filings and stuff, but that'll go away. If it doesn't, give me a call and I'll take care of it. Do you want an invoice?"

"Don't worry about it."

Kris pays in cash and adds twenty.

"Enjoy the rest of your Sunday," says the man from the key service. His steps ring out on the stairs. Kris stands in the doorway for a moment before going inside and closing the door behind him.

Whatever happens now, he thinks, *Meybach belongs to me.*

And he doesn't come.

And he still doesn't bloody come.

Kris sits in the dark. He has taken a look around the apartment. He's taken a flashlight from a drawer. He has found photographs of Meybach and now he understands everything. Twice he's tempted to call Tamara. To calm her down, to tell her what really happened.

But he decides not to.

The chair is placed in such a way that Kris can see the apartment door. It's like in one of those thrillers. Guy comes home, and his killer's sitting there. They talk a bit, then the killer says that's it. The camera wanders to one of the windows, we hear the shot offscreen, and that really is it. And on a distant soundtrack we hear the thoughts of our main character. The same three sentences over and over.

I know I'm not a killer.
I know I can do this.
I wish Wolf were here.

PART VIII

After

AND AGAIN AND AGAIN the question arises of where we made our mistake. I don't know, I don't get it, and it's killing me and it hurts all the way into my bones that I don't know, because we must have made some sort of mistake.

I just woke up breathlessly, grief flooded over me in my sleep, the inside of the car is filled with an acrid smell. My face is wet with tears. I think *Wolf.* I think *Frauke.* And my fists hammer against the steering wheel, again and again.

It's the fifth or sixth day. I can't remember. Like drifting through fog. Disoriented, uncomprehending. Outside dusk is falling, and there are a number of cars at the rest stop. I'm beginning to get careless. It's exhaustion. Thoughts are weary of constantly thinking the same thing. *Show me the mistake and I'll give up.* I'm lying, I won't give up. I've got to do something. I've got to finish this story, or it will finish me.

I start the car and drive away from the rest stop.

Two hours later. Off the highway. Into the patch of forest. If only I had a spade with me. If only I had a gun. Or an axe. I open the trunk. He doesn't wake up. He doesn't hear me. I don't want to touch him. I stand there and can't touch him. He's no longer a human being. No eyes, no mouth. The tape turns him into a thing. Only his nose is free, and his nostrils are flaring. He's breathing, he's still breathing. And I can't touch him. I can't end it. The trees are moving over my head. Always in one direction. Nothing but signposts. *That way.* I sit down in the grass, I lie down in the grass. Now I know where my path is taking me. I understand. The knowledge is such a relief that I close my eyes and go to sleep.

That way.

Yes.

Before

YOU

WE HAVEN'T HEARD FROM you for so long that we've almost forgotten you exist. How many days ago is it? Three? Or is it four already? You're aware that you've created a lot of confusion, and then you seriously thought you could just disappear invisibly back into your life and disconnect the line? You were probably really pleased to be allowed to disappear like that. *Forgiveness and peace and goodbye.* But that's not how things work. You can't conjure up ghosts and then turn away when they're suddenly standing in front of you. That's just not how it works.

They all made mistakes. Really, all of them. Trivial things, false steps, wrong decisions. Your mistake was to think it was over. The brothers came closer to you than ever before. During that time your existence reached a new level. A level of freedom. It's that exquisite taste of freedom that makes you feel every moment differently. The freedom to be you. The freedom to be. You.

But let's not leap ahead. Let's take a look at your Saturday, before it turns into Sunday and we can welcome you back into our circle.

On Saturday you gathered your papers together and terminated contracts. It was a lot of work, but you sorted everything out and began meticulously erasing clues. In the evening you went into a bar and met Natascha. It was your farewell present. You took her into the apartment, you had sex, and later you watched a film on television. It was a good finale.

On Sunday you caught up on the work of the last week and went into your office. At about eight o'clock in the evening you realized you'd forgotten your gym bag. You wanted to go to the new fitness center after work, and now you had no option but to go home. In your apartment you walked uneasily through the rooms and felt uncomfortable. Farewell is farewell. You were like a junkie who has to do without his fix for a day and tries to distract himself with trivia. At that moment you decided to go running. *Movement will be good for the restlessness,* you thought. Perhaps it would have been cleverer to yield to grief. Grief at the fact that the imprisonment is over. Honesty with yourself would have kept you at home. In grief. But you're not really that honest. And no one can help you if you're not honest with yourself.

It's late now. There are no joggers in the park. There's something reassuring about being the only one running through the darkness. Energy turns to peace, you're nothing but breath and rhythm, your head feels clear and free. You remember Frauke. How she sometimes ran along the water of the Wannsee. Self-contained. You watched her from a distance, and once you were on the point of running alongside her. *Am I disturbing you?* But then your courage failed you, and you stopped watching her running.

After the second circuit you decide that's enough for today. You walk down the pedestrian underpass, the traffic on Kantstrasse throbs above your head. You run to the end of the park and are about to leave it when you notice the man.

He's sitting slumped on a park bench, chin on his chest, arms in his lap. He reminds you of your grandfather, who could sleep anywhere and left the world like that—in his chair by the window, one arm on the armrest, the other on the windowsill, as if he were about to get up and cast one last glance.

You stop in front of him. You're not one of those idiots who have to dance up and down on the spot like restless horses every time they take a break.

"Is everything okay?" you ask.

The old man twitches, then lifts his head. Sixty, maybe seventy years old. A face that has seen everything. Marked by the sun. His look is weary and surprised.

"What?"

"You fell asleep. You should go home, it's late."

The man looks around. He isn't surprised now, he's startled.

"What . . . what time is it?" he asks and licks his lips.

You'd like to look after him, fetch him a glass of water, put his feet up. You push back the sleeves of your hoodie jacket and look at your watch.

"Just before ten."

"Oh my goodness," says the man, but doesn't move. He suddenly smiles at you. His smile is infectious.

"Do we know each other?" you ask and smile back.

"No, I don't think so."

The man shakes his head as if he's still deliberating, then he tries to stand up, trembling and unsteady. He looks at you apologetically and holds his hand out. You step forward. His fingers close around your wrist. For a moment it's embarrassing having him touch your sweat-drenched skin, but that moment loses its meaning when the darkness around you suddenly explodes in a dazzling light. Your bladder empties as you open your eyes wide and clearly and distinctly see the man's face. There's something almost religious about it. A revelation. As if you were seeing God.

"That's good," says the man, but you don't hear him now. You're just a quivering bundle on the forest path. Your nerves are jangling, your synapses are firing uselessly, and in a corner of your mind a voice calls loud, shrill warnings to you, but you don't understand a single syllable.

TAMARA

TAMARA WAITS. She spends the hours in the living room in the armchair. Now she understands why people keep vigil by the dead. It's the separation that's so hard. There's no going back. *Maybe being dead means being abandoned by everyone. And the longer you stay with the dead, the longer they stay alive.*

She tries to read. She tries to think. For a while she also tries to sleep, but the thoughts come creeping in. Something is gnawing at her, hazy and vague like the fragment of a dream. She turns on the television and hops from channel to channel, she wants to be distracted.

When night falls and she still hasn't heard from Kris, Tamara roams through the villa and is tempted several times to sit in the car. *And then?* She doesn't know where to drive to. For a few minutes she stares out of the window at the drive. Every approaching car fills her with hope; every car that drives past makes her even more insecure than she is already.

Did I misunderstand him? He said he needed a moment to himself. He didn't say it would turn into a whole night.

Tamara looks over at the television. In a field a woman is hanging up a hundred yards of washing. It looks silly, the woman is working like a hamster. Tamara turns off the television and is about to go upstairs to take a cold shower. A storm of images goes rushing through her head.

Kris leaning forward and pushing dirt away from Wolf's corpse.

Kris pressing Wolf's hand to his cheek.

Tamara using her teeth to . . .

She rushes to the remote and turns the television back on.

The detergent ad is over, the next commercial shows a cat that looks like a person. But Tamara has found the connection. She sees the memory clearly before her eyes. She sees Helena in her garden. She sees the taut clothesline, the basket of washing, the calm with which Helena hung out each individual piece. Kris joking that there was probably no one in the world who hung her washing out as slowly as the lady opposite. And Wolf added that as soon as Helena had hung out the last piece the first row was bound to be dry.

Tamara shuts her eyes tight and sees still more.

The Belzens' garden appears before her very clearly.

The clothesline and the wind moving the wet pieces of washing.

Pale green.

She opens her eyes, gets the flashlight from the chest of drawers in the hall and runs into the garden. She kneels in the dirt and doesn't have to look for too long. A corner of the pillowcase peeps out from the churned-up soil. *Pale green. Embroidered with lilies.* Tamara pulls out the pillowcase. She hears Helena calling out to her that there's nothing better than laundry drying in the sun. Helena raving about the smell as if every day had its own smell, while behind her the sheets and covers flicker pale green in the light. Tamara lowers the pillowcase and looks across at the Belzens' dark house.

She calls the Belzens'. She stands in the kitchen and watches the house. Kris still hasn't answered his cell phone. It turns nine, then ten. Tamara knows she can't sit idly around. There's something wrong over there. She sees the old man's face in front of her eyes, standing on the opposite shore and talking to her. She tries to remember the words, but it was only small talk, nothing significant.

He's an old man, what could he have to do with it?

And the pillowcase? What kind of coincidence is that?

Lilies again. Time and again, those damned lilies.

Tamara had only visited the Belzens once, they sat on the terrace and drank coffee. They hadn't talked about lilies, and no lilies grew in the Belzens' house.

They've been away for over a week and didn't tell us before they left.

Tamara goes upstairs and finds the gun in one of the boxes. Frauke was given the gas pistol by a friend years ago, and never used it. The gas pistol is an imitation revolver. No one would think of a gas pistol when they saw that gun. Tamara has no idea how the thing works. What matters is the first impression.

I could wait until Kris comes.

I could pull a blanket over my head and hide under it.

I could . . .

That's enough.

Tamara snaps open the barrel. It contains a yellow cartridge. She looks through the box, rummages through Frauke's things. There are no more cartridges to be found.

"Better than nothing," she murmurs and takes the gas pistol downstairs.

She drives across the Wannsee Bridge, turns into Conradstrasse and stops by the Kleine Wannsee, right in front of the Belzens' house. Her car is the only one in a ten-yard radius. No one opens the door when she rings the bell. Tamara walks through the garden and around the house. It's a strange feeling, seeing the villa on the opposite shore. That time with Astrid in the rowboat everything was new and exciting, now the villa seems familiar to her, and she's startled to see how desolate and deserted her home looks in the distance.

The motion detector reacts, the lights come on. Two beams illuminate Tamara and she tries not to look startled.

You know the Belzens, you're not a stranger, so don't act like one.

She looks up at the house. Three windows are ajar, and the terrace door is open a crack as well. Tamara reaches into the crack and pushes the door fully open. The stench makes her shrink back. She stays on the terrace and greedily breathes in the fresh air. When she steps to the door for the second time, she holds the sleeves of her blouse over her mouth. The stench reminds her of a summer on Norderney. Her parents had a holiday home that they visited twice a year. She found a dead cat under a bed. It had a wound in its head and its left ear was missing. It must have come into the house via the roof, to die in peace. In the Belzens' house it stinks as if a hundred cats had died.

Tamara turns on the flashlight. Everything looks normal. The sofa is in its place, no chairs have been overturned.

If it wasn't for that stench . . .

There's a glass in the kitchen sink. In the fridge there's cheese, milk, a loaf of bread. *Definitely away,* thinks Tamara, and follows the smell upstairs. Someone has taped the two doors closed with duct tape, as if to make sure that no one leaves the rooms. Tamara stops by one of the doors, reaches for the handle and presses it down. The door isn't locked, the handle pulls without resistance. The only resistance is coming from the tape, which stretches with a sigh as Tamara pulls on the door.

The stench gets worse. Tamara sets the flashlight down on the floor, turns her face away and pulls on the handle with both hands. A rasp, a crack, then the tape comes away and Tamara loses her balance for a moment.

The room is in darkness. The shutters are down, and no light comes in from outside. Tamara points the beam in front of her. Something comes flying at her, she jerks back. Flies, loads of flies. They beat against the glass of the flashlight. Tamara tries to keep the beam steady. She can see that she's in a bedroom. On the bed there are two figures covered with blankets; under the blanket something is twitching and trembling.

Get out of here, says a voice in Tamara's head. *You don't need to see what's hidden there. You know what it is, why do you have to look at it? What's wrong with you?*

Tamara throws the blanket aside.

Flies. Maggots. And what was once the Belzens.

* * *

After Tamara has thrown up, she hangs over the sink and splashes water in her face, rinses her mouth out and breathes frantically in and out. On no account does she want to see what lies behind the second sealed door. She's sure it's the old man who was looking after the house.

Meybach, you sick bastard, how could you?

So many things are being explained. How Meybach knew what they were doing. How he was so well informed. *He must have been watching us. He talked about us to the Belzens, and when he didn't need them any more, he killed them. He was watching us the whole time. Even when the police were there. All that time. He never had any intention of leaving us in peace.*

In the medicine cupboard Tamara finds a tube of tiger balm. She rubs a strip of it under her nose and inhales the sharp smell.

I've got to talk to Kris. I've got to call Gerald, and if Gerald isn't there, I'll talk to one of his colleagues. I'll tell him what I've seen. I'll—

One of the doors on the ground floor strikes the wall with a dull crash. The sound of footsteps. The door clicks shut again. Silence.

Tamara stands motionlessly in the bathroom. She looks at the ceiling, from which the light shines brightly and clearly down on her.

Whoever has come into the Belzens' house will see that there's a light on in the bathroom.

Tamara turns out the light and creeps to the door to close it. She holds her breath and is as quiet and still as the door behind her.

No one comes up the stairs.

Tamara exhales carefully, wishes she could close her eyes, her eyes are wide open. For one ridiculous moment she thinks the Belzens have had enough of lying on their bed and have gone downstairs to make a sandwich. Tamara holds back an explosion of hysterical laughter.

Pull yourself together!

She doesn't know how much time passes. The sweat on her

face has dried. No more doors bang. Just silence. Tamara counts the seconds. Reaching three hundred she shuts the door and leaves the bathroom.

The smell hasn't changed, the tiger balm barely helps. Tamara thinks she can taste the stench of putrefaction in her mouth, and suppresses a fresh urge to retch. Her eyes have gotten used to the dark, but she keeps one hand on the wall and starts creeping down the stairs.

Maybe I only imagined it.

Maybe the terrace door just blew shut.

She reaches the bottom stair, the door to the hall is shut, the terrace door is open. She sees the lights of the villa opposite.

If I set off running now, in ten seconds I'll be at the water, and once I'm in the water I can swim to the opposite shore in a few minutes and—

There is the sound of footsteps from the hall, the handle lowers, and the living room door opens.

YOU

NO ONE WOULD really want to know how you feel, but anyone could imagine. First 600,000 volts were shot through your body, then you were put on the back seat of a car, transported across Berlin, pulled from the back seat again, and dragged down some cellar steps. Before the last step you were dropped, and the ground received you roughly. For a while you just lay there, and the rough carpet imprinted its pattern on your face. Your consciousness was blank, so you weren't aware of being pressed to the wall. You felt nothing, smelled nothing, heard nothing. And as you were waking from your blackout, a nail was driven through your joined palms with two blows.

What you sow, you reap.

You scream from the depths of your unconscious. You're like a diver who has only seconds to escape the depths. Your screaming is the rope on which you pull yourself out of the darkness. Your screaming is your life, summed up in a breath.

You open your eyes and breathe frantically, your arms are stretched up, your fingertips touch the ceiling, you feel your weight pulling on the nail that's been driven through your hand. It feels as if you're burning from top to bottom. You try to calm your breathing, and look up. Above you are your hands, nailed together, below you your tracksuit, your legs, your running shoes. They just touch the floor.

I went jogging, you think, *I went jogging and then . . .*

You don't remember any more than that. The pain in your palms destroys all thought. You try to hang motionless from the wall and banish the pain. You succeed for thirty seconds, you succeed for a minute, and then the will to survive kicks in and you move, and the flames travel down your hands, and it's like dying and dying again and then again.

As if you knew what dying is.

As if.

Calm.

Calm down.

Now.

You relax, you hang there quietly again.

"Hello!"

You don't want to call for help, you don't want to plead, you just want to be noticed.

"Hello, is anyone there?"

You listen for footsteps, you wait and blink the sweat out of your eyes. It's unpleasantly warm down here. You try to concentrate. There's the sound of footsteps, a door opens, and then a man comes into the cellar. There's something familiar about him, but you can't grasp it.

"Ah, you're awake, that's good."

Your brain hunts for information.

Where ... Where do I know him from?

You really don't remember? Jogging, park bench, old man ...

The old man?

You've got it.

The man sits on a stool and looks at you.

"Fanni and Karl," he says. "Why?"

You don't mean to, but you burst out laughing.

The man tilts his head to one side.

You stop laughing and say, "Why? What sort of question is that? You're one of them, aren't you? What sort of stupid question is that? I'll tell you why. Because of everything they did to me. That's why. Because of everything."

"And who are you to dare to condemn others?" the man asks.

"You know very well who I am."

"Little Lars."

"That's right, little Lars."

The man shakes his head.

"Little Lars would never do anything like that. Never. He's one of us, he belongs to us. Lars is like a son to me. Who are you really?"

You spit and hit him on the shoulder. He looks at you, he looks at you for a long time as if he could see through everything you think and feel. You have to make an effort not to look away.

"At any rate you aren't one of my sons," says the man. "You have no respect, and you haven't got a spark of honor in you. Haven't you understood that we're your family, which sticks together?"

You feel the gall rising from your stomach. *Family. How dare he? How can he . . .*There's so much you could hurl at him, but all that comes out of your mouth is:

"You're a bunch of pedophiles who snatch innocent children from the streets. You're sick people who destroy souls. No more, no less."

The man looks surprised. *How can he be surprised?* You wish both your hands were free. Your legs twitch, but you don't think you could catch him with a kick.

"Pedophiles?" says the man as if the word were an insect that he would never catch. "You've got a few things wrong there. We teach the children something. We're good to them, because we teach them obedience. We catch them and teach them pain. How are they supposed to survive in our chaotic world without obedience and pain?"

He seriously expects an answer from you. You're bewildered. Why are you even talking to him? What is there to talk about? *Nothing.* What do you think you'll get from it? *Nothing.* There's no foundation to any of it. You could ask a stone why it's a stone. You could talk to yourself and you'd get more out of it. And if you're quite honest, you aren't really interested in what this man thinks and feels and why he became what he is. Forget his story, forget his roots. History and roots are no excuse for what's happening now. They just make it more comprehensible. Once you cross a particular boundary, explanations are unnecessary. Children are a boundary. No one can undo what's been done and go back to how things were. All you can do is stop it, so it doesn't spread like a virus. So concentrate on what's right now. You, hanging from a nail in a wall.

"... Why?"

"What?"

"Why did you nail them to the wall?"

You just look at him. You aren't going to answer that question.

"Did Lars tell you all that?" the man asks. "Did he tell you they did the same thing to him?"

He laughs.

"And you believed him?"

Your answer is a whisper.

"I know what you've done to me. I was there. You tied me up. You hung me from the wall like a hunk of meat. I know what I know."

The man smiles ruefully.

"Of course Lars lied to you because he didn't want you to learn the truth."

You don't listen, you tense your arms. The man makes you tremble. The man may have nailed you to the wall, but he left out one important detail. So that Fanni and Karl really stayed in place, you drove an additional nail through their foreheads. That detail is very important, because with your weight, if you—

The man hits you in the face as if reading your mind.

"Are you listening to me? Do you know why Lars would never have done something like that?"

You have no idea what he's talking about. If your hands were free, you could break his neck within seconds. The man lays a hand on your chest. He unzips your tracksuit jacket, pulls your T-shirt out of your trousers, and shoves it upwards to reveal your chest. You feel his cold fingers. His breath on your skin. You look down, the man looks up. His hand covers your heart.

"Tell me who you really are," he whispers.

"I'm your little Lars, you asshole."

The man shakes his head. His hand rests on your chest.

"Here," he says, patting you like a good dog, "you're missing something here."

He lets your T-shirt fall again and steps back. He looks at the hand that touched you, then he says:

"If you ask me, you don't know Lars at all, because if you knew him, you'd know that he's part of the family. Why do you think he's told you so little about himself?"

He touches his own heart.

"We branded him. All the sons, all the daughters bear the mark. Here. You haven't the faintest idea what I'm talking about, do you? You think you know so much about Lars, but you have no idea who he really is. Do you know who I am? I'm a mystery to you, aren't I? Come on, tell me. Who am I?"

You look away, you have no answer. So the man tells you who he is.

When Butch turned fourteen, Fanni and Karl told him he was one of their brothers now. They brought him presents that day and laid them at his feet. They were as affectionate as siblings, and for the first time Butch felt protected by their presence. Fanni bound his eyes and said they had a surprise for him. They left the room, then it was still. Minutes passed. Then Butch heard a movement and knew he was no longer alone in the room. He held his breath, everything inside him cramped up. A man's voice spoke close to his ear. It only spoke once. It said: *Lars.*

Butch started to pee. He was so scared that he simply started to pee. A hand wrapped itself around his penis and milked it as if Butch were peeing only for that hand. When nothing more came, the hand disappeared, and it was still again. For a few minutes, then Butch heard someone sniffing at him. Deep breaths in, sighing breaths out.

After that the man never touched Butch again. He just sniffed him repeatedly. All over. And he stayed for a long time. When he left, his lips were at Butch's ear again. He spoke quietly and said, *If anyone asks you, I was never here.*

The man looks up at him. He's pleased with himself.

"Lars told you about Fanni and Karl, but he didn't say a word about me. And you know why? Because I'm his secret. No one is supposed to find out about me. I asked and he promised. We're close. We trust each other, you understand?"

You don't take your eyes off him. You mustn't show any emotion now. The man knows where your sore point is.

"So who are you?" he asks.

"Lars Meybach."

"And you're sure of that?"

"I'm sure."

The man takes a hammer from the workbench and starts breaking your ribs.

Autumn was the end, not winter. In the autumn the lights went out and the shadows came to life. It was the time of transformation. Back then you didn't know that it would also be the time of your transformation.

You remember the smells. You still remember what life felt like. Everything was possible. Sundance was filled with hope, Butch was fine.

During the holiday they spent together in Sweden, Sundance had sprained an ankle and met a woman doctor in the hospital. In early autumn he had a week free and visited the doctor in Stockholm. Because his return flight was canceled, it was rebooked and he came back from Sweden a day early. Butch didn't know anything about it, Sundance wanted to surprise him.

After driving home from the airport, he went to the supermarket and did his shopping. He wanted to cook, and if Butch came home in the evening, they would celebrate his return.

At about three o'clock in the afternoon Sundance heard footsteps in the apartment above his own. Some days Butch came home early from work. Sundance got on with his cooking. He laid the table and turned on the oven, then took the two presents he'd bought for Butch in Stockholm and went upstairs.

No one opened the door.

Sundance rang again and wondered if he should go and get his key. He didn't think he'd imagined the noises before. On the other hand he didn't want to burst into the apartment when Butch was sitting on the toilet. He had sworn he would trust Butch and respect his privacy. He rang again. The sound of pounding footsteps, then the door opened.

Little Butch was standing in front of him. As if he'd traveled from the past to show himself to big Sundance. But the hair color was wrong, the eyes were different, and the longer Sundance looked, the more surprised he was that he could have mistaken the boy for little Butch.

"Get away from the door," he heard Butch's voice from the apartment.

The boy just looked at Sundance, then retreated into the shadows, walked backward down the hall touching one wall with his fingertips to get his bearings. When he had reached the doorway to the bedroom, he stopped.

"Who's at the door?" asked Butch.

"A man."

"What sort of man?"

The boy shrugged.

Butch told the boy to look at him.

The boy looked at him.

"You're lying, aren't you?"

The boy shook his head.

Butch stepped out of the bedroom.

The door to the apartment was still open, but there was no one there.

Butch looked out into the corridor.

"Fucking salesmen," he said, and shut the door.

Sundance went into action. He thought through every step. There were to be no mistakes. Once he was back in his apartment, he turned off the oven and sat down at the kitchen table. He thought. He had two kinds of sleeping pills in his medicine cabinet. He opened a bottle of wine. At half past seven he called Butch's cell phone and told him he'd just landed and was about to take a taxi. And did Butch fancy having dinner with him at nine.

"What are you having?" asked Butch.

"I'll scrape something together," Sundance promised and hung up.

For the next half hour he sat motionless on a chair, then walked to the front door, opened it and slammed it shut.

He was home again.

They hugged, they sat down for dinner, he got out Butch's presents, and they laughed at the nonsense he'd bought. A sweater with a red reindeer on the front, a cap with earflaps. They drank wine, and Sundance talked about his time in Sweden; Butch told him about all his work and how he'd almost not made it home from the advertising agency that day. Once Sundance disappeared into the bathroom. He picked up a towel, pressed it to his face, and screamed into it. After that he waited until the color of his face was back to normal, and went back to the table.

The sleeping pills started working after the third glass. Butch felt warm at first, then he felt strange and couldn't concentrate.

Sundance helped him onto the sofa, where Butch fell asleep after a few minutes.

Sundance went upstairs and opened the door to Butch's apartment. He left it open and went back downstairs to get Butch. He carried him as you would carry a bride. He laid him on the bed in the bedroom, then went to the bathroom and filled the tub. He wore gloves, he wasn't stupid. After lighting some candles, he put the wine bottle on the floor and the wineglass on the edge of the tub. It was a fresh glass, so that if anyone went looking they wouldn't find out that the sleeping pills had been dissolved in the wine.

In the bedroom he undressed Butch and noticed some scars under his left nipple. Four dots that looked like a Y. He laid Butch's clothes on a chair and carried his friend into the bathroom. Butch went on sleeping, the hot water didn't even make him flinch. It was all as it should be. Sundance pulled up a chair. He studied Butch in the candlelight. The way the hot vapor from the surface of the water swirled around his neck. The way his heart thumped in his chest. The peace exuded by his friend.

Sundance laid a hand on his head and pushed him gently underwater. Silence. Bubbles of air rose from Butch's nose. He coughed once, twitched. Sundance went on being gentle. When he took his hand off Butch's head, nothing had outwardly changed. Butch was underwater, hot vapor rose from Sundance's arm. He wished for a moment that Butch would open his eyes and look at him. He wanted to explain himself. There was nothing to explain. Sundance was convinced that his friend understood why he had to do it. Love. It was pure love.

And they had never once talked about it.

"Tell me your name."

You cough, the pain is so extreme that you've already thrown up twice. Every time you breathe you can feel your shattered ribs.

The man has started on the lower sections and explained to you that he's going to save the upper ribs for last.

"Otherwise they'll pierce your heart, and I'm not going to let it happen that quickly."

The man wipes his sweaty hands on a towel. Green with white lilies. He drinks from a bottle of water and takes two pills. He promises you that he will be back in a moment.

You shut your eyes and go back to the past.

You were the one who found the corpse the next morning. You were the one who called an ambulance, talked to the police, and offered them coffee. You, not Sundance, because that same night Sundance had died along with Butch. There was no longer any reason for him to exist. Butch and Sundance were no more. Extinguished.

A lot was expected of you. You promised his family you would take care of everything. His parents gave you power of attorney. The apartment, the bank account, the insurance. It all had to be administered, you had a lot of work ahead of you, but that was fine. Taking care of everything was your way of atoning for what his family didn't know.

"How on earth could he kill himself?" asked Lars's father. "What kind of person does something like that to his parents?"

As if everything revolved only around them, as if children existed so their parents would be seen in a good light. It made you bitter that Lars's family turned away from him in death. You'd expected more from them.

The day after the funeral you went to work. No one knew what had happened to your best friend, and that was how it was supposed to stay. There was the job, and there was private life. That was the day it first happened. In the bathroom you stood by the basin to wash your hands. Your eye fell on your unshaven face in the mirror, your cheeks were a bit hollow and there were shadows under your eyes. You were about to dry your hands when your eye slipped away. You tried again. It didn't work. You could no longer look yourself in the eye. Startled, you laughed out loud and were bringing your face close to the mirror when one of your colleagues came in.

You left work early that day and drove home. You couldn't focus your eyes on yourself. Your eyes avoided you. You were so frightened that you took two days off. You sat in your apartment and wondered what it meant. And during that period of calm the realization came to you. You were overwhelmed with guilt and you cried, you got drunk and barely stirred from bed. But whatever you did, your eyes avoided you.

Four days after his death you had reached bottom. Ghosts pursued you. *What if I'd talked to Lars? We could have talked about everything. Would we have? Was there another way?* Your rhetorical questions didn't help. You had chosen one course of action and you had to live with the consequences.

On the fourth night you started with wine and later switched to tequila. At about nine in the evening you drunkenly went upstairs to Lars's flat. You wept, you sat on a sofa and howled and wept. There were photographs of the two of you, there was the life that would never be again. You touched his belongings, you even sniffed his clothes, abandoned and lonely. In the bathroom you stood in the doorway for a moment before getting the cleaning things from the kitchen and starting to scrub out the bathtub. Your mouth moved of its own accord, all the words and excuses came out and came back to you because there was no one who wanted to hear them.

How you finally ended up in the bathtub, you can't remember. You remember that from one moment to the next the candles were lit, the foam made little crackling noises, and you were up to your neck in the water, your face wet with tears and steam.

When the water turned cold, you climbed out of the tub and

dried yourself. You left your clothes lying on the lid of the toilet and went naked into the living room. There was no thought, there was only the action. Lars was a bit bigger than you, but it was barely noticeable. You took clothes out of his wardrobe. As you did so you couldn't stop crying. You got dressed and sat on the sofa until no more tears came. Then you went out into the night.

The new club was at the end of Bleibtreustrasse, just before the Ku'damm. You found a table that was free and went on drinking. Later, you spoke to a woman while dancing. It was nice, it was natural. You stood at the bar drinking companionably, when she leaned forward and asked your name. And that's when it happened, you deliberately brought him back to life. *Lars,* you replied. You just said his first name, and the woman had no problem with that. Why should she? It was fascinating. She didn't doubt it for a second. Why should she?

Lars.

You went to his flat. You slept together in his bed and later sat at his kitchen table and drank his wine. You had sex again in the bath. Her hands on the tiles, your hands on her hips.

Fuck me, Lars, fuck me!

You had already had sex with a number of women, but never before had one of them ever called out your name. So you did as she asked. Lars fucked her. Lars lay in bed with her and slept deeply and soundly and dreamlessly. In the morning you woke up with a clear head. You let the woman go on sleeping.

The euphoria made you nervous. What did it mean? Were you psychotic? Were you going mad? Was that the course of action you wanted to take? Tribute. Every friendship expects tribute. So you opted for the tribute and went into the bathroom and bent over your dead best friend's sink and held your face under the tap. As you lifted your head again, you still couldn't meet your gaze in the mirror. Your eyes avoided you, jerked to the left, jerked away.

It's me, you wanted to say, but you didn't know if it really was.

Your first reaction was to laugh. *Christ, I'm exhausted,* you thought and shook your head. Then you went closer to the mirror. It still didn't work. Like two identical poles making contact. You couldn't focus your gaze on yourself.

That day you started paying your tribute.

You spoke to the owner of the house and rented Lars's flat as well as your own. There were no problems, people don't make problems for someone in your position. You neglected to tell the bank that Lars was dead. You faked his signatures and brought a myth to life. Among his papers you found all the information about his bank accounts, his health insurance and so on. You quit his job with the explanation that Lars wanted to look after his sick mother. You did everything necessary to make Lars disappear from the picture. And then you did everything you could so that no one would forget him. As a result Lars became someone who remained present through his absence. Not forgotten, not dead, but alive.

One morning the phone rang, and you automatically picked up the receiver. It was a friend of Lars, and you didn't know why he'd called you of all people. Before you could ask him the question, he started chattering and asked you what Berlin was going to be like in this mild winter. It was only then that you realized that you weren't in your bed. *Since when have I been sleeping up here?* You didn't know. After a brief moment's hesitation you gave Lars's friend the right answers. He didn't doubt for a moment who he was speaking to.

Even though you were paying tribute, your condition didn't improve. Your eyes kept avoiding you. You cried, you hit the mirror until shards fell into the sink. Nothing helped. You revitalized Lars's apartment as if it were your own. Your private life dissolved into nothing. You had only one goal now—to do justice to Lars. He would go on living through you. Until the point when he let you go. Perhaps no one can understand that, but you were shaken to the marrow by the fact that you could no longer look into your own eyes. You were surrounded by guilt.

Am I going mad? Should I go and see a doctor?

You covered the mirrors, even the ones in your own apartment. Women thought it was eccentric, you told them about a Jewish uncle who had passed away, and they were surprised that you weren't circumcised.

How long could it have gone on? Who knows? How long could you have lived those two lives? A year? Longer? You were relieved of the decision when you discovered the octavo notebook on the bedside table. Names, loads of names. Two of them were underlined, two of them you knew. At that moment you understood what a farce you were living. And you became furious, furious with Lars, because he wouldn't let you go. What else did he want from you? What else could you give him?

The realization was like a clear slice through your thoughts. It was up to you to make everything right. To create equilibrium.

I'll give you Fanni and Karl. And you let me go.

The man hits you in the face. Your eyes snap open, you don't know how long you were unconscious. The man tells you to concentrate. He repeats himself. An endless litany. *Who? Are? You?* You shake your head, you no longer know who you are. He lifts the hammer. The shadow of his arm. You turn your head away and answer. He doesn't understand you, you whispered. You whisper again. *Quietly.* Vomit flows from your mouth, you cough. The man stands on tiptoe. *Closer.* His ear is close to your mouth. Every word is like a sentence when you say:

"I'm going to kill you."

"No, you aren't," the man whispers back. "And shall I tell you why you aren't going to kill me? Because I'm not really here."

"Yes, you're here," you say, and at that moment your legs shoot upwards and close around the man's back. You scream, you scream into his face, because your body is pure pain, as if not only your whole weight, but all your nerves were hanging on that one nail, as if nothing existed any longer but that damned nail in your damned hands. Go on, scream, let it out, because this may be your only chance, so don't fuck it up, let it all out.

You can only hope the angle's right. You tense your arm muscles, a red-hot wire scrapes up your spine, your backside presses against the wall, the man struggles against your scissors grip and swings his hammer wildly, but it's too late, there's a jerk and the nail stays in the wall, and your hands come lose like meat from a kebab spit, and at last you're free.

TAMARA

A BEAM OF LIGHT falls into the dark living room. Tamara hears heavy breathing, then footsteps approach and the terrace door is closed. She hears the jangle of keys; in the minute that follows nothing happens. Whoever it is standing in the living room, all he's doing is standing in the living room as Tamara crouches behind the sofa, knees to her chest, holding her breath. At last the footsteps move away again.

Silence.

The light in the hall goes out. Tamara waits for the front door to close. Nothing happens. She stays in the darkness. Seconds turn to minutes.

One more minute. Maybe two.

Tamara waits five minutes before venturing out from behind the sofa. She creeps to the terrace and tries to open the door. The door is locked. Tamara could weep. She wonders what she can smash the glass pane with, and picks up a standard lamp. She swings the lamp. The gas pistol slips from the waistband of her trousers and falls on the floor. Tamara freezes. She looks from the pistol to the open living room door. *No one heard me, no one . . .* And it's at that moment that voices reach her ear. Quiet, restrained, then a scream, muted, far away, like a radio station sending faint signals. Tamara listens. The blood whispers in her ears, her heart hammers. She concentrates and follows the source to the heating. She leans forward. The voices are coming from the radiator. Tamara presses her ear to it and gives a start. *Why is the heat on?* Her ear touches the hot metal again. She hears a groan and then blows, and then it's silent again. Break in transmission. And suddenly she knows why Kris isn't answering the phone. *Because he's here.* Why she can't get through to him. *Because Meybach's got him.* A voice speaks. *Kris?* Tamara can't make out a word. Her hand reaches along the radiator. The pipes lead downwards.

YOU

THE IMPACT IS VIOLENT. The back of your head scrapes against the wall, then you land on your left shoulder and try to get away from the man as fast as possible. You have released your legs from him, which wasn't all that clever, because now the man's free and he's going apeshit. The hand with the hammer is swinging relentlessly up and down. You've been lucky so far. He grazes your arm, he grazes your leg, he misses your face by half an inch. You turn into a crab and scuttle backward. Your foot shoots out. The man wheezes, he has difficulty getting to his feet, and he rubs his chest. His face is white as chalk. You pull yourself up by the workbench. Your hands find a broken table leg, it's not a match for the hammer, but it's better than nothing. Now you're ready for him.

"Come on then," you say.

He doesn't hesitate, the hammer hisses through the air, you dodge it, the hammer misses your chin, then the man throws himself forwards and his shoulders ram into you. The table leg flies out of your hands, and you fall backward.

How can he be so fast?

You don't know, you smash him in the kidneys, hit his stomach, hit his chest, and try in vain to hit him in the face as you gradually realize that you're weaker than you thought. *He's wearing me out.* Your blows have no visible effect.

There's a strange sound, and it's a moment before you work out that it's the man. He laughs hoarsely and presses one hand to your throat so that the back of your head hits the floor, the hammer swings up, reaches its highest point and is on the way back down when the cellar door flies open with a crash. The man turns his head, your fist catches his neck, and you feel his sinews giving under your knuckles. The man falls back with a groan. Tamara Berger is standing in the doorway, and now it's your turn to laugh, because the scene looks like something out of a bad action movie, except that even in a bad action film the heroine would never look so terrified when making her entrance.

TAMARA

"STAY ON THE FLOOR! You hear me? Stay on the floor!"

The man in the tracksuit is so exhausted that he can barely move. He stays on the floor and raises his arms in self-defense. Tamara doesn't know where to look first. She recognizes the man who is looking after the Belzens' house. She remembers his name. Samuel. Tamara is relieved that he's still alive, and aims her gun back at the man in the tracksuit.

I know this guy too. That face, where . . .

And then she has it. In the kitchen. One of the two policemen; the one she asked to sit down.

Who was so young that I couldn't take him seriously.

"You're a policeman," she says in surprise.

"Criminal investigation," says the man.

"You . . . You were with Gerald."

"That's right. Gerald's my boss. I'm Jonas. Jonas Kronauer."

Tamara doesn't understand anything any more.

"What . . . what are you doing here?"

"That's a long story," says Kronauer and tries to get up.

"Don't," says Tamara.

"What?"

"How dumb do you think I am? Sit right where you are. First I want to hear what's happened here from him."

She notices that the policeman is looking at her gun.

"This isn't a toy," she says.

"I know," says Kronauer. "I didn't think you'd aim a toy at me."

Tamara waits to hear if Kronauer has anything more to say. He sits there in silence.

Good.

Tamara crouches beside Samuel.

"Everything all right?"

"I can . . . hardly breathe . . . He . . . my throat . . . But it'll . . ."

· 364 ·

He coughs, clears his throat, and asks, "Have you . . . found . . . Helena and Joachim?"

Tamara nods.

"Thank God," says Samuel and coughs again. "I thought—"

"I'm sorry," she interrupts, "Helena and Joachim are dead."

Samuel lowers his head and shakes it slowly in disbelief; when he looks up again, tears shimmer in his eyes. He looks over at Kronauer.

"What happened here?" asks Tamara.

Samuel speaks without taking his eyes off Kronauer.

"Helena and Joachim came back from their trip two days ago, and he turned up here the same evening. He identified himself as a policeman and said the criminal investigation department was keeping the villa under surveillance. He overpowered me and locked me in the cellar. I've been sitting down here for two days, not knowing what he'd done to Helena and Joachim. When he came down here just now, I caught him by surprise."

Now he looks at Tamara.

"I'm glad you found us, because I don't think I'd have got out of here alive."

"He's lying to you," says Kronauer. "It's a lie from start to finish."

"Will you please help me up?" says Samuel and holds his hand out to her. Tamara takes it and helps him to his feet.

"We should call the police," says Samuel.

"I AM THE POLICE!" Kronauer yells suddenly, then turns calmly back to Tamara. "Call my boss. Gerald will tell you who I am. This old guy lay in wait for me in the park . . ."

"That's ridiculous," says Samuel.

" . . . and dragged me here. I don't even know where I am. Please call Gerald."

Samuel leans against the wall. He's pale and trembling.

"Look at me," he says to Tamara. "Do I look like someone who can drag people around the place?"

"Don't listen to him," says Kronauer.

"We should tie him up until everything's sorted out," says Samuel.

"Listen to me, I'm a policeman. This man is a pedophile, and he won't wait a second before—"

"How dare you?" Samuel interrupts. "Haven't you a shred of decency?"

"SHUT UP!"

The men fall silent. Tamara holds the gun between them. She feels herself losing her balance. She has backed away from the men and now her back is against the wall. Nothing's working as it's supposed to. She was sure she would come storming down here and rescue Kris. *Where on earth is he?* What she'd really like to do is rewind and rethink her decision. And call the police.

I've got to call the police, I've got to—

As if from a great distance she hears a voice saying, "You've got to decide."

Tamara focuses on Kronauer. There's a memory that eludes her. *How does he know my name?* Kronauer tilts his head and waits for her decision. *He was in the villa, he's from the police. But how does he know my name?* Samuel coughs. The heating pipes hum. *I wish I were somewhere else,* thinks Tamara and makes her decision. She tells Kronauer to sit where he is and turn around. And she tells Samuel to tie him up. Kronauer curses. Samuel reaches into one of the shelves and takes out a roll of nylon tape. He ties Kronauer's hands to his back and steps away from him.

"Thank you," he says to Tamara.

YOU

THE NYLON TAPE CUTS into your wrists, every breath hurts. How did all this happen? How could you think there was no one but Fanni and Karl? Dammit, how could you be so naïve?

You turn around and see that Tamara and the man are leaving the cellar. Tamara isn't stupid, she makes the man walk ahead of her. You only wish she wouldn't hold the gun in such an amateurish way.

"Hey, Tamara."

She turns around.

"You're making a mistake, do you know that?"

She hesitates. You want to warn her, you want to tell her you know her and you don't want anything to happen to her. She's quicker:

"How do you know my name?"

You have no answer. For a few seconds you just look at her, then at last you react and say you were with your criminal investigation colleagues at the villa and—

"I was never introduced to you," Tamara interrupts. "You were never introduced to me. It makes no sense. I'd really love to know how you know my name."

She turns away and follows the man upstairs. She doesn't even think of closing the door behind her. She's so careless that she won't survive five minutes with the man.

You start trying to pull your bound hands out from under your legs. Your back hurts, and it doesn't exactly help that four ribs are broken. Every movement takes your breath away, and as you're working on your tied hands you wonder why Tamara didn't believe you. She saw you in the villa, she knows you're a policeman. And still.

And how does she know the man? What have I missed? Who are Helena and Joachim? And where am I?

Your hands are in front of you. Your whole body is drenched in sweat, and you stagger to your feet. The cellar door is only half-shut, you could run upstairs and then . . .

The shot makes you jump. You stare speechlessly at the ceiling of the cellar, as if it were possible to see through the concrete into the rooms above. You wait for the next shot, and when you realize that one shot must have been enough, you start frantically rubbing the tape against the edge of the table.

He's killed her, that bastard has killed her, and I'm still standing down here like an idiot and I'm tied up and there's nothing I can do.

You're too slow. There's the sound of footsteps on the stairs, and you're standing by the edge of the table like an idiot with your hands tied and there's nothing you can do.

THE MAN WHO WASN'T THERE

IT'S ALMOST TOO EASY. It's almost too disturbingly easy.

He goes upstairs with the girl and fills a glass with water in the kitchen. He gulps it down greedily. The girl stands behind him and asks if he's feeling better. He nods and says he hasn't eaten or drunk for two days. He fills the glass again and enjoys his role.

"We should call the police," says the girl.

He nods again and walks past her into the living room. The stench of the corpses is unbearable. He switches on one of the standard lamps, unlocks the terrace door, and gratefully breathes in the night air. He wonders where the girl has come from so suddenly. How long has she been in the house? The front door is bolted. How could he have failed to notice her? *And why is she so quiet?* He turns around. The girl is standing in the living room doorway looking at him.

"Why Wolf?" she asks.

He's a bit surprised. He thought she was more naïve, but she's clever and she notices things. She would have made a good member of the family. It's a lovely thought. She and Fanni would have been sisters.

"Can I sit down?"

He doesn't wait for her answer. He sits down in one of the chairs and crosses his legs.

"Why Wolf?"

"You haven't got any children, have you? You're thirty, mid-thirties? You wouldn't understand what I'm talking about. Without children the world stops turning. I was just defending my children. I didn't know what was really happening. I was sure you and your friends were to blame for everything. And if you're quite honest . . ."

He tilts his head to one side.

" . . . you are partly responsible. Why an agency that apologizes for other people? Shouldn't people do that for themselves? What's the church for? If you do a rain dance you shouldn't be surprised if it starts raining."

"What kind of bullshit are you talking about?"

"The good news is," he goes on as if he hadn't heard her, "that I forgive you. You're definitely a good girl and didn't know what you were getting into. So let's leave it there."

He stands up.

"Sit down!"

He doesn't sit down, he stands where he is, the gun is aimed at his chest.

"What gave me away?" he asks, although he isn't really interested. He wants her to talk, he wants her to think and not feel.

"The Belzens don't look as if they've only been dead for two days. And you don't look as if anyone's been keeping you prisoner. And you could have escaped through one of the cellar windows."

"Maybe I was tied up?"

"And why did you have the terrace key?"

"Because I'm looking after the house and—"

"I came in through the terrace," the girl breaks in. "I was here in the living room when you closed the terrace from inside."

"Ah," he says. "Clever girl."

The man comes closer. He can see that she's shaking.

"What did you do to Wolf?"

"I didn't do anything to him. He went to sleep and didn't wake up again. But I protected his face. The face of an angel. In his sleep he looked like a little boy. Who would want to cover a face like that with soil? It would be inhuman. No, I couldn't bring myself to do that."

The man remembers the heavy weight of the boy in his arms. He really couldn't do him any harm.

"He didn't suffer," says the man. "He went to sleep and didn't wake up."

The man sees that the girl's crying. He knows she won't fire at him. He feels sorry for her. How hard it must be to face the truth head-on, and understand that you've done everything wrong.

"It's fine," he says, "I know what it feels like."

"What?"

"I said—"

"I understood you. How could you say something like that?"

"I've experienced it myself, I've grieved for my children, I know how bad it is."

He comes still closer.

"Don't."

"You're a good girl, and I'm a good man. We can sort this out without using a gun."

"Please," the girl says and takes a step back.

"Just stay calm."

He will take the gun from her hand. He will take the girl in his arms and reassure her. Then he will deal with the policeman in the cellar. He isn't done with him yet, not by a long shot. He will put the girl and the policeman in the room with the Belzens. There will be a fire. A fire is the cleanest solution. There will be a fire, and the whole story will be over.

"Wolf was my friend," says the girl.

"Fanni and Karl were my children," he replies.

"Don't," says the girl and raises her arm.

"Fine," says the man and stops. The gun is a foot away from his face. He looks down the barrel. He sees the barrel trembling. The girl has her finger on the trigger. The finger isn't tensed. It's just sitting as if it doesn't know what it's doing there.

Good, thinks the man and says, "I have no guilt."

The girl doesn't react. The man smiles. The girl has stopped crying. She looks at the man as if seeing him for the first time.

"I'm sorry," she says.

"I know," says the man, "I do know."

He puts his hand around the gun. The girl shuts her eyes and pulls the trigger.

It's as if someone had torn his head back with a jolt. His body follows sluggishly, then the man lands on his back and his face is in flames. It feels as if everything he feels and thinks and sees is a sea of flames. No oxygen comes through it, just the constant throbbing of the fire. A croak emerges from his throat, his hands strike at the flames, and at last, at last pain overwhelms him, and his mind sinks into unconsciousness, while his body still twitches once, twice on the carpet and then lies still. His arms subside, his hands come to rest.

The girl jumps back when the shot goes off. For a while she stands in the hall and waits for the gas to be sucked outside and across the terrace. The man isn't aware of any of this. He lies on the ground with his half-burnt face twisted to the side. Spittle runs from his mouth, his heartbeat is barely perceptible. The girl bends over him. She smells the burnt flesh, she sees the blood and feels no regret.

TAMARA

SHE STAYS ON THE cellar steps and sees through the half-open door that Kronauer is no longer sitting on the floor. She is tired. She holds an empty gas pistol in her hand and is dog-tired. She crouches on the steps and waits. When no sound comes from the cellar, she says after a while:

"Hello?"

A shadow moves through the room. Then Kronauer appears in the chink of the door. His bound hands are no longer behind his back. He holds them out like a gift.

"I made my decision," says Tamara.

"And what made your mind up?"

She shrugs. Even though she feels like crying, she doesn't want to look weak in front of Kronauer.

"I didn't like him."

"Good enough," says Kronauer and enlarges the gap in the door with his foot.

Tamara goes on crouching on the steps. Kronauer isn't a threat to her, no one is a threat to her now.

Sleep, how lovely it would be to go to sleep here on the steps.

" . . . dead?"

Tamara gives a start; for a second she was gone, submerged. "What?"

"Is he dead?"

Tamara shakes her head.

"I don't think so."

Kronauer holds his bound hands out to Tamara.

"Could you—"

"What'll happen to him now?"

"Is that a loaded question?"

"No, it's not a loaded question."

"He'll be arrested, he'll be sentenced, he'll end up in jail."

"End of story?"

"End of story."

Tamara stands up.

Wrong, that's wrong.

"I don't think that's right," she says and aims the pistol at Kronauer. "Take two steps back please."

"That's not necessary now," says Kronauer.

"I don't want him to go to jail."

"You can't just let him go, don't be ridiculous!"

"Two steps back," Tamara commands.

Kronauer retreats, he doesn't understand what's going on. *And I don't want him to,* Tamara thinks and points with her free hand at the cellar window.

"You see those windows? You can do it."

Then she reaches for the cellar door and slams it shut with a crash. She turns the key and leaves it in the lock. Then she sits back down on the steps and doesn't expect Kronauer to hammer against the door. If she's being honest, she didn't expect much from the police.

He'll be arrested, he'll be sentenced, he'll go to jail. End of story.

Tamara sits on the steps in the dark and thinks.

YOU

THE DOOR CRASHES SHUT, you hear the turn of the key, and you're locked in again. Try and see the funny side; it's better than a bullet in the head.

That silly tart.

You're so exhausted that at first you just sit down on the floor and slowly slump back. For a while you lie on the floor with your eyes closed. You doze off, you land somewhere between before and after. In an intermediate realm in which nothing can happen outside of your control. You awake with a start. It's all the same. The cellar, the pain, you. Your attempt to sit up is a failure. You roll to the side and reach for the wall. Your hands feel as if they've been pumped up. At least the bleeding has stopped. Inch by inch you get up on your feet. A few years ago there was a very bad Bruce Willis movie. You can't remember the plot, just that one of the characters had fragile bones, bones made of glass. Bruce should see you now. There's nothing inside you but shards.

It takes you five minutes to free your hands, another ten minutes and you've crept out through the cellar window and you're lying on the cool grass.

You look like the lowest kind of tramp; your tracksuit is torn in two places, your trousers are smeared with vomit, and your hands are covered with blood.

After you have pulled yourself up on the wall of the house, you look to the right, and a hoarse laugh explodes from you. There's the villa, on the opposite shore. You recognize the tower and the shed. You drove through that front gate with your unit eight days ago, after Gerald had rounded you all up. You were completely naïve that day. It all happened so quickly. Suddenly they were standing there in front of you. Frauke Lewin, Tamara Berger, Wolf Marrer. You expected one of them to point at you at any moment.

Hi, I'm Lars Meybach, how's it going?

Only Kris was missing that day. As if someone had removed the most important piece of the puzzle that turns all the fragments into a whole. If Kris had been there, your meeting a week later in the corridor of your apartment block would have been a fiasco.

Maybe you were lucky, perhaps fate was only playing with you.

You turn away from the villa and walk diagonally across the garden to the street. A car drives past, you opt for the same direction and follow it. Your steps are unsteady at first, but after a hundred yards it gets better. You carefully stretch the small of your back and breathe deeply in and out. Your body slowly realizes that life has resumed.

When the suburban train station appears in front of you, you lean your back against a parked car for a moment and rest. It strikes you as pure irony that the old man carted you off to the Wannsee. How did all of this happen to you? You'd planned it differently, you thought you'd be in control. You have absolutely no idea what it means to be in control.

The people on the train keep their distance from you. You really hope no one's going to want to see your ticket. A homeless man walks down the carriage and ignores you.

For a while you sit there leaning forward staring at the wounds in your palms. *Tetanus,* you think, *I urgently need a tetanus injection.* You have a sense that the train is stopping twice as long as usual at every station. You look up and see that you're at the Nikolassee. The train goes on. The station disappears, your reflection suddenly appears in the window. Your eyes. How good it feels to be able to look at yourself again. No one would believe how important it is for a person to really see themselves. Absolutely vital. You wink at yourself. You clench your fists. The pain is so clarifying that tears run down your cheeks.

*   *   *

You aren't a murderer, you're just a lost human being in search of himself. He can be terribly lost but as soon as he has the chance to find himself, he will take advantage of it. And murder. And turn wrong into right. That's the justice of this world, as you see it.

Fanni and Karl.

You found out everything about their lives. You weren't interested in the other names in the address book. It was just about Fanni and Karl. And right in the middle of your investigations, in the middle of your perennial feeling of guilt and remorse, one lunchtime your boss sat down to eat with you and three other colleagues in one of those smart restaurants. You'd just ordered when Gerald told you about a friend of his who had set up an agency. An agency that apologized. For other people. You laughed, and yours was the only laughter that sounded false. You were sure you'd misheard. You remembered the story of a car engine that ran on one part gasoline and nine parts water. Myths. But as with all myths, the question immediately arose: *What if?* You went on eating and digested the information. Gerald saw your doubts and advised you to look on the internet. That's how it all started.

It's a weird feeling, getting out at the Charlottenburg station just before midnight and walking the three hundred yards home as if nothing had happened. Past the people in the cafés and restaurants, past all those mortals casting you suspicious glances and not knowing what it's like to be almost killed by an old man.

On the second floor you stop by at your open apartment door and hesitate. Everything has changed; everything has stayed as it was. You slowly understand why it's so hard to let Lars go. You haven't denied that name a single time tonight. Although the man broke your ribs. What is that? Can't you or won't you let him go? *I can't. I won't.* What's wrong with you? You've paid your tribute and you're free. And still you're asking yourself this question: *Who says I can't maintain this illusion a little longer?* It's separation, it's farewell, it's over. *Yes, but Lars belongs to me.* And at that point you're not quite honest with yourself. Of course there is a fascination in living two lives at once. *One more night,* you say to yourself, *and if I feel different in the morning, I'll end it all.*

And thus Jonas Kronauer pulls his apartment door closed again, and thus Lars Meybach climbs the stairs to the next floor.

You try to open the apartment door, the key jams. You pull it out, try a second time. The key bites, you open the door and reach automatically to the right to turn on the light. The switch reacts with a dry click, the light stays off. You curse, step into the apartment, and close the door behind you. Just as you're about to head for the fuse box, the first shot hits you in the stomach. The momentum carries you upwards, your feet lose contact with the floor for a moment. The second shot shatters your forearm. You collapse against the apartment door and slide down it. You're bewildered. The pain hasn't yet reached you. You lack all comprehension. You sit on the floor and don't know what's going on. Then your body registers the entry wounds, and your nerves react. A sigh escapes your mouth, and a wave of pain rolls over you.

TAMARA

HE LIES THERE, not moving. She goes through his trousers. Empty. She goes into the hall and rummages through the coats and jackets in the wardrobe. The fourth jacket belongs to him. His first name really is Samuel. In his right pocket is a bunch of keys, the car registration papers are in his wallet.

She takes them all.

One of the keys shows the brand of automobile. It takes Tamara less than two minutes to find his car. She reverses into the Belzens' driveway. In the trunk there are two boxes of empty mineral-water bottles, an umbrella, and a blanket. She sets the things down beside the car and leaves the trunk open. She's on autopilot, she circles the house once and is suddenly sure that Samuel has disappeared.

If he's gone, I'll look for him. I'll . . .

He's still lying on the carpet. Tamara grabs him under the arms and drags him across the terrace, through the garden to the car. She doesn't care if anyone sees her. She heaves his body through the hatch. The trunk shuts with a boom. Tamara gets into the car and drives off.

Her first stop is the villa. She gets her papers and a big roll of tape. She stuffs clothes in a bag. In the shed she finds cushions and woollen blankets.

She goes back to the car and opens the trunk.

He's still unconscious.

I could bury him. I could bury him here and now. The hole is still open, it would be very easy.

Tamara shakes her head, she doesn't want to have him anywhere near her.

She ties him up with the tape. First his arms, then his legs.

She makes a parcel out of him. Finally she tapes up his mouth and packs the blanket and cushions firmly around him. She shakes him by the shoulder, he doesn't move an inch.

All wrapped up.

In the villa Tamara hesitates for a moment. She wants to leave Kris a message and wonders what to write. *Hi, I've got an old man in the trunk, and if you're unlucky, you'll never see me again.* She finds a pen and looks for paper. Her eye falls on the note above the sink. *In the darkness of your thoughts . . .* She doesn't know who wrote this nonsense or why she's overlooked it before.

Tamara pulls down the note, crosses through the words, and tries to write, but her handwriting is a scrawl, her hand is shaking. *Pull yourself together!* Finally she scribbles in capital letters:

DON'T WORRY I KNOW WHAT I'M DOING. TAMMI

That's enough. She leaves the note on the kitchen table and goes outside. When she reaches the car she hears a dull knocking from the trunk. She doesn't want to look inside. She gets into the car and starts the engine.

KRIS

KRIS GIVES A START when he hears the key in the lock. The man from the emergency service is right, the key jams. Kris hears a curse, then someone shakes the door and the key bites. The door swings open. A hand reaches for the light switch. The light doesn't come on. Kris has learned from films.

"Shit."

Kris sees Meybach's silhouette. The door is closed. Meybach takes two steps into the room and stops. He waits for his eyes to get used to the dark. Kris waits for Meybach to take the next step. Meybach has to get past him if he wants to get to the fuse box.

Why is he hesitating?

And then Meybach takes the next step.

The shots are loud. Two explosions that sound as if they've bypassed the silencer. Kris aimed at Meybach's lower body. He's surprised how calm he is after firing the shots. His ears ring, but he is calm. Meybach slides down the door. He's still, then a groan comes from his mouth, sounding a little like a sigh.

Kris aims his flashlight at him and turns it on.

"It's you," he says.

Blood. A tracksuit. Running shoes. Meybach looks into the light as if Kris weren't there, as if the light were a presence of its own in the room, calling him into question. His pupils are pinheads, his mouth is half open.

"It's me," whispers Meybach and breathes in and repeats, louder: "It's me!"

YOU

IT REALLY IS YOU, even if you wish it wasn't, it really is you—with four broken ribs, a shattered arm, holes in both hands, and a bullet in your belly. Who would want to be in your place?

You sit facing one another. You with your back against the door, Kris Marrer on a chair. The flashlight is on the floor in front of him, lighting up the ceiling. The light is like the light in a badly lit aquarium. Your vision blurs, you try to see clearly, the light doesn't exactly help. A puddle of blood is spreading around you, you can't feel anything from your pelvis down. If your legs got up and walked away right now, you wouldn't be surprised.

"I hope it hurts," says Kris Marrer.

"It's okay," you say and mean it. The pain has turned into a background pulse. No, the pain isn't your problem, what's much worse is that you feel so weak. Sleep, you can think of nothing but sleep.

"I don't care who you really are," Kris goes on. "I don't care if you died three months ago or if it's all been a big act. And I don't want to know why you made it so easy for us to find you."

You cough, blood spills thick and warm from your mouth, you try to lift your good arm to wipe the blood from your chin, you can't do it. You're glad you can't see yourself. Kris Marrer goes on talking. *Concentration.* You feel yourself losing the thread. Concentrate!

" . . . you're one of those psychopaths who give themselves up to have the stops put on them. I don't care about that either. I just want to know one thing: why did you have to drag us into it?"

A jolt runs through you. Oh, look, now we've got your attention. This is about the truth. This is about what happened. So give him an answer, calmly tell him the whole truth.

"Because . . . because of your presumption."

"What?"

Kris Marrer has to lean forward to hear you better. You didn't know you were whispering. You clear your throat, more blood, you spit, try to sit more comfortably, give up.

"Because of the . . . because of the position you put yourselves in. You . . . Everyone lives with guilt . . . tortures himself over the way he . . . And then . . . then along come you little jerks . . ."

You grin, the white teeth, the film of blood on your white teeth, the smile of a wolf. And for a moment your strength comes back to you. Like a fluctuating pulse. Your heart thumps. The power of the just.

"I was . . . punishing you, get it? I punished you for your presumption. Because I . . . I know what guilt is. I . . . I was guilty. I was so guilty . . ."

You aren't aware of the tears. They flow down your filthy cheeks. You wish you could stand. Proud, dignified, and not sitting pitifully on the floor like an idiot who's just been shot in the stomach.

" . . . I was . . . I couldn't do anything, anything at all. I thought I'd found a way, and then . . . then I heard about you. You . . . you gave absolution and took other people's guilt away as if it was as simple as that. I . . . I knew you couldn't help me. And I wouldn't have wanted help. Guilt is personal. Guilt is private. And no one can apologize to a dead person, can they? No one . . . no one can give a dead person satisfaction . . . No one. That's why I taunted you. I made you talk to the dead. How . . . Christ, how ridiculous must you have seemed to each other. Did you really think I needed an apology for what I did? That was what you thought, wasn't it? You . . ."

You burst out laughing, you can see how painful your laughter is to Marrer. Perhaps you shouldn't overdo it, or he'll fire the next bullet at you before you're through with laughing.

"Tell me, how silly did you feel standing in front of those corpses and mechanically reciting those texts? The words were written just for you . . . You didn't understand a thing . . . You—"

"You were *punishing* us?" Marrer interrupts you in disbelief. "That's all?"

"That's all."

"You're messing with me, right?"

He doesn't believe you, he doesn't want to believe you. He's an idiot, but he's an idiot with a gun in his hand.

"Your presumption, your arrogance," you say, each word like spitting. "Why should I mess you around? What you have done in the name of remorse and guilt should be forbidden. How dare you be so presumptuous?"

"But we wanted to help, we—"

"YOU JERKS WANTED TO PLAY GOD!" you suddenly explode, knowing of course that you're overdoing it a bit. But you can't think of anything better. You know they never wanted to play God. You're just bitter that while you were engaged in the arduous struggle with your own guilt, four people came along to be paid for something that had cost you your entire identity. No one should have it so easy, so you made it hard for them.

"I was so guilty," you go on, "that I lost myself. I couldn't look myself in the eye any more, do you understand that? How are you going to solve that one? I looked for a solution. And when I did that, I became your mirror."

"And for that two people had to die?"

You laugh. You thought Marrer was more intelligent.

"I would have done what I did to those two even if you hadn't existed. You fit into my schedule."

"Timetable?"

"Right. Timetable."

"And Wolf? Did he fit into your timetable as well?"

"What?"

"We found him yesterday in the ground by the villa. What

· 384 ·

were you trying to tell us with *that*? What can a sick mind be trying to tell me by burying my brother alive?"

You try to concentrate; you have no idea what happened to Wolf Marrer.

"I . . ."

"You know something? If I'm being perfectly honest, I don't want to hear your answer. You've talked enough crap. Is this the source of your guilt?"

Kris holds the photograph up to you. Butch and Sundance on the bicycle.

"You know what I think of your guilt?" Kris goes on. "It belongs to you alone. No one will take it from you. And this is what I think of your guilt: nothing."

You stare at the photograph. Everything comes together into this moment. There it is again. The ringing in your ears and reality starting to jerk and tremble before it freezes with a scraping noise. You look at the photograph in Marrer's hand, you see his face behind it. The grief, the rage. He's here to kill you. He doesn't care whether it's right or wrong. He just knows one thing: *You must cease to be.*

Remember the moment in the restaurant when you first heard about the agency. Reality froze then too and you wondered what would happen if you died at such a moment. Would you simply disappear? It was a premonition of this moment. No bullets are needed now. Everything has frozen.

You feel the darkness around you; you wait for Marrer to go on talking, to put the photograph down and shout at you. Nothing happens. The photograph floats in front of your eyes, Marrer's mouth doesn't move, and then the darkness surges closer. It comes from every corner, it fills the room like liquid, like warm black blood. Slow and sluggish. The darkness creeps down the walls, it comes away from the ceiling and starts to flow around Marrer's feet and comes at you from all sides. You are nothing now but a silent particle in a silent world that will never again be set in motion. And as the darkness completely enfolds you, you disappear just as silently, leaving no traces, from this reality.

After

IT'S OVER. Time has ceased to exist. I wait for sunrise. When the sun has risen, I will get out of the car, and then it'll be over. I haven't opened the trunk since yesterday, and that's how it's going to stay, I will never open it again. I bought wet wipes and glass cleaner at a gas station. At another gas station I vacuumed the car. I cleaned the interior, and since then I've been sitting here waiting for the sun to rise.

The view is enchanting. I know Frauke would like it. All the light and the peace that lie over a city at the start of the day. I know what Wolf would say now. He would hug me close and give me warmth. He would say: *Are you cold?* And I would nod and his hands would be everywhere, warming me.

How I miss his warmth.

How I miss his warmth.

The sky has a purple glow, and slowly the purple dissolves and turns pale and fades to a matte blue. The sun is like liquid mercury. I can't take my eyes off it. I persevere until my eyes are swimming with tears, then I close them tight and the sun reappears behind my closed lids.

Cars go past. A bus. A rattling moped. More cars. I wait for the lights to change, pick up my bag and get out. The morning air is fresh and clear. Maybe I'll stroll down to Friedenau. I can do that whenever I like. Maybe I'll go and stand below Jenni's window and call her name. *Maybe not.*

I lock the car, walk a few yards, and stop on the bridge. I

look down on to the Lietzensee. Everyone's still asleep. There are individual lights burning in the hotel, the trees don't yet cast shadows. Even though it's so early, a few people are sitting by the water. Perhaps they slept here, perhaps the spring nights are already so warm that you can sleep outside. They're sitting on a blanket with their legs outstretched, their voices are faint and thin. One of them squats by the shore smoking a cigarette. One of them looks up and sees me. Wolf. He raises both arms as if he were bringing in a plane to land. I wave back to him. The others look up now. And there is Frauke, dressed head to toe in black and tired, but she laughs, I can see her laughter, warm as sunlight, warm and everywhere all at once. She waves, she presses a hand to her heart, then she presses the hand to her mouth and blows me a kiss. And I know I should walk on, but I can't leave her alone, it's so hard. And Wolf lays his arm around Frauke, and the man by the shore flicks his cigarette away and reaches his arm back and throws a stone over the water, and the others go on talking as if nothing had happened, while the stone jumps once, twice, three times over the surface of the water before disappearing silently into the depths.

My Thanks To

Gregor, I've tormented you over and over again with this novel, until you found out how much I was tormenting myself with it and took me aside and told me it would all be okay.

Peter and Kathrin, for your enthusiasm and your criticism.

Daniela, because you never had any doubts when I was full of doubts, because you love the darkness and forgive me my evil self.

Ana and Christina and Janna and Martina, you took the sting out of my nervousness.

Ulrike, because you were committed to every sentence and every thought.

Felix, my very personal secret agent, who kept the fire burning, who covered my back and was always there.

Eva, you touched me with your words and believed in me when times were dark.

Patrick, who made me remember why writing is so beautiful.

Shaun, who made me sound like myself.

Ullstein Verlag, your enthusiasm healed wounds.

Andrew Vachss and Jonathan Nasaw and Jonathan Carroll, for the thoughts that shouldn't be.

Ghinzu and Tunng and Archive and Mugison and The National, for the rhythm and the all-night stints.

Corinna, two hard years working as a Muse and you never once complained. *Love ya.*

A Note About The Translator

Shaun Whiteside's translations from German include works by Freud, Nietzsche, Schnitzler, and Musil. His translation of *Magdalene the Sinner,* by Lilian Faschinger, was awarded the Tieck Prize in 1996.